I0822146

"I AM THE ALPHA AND THE OMEGA,
THE FIRST AND THE LAST,
THE BEGINNING AND THE END."

THE CLOCK AND THE CARNIVAL

BOOK FIVE

BRANDI ELISE SZEKER

99 Hudson St
5th floor New York, NY 10013

ISBN:979-8-9894436-8-0
Cover Art: Seventh Star
Editor: My Brother's Editor
Proofreading: My Brother's Editor
Formatting: Imagine Ink Designs

The Pawn and The Puppet Series

(1)The Pawn and The Puppet
(2) The Master and The Marionette
(3) The Puppeteer and The Poisoned Pawn
(4) The Doll and The Domination
(4.5) The Fortress and The Figurine (novella)
(5) The Clock and The Carnival

Content Warning:

Disclaimer: This book contains explicit content and dark elements and may be considered offensive to some readers. Check trigger warnings before reading. It is not intended for anyone under 18 years of age. Please store your files wisely, where they cannot be accessed by underage readers.

Triggers: Abduction, captivity, imprisonment, psychological manipulation, gaslighting, delusional captor behavior, coerced bonding, trauma bonding undertones, forced proximity in captivity, physical torture, beatings, restraint, non-consensual medical procedures, injections, witnessing torture, threats of violence, fear-based manipulation, intense emotional distress, PTSD symptoms, dissociation, hallucinations, body horror, bruising and injuries, vomiting, fainting, carnival/circus horror elements, drug-induced sexual assault, chemical coercion (sexual), non-consensual, drug-facilitated arousal and sexual contact.

Do not continue if you are unsure of the contents of this book.

Is it breaking some sort of author rulebook to add more than one dedication?

Oh, yeah. I don't care.

For my baby, Lucinda Belle.
Without you, this book would
have been finished and
published a year ago.

Lastly, for my readers,
I am so sorry for hurting you with the cliffhangers.

HAHAHAHAHAHAH, no I'm not.

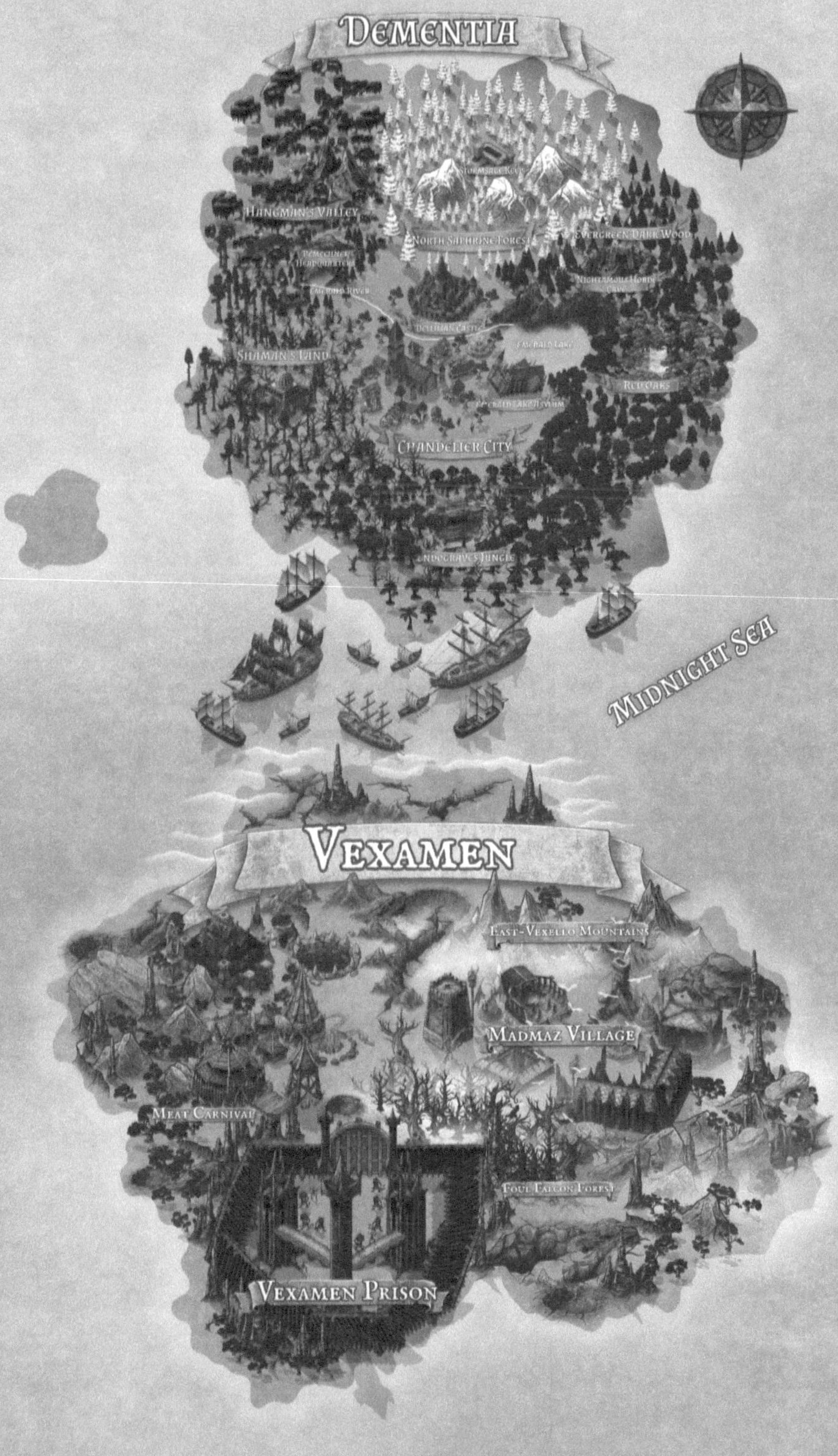

DEMENTIA
Hangman's Valley
Evergreen Dark Wood
Emerald Lake
Shaman's Land
Red Oaks
Chandelier City
MIDNIGHT SEA
VEXAMEN
East-Vexello Mountains
Madmaz Village
Meat Carnival
Foul Falcon Forest
Vexamen Prison

"Time heals nothing."
-Rose Kennedy

Author's Note

If you have made it this far, you know what to expect.

As you may know, this series isn't any ordinary dark fantasy romance series… It is a labor of love. A cry into the void to reach that reader who desperately needs something more. I hope Dessin and Skylenna's story delivered. I hope they transported you to their world and ensured without a shadow of a doubt that you will leave it believing that soulmates do exist.

Now, I have to ask of you three things:

One: Be an advocate for those with DID. Take one hour of your week to do just a little more research. This disorder is misunderstood and villainized. Let's change that by the time you finish this book. Let's be their shield against a world that has already failed them.

Two: Adopt a pet, volunteer at an animal shelter, or donate. The animals in my books were placed there to show you their worth. They are angels scattered amongst our world to endure our evil and comfort us through many storms. Go find your DaiSzek that has been abandoned at your local shelter. Donate to feed the Knightingale at your humane society.

Three: Make a daily effort not to add to the hate you see on the internet. People are being cyberbullied and canceled daily. A rule of thumb I now live by is, I will never know every detail to the story being shared in videos and posts. So why add to the hate? I will only ever choose to spread love and kindness in my comments and messages. I hope you will do the same.

"In this madness, he found her."
-Edgar Allan Poe

Playlists

Bad Guy by Vitamin String Quartet
Another Love x Summertime Sadness by TommyMuzzic, ZeddMusique
Evermore by Dizaro, WLZN
FU in My Head by Cloudy June
King of Disappointment by Echos
Genius (feat. Sia, Diplo, and Labrinth)
Three Seasons in Wyoming by Nick Cave & Warren Ellis
Second Journey by Nick Cave & Warren Ellis
You Failed Me Finn by James Newton Howard
Remembrance by Bryce Dessner
Lost at Sea by Thomas Newman
The Seed by AURORA
Girl With One Eye by Florence + The Machine
Me and the Devil by Soap&Skin
Pretty Little Devil by Shaya Zamora
Lament by Tommee Profitt, Sam Tinnesz, Shaya Zamora
Beautiful Things by Benson Boone
The Death and Resurrection Show by Killing Joke
I Forgive You for Me by Good Vibes Tribe 11:11
The Green Mile by Thomas Newman
A Charge to Keep I Have by Thomas Newman, Marion Williams
It's OK – Slowed by Edith Whiskers
Not About Angels by Birdy
If I Could Fly by One Direction
Broken (Acoustic) by Jonah Kagen
I'll Be Seeing You by Billie Holiday

The playlist can be found on Spotify by searching for "The Clock and the Carnival"

“He was gone, and my world grew quiet.”
-Hope Edelman

Prologue

Sapphire S. Valdawell

Five Years Old

I was five when my little crush on him was *extinguished.*

I was five when I gave him a wooden carving I made from a red oak tree, a beacon, just like the ones my father made for my mother when they were young.

I was five when he held it in his hands during class, examining it while I said the carefully rehearsed words. *I'm gonna love you until hell freezes over.* Again, just like my mother and father would say to each other long ago.

I was five when hell turned to a solid block of ice in the bed of my chest.

I was five when he looked at me with those cold, ocean-blue eyes and spit in my face. The act itself was too vicious and cruel to be from another five-year-old. It was thought out and intended to wound. It was followed by a smirk sharper than a Vexamen sickle.

I was five when Niklaus Demechnef broke my heart.

Letter #86

Skylenna

Dear Dessin,

I can't soothe my own babies.

It's only been three days since I've given birth, but I just feel...lost. My heart wilts when I look into our son's sleepy eyes, and I see Kane. Or when Sapphire sleeps, it reminds me of the concentration on your face when you solve a problem. These similarities make me yearn for you in the time I lie awake to breastfeed every two hours.

Chekiss helps me around the clock. Niles and Marilynn are in the trenches with their own baby boy, Niklaus, but still make time to help when they can.

Ruth and Warrose are here often too. But it's not the same. We were robbed, weren't we? These moments with our newborns we will never get back. Sometimes I imagine you changing Sapphire's diaper in the nursery. Sometimes I picture Kane sleep deprived with me, cracking jokes about the hardships of having twins.

When I do sleep, I see your face, and when I jolt awake, I can still smell your clothes. I can't stop crying. Please come back. I need you. Your babies need you. How am I supposed to go on without you?

My love for you doesn't fade, it only grows more painful.

Sincerely,

Your Soulmate,
Skylenna

1. The Wolf Beneath the Silverware

Sapphire

Twenty-One Years Old

Grief is no strangeR IN the Valdawell house.

It lives down the hall in my father's room. It sleeps on the right side of my mother's bed on a cold night amid a winter storm. It haunts the pages of our family photo albums.

And we let it reside here because there is nowhere else for it to go.

I think on that as I trace the uneven edge of the wooden table. The imperfect carvings of a wolf sprinting through a mass of trees along its perimeter. I admire the careful details and the precision it must have taken the artist to draw the lines with the pointed end of the knife. It must have taken days to complete.

Though I'm careful not to let my mother see how my index

finger caresses the paws of the wolf. Any time she sees me giving this table the slightest bit of attention, she starts to explain how my father built it himself. Carved it from a red oak tree and spent all night drawing those designs of DaiSzek running through the forest.

I've heard it as a child.

I've heard it as a teenager.

I've heard it at holiday gatherings.

I've heard it.

I've heard it.

I've heard it.

"Set out the candles, please," Mom calls over her shoulder, seasoning the meat before she slides it into the oven.

I raise my eyebrow at my brother, jerking my chin toward the dining table. "You heard her."

Krimson swings his glare back to me, narrowing those dark, heterochromatic eyes in annoyance. The orange glow of the oven fire flickers along his chocolate brown hair, casting a rich glimmer in this depressing house.

"You know who I was talking to," Mom clarifies, wiping down the glossy, garnet countertops. "Krimson is peeling potatoes. How are you contributing?"

I contemplate how I'd like to respond as Mom organizes the glass jars of herbs and seasoning lining the backsplash next to the stove. She's always so quick to clean up after preparing each dish for dinner. If she doesn't, Grandpa almost always cleans the entire kitchen, though it's small, Mom doesn't like him doing additional work.

"I'm using all of my energy not to bitch and complain." I sit on the chair next to my brother, arms crossed, jaw locked, staring at that front door that seems to mock me as the winter winds bustle against its barrier.

We are twenty-one years old. Why am I letting our mother pressure me into continuing to attend these dinners?

"He's not going to be that bad this time. Seriously. He'll be on his best behavior," Krimson says calmly, tossing potato skins in a bowl.

I raise my grimace slowly, pointedly. My brother meets my eyes and sighs.

"You're a fool."

They know why I hate these dinners. They know I can't stand to be in the same room as Niklaus. They know why I get into a shit mood when Sundays come around. But family is everything here, isn't it? A toxic idea my mother and her friends inherited from their time behind bars.

"He's right, Sapphire. Uncle Warrose and Aunt Ruth are coming too."

Thank fucking heavens.

Almost every Sunday evening Aunt Marilynn, Uncle Niles, and their deranged son come over for family dinner. Regardless of our parents' epic familial bond, the night always ends with Niklaus saying something subtle, something atrocious to provoke me. I'm apparently not smart enough to ignore the bait. He's crafty with his words, careful not to alert the parents that he's tormenting me. I usually hold it together. Simmer in unbearable silence. But there has been the occasional outburst.

Krimson is the only one who can pick up on the subtle digs. He's the only one who believes me when I come home crying.

He's gotten in a few fights with Niklaus over the years because of it.

"He's scared of Uncle Warrose," I mutter, continuing to study the carvings of trees in the old wood.

"I would too if he threw me off a cliff." Krimson chuckles.

Mom shoots us a warning look from her crouched position by the oven. But it's too late, I relish in the memory as it settles into my thoughts.

When I was eleven, Niklaus found me sitting on the cliff of the lagoon, praying to God to wake my daddy up. Praying that I'd get to see his brown eyes that my mother speaks so fondly of. Praying that he'd get to watch me grow up. I was in tears, and Niklaus still said what he said.

"Your daddy would have been a terrible father. He's got demons in his head and would have killed you for fun, I'm sure! You should be thanking God he's in that coma, rotting!"

It was the cruelest thing he's ever said to me.

And at such a low moment too.

But what he didn't know was that Uncle Warrose had just come back from Vexamen and was standing right behind him. I froze at the look on my uncle's face, the expression coated in ice, in war, in insurmountable rage. He lifted Niklaus off the ground with one hand by his throat and dangled him over the edge of the cliff.

And his rigid words have haunted me since.

"The man you speak of is my oldest and best friend in this world. He has given up more than you will ever know. Has endured more pain, more suffering than you could ever imagine. That includes not getting to raise the little girl you treat with such disrespect. If you weren't a child, I would have skinned you alive and fed you to my wolves for saying one ill word about my best friend. If I ever hear you disrespect his name or his children again, I'll do much worse than this…" And with a slight shift of his hand, he let the stunned eleven-year-old boy go, dropping him in the chilly lagoon in the middle of autumn.

My mom glances at me daydreaming, wiping her hands off on a towel.

"Aunt Marilynn says he's been a lot better lately. Having a girlfriend has really helped."

Why is she so naïve? So blind?

Has she never had to deal with a heartless man in her life?

I sigh loudly. "How long until they're here?"

"One hour."

I don't dare to greet them at the door.

Nope, my ass is planted firmly in my chair.

The plan for this evening is to ignore, deflect, and to just leave if he pokes and prods at my patience.

He does not exist.

He's dead.

Died.

Corpse.

I breathe in and out. Why am I already angry?

"*Ahem*!"

I jerk my head toward the dining room entryway.

"No one took my coat at the door. No one announced my title and arrival. No one escorted me to my dining seat. What kind of an event are you running here?"

I lose a little steam at the sight of his hand on his hip. Flecks of snow melting on top of his golden hair.

"Hi, Uncle Niles."

"I'm pretty important," he adds with narrowing eyes.

I crack a smile and get up to hug him. Wrapping my arms around his neck, my frigid heart thaws out as he hugs me back. It's expected when hugging Uncle Niles. It's a natural law when being embraced by someone like him. These hugs are the warmest. The sweetest. And he almost always has a joke lined up to make me laugh.

Why does his son have to be a narcissistic—

"You're insulting my son again in your head, aren't you?" Uncle Niles kisses the side of my hair.

"No…"

"Can I help?"

"Give it your best shot." I grin against his shoulder.

"Niklaus was a slippery baby," he says seriously.

I crack a smile. "Was he now?"

"Yes. Always lathered in too much oil after his bath."

"Oh. I sure hope he wasn't—"

"Dropped? Several times? No. No, no, no, no…" Uncle Niles smiles innocently.

I burst into laughter.

"I heard my name."

The devil himself enters my kitchen bringing with him plagues, famine, everlasting darkness, and the temptation to end it all right now just to get away from him.

"No one said your name," Uncle Niles responds.

My arms cross as I separate from the warmest hug. It seems you *can* summon evil by calling upon a demon's name.

"Don't I get a hug, Spitfire?"

I stare impassively.

"Niklaus," Uncle Niles warns. "You know she doesn't like being called that."

"No, not at all." I wave my hand nonchalantly, taking two careful steps toward his tall, cocky stance.

Niklaus's eyebrows raise a fraction of an inch as I hug him stiffly. He doesn't react right away. There's a pause in the slow-moving pattern of his brain.

We *never* hug.

Maybe three or four times in my life. Once for my sixth birthday when Aunt Marilynn forced him to. Other times when he was made to apologize for bullying the shit out of me.

But I don't let go until he hugs back. His lean arms circle my waist. It's intimate…and my skin crawls at the interaction.

Reaching up to my tiptoes, I hover my lips over his ear, and with a tone so sensual, so soothing, I whisper… "Out of all the sperm to win the race…"

Niklaus pauses before he laughs, tossing his head back as his upper body rumbles against my chest. I immediately pull away from our embrace to walk back to my seat. The sound of his laughter is confusing to me. It's the kind of wheezing laugh that gets everyone else to laugh. It's the laugh that you look for when you're trying to decide if something is funny or not. But unfortunately for me, it's also the sound I've grown accustomed to when he's getting a classroom to make fun of me.

"Wow. You never laugh that hard at my jokes." Uncle Niles pouts, finding his place at the table.

"I don't laugh at all at your jokes," Niklaus retorts.

I have never understood how he could be so callous toward his dad. It's always been this way since he was a little boy. My mom assumed it was after Niklaus learned about how his birth father, Aurick Demechnef, died—saving Uncle Niles's life.

Though Uncle Niles has been such a good father that I would find myself hot with rage and envy. It used to make me wonder what kind of dad mine would have been. Was he funny like Uncle Niles? Was he warm and sweet?

Or was he cold and heartless the way Niklaus has always taunted me with?

I wish I knew.

Uncle Niles shrugs. "It's not your fault, son." Following me to my seat, he leans in. "Slippery baby. Long-term side effects. No sense of humor."

I snicker, giving him a grateful pat on the back.

"When did you two start dating?" Mom's voice echoes from down the hall.

Did Krimson bring a girl over?

To my confusion, my brother saunters in with a strange look widening his heterochromatic eyes. His giant, muscular frame takes up the entryway as he pauses to communicate something. A warning directed to me. And as his twin, I know I'm about to be sucker-punched.

"Sapphire!" Mom trails in behind Krimson, holding someone's hand. "Look who's joining us for dinner!"

Short, white-blonde, baby-blue-eyed, gorgeous *Mabel Rose*.

My. Best. Friend.

Our eyes clash as she greets everyone with that bright, glittering smile of hers. Those pink cheeks, glossy lips, and thick eyebrows captivate any audience. Though that grin slips as she processes my face. My look of shock. *Her* look of shock. It's as if *she's* surprised to see *me*.

In my own house!

Mabel Rose parts her lips, glances at Niklaus who has taken his seat across from me. *Why is she looking at him?*

"You didn't tell me Mabel Rose and Niklaus were dating, Sapph!" Mom says, ushering my *dead* best friend to her seat next to the clinical-grade malignant narcissist.

Dating.

They're dating.

The shock sitting in my stomach like a rock, turns to hot, burning coals.

"*What the fuck?*" The sound barely makes its way past my lips.

"Respond *after* dinner," Krimson whispers next to me.

Respond. Don't react. It's his award-winning advice when I have a meltdown. I've had these quick bursts of fury that get the best of me since I was five.

But how the hell am I supposed to sit here and pretend like someone didn't just perform open-heart surgery on me while I'm wide awake?

"What. The. Fuck…" I whisper again.

"It's still pretty new," Mabel Rose responds to my mother. She walks with her head down until claiming the seat next to Niklaus. They exchange a look, and he pats her thigh reassuringly.

Anger lashes through me, sawing my molars together, launching a flare-up of acid reflux. I stare at them together with bulging, unrelenting eyes.

Krimson's foot brushes mine. "You're going to burst a blood vessel."

My heart bucks in my chest as Mabel Rose meets my eyes again, then turns away to scratch a fictional itch on her ankle.

"Let's hope I die of internal bleeding then," I respond.

He chuckles.

Mabel Rose has been my best friend since starting school when we were five. She helped me wipe the saliva off my face after I moronically confessed my love for the slippery baby. She was there almost every time he made me cry. She might be the only person, other than my brother, that knows of how evil and horrendous Niklaus Demechnef has been to me.

And yet…

"So, how the hell did this cute little…*thing* start between you two?" I ask with a critical smile.

"*Sapphire*," Krimson warns.

"The night of your birthday party," Niklaus answers like he's been waiting his entire life to hit me with this one. Right in the jugular. And it fucking *stings*.

My innards buckle down as I catch fire.

"Eight. *Months*. Ago?" I grit through my teeth.

Mabel-The-Coward-Rose doesn't look up from her hands twisting in her lap.

I'll gut her.

Under the table, Krimson snatches my clenched fist. He squeezes over and over again. The act makes me want to cry in his arms. My best friend has been hiding a secret relationship with Niklaus Demechnef for eight fucking months?! My mind zooms through different insignificant moments I should have caught on to. Her not wanting to talk about secret meetings with a crush she's had for a while. I didn't press because I figured he was ugly, and she was embarrassed. But *this* makes far more sense.

"Very good, Spitfire. And here I wasn't sure if you were any good in mathematics."

I rise from my seat. But a ginormous hand lands on my shoulder to keep me from moving.

"Who the fuck taught you to speak to a woman like that?" A gravelly, masculine voice slices through the tension in the air. An alpha presence. A booming tone of authority.

It reminds me of what everyone says my dad was like.

But of course, it couldn't be him.

It's his best friend.

I whip my head around to see Uncle Warrose standing behind me, burning his stare into Niklaus like he's about to beat me to that steak knife. He's still in his raven-black General's uniform. Sleek feathers, weapons strapped across his body, and ferocious tattoos trailing up the sides of his neck.

"Hello, Uncle Warrose," Niklaus purrs like he isn't sweating his ass off at the size of the great oak behind me. Like he isn't contemplating leaving the dinner early.

"Don't *hello* me." My uncle turns to the right. "Niles, that's some real parental authority you're exhibiting right now. I walk in for two seconds and already hear the immediate disrespect spewing out of your kid."

For a moment, I feel bad for the way my Uncle Niles opens and closes his mouth. He looks just as helpless as I feel in his son's presence.

"What'd he do now?" Aunt Marilynn walks in with Aunt Ruth coming up behind her in that beautifully carved chair.

"Just insulting Sapphire again," I mutter in her direction.

Aunt Marilynn casually walks around the table, lifts her milky white hand, and smacks Niklaus on the back of his stupid head. Exactly like how Grandpa always does to Uncle Niles.

"Apologize," she says calmly, with radiant blue eyes that puncture through him.

Niklaus cracks his neck, redirects those deceivingly beautiful ocean eyes toward me, and smirks. "I'm sorry, Spitfire. I'm sure you're very good in mathematics."

But oh, that stare is communicating a thousand other insults.

With just my thumb, I trace the carvings on the table again.

The carvings my father made with a steady hand.

How different from him I feel as mine isn't steady at all.

It's trembling.

2. Mabel Rose

I turn to Uncle Warrose, throwing my arms around his waist in relief.

"Hey, kid," he breathes.

"Missed you," I grumble into his massive shoulder. He smells like a winter storm and a heated cabin.

"Feeling a little neglected over here," Aunt Ruth announces.

Uncle Warrose and I both chuckle. But Krimson leaps from his chair to rush to her with wide, open arms. He hugs her so hard and so fast that her wheels roll backward a few inches. She lets out that beautiful fairy laugh I love so much.

Everyone rises from their seats to greet them. Grandpa trudges in shortly after, bringing in firewood as DaiSzek moseys in to casually nudge his nose against his house guests. I scratch his head as he passes by.

I tune in and out of the conversations, my eyes trailing over anything else in the house to mentally escape the two individuals I want nothing to do with at the table. I look to the stone hearth in the center of the living room. The mantel's lined with trinkets Uncle Warrose and Aunt Ruth brought back from Vexamen. Dried herbs hang from the fireplace, filling the house with the gentle scent of lavender and sage.

For a while, I watch the fire dance absently, wishing I was alone in the woods. To cry over a ruined friendship. To process the knife to the back I just received.

The dinner carries on with stories of the prison or the asylum, and it all sounds dramatized for our entertainment. We're old enough to hear some details now, but they still manage to hide most of the horror we learn about in school. Their adventures together as a group sound like a grim fairy tale.

"The only dining party I wish I could seriously attend was Meridei's little get-together…" Uncle Niles reminisces. "God, she was a psychopath. Hey, Ruthie, didn't you have a run-in with her mother?"

Aunt Ruth stops chewing her food to roll her eyes. "Apple May, yes. Don't remind me."

"You did?" My mother looks surprised.

"Yeah. At the infirmary during my recovery. She really had it out for me."

"What? You never told me that. What happened?" Mom asks.

Uncle Warrose and Aunt Ruth exchange a look before she responds.

"We all had a lot going on during that time. After the war. Ah, let's see." Aunt Ruth dabs her napkin along her lips. "She tormented me a few times."

"Details," my mother insists.

"Not at the dinner table."

"Why was she tormenting you?!" I ask.

"A couple reasons. I was getting more attention than her for my injuries. And, well, she was an incredibly vain woman. She was attracted to Uncle Warrose, and he clearly didn't feel the same."

Krimson and I bust out laughing. The distraction of a positive feeling doesn't outweigh the bad ones, but it does help.

"No need to laugh that hard," Uncle Warrose says with a glare.

We laugh harder.

"Then when she threatened to go after *you*, Skylenna, I..."

We all lean forward, collectively very invested in this story.

"What?" My mother blurts out.

"Aunt Ruth clawed Apple May's eyes out with her thumbs," Uncle Warrose finally reveals.

"Jesus!" I slap my hand down on the table.

Aunt Ruth waves off the gasps. "Back to that dining party with Meridei. He *loved* to put on a performance, didn't he?" she snickers into her hand.

I glance down the hall paneled with dark red oak, exhaling against the ominous energy floating along the walls and into his room like a cemetery of disgruntled spirits.

"What'd he do?" my brother asks. This part is not in the history books. So, when we hear about new stories regarding our father, Krimson is always the first to ask. I'd rather leave well enough alone.

My mom shifts in her seat. "It's not appropriate for the dinner ta—"

"He made them think he poisoned their champagne!" Uncle Niles announces excitedly. "But he just made them puke their guts out and have...you know, diarrhea!"

Grandpa promptly pinches the back of his arm to which Uncle Niles hisses and pulls away.

"Why'd he do that?" Niklaus asks on this rare occasion. He never wants to hear about my father. In fact, neither of us do. It's the one thing we have in common.

Grandpa and my aunts and uncles all turn to look at Mom. And there's this weight in the air. A blanket of respect that seems to fall over the table.

Mom sets her glass down. "They were mistreating and bullying me for trying to stop the cruel treatments in the asylum."

Niklaus levels his gaze with hers. "And he came up with that plan to ruin their dinner party when you told him about their mistreatment?"

"I didn't have to. He saved me from their hazing methods every time. He saw what they were doing to me and wanted to make them suffer for it."

Aunt Ruth turns to Krimson and me. "Your father was a cold, calculating man… But when your mother walked into a room, that ice would melt for her. He was terrifying to all except her."

Something like admiration glimmers across Krimson's face. He's always craved stories about our father, always wanted to be strong, fearless, and powerful just like him.

"Sounds like a real stick-in-the-mud," I say with a flat tone and blank expression.

Uncle Warrose burns me with his hazel glare. "You certainly have his sour, stick-in-the-mud personality. So go on, keep insulting his memory."

My blood goes cold in my seat.

Mom usually lets me make dry comments or insults about my father in her presence because she feels bad I'll never get to know him. She thinks this is a coping mechanism.

But Uncle Warrose has no such leniency.

"Why're you sitting all the way over there?" Uncle Niles barks, changing the subject to relieve the tension.

Uncle Warrose does not tear his roasting glare away from me.

I slouch under the weight of it.

"I'm right next to you," Aunt Marilynn laughs.

"Too far." He scoops her up from her seat and plops her butt down on his lap. "Much better. Niles happy."

"*Christ*," Niklaus hisses, dropping his fork down with a clank.

Mom shifts around the table, serving everyone this weird, pancake-glazed cake. It's an inside joke. Something about the prison for Uncle Niles's birthday. Forks scrape against plates. The heat of the oven permeates the dining room in subtle waves.

"So, how serious is this, Niklaus? Love? Fling? Getting married soon?" Mom asks with a small laugh.

The redirection to the two people in the room I'm refusing to look at tugs at an old feeling that has been buried. Something that makes me feel small and insignificant.

It reminds me of a time when I was little, sitting at my father's bedside, watching the snow fall across his frosted window.

I held that limp hand close to my chest, trying to go into the void like Mom. I was trying to find him in Ambrose Oasis. But to my immediate disappointment, I'm not like my parents at all. There isn't anything special about me. And when I realized that I was holding the dead, limp hand of a man I would never meet…

I threw a fit.

I screamed and cried and destroyed his room. Dresser drawers were yanked from their slots, chucked into walls. Picture frames were shattered. Curtains ripped from windows.

And Uncle Warrose just happened to return home to surprise me.

He found me screaming cruel, cruel words in my father's face.

All I remember after that was being held in his lap while I cried. He rocked me back and forth in front of the fireplace, singing a sad song, reminding me that he's always going to look out for me.

Mabel Rose opens her mouth to answer. Her pink lips curling into a grin of utter happiness, like this is one topic she's been eager to talk about. And clearly, she's forgotten I'm in the room, sneering in her filthy direction.

"Fling." The word comes out with such finality to it in Niklaus's smooth voice.

Fling.

Mabel Rose isn't subtle in the twist of her frame, creaking the chair as she gawks at his lean profile. The betrayal darkening her gaze is unmistakable. She's mirroring the expression that has yet to slip from my grasp. That has yet to remove its dirty claws from my spine.

"Oh, okay." Mom nods as she sits down. "Nothing serious then."

I bite my tongue in sickened disbelief. It's as if I'm meeting Mabel Rose for the first. A devious version of her. A liar. A soulless individual who takes pride in watching me burn.

How did I not see it?

Embarrassment hits me square in the face as tears glide over my eyes.

It was right there in front of me…

Niklaus eyes me before he replies. Like he is enjoying my reaction as he pokes at a bruise.

Don't you fucking cry in front of him. Don't you dare.

"Just having fun."

Mabel Rose is a statue. No longer a human woman with a splitting, aching heart.

My upper body quivers first, then I bubble into hysterical laughter. It weaves and flutters up my throat in a contagious fit.

"Fun?" I place my hand over my mouth to contain myself.

Niklaus glides his stare to me. Cold, curious, creeping amusement.

"You think you're showing her a good time?" I swat Krimson's steadying hand away. "Fun would require your dick to be bigger than a pencil. Fun would require you to know what to do with a woman's pussy in order to make her come. Fucking you wouldn't be *fun*. It would be *charity*."

I smile wider as my mom rises from her chair to stop me. The rest of the table does something similar.

Niklaus raises a devious brow. "You want me to pull it out to measure, Spitfire?"

I don't pay him a second glance. "And you." I rise from my seat to point at the traitor. "My best friend? You *actually* fell for him, didn't you?"

But it's the way she stares back at me, unyielding and prepared for this reaction that summons a thought. My brother once warned me about Mabel Rose when we were twelve. He connected the dots when we met her parents. He told me she is the distant cousin of someone our mother killed in the asylum.

Belinda was her name.

I told Krimson that meant nothing. Mabel Rose swore to me she didn't even know Belinda and their families weren't close… But what if they were?

And all I can see is red. Fire. Brimstone. Ash. *Betrayal. Betrayal. Betrayal.*

"Come on, sit down," my mother barks.

But Mabel Rose continues staring at me. The vacant eyes of a trickster that has little regard for their victim. A mask of innocence with a hint of relief that I'm making a fool of myself in front of my family.

It's what Krimson warned against, isn't it?

Belinda.

Belinda.

Belinda.

"You did it on purpose…didn't you?" I say breathlessly.

My throat tightens up as I wait for her answer.

Krimson's chair groans under him as he adjusts his weight.

Mabel Rose holds my gaze without blinking.

"You should drink some water, Sapphire. You're becoming hysterical."

My last bit of patience explodes.

The glowing memories I had of our childhood together melts under a flame. The edges of each fond recollection I have of her curls and blackens at the corners, burning and fraying. This new Mabel Rose I have yet to see. Yet to interact with.

She is no longer my childhood best friend.

Mabel Rose is Belinda's cousin.

And as my face turns bright red, Mabel Rose lowers her lashes to smile, perfect and porcelain at my expense.

A wolf stirs inside of me.

The same carving under my thumb.

And I let it loose.

I allow another beat of uncomfortable silence to suck the oxygen from the air before I respond with what I deem to be appropriate.

"I'm so glad my mother killed your cousin like a rabid dog. Let's hope you're not next."

3. "Your Father Was a Great Man."

Snowflakes sting my cheeks as I breathe them in.

In and out.

In and out.

The fear of crying looms over me. I ignore it by taking in the Red Oaks crystalized with snow and ice. The chimney of my house expels clouds of smoke, carrying the fragrance of burning wood, pine, and cloves. The stars glimmer so brightly, their white light pings off the frozen body of water by the dry waterfall.

My feet dangle over the cliff of the lagoon. And I wonder how badly it would hurt to jump in winter water and crash through that plate of ice protecting its current.

In and out.

Once I gather the courage and learn more about the outside countries, I'm getting the hell out of here. I'm buying passage on a boat and venturing far away for a new life. I'm changing my name. I'm going somewhere where no one knows my family. Where no one has ever heard of Valdawell. Of Patient Thirteen. I'll be a nameless stranger who gets to live out my life in peace and solitude. Demechnef will not mean anything to me.

"You always know how to make these dinners entertaining, don't you? Just like your father." Uncle Warrose wraps a heavy fur blanket around me before taking a seat.

I fidget with a crispy red leaf between my fingers.

"I could have killed Niklaus as a grand finale. That also sounds like something my dad would have done."

He chuckles. "Yeah. I'm not going to disagree with you on that."

"You know I don't like talking about him," I say quietly.

"Which him are we referring to?"

"My father."

"I know."

For some strange reason, my eyes start to water.

"But sometimes when I'm going head-to-head with Niklaus…I wish my dad was standing next to me. Standing *up* for me." I bow my head at the unwanted confession.

Why am I getting choked up?

"I hear you," Uncle Warrose rasps. "But here's how I see it. Your father was a great man. When he walked into a room, it was as if a king was returning to his throne. He demanded fear and respect and admiration from anyone who set foot in his presence. And the beauty is…*you* are *his* daughter. Just like him, you don't *need* anyone to stand up for you. In fact, he preferred it that way."

My eyes well with more tears. Hot and thick against the winter chill.

"But I'm not like him at all! I'm not special. I'm ordinary with a bad temper. That's it!"

A large hand rubs circles over my back. And there's that pang in my stomach again, that zing up my spine, that for a split-second, I wish the hand was my father's.

"Where do you think you get your temper from?"

"Certainly not my mom."

He sighs. "I think you might be mistaking patience and kindness for weakness when it comes to her."

"Am I though? Look at her! She's naïve and clueless. That woman spends so much time in that sad, dreary room holding my father's hand. What part of that screams *power* and *warrior* to you like everything I've been taught in school? There's no way history reported any of what she did accurately."

I glance over at my uncle's face as he smirks to himself, shaking his head.

"What?" I ask.

"It's a shame you'll never see what I've seen." His glittering hazel eyes trace over the icy lagoon in thought. "Your father was a force, yes. But your mother is the one who led armies to save us. She's the one who played the enemy like a puppet. Who dragged their subconsciouses to hell and back. *She's* the one who won the war."

I try to picture that beautiful blonde woman hurting anyone. Saving anyone. I mean, sure, I've seen the illustrations. I've read the descriptions of the part she's played. But I can never see it in my head. She's always just that sad woman sitting at his bedside.

"And if you think your father was the only one with a bad temper, you're wrong. The day she destroyed that asylum was more pain and fury than you might ever see in your lifetime."

Not a lot of detail for that story. They said it was a slaughter from the Fallen Saint. They said it was exacted revenge, and she gave each member what they deserved.

"I plan on doing something similar to Niklaus," I grumble.

"Is that a fact?"

"It is."

He's quiet for several seconds. "I know he seems like the enemy now. But there are far worse people in this world, Sapphire. And you two will have to be on the same team to defeat them."

Over my dead body.

Niklaus and the traitor have left.

But everyone else stays to say goodbye to my dad. Even though it makes me deeply uncomfortable and angry for some reason, Krimson and I always stand in the doorway to watch the interaction.

They sit around his bed, talking, sharing updates on their lives, and reminiscing.

Why? I have no idea. He's brain-dead. He cannot hear them. He cannot feel them hold his hand. He can't interact. But I suppose this little ritual of theirs is more to make them feel better than anything else.

"That's how my week went, Dess." Uncle Niles pats the top of Dad's hand, then snickers. "I love that I can call you by that nickname now without getting the death glare."

Though his smile fades. And he's left with a vacant look that tells me he doesn't love it at all. He misses that glare from my father.

However, this starts a new conversation about how mad my father was when Uncle Warrose brought up the nicknames he used to give himself as a child. Dess-aster. Dess-truction.

The room trembles with laughter.

"I hope we have a group of friends like this one day," Krimson whispers.

I shrug. I'll be long gone by then.

"I wonder what he was like with all of them. I mean, I know how Kane was. He liked them. Was nice. Patient," he goes on, watching their banter with thoughtful eyes.

"And now brain-dead," I add.

It's disturbing how they all sit around his lifeless body like this. It's not right. Just let him go. Let him be.

"Bite your tongue. Jesus. Sometimes I wonder if we were raised by the same woman." Krimson furrows his brow, crosses his arms, and broods to himself. It's the same expression Mom always says makes him look just like our father.

I turn away. Every time he's upset with me, a knot forms in my gut. Tight and unwanted.

"I don't know why I'm like this," I murmur.

His arms slacken an inch.

I wish I was more like you.

"It's okay."

The room begins clearing, but Uncle Warrose stays to talk to my dad. Shoulders slumped, husky, quivering voice. And Aunt Ruth gives us a quick pat to give him some privacy.

"Why does he always want to talk to him alone after?" I ask.

"To catch him up on everything that's going on in Vexamen."

Aunt Ruth shrugs a petite, pointed shoulder, ruffling her curly brown hair.

"Why?" I push again.

Krimson gives me a shoulder bump.

Aunt Ruth studies my face for a moment too long, making me feel small and arrogant in her line of sight. She's always had this elven-like beauty. I used to tell Mom that I wanted to look just like her. I wanted curly brunette hair, rich brown eyes, freckles, and to be a queen too. I even had Krimson push me around in a dining table chair to pretend it was her beautifully carved moving chair. If Aunt Ruth had to use one, it must be something to strive for. A tool for queens.

When Mom told Aunt Ruth about it, she laughed, hugged me, and said "*that's a beautiful compliment to give, little Sapphire.*"

"Are you asking that question to make another insensitive dig at your father's condition, or do you genuinely want to know why he would want to share that information?"

I shrink a little.

She nods like that small movement answered her question.

"Just because your father is in a coma, is unresponsive, and your mother can't find him or any of his alters in the void... That doesn't mean a damn thing." She runs her thin hands over the wrinkles in her blood red winter dress. "Why? Because his heart is still beating. His lungs are still filling with air. He's still alive. I've seen that man rise from the fucking grave. I've seen him take on leagues of men and win. I've seen him save the woman he loves with impossible odds. And in all that time, I've learned one lesson that remains the same."

Her round, beautiful eyes bounce back and forth between me and my twin.

"To never underestimate the lengths Dessin will go to be with the woman he loves. Nothing is impossible for him. And after all he's done for us, holding out hope until my dying breath is the least I can do."

They speak of him like he is a god. I'll never understand it.

"I've read about his adventures. All the myths and legends that are attached to his name," I say coldly. Why am I like this? Why can't I just respect their opinions and move on? Why must I always have this undying urge to prove that he isn't as impressive as they all claim?

Aunt Ruth laughs, but there isn't any humor in her eyes. "Read? Your eyes trailed over words on paper, and you think that does him justice? It's one thing to hear about Patient Thirteen in a lecture at school. It's another to witness it when death is biting at your heels." She looks down at her lap, thinking quietly to herself. "I wish you could have been there, little Sapphire. Maybe then you'd understand the gravity of love and respect we all have for him."

I continue to shrink.

"I understand, Aunt Ruth. I've always known my father was a great man," Krimson says with both sadness and impenetrable pride.

"The greatest." She nods in agreement.

After everyone leaves, and I say good night to Mom, Krimson, and Grandpa, I walk through the dark house and stand in the doorway of my father's room. It still carries that haunting scent of old books, sandalwood, and fresh linen blankets.

I watch his chest rising and falling for what feels like several minutes.

"You have them all fooled," I say in a low, hushed voice.

He continues to breathe. To sleep. To take up space.

"They all think you're this great hero."

I do not often address him directly. In fact, I try to avoid this area as much as I can. But tonight was too much to handle alone. I only talk to him when I've had enough. When I want someone to blame. When I need to lash out without judgment.

"But where were you when Niklaus Demechnef pushed me over the Chandelier Bridge, and I had to fight the current to make it out without drowning when I was ten? Where were you when I fell out of the treehouse and broke my ankle? What about last year when Niklaus soaked my dress in ink at the ball and I left in tears?"

My blood rushes to my face in mortification and hatred. Hot, angry fireworks go off in my arteries. And I want to cry. I want to scream. I want to throw things. I want him to feel how much this *hurts.*

"Where were you then? If my father is supposedly the most powerful man our country has ever known, then where was he when his only daughter needed him?" Tears roll down my cheeks. I wipe them away furiously. "Where were you, Dad?"

As the hiccuping sobs barrel through my throat, a pair of hands turn me around by my shoulders and pull me into a wide, hard chest.

"I've got you," Krimson breathes, strained and labored.

"I hate him," I cry.

"I know."

"He's saved everyone. He's been there for everyone. Why not me?"

"I know," he says again.

"It's not fair."

Krimson holds me while my tears soak his gray nightshirt. He holds me because he's the only one who knows where my fury comes from. Where my insensitive comments originate. Right here. In the doorway of a great man who no longer can do great things.

Not even for his children.

4. Homicidal Mania

Apparently, the city we live in is very different from what it looked like twenty years ago.

My brother and I go to a savant school for adults now, between the ages of twenty and twenty-five, close to the Dellilian Castle. There's a beautiful reform estate where the Emerald Lake Asylum used to sit. It now acts as a sanctuary, a rehabilitation home for those with mental illness, trauma from the old days of Demechnef law. My grandfather, Chekiss, runs it with so much compassion and care, no one would ever know the dark secrets that land still holds from the old asylum.

Women no longer have to starve themselves, although many older women still do.

Since Aunt Marilynn and Uncle Niles have taken Aurick Demechnef's place, many laws were abolished and new ones were created to protect women, the mentally ill, and equality.

Apparently, my parents made this all possible.

Apparently, this city used to be filled with manic dolls, fainting couches, and boutiques filled with concoctions of creams and oils for nightly routines. Mints to help a woman purge her food if she ate too much. Brass corsets that helped reshape a ribcage to permanently give that hourglass figure.

I get told often by our professor how lucky I should feel.

"Women used to be oppressed."

"Women used to be monitored."

"Women used to be judged by their menstrual hysteria."

It's hard to feel lucky when I've only ever seen the good side of this country. Everything else feels like a dark and disturbing fairytale. Not to mention…*fictional*.

"Niklaus, what do you think? I'm certain you have a unique take on this," Professor Nundy turns from his chalkboard.

Niklaus sits one row behind me. I try to ignore him back there, but paranoia gets the best of me. How could it not? He used to stick gum in my hair or just glare at me until I turned around.

"We wouldn't have won the war without Mind Phantoms," he answers in boredom.

Krimson scoffs next to me.

"Interesting take," Nundy comments. "Mr. Valdawell, you don't agree?"

Don't agree? God, this is going to open a can of worms. Look who you're talking to. We're the children of Skylenna and Dessin and Kane Valdawell. Mind Phantoms destroyed our parents' lives.

"I'd say not," Krimson responds with a venomous chill to his tone. "Poisoning children and their parents so that they can be raised like pigs for slaughter? Can grown men not win their own wars anymore?"

My brother is so often calm and collected. Unless it comes to defending our parents. My mom always says those are the moments she can see the avenging alter in him. Dessin always showed his anger and ill-intent through cool, cutting words and an indifferent expression.

"War is war. There are no shortcuts." Niklaus sounds like he's on the verge of smiling. Krimson can hear it too.

"You're right. Far be it for the Demechnef family to have

enough balls to fight a war themselves. Let the Valdawell family continue to do the heavy lifting," Krimson replies with a cruel smirk.

A chair screeches behind us. Niklaus is on his feet, but neither of us turn to look.

"Conveniently leaving out moments of history for debate, I see. Or have you forgotten that Aurick Demechnef died in that war."

A thought sparks behind Krimson's punishing gaze. "Someone had to pay for the sins of the Demechnef dynasty, didn't they?"

Oof. Cold, Krim. Fucking cold.

Hey, I'm just happy I'm not the one doing the fighting this time.

Niklaus remains standing, somehow keeping his composure. Keeping his loud, violent silence.

"I suppose you're right. Considering he and Vlademur Demechnef are the reason we even had great, supernatural warriors to win this war, why shouldn't he be punished for such a heroic war plan?" Sarcasm. Heavy, condescending sarcasm. "Because once again, without Mind Phantoms, there wouldn't have been a great war to begin with. There would have been genocide of our country. But go on, Krimson. Continue telling me how the good of two outweighs the good of the many."

An icy fire roars under my brother's flesh. But he keeps it contained. He always does.

"You know, your own father was a victim of Mind Phantoms. So was your grandfather," Krimson breathes. The killing blow.

I turn around to see Niklaus's face, because right now...my interest is peaked. His furtive ocean eyes make a single sweep in my direction. It's quick but lands like a crashing avalanche over my body. The pang from its landing hits my stomach. What I see in his heavy stare isn't cruelty or coldness. It's a deeply embedded burden. The same discomfort I've seen in Niklaus since he was a little boy.

He covers it well.

Ultimately, he shifts his gaze back to my brother.

And that look morphs back to rigid spite.

"Niles Offborth is not my father. I'm a Demechnef. And he is nothing more than an asylum patient who should have never been released."

Oh, yeah.

He's a dead man.

The burst of rage is a flaming drug that turns my muscles into unfeeling iron. I rise from my seat slowly, snatching my textbook before Krimson has a chance to stop me. Without a word, I spin around and launch the heavy book at his face. It makes perfect contact with a loud thump followed by his deep, erupting snarl.

The classroom chuckles, gasps, and whispers.

Before he can retaliate, I make my way for the exit, turn on my heels and give him a glance of uncaring steel. "I hope you die alone, just like your father."

I wait outside in the glittering snow for my brother to get out of class. The small park is just outside of the Emerald Savant Estate. The central fountain is frozen, the stone walkway is covered in ice. But I don't move from this black iron bench. Even if it is named after my father.

My toes are numb, and my nose is the color of a cherry, but I refuse to show my face in there after throwing the book.

An angry chuckle ripples through my lungs, and I smirk back at the memory of his red face. *I threw a book at him. Ha!*

"Can we talk?"

My smile is peeled off my face.

The traitor stands to my left, shivering in her plush, white coat and blush-pink mittens.

"Can I get buried alive first?" I say without blinking.

"Sapphire," Mabel Rose says critically.

"What possesses you to believe you're safe in my presence right now?"

She shrugs. "Because I know you. Yes, you're grumpy, but

you'd never hurt anyone."

Wow. Maybe we were never friends. Does she know me at all? I stabbed Niklaus once with a pencil. And moments ago, I threw a heavy fucking book at his face.

"Do you know who my father was to the world, Mabel Rose?" *This*. This is one of the only times and occasions I use his reputation in my favor.

"A hero," she says.

"A monster."

She blinks in surprise. I don't let go of our eye contact. In fact, I let my stare make her undeniably uncomfortable. I let my inner monster gleam through my different colored eyes.

"They say he mutilated people who pissed him off. Albatross Ivast? Removed his penis and carved his name in his forehead. The head cook who starved him in the Vexamen Prison? Burned alive in her own oven." I rise from my father's dedicated bench. "Sometimes I feel those same sociopathic tendencies. Should we test my temper today?"

"You really don't think you deserve this after what your family has done to mine?" She takes a step away from me. "I mean, I know you had nothing to do with it…but am I not allowed to be angry and hold you accountable?"

I flex my abdomen as if she's just punched me.

"Eight. Months." My molars scrape together.

"I shouldn't have kept it from you for that long… I should have told you right away and that would have surely satisfied my need for retribution, and we could have moved on as friends. I just knew what you would say. I knew you'd hold a grudge instead of just accepting that this was purely out of vengeance."

"What would I say? That Niklaus Demechnef has tortured me for years. Has spoken unforgiveable statements about my father, not just to me but to everyone?!"

"You talk way more shit about your dad than he does!"

"BECAUSE HE'S *MY* FATHER! I'M ALLOWED TO HATE HIM! I'M ALLOWED TO TALK SHIT!"

Mabel Rose takes another vigilant step back, brushing her white-blonde bangs away from her face with nervous, trembling fingers.

"I know that. I'm sorry."

"What about when I was seven, and he dumped his glass of milk down my back at lunch? Or wait, no, I've got a good one." I hold my hand up and laugh. "How about last year when I cried at the picture of my father in that history book? I stepped out of class to have one fucking moment alone. And what did he do? He ripped the picture of him out and set it on fire to turn to ash on my desk."

"Krimson gave him a nasty black eye for that one, though," the traitor counters.

"So?!? That's the least of what he deserved! My father would have made him eat his own intestines for treating me this way!" I bite my own tongue. I don't normally speak so highly of him. But deep down…I think it might be true. If Uncle Warrose was willing to dangle a skinny eleven-year-old over the cliff of the lagoon by his neck, who knows what Patient Thirteen would have done for half of these offenses toward me.

"I don't think he's as bad as he portrays himself to be in front of everyone, Sapphire. Can't you just apologize for what your mother has done, and we can be even now?"

Hell pummels through my core in a firestorm of murderous thoughts.

"You think I deserved this to pay for the actions of my mother?"

"I do."

I hold my breath.

"Okay. Let's say that's true. Are you aware of what Belinda's crimes were? Torturing, maiming, and killing innocent people in the asylum?"

Mabel Rose does not have a rebuttal to that.

"Either way, what's done is done. I hope it made you feel better. Because I will never speak to you again."

"Is this because you're jealous of us?" She stomps her small foot in the crunchy snow.

Oh. Ohhh.

"I beg your pardon?"

"That's what this is all about, isn't it? You had the biggest crush on him all those years ago, and now you're just jealous that I got him, and you didn't!" I've never seen Mabel Rose's face so red, so pinched, so *ugly*.

"Got him? You *got* him?!" I bark out a hateful laugh. "He just admitted that you're an easy fuck at my house last night! In front of our families."

The length of her throat stretches and shifts. The insecurity stewing in her thoughts is bleeding into the minute changes in her body language. The twitching of her thumbs, licking of her lips, and uneven motion of her breathing.

"Did you really think we could still be friends after this? Even if I could get past the fact that you're sleeping with the man who has made it his mission to cause me great pain and humiliation, you lied to me for eight months. You are no friend of mine, Mabel Rose."

Off in the wintery distance of the estate, my brother and Niklaus make their way toward us. Their eyes are firmly on us with alarm and heightened interest.

"Then thank you for helping me realize something today," the traitor says calmly, schooling her features to appear poised and indifferent.

"And what's that?"

"I guess I'd rather be his easy fuck then your friend." White-hot venom. And she isn't done yet. Her white eyebrow lifts with a menacing thought. "Oh, and Sapphire? Your father is in a coma and is never going to wake. Get the fuck over it."

If I wasn't so shocked by her malice, I would act on the tendrils of resentment and wrath binding my organs in a chokehold. She didn't. She wouldn't. Unforgiveable. Dead to me.

"What are you two talking about?" Niklaus closes the distance behind Mabel Rose, consuming her small frame with his bulking height.

"You okay?" Krimson asks close to my ear.

I barely shake my head.

I'm not okay.

Niklaus holds my gaze like he's trying to pass me a secret message. With one arm draped over the traitor's shoulders, his smirk is slight. It tugs on the strong jawline covered in black whiskers, revealing a dimple on his left cheek. If I didn't know of the dark, dirty contours of his soul at every angle, I'd think he was the most beautiful man I'd ever seen.

A deceiving devil dressed as an angel.

And he's just taken my best friend away from me.

Murder dances behind my eyes, showering my thoughts with creative, delicious, substantial forms of torture and death.

Maybe I'm more like my father than I realized.

Letter #675

Skylenna

Dear Kane,

It's been a long week of temper tantrums from Sapphire. She's only four years old, but her mean streak is dramatically advanced. And the cruel things she's said to me? I didn't know a child could have such strong opinions. Last night she told me she wished I was in the coma instead of you. I just looked at her red face and nodded with tears pooling in my eyes. "Me too, baby. Me too."

Sometimes I watch these meltdowns, though, and want to laugh. The thought of you attempting to quell the theatrical outbursts and trying to keep your composure is hilarious. And don't get me started about the thought of Dessin trying his luck with her.

We had a good day though. I took Krimson and Sapphire to a small farm in the Bear Traps. They held chickens, milked a cow, and held baby goats. Sapphire held my hand for half of the trip.

I wish you could have seen it. I was so happy.

I'm working so hard to take care of your babies, honey. I put everything I have into loving them, caring for them, never letting them see me cry over your absence.

I hope I'm making you proud.

I love you still.

Sincerely,

Your Soulmate,
Skylenna

5. "You'll Get Yours."

"Why are you avoiding eye contact? Are you having a seizure? What's happening?" I ask Krimson.

He keeps his strained stare on the glittering night sky. Chin raised. Lips pursed.

"I'm not going to look at you when you have everything out on display like that," he grumbles, clenching his jaw.

I look down at my plunging square neckline. My dress is made of onyx silk, short and flowy around my mid-thigh, tight and tied off around my waist. My candy apple red winter cloak takes the bite out of the frost in the air, but yes, I'm freezing my ass off.

Do I look like an evil seductress coming to take a nice, juicy bite out of a boy's heart? Also, yes. Worth the discomfort.

"I look like old money and expensive sex. It's all a part of the plan."

Krimson huffs. "Never say that again."

We're walking along Main Street to the Chandelier Tavern. It was built seven years ago, encouraging women to dress less proper and express themselves and their sexuality. Apparently, dresses this short and lowcut weren't allowed in my mother's time.

Boring.

"I'm going to make him bleed." *Did I say that out loud?*

"You may be giving him the wrong idea with how you look."

My copper-blonde hair hangs in long spirals down my back, decorated with small rubies gifted to my mom by Aunt Ruth. (She doesn't know I took them, *whoops*.) My makeup was done with a precise hand, gold glitter on the inner corners of my eyes, black ink pointed like small knives on the outer corners. Long, wispy lashes, and blood red lips.

"Don't ruin my high," I tell him as he opens the tavern door for me.

The tavern is dim with candle-lit chandeliers, black marble surfaces, glossy espresso floors, and the strong scent of cigars and horny men.

Krimson laughs, signaling to the bar. "What'll it be?"

"Two shots of cognac." In the corner of my eye, I see Niklaus sitting with his inner circle. The traitor planted on his lap like a ridiculous decoration. "Make that three."

"Dear God," Krimson groans.

I hang my red cloak on the rack by the front door. And I'd be lying if I said I don't immediately notice the heads turn in the glowing, crystal tavern. My legs are shiny with gold shimmery body cream, breasts are two heavy swells above my low neckline, and this dress is stunning. It's a show or armor.

I can feel his eyes on me.

Let the games begin.

"Sapphire, you're a vision." Trexon Parlomon. The son of the late Suseas Parlomon. Former head conformist of the Emerald Lake Asylum. You'd think he'd hate me for what my mother did to his.

But of course, he's a man. And he's always made it clear he wants to buy me flowers, kiss my hand, and take me on lavish dates.

"Well, aren't you sweet?" I gaze up at him from under my lashes. I'm laying it on thick.

"Can I get you a drink?" he asks with a little too much excitement in his eyes. Trexon isn't very tall. About my height with skinny arms, chapped lips, and curly yellow hair. He has no idea that he's currently a pawn.

"She has one." My brother hands me my three shots, glaring down at Trexon with those eyes. The ones that big brothers and fathers have when they're hit with that horrid territorial urge to protect.

With one hand on my back, Krimson guides me deeper into the tavern.

One down.

"You must be psychic. That happened exactly how you planned," he murmurs over the loud music of saxophones and piano.

"And we're just getting started." I clink my glass to his, and we down our first shot. My throat, chest, and stomach buzz with a fierce chemical burn, but I don't let my face show it. It's water. *Water. Water. Water.*

"Did you wear that dress for me?" Ernest, the Chandelier City rake whispers in my ear.

He hits on me occasionally, but it isn't usually in front of large crowds like this. Ernest has old money, regularly throws ridiculously expensive parties, has had sex with basically every woman with a heartbeat. Even women older than his mother.

"I wore it for me," I say with a soft smile.

"Then maybe you could take it off for *me*. Later?"

"Perhaps. But you won't be able to enjoy the view without your eyes," Krimson growls, taking a step toward me.

Ernest is a good-looking man. Muscular and in shape, but he's no match for my brother. And he's certainly no match for the reputation attached to our last name.

Ernest backs away with an apologetic look. I shrug a shoulder and mouth the word *sorry*.

"This plan is starting to turn my stomach," my brother complains. And although he likes to pretend otherwise, Krimson has a temper when it comes to defending me or my mother. I know this is actually boiling his blood.

"Don't worry. Your part is almost over. Then you get to go flirt with the precious Genevieve watching you in the corner."

Krimson straightens, peeking over my shoulder to catch a glimpse of her.

"Good."

"Are they watching me?" I ask.

My twin's brown and green eyes slide to the left side of the tavern. He nods twice.

"Beautiful." I grin.

We take another shot. Krimson orders us two more. A shadow shifts behind me, and a finger taps me on the shoulder.

"No," Krimson barks at the faceless figure.

I grin wider. And that was the last one I needed. Here's the thing. Men want what other men want. If I walk into this tavern turning heads, and shooting down every suitor who comes tapping me on the shoulder…I'm twice as desirable. Even to the inner circle of my enemy.

Men are competitive. They want the chance to prove that they can claim what other men have tried and failed at. I'm playing them right into my hand.

Aunt Ruth taught me this.

"You're scary accurate. Quite the mastermind manipulator," Krimson mutters, giving me a quick kiss on my cheek before he makes his way to sweet Genevieve in the corner.

Game time.

I hold two shots in my hands, feeling the downpour of a great buzz filling my mind with temporary bliss. Careful not to appear too intoxicated, I start walking toward enemy lines. Niklaus's usual table. To his gang of friends that have helped make my life hell.

Although there is one man left who I'm waiting on to approach me. Ralik Marvelan. He's the only Demechnef swordsman who gives Niklaus a run for his money. They *hate* each other. Maybe more than he hates me. But the thing about Ralik is—he'd never approach me with Krimson at my side. He may be good with a sword, but everyone knows that no one can take Krimson on in hand-to-hand combat. He really is our father's son.

So, where does that leave me? Waiting on Ralik to approach now that I'm without my twin bodyguard. I'm banking on this exact move to put the pieces exactly where I want them.

And like a well-dressed puppeteer, a single step away from crossing Niklaus's table, Ralik stops me, holding a glass of champagne and that dangerously beautiful smile of his.

Please, please, please ask me what I want you to ask.

"Did you come here all by yourself, Valdawell?" Ralik purrs, those stunning white teeth contrasting with his dark skin.

There it is.

Even in the hazy shadows of the tavern, Niklaus's intrigued stare is boring into my spine. The weight of it alone sends a tingle of adrenaline scorching my toes and fingertips.

"Sorry, Marvelan. I'm actually here with my boyfriend." I point my chin to Niklaus's best friend, Stark. Broad-backed, long chestnut hair, pale skin, amber eyes, and apparently sporting a huge dick. I've chosen my puppet with careful consideration and distinct precision.

Stark and Niklaus have mirroring expressions. Wide eyes. Raised brows.

I smile sweetly to him, holding out the cognac. "Here's your shot, handsome." *And for the killing blow…*I give him the "*help me*" eyes. What man can resist swooping in and laying false claim to the woman in the tavern who's getting the most attention? Especially from their sworn swordsman opponent.

Stark takes a second too long to think about this. His glowing amber eyes shift from me to Ralik. My stomach sinks at the possibility of this plan failing miserably. How would I play it off? How would I recover?

"Rotten luck, Marvelan," Stark says, standing to take the shot out of my hands. "She's coming home with me tonight."

I give Ralik an apologetic look as he storms off.

Taking a seat next to my victim posing as a white knight, I delicately place my hand on his thigh, leaning close to his ear.

"You're a lifesaver," I breathe against his skin.

Stark freezes up, then clinks his glass against mine. "Need a fake boyfriend tonight to keep these horny men off you, little Valdawell?"

I'm tempted to roll my eyes at the nickname. I'm five foot ten, much taller than the average woman here.

I gaze up at him from under my lashes and nod. "Would you mind?"

Stark is particularly attractive as he nods. Amber eyes, plush full lips, and hair that might be shinier than mine. It goes down to his collarbone, pin straight and tousled to one side.

He's gorgeous.

Unfortunately, nothing compares to the icy blades that are Niklaus's searing eyes. His face, holding no shame, is turned toward me. A portrait of disbelief. Raw, unblemished beauty. Disagreement written across his pinched brow.

The sight is victory. It only spurs me on.

"To being your fake girlfriend for the night?" I hold up my glass.

"To making every man in this bar sick with jealousy." He smiles, tossing back the shot.

Now that I have a solid buzz, keeping my face emotionless as I let the fire slip down my throat is fairly easy. However, even I know I shouldn't have taken this next shot. The fear of getting too happy, too friendly sits unwelcomed on the precipice of this plan.

"How should we keep up the ruse of convincing everyone here that we're together?" I ask, pulling the hem of my dress down an inch.

Keep your faculties, Sapphire.

"Well," Stark sits up a little straighter, "I'd normally have my girlfriend sit in my lap."

I must be a fucking wizard.

"I guess I could—"

"No." Niklaus's silky voice cuts through my buzz.

Stark shoots him with a grimace. "And you can shut the fuck up."

"I said no," Niklaus repeats, stroking Mabel Rose's thigh.

Ha! Faculties gone.

I pop up from my seat, straighten my dress, and slide onto Stark's lap like a lady. Right hand clasping his neck, I take his wrists and circle them around my legs and waist. All while facing Niklaus and the traitor.

Does he see right through this? Without a doubt.

Is that the point? No.

This is.

"You know…I could use a fake boyfriend to the Emerald Lake Ball next week," I murmur so *so* close to Stark's face.

"Need me to fend off more horny men, little Valdawell?" An eagerness is sparked in those amber eyes.

"Mmm-hmm. If you're not careful, I may start needing you more often. Day *and* night."

Niklaus is still staring. Seething. Smoke pouring from his skin in lethal waves.

"I think I'm up for the job," he says.

Mabel Rose makes several attempts to get Niklaus's attention to no avail.

"And what about right now? My boyfriend would have kissed me by now, don't you think?" Whose voice am I using? It's...*perfect!* Low, sultry, full of raspy spice.

Stark blinks before he processes my request. He doesn't smile. Doesn't respond. He doesn't waste this opportunity. Gripping his hands to my waist, he pulls me flush to his chest, lifting his chin so that I get the hint to lean in the rest of the way.

And I do.

My lips tease his at first. A light brushing of my skin to his. But then I let out a soft moan and lick his mouth lightly. That's enough to undo the stoic composure that he's known for. Stark takes me by the neck, opening his mouth to meet my tongue with his own. The kiss is hot, wet, and honestly? Delicious.

"Goddamn, little Valdawell," he groans into my mouth.

Make it hotter. Alcohol swims in my thoughts, taking the reins and leading me to go further. I slide my hand down the tight muscles of his stomach, caressing his belt buckle.

His kiss is bruising before it stops abruptly. My mouth is greeted by a violent gust of air as Stark is ripped from my lips, my hands, even my backside is no longer supported by his lap. I crash to the floor.

"Shit!" An ache shoots up my tailbone. I scramble to get back to my feet in case I'm drunkenly flashing anyone in this dress.

Niklaus has taken Stark to the ground. Foot on his throat. "I. Said. *No.*"

Internally, fireworks erupt, the sun rises, and I do a little dance.

"Stark?" I place a hand on Niklaus's shoulder, so I can get a better look at his best friend. "Pick me up at eight for the ball."

And I make my exit. With one last look at that storm of bewildered, ocean eyes, I send him a message that's made of hot coals and rusted blades.

What took you eight months, I can do in one night. To fuck my friend. To charm her pants off. To get into her heart.

Rot, Motherfucker.

6. Storm of The Void

I throw my red hood over my head with a victorious smile. Flecks of snow sprinkle over my lashes as I stare up at the winter starry night. It's past midnight, so the Chandelier City is quiet aside from this tavern. A peaceful setting for a walk back to my house in the Red Oaks.

As I move down the cobblestone street, I replay that look on his face over and over again. The confusion. The rage. The—

"Do you even realize how pathetic you look for that?" The Demechnef spawn shows up behind me, crunching through the snow until he's walking with me.

A slow smile creeps over my red lips. "Was he still hard when you tackled him to the ground?"

A muffled growl escapes his throat.

I smile wider.

"That entire act was transparent, Spitfire. Sad, even."

"What part exactly?"

"Having those men approach you one at a time. You don't think I saw right through that little act? Wasn't very creative, was it?" He keeps his sharp chin lifted as we walk, maintaining his dominant stance.

"You thought I orchestrated men approaching me?" I ask with a laugh, stopping dead in my tracks and opening my cloak to reveal my breasts plunging from my dress. "What part of my body makes you think I'd ever need to beg men to come crawling?"

Niklaus comes to a halt with me. And his angry eyes drop to my chest. One, two, three long moments pass, and he takes a deep, steadying breath. Still. *Staring*.

Victory floods my drunk brain.

His glazed stare flickers back up to my mocking expression.

"Do you want to see more of me?" I taunt with the sultriest voice I can manage.

Niklaus stiffens, dropping his line of sight back down to my chest. The frigid air pebbles my skin, causing my nipples to harden to fine points. And I know he can see it.

I take a dangerous, predatory step toward him. "You see? You'd crawl to taste me too."

He snaps out of it, clenching his jaw, and crossing his arms.

"You think I'd ever touch you?" He lets out a bewildered laugh. "I can't imagine any man getting hard for you, Spitfire. In fact…" He leans in, trying to intimidate me with his dwarfing height. "I'd rather fuck your mother."

"*Dezexez fir qasoi nexes.*"

These words. That daunting, bone-chilling language is the only thing that could break our focus right now. Niklaus and I turn abruptly to a lanky man with a top hat limping from the shadows holding a cane with a wolf head on the handle. He wears a red jacket with gold tassels, black matte shoulder armor, and a smile too wide and crooked to be natural.

He looks like a…*Ringmaster*.

"This is a private conversation," Niklaus tells the man.

"*Duséaz Demechnef!*"

We stay perfectly still.

No one speaks Old Alkadonian here.

And he's not alone. Men in strange uniforms start approaching us from all around. In a slow, calculated formation, these Vexamen strangers surround us, whispering in Old Alkadonian.

And I hear them say *Valdawell.*

"We're being targeted," I whisper.

Niklaus spares me a quick side glance. We assess the odds as they close in. There are thirteen of them. It's odd, I never once thought I'd need the combat training our parents and Uncle Warrose gave us. It seemed so silly. The time they came from was brutal, violent, chaotic. We're privileged here. Safe. Comfortable.

One by one, we watch them unsheathe weapons. Shining glints of metal.

"Fuck," Niklaus breathes. He doesn't have his sword. Though I wouldn't admit this to his face, the likeliness of Niklaus defeating all thirteen men is strong. He's *that* good with a sword. The greatest of our generation, in fact. Although, many say he would not have been a match for Patient Thirteen. They say my father was the greatest swordsman to ever live.

Niklaus has worked half his life to prove them wrong.

"How drunk are you?" he asks quietly.

"I'm not seeing double," I say, sobering up quickly.

We need my brother. His friends. There are too many of them. And we're unarmed.

"I have your back. You have mine." Niklaus looks down at me. It's the first time we don't make eye contact with bleeding hatred or tormenting amusement. Right now, we're all each other has.

"Yes."

They charge us. They're smart to rush us at once, overwhelming with sheer brute force and speed. I lower my stance, assessing each man. Who to strike first. Who has preexisting injuries. Whose weight I can use to my advantage.

And they strike harder than I expect. I'm thrown off my feet into a pile of snow, but crack into two kneecaps, and block a killing blow from a sword. Grunts come from behind me, but I can't see how well Niklaus is doing. I have to focus on the men coming after me.

With a sweep of my legs, I take two men to the ground. But to my shame, I'm not fast enough. The others start wailing on me. A foot thumping down on my stomach. Something jabs into my ribs over and over again. The hilt of a sword pops into my cheek.

"Sapphire!" Niklaus yells over the shrill chaos.

Krimson, we need your help!

My brother has always known when I'm hurt. He's always been able to sense when I need him. It's as if there's an invisible tunnel that connects our minds. If we yell loud enough down its echoing canal, our cries can be heard.

Blood smears into my vision as I'm struck across the face again.

It's all happening so fast. The blows keep coming. Somewhere behind me, I hear Niklaus fall to his knees.

"Hey!" a familiar voice shouts in the distance.

It's not my brother.

"Get off of her!" the voice calls again, closer now.

Before another jab can land in my stomach, a body is thrown over me. A golden face looks down at me before turning to face the swords and fists.

"Uncle Niles," I cough out wetly.

My uncle holds out his hands to greet the slashing of the blades swinging at us. He doesn't even grunt as his palms are torn to ribbons.

"No!" I cry, blood spraying across my face.

But my uncle stays steady over my body, taking the beating as Niklaus fights to gain control.

Krimson! Please!

A violent sensation vibrates up my spine as I realize what our future holds. Uncle Niles doesn't cry out in pain, he doesn't hold his protective stance with a whimper. He's strong and resilient in guarding my beaten body.

He's going to die.

A bottomless vibration molds into my bones at the thought. Deeper than pain or fear. Louder than the shouting of men and clanking of swords.

Something shifts.

The panic of watching my uncle use his body to defend mine sets an unnatural event in motion within my core. The world doesn't exactly spin—it *sinks*, like reality is being pulled apart at the seams.

Sounds of waves and astronomical winds slosh throughout the fighting. It's loud and clanking. I whip my head at the men focused on attacking Niklaus, staring in shock to see if anyone else feels it too.

Nothing. No one reacts the way I am.

It's like time slows down.

One second drags to the span of a minute.

And I'm the only one that notices.

The clock hand strikes at the town hall tower above me. And the whooshing is magnified. It grows and wells over my skin, a living, breathing entity. A foreign place where no one has ever gone.

I can taste the chilled particles of its air, smell its vast darkness, like seawater and stardust. And though *physically* nothing hits my stomach, it's as if I'm kicked again. Like a fishing hook slicing into my core, reeling my impaled body out to sea.

What is happening to me?!

I start to scream at the unbearable pain.

Uncle Niles grits his teeth at the rigorous assault.

The chaos decreases as my agonized howls distract a few individuals. But it doesn't matter. It's as if the hand of God is dragging me away by my ankles. And with that pull, something wild and berserk rolls out from my fingertips, casting a net. A net that blankets everyone here.

Am I being drugged?!

A starry night blots my vision as that hook tugs harder and faster, and I'm hauled away from the cobblestone street, like falling through quicksand—through space. No longer in the snow. No longer lying under my uncle's body.

My heart threatens to collapse at the thundering pulse hammering in my chest.

And time stops.

There's a lonely, dismal blackness that goes on for light years.

Each second is nonexistent.

It is all blank.

Muted.

Empty.

Yet I know I'm not alone. Something inhuman watches me with growing interest, a pair of eyes hiding in the leagues beyond sight.

It's a hallucination.

I've blacked out.

I *must* be blacking out. Maybe I'm dying? Maybe we're all dying.

"*You'll be all right*," a small voice says. "*I'm here*."

The light of the sky starts appearing in the form of a star, then it expands until the world around me is alive and breathing again.

But…I'm stunned.

The sun is at its peak. The sky is bright blue. And there are no boutiques or street lanterns. I lie under its beating heat in drowsy, paralyzed shock.

"What the hell?" I cough, wincing at the shooting pain climbing up my rib cage.

It was midnight. Did I black out? How long have I been unconscious?

"Niklaus," I wheeze.

A hand skims my arm. "Where the fuck are we?"

He's alive. Next to me. At least I'm not alone.

Not too far from where we're laying in the dirt and gravel, I hear grunts, heavy breathing, and the shifting of bodies. My eyes stretch wide as alarm fills my veins.

"Niklaus." I grab his wrist. "We—"

"I know." He reaches for something between us. "We're not alone."

My hazy eyes fall to a shiny piece of metal between our legs. Niklaus's hand searches its length until he finds the hilt. A sword. Thank God, he's found a sword. I tilt my head up to find he's already staring at me, blood trickling down the side of his forehead.

"Can you fight?" he asks.

Can I? My body feels like one giant, throbbing bruise.

"I can try."

He nods, trying to look at our surroundings without lifting his head. The sounds of movement become a little louder, as if people are starting to wake up.

"My dad is a few feet below you," he whispers, raising the sword off the ground. "Get him up. If we can take down a few of them, we make a run for it. Yeah?"

"Okay." This might be the first conversation that hasn't ended in insults with us. But right now, it's life or death. And clearly, we've been abducted. Not sure which forest we're in, but I'm mostly confused how it's so hot outside. It's winter. *This isn't right.*

"Now," he mouths.

We spring up at the same time, blood rushing to my skull, pain exploding down every nerve ending. I jump toward Uncle Niles as Niklaus impales two men while they're still on the ground.

"Hey! Wake up!" I shudder at the amount of blood dripping from his shredded hands and arms. Ribbons of severed skin hang from his palms. That bright red staining his white shirt, his coat, puddles being absorbed into the dirt.

"Uncle Niles!"

"Sapphire, come on!" Niklaus shouts over the clanking metal.

I shake his shoulders harder, getting his eyes to flutter open. He winces against the burning sunlight, fighting to understand his surroundings.

"We have to run!" I tell him, trying to pull my uncle to his feet. "Hurry!"

A stampede of footsteps thunders behind me. I pivot to a desert landscape of rocky terrain, and tall towers deep in the distance. But most importantly, the parade of soldiers running toward us.

Uncle Niles lifts his head, seeing it too.

"We're in Vexamen," he utters in cold, quiet horror.

"No, we're not—"

"Sapphire!" He grabs my arm with his bloody hand. "I still have nightmares about this country. We're in Vexamen, and I cannot run."

"What?!"

He points to his ankles. "They've cut my Achilles tendons."

Deep, gushing wounds are ripped open just above his heels. It's grotesque and shocking, and I begin to cry. *No. He can't run...*

"We have to go now!" Niklaus shouts.

"We'll carry you," I tell my uncle.

Niklaus drops down to a knee, panting and covered in splatters of red.

"We have to carry him." I point to my uncle's ankles.

Niklaus follows my hand with dread morphing his entire face. Those crushing blue orbs trail back up to his father. They lock eyes for a single, terrible, devastating moment.

"Leave me. Find Ruth and Warrose." Uncle Niles stares at his son without a sliver of doubt or fear. "Hey! Do you understand me? I'll be all right. But if you try to carry me, they'll catch us all!"

The soldiers grow dangerously close.

Niklaus nods tightly. Jaw clenched. Eyes shifting to me.

"No! *Hell no*!" I sob.

"I am not asking, Sapphire Valdawell. Go now, goddammit!" Uncle Niles barks.

And I'm being hauled to my feet, yanked by my elbow, and dragged away from my uncle as I scream for him. Tears bleeding down my face.

"Find my family!" he yells as the soldiers reach him. "They'll come for me! Do you hear me? They will come for me!"

Letter #1,458

Skylenna

Dear Dessin,

Today is my birthday.

Niles helped the kids bake me a cake. Though it wasn't a cake at all. It was blueberry pie, just like I used to make with Scarlett. He told them all about the time you figured out Niles was pouting in prison because he thought no one would know it was his birthday. But you did (with my insistence, of course-ha!).

The kids laughed when he told them about your secret best friend handshake.

When I blew out my candles, I wished you could come home to me. I'd like to see you do your secret best friend handshake with your best friend, Niles, one more time.

I'd like to see you make special handshakes with your children.

I love you.

Sincerely,

Your Soulmate,
Skylenna

7. Does Not Belong

"If we're in Vexamen…then why the fuck is *that* here?"

Niklaus and I hide behind the side of a great red archway. An entry to a carnival of fire dancers, smoking pits, cages, and animals on display. There are stained stages and racks of weapons. People walk in crowds through the layout, pointing, eating, and laughing.

My stomach drops to my feet.

This can't be…

"No…" I gasp, turning to Niklaus. "Aunt Ruth and Uncle Warrose outlawed this decades ago. There's no way this is…"

"The Meat Carnivals," Niklaus finishes.

"I don't understand," I whisper.

Niklaus looks just as horrified as I feel. We learned about The Meat Carnivals growing up. When we were seven, Niklaus got so mad, he threw his textbook across the room. Uncle Niles had to pick him up and explain how our aunt and uncle banned it from that country for good. No more animals would suffer.

Yet here we are.

I let my eyes wander a moment longer. Furry corpses. Severed animal parts. Fire. Fire. Fire. And the noises, *oh god, the noises!*

"Niklaus," I gasp, throwing my hand over my mouth. "What the fuck!"

"When we woke up here, I thought they drugged us, put us on a ship, and brought us to Vexamen. That we must have been out for days," Niklaus says, zoning out in thought.

"That's what happened, yeah."

"No. It's not." He looks at me with large blue eyes. Alarmed and sickened. "The blood on us hasn't dried yet. It's still fresh. And the Vexamen Breed soldiers were knocked out with us. They were just as shocked to be here as we were."

I touch my wet, bloody face. He's right. Our blood would have been dried on us by now. And everyone was unconscious.

"Then how did we get here?" I ask.

Niklaus shakes his head, having a thought that disturbed him too much. "We need to find Aunt Ruth and Uncle Warrose now."

I'm yanked backward by my hair. Sharp, stabbing pain splinters across my scalp, and I yelp. "Hey!"

Niklaus is grabbed from behind, knocking the sword out of his hands.

"*Demechnef vizezës!*" a man yells behind me.

It's the mob of soldiers. Too many of them. People in the carnival turn their heads. Animals bustle in their cages. And even though I'm too sore to fight, I remember my mother telling me the story of when she was stuck in a drainpipe in Vexamen. That if she didn't keep fighting, she would have starved and died down there.

I throw my head back, feeling a crack as those arms release me. Niklaus does something similar, maneuvering his way out of their hold. But they come at us too quickly, swords and sickles, whips and blades.

Two against dozens.

We back away in a panicked shuffle. My heart rattles inside my chest. I can't catch my breath. *This is it. This is it. This is it.*

But that familiar, agonizing hook slices back into my core. A stabbing puncture. And that world of black fog and starry night appears behind us, full of glittering pinholes of white light, and cosmic powder. Without any warning, a charcoal animal dives from its opening, dragging a trail of onyx smoke as it soars through the air. A small, shiny wolf made of dust and stars and the night sky.

Go now! I hear it speak to me in a small, inhuman voice.

The small shadow wolf attacks the soldiers, giving us enough time to…

"What the hell is that?!" Niklaus shouts. But the call of that tunnel, that astronomical mist is having me heave in torment. It blasts up my spine. A lightheadedness sways through my brain cells. Instinctually, I latch on to Niklaus's arm, and the sparkling black sky swallows us whole.

Bile spills from my mouth, leaving the taste of cognac to burn the back of my throat.

And…everything feels *wrong*.

I'm profoundly out of place, delirious, confused, and in shock.

A tremor runs through my systems, prickling my skin, jolting me awake. I reach up to my face, rubbing away the fog, and it stings. My face is pressed against the sharp ground, going numb and lighting up each individual nerve.

What just happened?

Cold. So cold.

Sleep is ripped from me as I stare at the endless sea of white on the ground and blasting in my throbbing face like a dust bowl through the hazy air.

Snow.

I shiver like a wet dog. Every muscle in my body begins to shudder at the sudden drop in temperature.

Glorious evergreen trees line the skies overhead. White capped mountains cascade in the horizon. I spit the rest of the bile out, using my arms to rise from the biting snow.

"We must have been drugged," I mutter to myself.

This has to be a drug-induced trip. What else could it be? We're clearly hallucinating. But then, why does it feel so real?

As I stand, still wearing my terribly uncomfortable red high heels, I see Niklaus already standing, staring off into the storm of snow with an unreadable expression.

"We're in the North Sapphrine Forest," I say quietly. "We must have been drugged."

Niklaus keeps his eyes forward. "I'm the only Blackforth family member who has never heard the prophecy of the seven forests. My mother would never tell me why…"

Has he lost it? How is this relevant right now?

"You did this to us, didn't you?" He rotates toward me, anger turning the whites of his eyes a light shade of pink. "You are just like your parents. You brought us here!"

I take a step back and nearly trip. "Me?!"

Does he have a brain injury from the fight?

"Yes, Spitfire! Look where the fuck we are! Look who your goddammed parents are!"

I choke out a furious laugh. "I'm nothing like my parents! I'm not an experiment! I'm *normal*. This wasn't my doing!"

There was a time, yes, where I wished I could be just like them. I wished I was special too. Maybe then I could talk to my father for the first time. Maybe then I could be a part of history too. But now? Hell no. I want to get as far away from our fucked-up family as possible. I want to build my own name, my own life.

Niklaus crunches through the snow to get a better look at me, glaring through the curtain of falling snow. "Have fun freezing to death out here in your short, slutty dress. I'm not staying with your defective brain another moment."

Something inside me withers before it lights on fire.

"Good! Leave! Enjoy your unmarked grave, coward!"

And he's gone. Abandoning me in this winter storm.

I know we have never gotten along, that we've always disliked each other greatly…but I am in a short dress. My legs are exposed. This thick cloak will only do so much to keep me warm. I *will* freeze to death out here without him. I never thought his hate for me was so pronounced that he actually wished me dead.

I stumble across the snow to find a cave, too stubborn to die before he does out here. All I need is to make a fire. If I can do that, maybe I can hunt. Get fur to keep warm, give myself a fighting chance to hike back to the city.

A few leagues away, I see it. A dark hole where a cave would exist. I pick up sticks and a couple logs of wood along the way. *I'm going to make it. I'm going to make it.*

The arctic chill in the air is paralyzing, drying out my skin, and causing my muscles to atrophy. The forest screams with eerie winds and rustling branches. And my view of the white landscape all blends together. I tuck deeper into my red cloak.

Krimson, where are you? I need help.

It feels like half an hour before I see that cave growing larger in the distance. If I can just start a fire…

There's a whooshing sound that zings through the air. Something slices into the top of my ear. I screech, throwing myself into the snow as ruby drops splatter across the ice. An arrow lands a few feet away from me.

"Fuck!" I whip my head around to see two of those same Vexamen soldiers who tried to grab us before. Did they come here with us when we…*traveled* again?

"*Whëx eiz Demechnef!*"

They throw two more objects in my direction. Metal balls that expand, casting a net in the air before sticking into the ground on either side of me.

Shit!

No amount of scrambling helps, I'm hogtied down, unable to wiggle out of the net they've closed me in. And the two soldiers are sprinting through the heavy snow, holding up a sickle in my direction.

"Hey! Wait a second! I—"

A fountain of blood bursts from the neck of the soldier to the right as his head isn't quite cut off, but close enough. The next is speared from behind. The shiny tip of a sword glides through his chest, coated in a thick layer of dark blood. As it slides back out, the soldier drops with a gaping red mouth.

Niklaus stands behind them, wiping off his sword.

Well, hell, I would rather have died.

"Are you hurt?" he asks, pissed and panting.

I shake my head. He ran to come find me. Through the snow.

His large deep-sea eyes trail over my tied-up body, then land on a spot at the side of my head. "Your ear is bleeding."

My momentary shock wears off. "So, freezing to death is acceptable for me, but being butchered by Vexamen soldiers isn't?"

"You're fucking ungrateful." He uses the tip of his sword to cut me loose. "But my saving your pathetic ass was entirely selfish. I don't know how you moved us across a great distance like this…but you may be our only way home."

He doesn't offer to help me to my feet. I wouldn't have taken his hand if he did.

"I didn't do anything," I huff, dusting the snow off my cloak. "You don't need me to get home. Just hike back to the city from here and try not to freeze or getting eaten by wild animals."

"I don't know if moving us to a different location is all you've done. What if you shifted us to a new reality? Or a…"

"A what?"

His piercing gaze meets mine. "A different time."

I laugh in his stupid fucking face. Cruelly. Coldly. Mockingly.

He raises an eyebrow. "I see you're still just as unimaginative and dense as when you were a child. Pity."

My smile falls.

"Great. So, we're stuck together." I pluck the sickle from the dead man's hand. I'm not going to let Niklaus inflate his own ego by saving me again. Besides, sickles hold a weird importance to my family. It's feels right to take it for myself now.

"Not for long. You still might freeze to death."

I look down at my exposed legs. "There's a cave that way."

He helps me gather the wood, following my lead to the gaping mouth of hollow murkiness. It's musty, covered in icicles, and pitch black the further in we go.

"At least this gets us away from the wind chill," I say with chattering teeth.

Shit, I really might die. Dropping to the ground, I start rocking back and forth to keep warm. Niklaus attempts to light the fire. He curses several times.

"The wood is wet. It's not going to work."

I'm going to die.

My entire body vibrates like a storm is shaking my skeletal system. I can't get warm. Rocking faster, I clutch my own core, breathing shallowly.

"Spitfire," Niklaus says with caution.

I can't answer. Keep rocking.

"Hey."

I roll onto my side, bringing my bare legs to my chest in the fetal position. My teeth clack together like high heels against a marble floor. Everything aches. Everything is numb.

Where's DaiSzek when you need him? With his bum leg, he's not good for much, but at least he's warm.

"I can't start the fire," Niklaus says at a loss for words, standing over me, staring like a fucking idiot.

I clutch my cloak tighter around my body. I used to think this thing was so warm. So thick and good at trapping heat. But right now, it feels like ice is coating my skin, layering over the chills and goose bumps.

Niklaus starts pacing, running his hand through his hair. He's wearing more clothes than me. It's not fair. Why did I have to go to that tavern wanting to look hot in a short dress?

Frozen tears leak from the corners of my eyes, dripping onto the cave floor.

His footsteps pause, and I can feel those radiant eyes boring into the side of my head, my quivering, curled up body.

"I'm not doing this because I want to," he clarifies, then begins taking off his clothes.

What is he doing exactly?

"But you're my only way home."

His pants drop next to my head.

Oh god!

I flinch as the metal from his belt buckle clanks against the stone floor. His shirt. His boots. And suddenly, Niklaus is kneeling at my side, undoing my cloak, pulling it away from my body.

"Yout-tryingtok-k-illmef-f-faster?"

"I know your mother taught you about wilderness survival too. You're just too fucking stubborn to offer the idea first." He reaches under my thighs, pulling my dress up.

"H-hey!"

"Would you rather me rip it right down the middle? Because I will."

Damn. I know what he's doing. Body heat. And right now, I'm not in a good position to argue. To come up with a plan that doesn't involve our naked bodies touching.

I stop struggling as he pulls my dress over my ass, tugging my arms to loosen as he unveils the rest of my body. I'm wearing red lace panties and a brassiere. *Please. Please don't remove them too.*

Niklaus positions himself behind me, tucking his legs behind my own, circling his body around mine like a quotation mark. There's a quick gust of air as he drapes our cloaks over top of us.

And for a quiet, awkward moment, he doesn't know what to do with his arms. With his hands. They remain close to his sides, as if I'm made of poison oak, as if touching me will burn him.

The heat from his chest pulses into my back, cutting through the vicious shivers in my bones. I melt a little against him, going to mush as some of the discomfort passes.

"J-just put them around m-me," I stammer. *Coward.*

Niklaus doesn't move, though his breathing finds a faster rhythm. After a few seconds, he sighs, and his breath tickles my ear. Those lean, muscular arms slide around my waist, circling over my chest. He pulls me closer, hugging me against the flexed, shivering planes of his frame.

Krimson, you wouldn't believe what I'm having to do to survive out here.

"We're not going to last like this," Niklaus breathes. "We need fire. Warm clothes."

I nod, shifting under the cloak.

Body heat can only get us so far.

"Do you think you can control it?" he asks.

"Control what?"

"Whatever you did to get us here."

I breathe hot air against my fingertips, remembering that strange onyx animal that helped us get away. Maybe I *did* do this to us.

I shake my head slowly.

Niklaus grunts, squeezing me tighter in frustration.

"Did you see that—*thing* that came out of the darkness?" I sound nuts.

He's quiet for three seconds. "Yes."

"It helped us."

He doesn't respond.

"Maybe it will again," I add.

Again, his silence leaves room for me to practically hear the subtle cues for what he wants to say about this topic. The rolling of his eyes. He thinks the idea is absurd and not worth wasting his breath on.

"Don't get yourself turned on right now." I feel something against my butt, and I'm not sure if it's just his pelvic bone or something else. "I'm only doing this, so I won't drop dead."

He chuckles unkindly, rumbling my back. "Not even lying with your naked body could get me off. Your best friend is what a man wants. Not. *You.*"

Blood rushes back to my numb limbs. Just when I started to think we could set aside our differences for this…

The stupid motherfucker proves me wrong.

Mabel Rose. Mabel Rose. Mabel Rose.

Hot, bitter acid splashes against my throat. A million malicious thoughts spring to life in my mind. Unforgivable phrases, below-the-belt comments. But instead of using my words, I arch my back against his groin, releasing a soft moan.

It can't be healthy how quick his erection presses against my backside.

He seems just as surprised and frozen with shock as I do. And to further dig into the roots of his humiliation, I roll my hips back again, rubbing up his bare shaft. I briefly pause at the length as it keeps going for longer than I was expecting.

Niklaus coils his arms around me tighter, like a snake preparing to strangle its victim. His fingers dig into the side of my waist, the soft space on the underside of my breast. The growl that rumbles up his chest, into the back of my head is embedded with sexual frustration.

With one quick jolt, he pulses that long erection against my ass. Pleasure tingles along my inner walls, causing me to clench and lose my breath. My mind shifts from vindictive to desperately wanting to chase that crazed feeling again.

"Fuck," he hisses against my neck.

What am I doing? Stop. You're supposed to tease, then blue balls the shit out of him!

"Spitfire," Niklaus grunts in my ear, rolling his hips into me again.

I moan despite him using the name I hate.

Causing me to choke on surprise, his cold hand latches onto my throat, tugging the side of my face in the direction of his mouth. "You think you're special because I got hard? We're in the middle of the frozen wilderness. Any hole would do."

My elbow flies into his rib cage before I have a chance to let the flood of anger pass through my system. "Die then."

I shimmy away from the warmth of his body, exposing my body to the deadly winter winds.

"What the hell are you doing?!"

"Isn't it obvious? I'd rather freeze to death than cuddle up next to a fucking sociopath."

We lie in shivering, haunting silence. And it dawns on me that I will in fact die of stubbornness. But Niklaus isn't stopping me. He's bearing the biting slice of the icy winds alone, without another terrible comment, without even attempting to pull me back in for the sake of heat.

He will also die of stubbornness.

I pull my cloak over my shoulders with stiff, aching fingers and pray for a quick death. I can hear his shallow breaths behind me, in and out, quick, pained. I should have an instinct to help him, to care for him. We both should, considering we grew up together. Considering we are practically family.

But I've never hated anyone more in my life.

"I'm glad your father is nothing more than a piece of limp meat."

"Patient Thirteen was incapable of real love. Especially not for you."

I tighten my grip around my own quivering frame, as if I'm slowly frosting over. My fingers, too stiff to uncurl, dig into the backs of my arms. The wind hisses along the floor, stinging my exposed skin until I'm numb and made of painful marble.

I glance out at the white curtain of snow whirling in a constant churn at the entrance, punching hard gusts into the cavern.

I'm going to die here.

My body already feels like a corpse.

Forgotten.

Alone.

Empty.

Numb.

The cold from outside settles into my heart. And I tremble so forcefully, my joints mold into an unbreakable position. Elbows hardly able to bend. Knees like metal grinding against each other.

I always thought being hot was the worst feeling. Sweating. Standing under a scalding sun. But it's not. Not even close. Lying under a cave ceiling, creaking under the weight of hardening ice is much worse.

My brain starts to shut down in choppy increments.

Stay awake.

My eyes flutter like a candle flittering against someone trying to blow it out.

I look at the skin on my arms, it's pale-bluish color. The agonizing pulses of cold air rolling over them.

Please, come find me, Mom. I won't make it much longer.

"Spitfire," Niklaus utters, gripping my elbow.

I jerk away.

But there's an urgency in his touch. A pause of the shrill, whistling winds that permeate the cave opening. And his spine goes taut behind me, sitting up as he tries to get me to follow his gaze.

Coming from the mouth of the cave, an animal snarls, ripping through the void of shrieking winds and falling snow.

I flinch as much as my numb neck and limbs will allow and peel open my watering eyes to get a better look.

White wolves. Seven of them. A full pack. And they aren't small either. Not as big as DaiSzek, but still, quite large.

"Come—here," he stammers once more.

I can't find it in my frozen brain to argue. Freezing to death is one thing. But being mauled by hungry wolves is another. I shimmy back against his bare skin, now lacking any body heat he had before.

We're cold flesh pressed against cold flesh, watching the pack with watering eyes as we wait for their next move.

Foggy air chuffs from their snouts.

They seem to linger in place, unfazed by the shooting squalls of flurries beating against their heavy coats of fur.

Another minute passes.

"Could—they be—"

"From—Stormsage?" Niklaus finishes.

As they approach, they don't stalk forward with lowered necks and predatory eyes. Their ears press back, and their tails starts to wag back and forth. A whooshing breath of relief leaves my tightening lungs as they lie down around us, snuggling against our bodies to create a warm cocoon of white fur and warm bodies.

"W-what aretheyd-doing?" I ask.

"Saving us."

8. Help Has a Name

The thick fur under my fingertips reminds me of DaiSzek.

When I was nine, I fell through the plate of ice on the surface of the frozen lagoon. DaiSzek pulled me out and curled his gigantic body around me to keep the hypothermia at bay. That's what these wolves remind me of. We did not ask them to keep us warm. They just are.

And now that I'm not chilled to the bone, I've been caressing the fur along their spines.

"We had a visitor," Niklaus says quietly.

The breeze has died somewhere between the mountains, and now all that remains is a frozen, eerie quiet. The wolves sleep in a ring around us, but I can feel the change in Niklaus's breath against my back.

I roll onto my back to see him. Niklaus is propped up on one elbow.

"Who?"

He shrugs. "I didn't see them. But they left us something."

Down by the opening of the cave is a leather backpack and a satchel canteen for water. Someone left us means for survival. Could it be Asena and members of the Stormsage Keep? Why wouldn't they stay to help us get home? They've known Niklaus and I since we were born.

Carefully slipping out from the cocoon of warmth the wolves have given us, Niklaus gets dressed, and goes to inspect the contents of the backpack.

"Change into these." He tosses me thick fur clothing and a pair of boots.

Hell yes. We'll be able to get out of here. But will we be able to hike all the way back to the Red Oaks in the snow?

The wolves wake up one at a time as we tie our boots, buckle our pants, and fasten our coats. They sit up, blink slowly, and begin to leave the cave in a single-file line.

"Thank you," I murmur as they leave, patting one on the head as it briefly rubs against my thigh.

The trek through the snow is long, exhausting, and lonely.

Niklaus refuses to acknowledge me in any way. Which normally I cherish. But this is an unusual time. We need to be a team whether I like it or not. Uncle Niles has been captured in Vexamen, and yet we're back in Dementia. I can't shake the disbelief in my bones that we've left him behind.

"I'm worried about Uncle Niles," I finally say as we cross over into the Evergreen Dark Wood.

His steps falter, and he has to roll his shoulders before he continues walking.

"Me too."

"I don't understand how he was so violently treated in Aunt Ruth's territory. She'd never allow that."

The muscles in Niklaus's jaw are working endlessly as he grinds his teeth.

"He's okay though, right? Surely Aunt Ruth and Uncle Warrose would have gotten word about his capture?"

But it all feels so wrong. My optimistic thoughts are figments of imagination. Of wishful thinking.

"Did that look like the same place Aunt Ruth has ruled over to you?" he growls.

No.

Niklaus scans the dimming horizon, glaring at the sun lowering below the tree line. What are we supposed to do once it gets dark? In this forest, it turns pitch black. And neither of us knows our way around or how to get out.

"Maybe we can find Runa? Ask for a place to stay?" I offer.

He stops walking, sighs loudly, a show of how agitated he is by my effort to communicate. Heat presses into my chest as my temper grows weary and inconsolable. This idiot *needs* me. He said it himself. Even though I know he's wrong about that theory, I'm not going to correct him and devalue myself. *I'm* the asset here, and he's pretty much deadweight.

"Fine. I'll go myself." Before I can stomp off, Niklaus catches my wrist.

I react out of pettiness. The sickle strapped to my back is pointed at his genitalia so quickly, Niklaus only has time to lower his eyes at the blade to observe the *almost*-castration.

"Hand. Off."

His iron jaw flexes, and though his stone expression does not change, I can feel the hateful seething behind his eyes.

"We camp here," he says, glaring down at me.

I look up at him, too close to his chest, which expands his aroma of fresh citrus, white musk, and aquatic wood. I take a disgusted step back.

With my best condescending smirk, I say, "No more naked cuddling?"

That grimace could burn a hole through my skull.

While Niklaus sets up camp and fire, I manage to hunt a jackrabbit. When Aunt Marilynn taught us how to hunt growing up, I remember thinking "*What situation am I ever going to need to know this for?*"

We eat in silence.

Stare blankly at the fire in silence.

Co-exist in silence, *barely*.

Aside from the light of the fire illuminating our faces, the world around us is an empty pit. This forest leaves no room for sight. It's just us and an eerie feeling in my chest growing hollow and uneasy.

"Your chewing is obnoxious," he comments.

Oh, here we go.

I start smacking my lips.

"God," he sighs.

"So crazy how my mouth annoys you so much," I say, still chewing.

Niklaus relaxes, unbothered and uncaring.

"Would you rather be stuck out here with Mabel Rose?" I ask and instantly regret it. Why? Oh god, why would I give him the impression of jealousy? It wasn't. Fuck, no, it wasn't.

"That is eating away at you, isn't it?"

"That my best friend was sucking the dick of the man who has been obsessed with hurting me my whole life? Yes. It's eating away at me."

He smirks, half amused, half disinterested as his eyes remain focused on a spot in the darkness beyond the fire. "And imagining your best friend riding me isn't making you furious with jealousy?"

That image collapses onto my thoughts. The brunt force of it scorching my insides. But I relax the lines on my forehead, steady my breath, mute the feeling of betrayal boiling over.

"It makes me sad." The muscles in my neck stiffen. I can't decide if I'm embarrassed or disgusted at my sudden confession.

"What?"

"Yes."

I continue digging a deeper hole for myself.

Niklaus shifts his attention to me slowly from the corner of his eye.

"Sad because I didn't see it. Not you two fucking. But that I didn't see how much she's hated me all these years."

He listens reluctantly.

"She's your best friend."

"I thought so too. But my mother killed her distant cousin, Belinda, in the asylum. Mabel Rose always attempted to convince me that fact meant nothing to her."

He peers away in deep thought. “I didn’t know that.”

Doubtful. “I knew it had a part to play in being with you when she looked at me that night.”

“Maybe you’re reading into it.”

I shake my head. “I’m not.”

“She would have mentioned it to me…”

“Then maybe you got played too.”

He chuckles. “That would mean I had any feelings invested in her at all. I did not.”

“Look.” I exhale sharply, wanting to talk about anything else right now. “You don’t want to be around me. I don’t want to be around you. But we’re family. Our parents would want us to look out for each other right now.”

“We are not family, Sapphire.” His expression is carved from stone.

“I’m inclined to agree. Your parents are my family. Either way, my point remains.”

A windless cold glides between us, prickling the hairs on my arms. I hold my hands to the fire, wishing I was with Krimson tonight, sitting on the couch, reading new books he picked up for us.

“Do you remember that night when we were playing in the woods as kids? Krimson was home sick, and I tagged along with your friends? You told everyone the night dawpers were emerging from hibernation?”

“No.”

“You do.” My voice cracks. I refuse to look at him. “You convinced the other kids to run home, screaming for their lives. But I knew I wasn’t as fast because you were all boys. So I…I climbed a tree and waited there all night. It was freezing, and I couldn’t stop shaking because every twig snapping in that dark forest made me think the night dawpers had found me.”

“What is your point?”

“You could have come back.” The little girl in me is speaking now. “You could have helped me down from the tree and told me it was all a joke. But you just left me there.”

He’s staring at me now. “I did.”

The admission stings.

"I was eight fucking years old."

"Yeah. And it worked."

"Huh?"

"You stopped trusting me."

"And that's what you wanted?"

"It is." No malice there. No satisfaction. Just a flat truth.

"Why?"

"Think about it," he says evenly.

The fire pops sharply between us.

"No answers are coming to mind," I say.

He draws in an inpatient breath. "I've had very upsetting thoughts about you since I was taken as a kid. Violent ones." There's a breath of silence that stretches unbearably long. "Toward you. You shouldn't have been allowed to simply wander the woods at night with me. I wasn't right in the head."

The sound of rapid breathing that doesn't belong to either of us, snags our attention. Our heads snap in the same direct straight ahead. We make eye contact briefly, then lower our food to the ground. The sound turns into something dragging across gravel and dirt, scratchy and quiet.

Niklaus grabs his sword slowly, communicating some silent message of attack with his eyes on me. With a shaky hand, I find my sickle, latching onto its handle as my heart drums against my breastbone. I don't know if I have it in me for another fight.

"*Rabbit good.*"

We freeze. It isn't words we heard with our ears but with our mind. An intrusive thought that doesn't match my own. A sound that seems to come from all around us, sticking to the cool, dry air. A soft echo.

Niklaus furrows his brow at me, then mouths, "Did you hear that too?"

I nod.

"*I hungry too,*" the voice adds. It's like that of a female child. Cute and high, innocent and pure even.

"What the fuck?" I mouth to Niklaus.

Is this a demon haunting these woods? I mean, we've heard stories growing up about how mystical beings used to live here a thousand years ago. But I've always thought it was bullshit.

The creature moves closer, taking steps in pure darkness toward us, sniffing the air and dirt obnoxiously.

I hold my sickle up with a shaky hand, straining my eyes to see past the black fog.

"Fuck this," Niklaus growls, tossing a flaming branch in front of us.

The creature whimpers, side-stepping the fire as the orange light shines across the beast's side. I move cautiously toward the dark figure still holding out my weapon.

It's a…dog? Small wolf?

Black shiny fur and funny white markings on its chest. Funny ears that don't stand upright but hang floppy against its cheeks.

"*Ouch.*" The voice echoes again. "*Hurt paw.*"

I lower my sickle.

"Could still be a demon," Niklaus warns.

"*Dellilian no demon*," the childlike voice says. I'm surprised that I have no impression of the sound being creepy or disturbing. It's sweet and somehow exactly what I would expect to be the voice of a small wolf.

"That is what a demon would say." I narrow my eyes.

The animal steps out into the light slowly, cautiously, as if it's trying not to spook us. With small brown eyes that look positively too human to be a beast, it watches us as it blinks curiously. Each paw is white and speckled like snowy boots, and that long tails sways back and forth happily.

I move closer, lowering myself to the ground to get eye level with it. On the edges of that dog-like frame, a glittery dust seems to dissolve from its charcoal fur. Like a midnight, mystical breeze. Like *magic*.

And I'm not sure what it is exactly, but a calmness washes over my chilled skin. Trust. Purity. Loyalty. *Safe. Safe. Safe.* I sense no threat or danger. In fact, the midnight creature lowers itself to the ground, sprawling out their hind legs and crawling on the dirt to get closer to me. A submissive attempt to ensure my feelings ring true.

"*Spitfire*," Niklaus warns under a hissing breath.

"What's your name?" I ask.

The animal blinks twice, then that small voice answers in my head, "*Dellilian.*"

"Her name is Dellilian," I tell Niklaus.

"Thanks." He slowly lowers his weapon in annoyance.

I glance over her features again, studying the way those human-like eyes study me back.

"What *are* you, Dellilian?"

"*A Morphing Onyx Short-Haired Windila!*"

Huh.

I glance back at Niklaus who can't wipe that stupid look of revulsion from his face.

"I've never heard of that one before. You're not here to harm us?"

She shakes her head with a chuff. "*No harm. Helped you escape, 'member?*"

I stare blankly, remembering the black puff of cosmic smoke that came soaring from that hole that sucked us out of Vexamen. Was that her?

"*Been sent to help you, Sapphy!*"

Me? I stare at her with a furrowed brow. This is a fever dream—it must be, right? I'm at home, sick and near death, probably. None of the recent events are logical. Nothing makes sense.

"Why?"

Dellilian tilts her head. "*Need Sapphy's help one day. Here to help Sapphy on time journey*!"

Niklaus leans forward. "*Time* journey?"

Oh, fuck.

Sinisterly, Niklaus slides his glare to land on me, jabbing into the side of my face like a hot fire poker. "Time?" he repeats himself slowly.

I swallow down the nauseated saliva building in my mouth.

"Dellilian…are we"—I clear my throat—"are we not in our own time anymore?"

Niklaus doesn't take his hateful eyes off of me as she answers.

"*Sapphy moves time. Time moves Sapphy.*" Her human-like eyes shoot over to the fire Niklaus stands in front of. "*Rabbit is yum.*"

My mind goes blank, then explodes into chaos. "Oh, shit! How?

Why? How?!"

I rise to my feet, hands in hair, pacing in front of her.

"Because you have a fucked-up head like your parents," Niklaus seethes, though he doesn't seem surprised by this revelation.

I don't even have it in me to snap at the comment. Maybe he's right? My mother can supposedly go into the void and peer back at old memories as if she's actually there. My father had the inner world with his many alters, I'm told. And those alters were split to suffer in different ways, bear different forms of trauma.

Could my DNA have been altered because of them?

"*Fallen Saint. Patient Thirteen.*" Dellilian nods her head, still fixated on that cooked rabbit.

"Fuck," I breathe.

Dellilian blinks up at me casually, then narrows her focus on the rabbit again.

"Send. Us. Back."

I turn to face Niklaus with my mouth still hanging open. Everything that's happened since those Vexamen Breed soldiers attacked us on the street hasn't made any sense. Waking up on Vexamen soil with blood still wet on my body. The Meat Carnivals active again. Waking up in the snow a moment later. This is truly the only explanation!

Niklaus takes a predatory step in my direction. "*Now.*"

Bewilderment lines the acidic bubbling in my stomach.

"Are you fucking deaf?"

"I don't know how!" I say in exasperation.

"Bullshit!"

I cough out a laugh. "You think I can control it?!"

"Yes," he answers, soft blue eyes turning vengeful and black.

"Why would I intentionally send us to Vexamen before Aunt Ruth and Uncle Warrose made it safe? Why would I leave Uncle Niles behind and not go back for him already?!"

The fire crackles and pops before he thinks of a reasonable answer.

"Because you're a psychopath like your parents."

Normally insults to my parents don't bother me. I say worse things in my head. But in this particular situation, that one *hurts.*.

"I don't know how to send us back." My hands clench into painful fists at my sides. "Can you help me control it, Dellilian?"

Sitting close to the fire, Dellilian finishes off the last of the rabbit, licking the bones clean. She's sort of adorable, blissfully unaware of us talking anymore.

Niklaus explodes.

"Did I say you could eat our food?" He stomps aggressively in her direction, forming a puff of dust and dirt around his boot. "Get out of here! Go!"

Dellilian scurries away from him, limping toward me as if she'd been struck. Her soft whimpers tug at my heart.

I glare up at the monster guarding the leftover rabbit bones. "And *I'm* the psychopath. She's here to help us, you idiot!"

Dellilian sits by herself in the dark, her head hanging, pouting in silence.

"Please," I whisper softly to her. "Can you help us get back?"

The midnight animal glances up at me in sorrow. "*Can follow and protect. Cannot lead.*"

"So, she's fucking useless."

Anger simmers under my skin, prickling at my nerves.

"Then leave! Have fun trying to get back to save your dad without me! Or getting back to our own time for that matter." I stare him down for several seconds. "No one's stopping you. Go on, leave!"

Niklaus moves toward me, dilating pupils, tightening jaw, like he has something evil to say. Something to wound me with. But after a single deep breath, he turns around.

"I'll find more firewood," he says coldly.

The rigorous tension in my muscles and bones begins to deflate. I fall to a seated position, unsure if I want to cry or scream. Wishing Krimson was here. Wondering with racing, unstable thoughts if I'll ever see my mother again.

"*Dellilian sleep right here?*" the gentle creature says, reaching into my mind to snag my attention.

My face drops into my hands as I nod. "Yes. Let's sleep now."

9. When She Screams

When I was nine, a squirrel ran up to DaiSzek as he was lying on the front porch, watching the sun set.

He was so still. The small rodent must have thought he was a majestic statue.

Krimson and I watched quietly, waiting for the great and powerful RottWeilen to pounce. To hunt that squirrel before we even would have a chance to blink. But instead, we witnessed the squirrel coming to the realization that there was breath puffing out of DaiSzek's nose. It stood upright, still, and unsure as understanding draped over its small body.

And just as it took off in a sprint of survival, Krimson and I jumped to our feet, hollering for DaiSzek to hunt it down. We were children desperate to see if the stories and legends about his power were true.

But DaiSzek adjusted positions to sleep on his side and closed his eyes for the next nap of the day.

I kicked dirt and swore up and down that he was no predator. Just an old pup.

Our trek in the daylight has been nauseating. Not because of Niklaus's sickening presence, but because we haven't come across any food at all. No berries. No animals to hunt. *Nothing.*

How did my parents survive out here when they were on the run? How did my father always provide food for them? Over the years, we heard stories of the time they escaped the asylum. How my mother took a leap of faith to break him out of confinement. Krimson and I always laughed at the fact that he could have left anytime he wanted. Our father was simply waiting on her.

My feet are blistering. Fire smolders in my joints, creeping into my lower back until there's a constant ache. And god, I'm so hungry.

What is it now? Late afternoon? Is the sun setting? How long are we going to go without eating?

"*Dellilian hungry.*" The Morphing Onyx Short-Haired Windila trails behind us, still mildly pouting at Niklaus's cruel mood toward her.

Niklaus's back tenses at her small voice entering our minds like a puff of smoke. He rolls his shoulders and keeps walking. I silently applaud him for not saying anything else callous to her. I'm in no mood for it. With this empty stomach, I feel mean, resentful, and harboring a dark cloud of hate toward him.

After another hour, the ill-mannered man I'm traveling with slows his pace suddenly, staring off at something ahead with unbreakable focus.

Speeding my aching pace to take his place in the lead, I bump his arm with my shoulder. Hungry. Pissed. Pained. Exhausted.

But a hand snatches my hair from the back of my head, knotting it in a tight fist, and yanking me backward.

"What the fuck!" I shriek.

His mouth is pressed against my ear with bristly facial hair scratching against my soft skin. "Would you rather I let you fall into that hunter's trap?"

I shiver against his smooth, ice-cold tone.

His spare hand points to the ground a few feet in front of us, outlining a space covered in giant leaves, twigs, branches, and moss. A distinct patch of earth that is meant to fool an animal.

"I already saw that," I lie.

"Mmm-hmm." Niklaus releases his grip on my hair, investigating the area.

"*Dellilian very hungry.*"

Niklaus turns his neck slowly, glaring in her direction with a wild storm of cruel ideas churning in his icy eyes.

"Easy," I warn him, standing in front of the innocent dog-wolf to prevent her from interpreting his expression any further.

A nasally growl is muffled from inside the hole. A sleepy, gruff noise that brings our rising argument to a halting stop. Niklaus squats in front of the covered hunter's hole, listening closely to analyze what is most likely an injured animal.

The growling turns into a weighted breath, much like snoring.

Niklaus gives me a sidelong glance. "That sounds like a large meal to me."

I nod timidly.

It sounds *massive*.

"Aurick is very lucky that he kept his genitalia that night." A deep, booming voice punctures our quiet bubble of discovery.

Wait. Did I just hear the name…

Niklaus pops his head up, looking south into the woods.

That name…

"Did you just hear Aurick's name?" I whisper to Niklaus kneeling before the hunter's trap.

He doesn't spare me a look of acknowledgment.

"You're so slow, we could have been there by now if we didn't have to move like snails!"

My blood runs cold.

I know that voice. It's lighter. Younger. Softer. The innocence and gentle nature of that tone is almost unrecognizable from the voice of the woman I grew up knowing.

That's my mother's voice.

Niklaus recognizes it too. He shifts his distant stare back to me in muted surprise.

"*Oh my god!*" I mouth to him.

"Oh, so it's me holding us back, huh?" the baritone voice says to my mother.

My back goes rigid as I pause to think back on the history we learned about my parents' journey during the years of the asylum and the war. She traveled through these forests with…

"Impossible," Niklaus hisses, stumbling back. The color drains from his face, and behind that palpable look of shock—he's scared.

My father.

Chills sprinkle over my back and legs as I gasp cold air into my lungs. I've never heard his voice before. I've never seen him walk. I've never seen him *awake*.

A sob crawls up my throat.

"We need to hide!" Niklaus grips my arm, tugging me to the blanket of a nearby tree, bushy with overgrown leaves, vines, and shrubs. "We can't know what happens if we're seen!"

Dellilian sits quietly to my left, observing two individuals appear through the shadows of the evergreen trees. My mother, dressed in a black lace and cloak, comes jogging forward playfully. The grin on her rosy cheeks is one I haven't seen before. Yes, she's smiled, laughed, been happy. But this grin is dressed in desire and giddiness.

"Yeah! We need to get you in shape! Have you lost all of those big muscles or something?" my mother teases breathlessly.

And right behind her comes a man who seems to eat up the space in the forest with his dark presence. He's taller than Niklaus, broader, stronger, unyielding with heavy muscle. His chocolate brown hair is without the speckles of gray and white strands I'm used to seeing.

I peer at him through the wispy leaves swaying in my view. I blink at the tears gathering in my straining eyes.

It's him…

He looks like Krimson with his eyes open.

My dad.

The muscles in my thighs begin to tremble as I try to overcome the urge to cry.

"Oh, so you think my muscles are big?" my father, Patient Thirteen, calls to my mother with a half-smile.

Something soft tears open in my chest. His voice, warm and

strong, I somehow recognize within the marrow of my bones.

It hurts.

Oh god, it hurts.

The tingling tautness coating my nerve endings is cut off by the sound of my mother's laughter as she falls through the hunter's trap. My posture straightens as I witness a wave of golden hair disappear into the hole.

Niklaus slaps his hand over my mouth before I have the chance to scream for her.

There's a whoosh, then a thump as her body hits the bottom.

"Skylenna!" Patient Thirteen yells, diving into the hole after her.

I thrash against Niklaus's arms and hand covering my mouth. His hold is unyielding, as sure as stone surrounding my core.

"We have to help them!" I grumble into his palm.

"You don't think your father can handle himself?" he mocks against the shell of my ear.

I can't blame his tone. We're both non-believers of the endless stories. The sleepy growl of that trapped beast sounded like a caged titan. My father is no match for that kind of feral, brute strength. He's only a man.

There are muffled words coming from the hole. The feline snarl of the creature. Dellilian leans forward with perked ears, waiting for something.

A thick drop of chilled sweat runs down my spine. What's the right thing to do here? Help? What if this wasn't supposed to happen? What if we've already changed something and kill my parents before I've been conceived?

My mother lets out a blood-curdling scream.

Shit!

Niklaus lurches forward first, acting on instinct to help before I get the chance to react. But something snaps like a whip through the trees, cracking through branches, and splitting leaves in half with the sheer ferocity behind a blast of movement.

The blur of blackness shoots across the forest floor like a train.

An animal.

A wolf.

A *RottWeilen.*

I stumble back into Niklaus's hard chest as DaiSzek—*my* DaiSzek—gallops like a rabid stallion into the hunter's trap after my parents. His roar and attack can be heard miles away. Teeth ripping through flesh, bones, and vital organs.

Goose bumps ripple over my cool skin, and a ringing echoes violently through my ears.

"Holy shit," I breathe.

He looks so much…younger. That can't be the old boy DaiSzek I grew up with. The same sweet boy who sleeps on the porch at sunset, eats scraps out of Grandpa's hand under the table, and always gets in the way when we're trying to cook.

My parents climb out of the hole, covered in dirt and splatters of blood.

"Just don't look at it," Patient Thirteen says as he peels off his shirt. "I'll patch it up when we get out of here."

My mother stares at him with parted lips, gawking as if her brain has temporarily fried. I've never seen that look on her face before.

The beast in the pit yelps, snapping my mother out of her trance as she whips her head to the left. "DaiSzek!" she yells. "Oh, Dessin! Is he okay?"

My father leans over to examine the inside of the hole, exposing his bare back to my side of the forest. Scars. Huge, raised scars in the shape of wooden slats. Burn scars. I narrow my eyes and glance back at Niklaus. He looks away quickly, as if those marks are none of his business to inspect.

I've never seen them before.

My mother shrieks as DaiSzek leaps gracefully from the hunter's trap. Blood drips down his chin, and he does his best to shake it off like an unwanted insect.

"Is he hurt?" my mother gasps.

But my father doesn't seem too concerned as he checks DaiSzek for any injuries, then slaps him on the butt.

"We need to put as much distance between us and your parents as possible." Niklaus spins me around to meet my eyes. "We're not going to want to have a run-in with your dad."

It looks like it pains him to admit he's scared of the infamous Patient Thirteen.

"Thought you didn't believe the lore about him?" I taunt.

"I don't. But are you prepared to gamble with your life on his temper and paranoia for strangers watching him in the forest?"

My eyes dart back to my father, lifting Mom off the ground and carrying her away.

"I guess not."

Niklaus's cold blue eyes track their movements until they're out of sight. He lets go of my shoulders and takes a step back. "The world we were raised in is a lot safer than the one our parents grew up in."

Obviously.

"We need to stay out of sight," he adds.

"*Out of sight,*" Dellilian agrees with that innocent, soft voice floating through our minds.

I flinch, forgetting she's been by my side observing this whole time. Looking down at her curious little eyes, I smile at her comment. She blinks in surprise, wagging her tail, then going abruptly stiff.

My smile falls.

"Spitfire." Niklaus's voice rings with a warning, raising the hairs on the back of my neck.

I turn to see a great RottWeilen standing behind us. Large cinnamon eyes. Mahogany markings on his brows, chest, and paws. Residual blood still dripping from his mouth in long, goopy strings.

I've never seen him like this.

Shit. He'll know me in a few decades. Not now. I'm a threat.

"DaiSzek," I mutter.

The RottWeilen's lip curls up, showcasing his sharp incisors. He snarls, taking slow predatory steps closer. I sense Niklaus shift his wide-eyed stare to me, probably expecting me to call him off. To command my massive *future* pet to stand down.

"Do something," Niklaus says through clenched teeth.

"He doesn't know me yet!" I hiss under my breath.

I think back to when I was eleven, and I tripped over DaiSzek in the hallway, falling on my tailbone. It was the first time I cursed. My mom heard me call him a big, stupid animal. She told me to be careful with how I speak to him.

"*He isn't like most animals, Sapphire. He can understand your words clearly. The same way you're understanding me now. It's what makes him so wonderful, and so dangerous...*"

"DaiSzek," I say again, forcing the shakiness from my voice. "You don't know who I am yet. You don't know if I'm a threat or not."

He snaps his thick teeth at us with a growl that could make a lion bow to him.

How am I supposed to prove to him that he can trust me?!

I hear my mom's voice again. "*DaiSzek spent so much time lying his head on my pregnant belly before you two were born. He could catch your scent and Krimson's miles away when I gave birth.*"

"*But how could he recognize our scents if we were in your belly?*" little Krimson asked.

"*Because you have the same blood in your veins as his two favorite people in the whole world. Me and your dad.*"

Of course!

"Wait!" I hold up my hand as he lunges forward again. "You can trust me, DaiSzek! You *know* me! Just smell me! Look into my eyes. Can't you see it? I look like your two favorite people in the whole world." My vision blurs. I lay a splayed-out hand across my chest, clutching at my heart. Why does this make me so sad? I point to my left brown eye and the right green one.

Can he sense the heavy emotion pouring off of me? I didn't realize how much it would sting to have my sweet, lazy boy not know me as he stares into my eyes.

That gargantuan head leans in, nostrils flaring as he huffs and sniffs an inch away from my forehead.

"Please believe me, Big Guy." My chin trembles. The rusty odor of fresh blood crawls up my nostrils. The wind calms. The trees stop whispering. No one moves a muscle.

DaiSzek's wise, ancient eyes turn down as he registers my scent, then they snap up to meet mine abruptly. He is stiff and unflinching, quiet with slow breaths. And then there is his famous head tilt. It's the small movement of his neck, making those ears twitch when Mom talks about my father. When she says *his* name.

Dessin. Kane.

And he always checks the house as if his old friend has finally come home.

It's that head tilt that tells me he knows me. DaiSzek may not understand how he recognizes my scent, my eyes, my face…but he does. All of it carries strong, unbreakable ties to his two favorite beings in the whole world.

My parents.

The enormous beast sighs, accepting that I'm not a threat to him or the people he protects. And with that, I lift my hand like I have done all my life and stroke the sleek fur up his snout and between his eyes.

"Thank you," I whisper.

Those eyes filled with simmering coals and ageless awareness share one final look with me before he chuffs, turns away, and vanishes into the trees.

10. Run

Dellilian is gone.

I'm not sure if the interaction with DaiSzek scared her, or if she's abandoned us for good. But she's left us alone in the woods, searching for a way to return home on our own.

Niklaus glares back at me as we continue to trudge with sore, aching legs and feet through the pine needles, wild vines, and damp soil from an early morning rain.

"What?" I snap.

His piercing avalanche of a stare returns to the forest ahead. "How'd you know that was going to work?"

I blink at the back of his head incredulously, watching his almost-shoulder-length hair get tousled in the cool breeze. Does he think I'm going to explain that to him? Does he think I'm going to reminisce over memories of DaiSzek? Of the stories my mom has told me about him? About how my blood is her blood and DaiSzek is smarter than he is, clearly, and would be able to recognize the scent alone?

"You're welcome," I say.

"Not an answer."

"Not going to give one."

Why does he care? He's never liked DaiSzek. And I've never for the life of me understood that. When we were children, Niklaus was kidnapped for four days while he was supposed to be on a hunting trip in the woods with his neighbor and their parents. A few Demechnef extremists killed the family and took Niklaus to a hideout deep in the Emerald Lake woods, and as far as we know…they tried to brainwash him.

On the fourth day, he was supposed to return from the hunting trip with his neighbors, but the sun began to set and there was no sign of him. Before anyone had a chance to even begin to panic, Uncle Warrose took off to the woods to find him. He didn't waste a moment of speculation to wait around to see if they showed up. My mom told Krimson and me that Uncle Warrose knows the forests better than anyone, knows how to track better than the rest of our family. Well, with the exception of one.

DaiSzek beat him to the woods where Niklaus was supposed to be. DaiSzek had already begun the hunt for who took him. He clearly understood when Aunt Marilynn and Uncle Niles were expecting their son to return, and his instincts told him to act immediately.

When Uncle Warrose made it to the woods to search, DaiSzek growled and barked to get his attention, urging him to follow. It was midnight when Uncle Warrose and DaiSzek raided a condemned cottage to free Niklaus from his captors. And I didn't realize it then as a child, but my uncle and DaiSzek never brought back anyone living to punish. They clearly took care of the problem themselves.

Niklaus returned completely silent. He wouldn't speak for several days. Uncle Niles didn't make any jokes or laugh for what felt like years. My mom blamed herself for not seeing it sooner, for not figuring it out through the void.

He never spoke about what happened. Never told anyone what was said to him. Never spoke about the murder of that family who was killed on the hunting trip. And I used to feel bad for him—and even made him a card and sock puppet to make him feel better. He threw both away in front of the other kids, glaring at me like I couldn't have been more pathetic for taking the time to make both.

The point is, even after DaiSzek saved him, he still was cold toward my gentle giant. Hardly ever acknowledged him. Not really noticing his presence in a room. And how the hell can that be? I'd forever be grateful to him for saving my life.

"You still scared of DaiSzek?" I break the silence.

I can hear Niklaus roll his eyes from the back of his head.

"I have never been scared of him."

"Liar."

"I just don't like him," he says.

"Everyone likes DaiSzek." They are in awe of him. Speechless. Tempted to caress his fur and gaze into his russet eyes. Niklaus is the only one who avoids him even though DaiSzek has never been a threat or shown him harm.

"I am not a fan of animals," he explains in that dark, baritone voice of light agitation.

"Then you are a sociopath. No other explanation."

He continues walking without acknowledging that dig.

After a few minutes of complete silence, I let out an exhausted sigh and call out for Dellilian again. Is it possible she's been taken? Hurt? Scared? Wandered off like a small child?

"Dellilian! We're safe! Big bad DaiSzek is gone now!" I holler again, sending echoes of my voice to nearby caves.

Niklaus's upper stiffens and his steps slow down. Here we go again, another outburst of annoyance.

"Dellilian!" I shout again, louder this time to piss him off a step further.

"Shut. The. Fuck. Up!" Niklaus hisses over his shoulder.

"*Ohhh,*" I say incredulously. "When I figure out how to travel back home, I'm leaving your ass behind!"

What part of his stupid little brain is telling him that it's a good idea to bite the hand that feeds him? I'm our *only* way home!

Niklaus spins on his heels to get in my face, scowling down at me with an alarmed expression. He presses one finger to his lips, drawing my attention to the stubble growing on his face, the faint trace of five o'clock shadow.

The idiot is shushing me now. He's *shushing* me.

The hairs on the back of my neck rise at the loud silence, then a shuffling sound slicing through it like a scalpel, dissecting the stillness of the forest.

It's not the shuffling of an animal. It's the movement of boots.

My eyes widen, and as I lock eyes with Niklaus, we seem to share a thought, silently communicating our exhaustion and confusion as to why this is happening to us. Even through time, why can't we seem to escape being followed? How could this even be a factor we're worrying about? We don't even technically exist here…

The trees creak in the strengthening wind, carrying the heavy, humid scent of an upcoming storm. In the corner of my vision, a tall figure shifts behind a distant tree.

I sigh.

"What'll it be, gentlemen? You've already lost the element of surprise." Niklaus raises his voice, scanning the trees.

It's as if he's talking to himself, yet we can practically hear their shallow breaths wisping through the falling leaves and spindly twigs.

Niklaus looks into the distance with narrowing eyes, tugging his black eyebrows together as he concentrates.

"What is it?" I whisper.

His arm snaps upward, wrist locking into place against a small gust of wind that whooshes past my cheek. The blade of a small throwing knife slices into his palm. A throwing knife he intercepts before it lodges in his shoulder. Gritting his teeth, he throws it back in the same direction it came, hitting something that groans and falls to the ground.

The men dart from their hiding places all at once, kicking up dirt as they charge us from every angle. The attack this time is different than the last two. I thought there were only a couple of assailants hiding among us. But there are a little over a dozen this time.

"Oh my god," I mutter.

Niklaus and I release our weapons even though we both can feel it. The only reason I wasn't overpowered and killed last time was because Uncle Niles threw himself in the line of fire—using his hands to block the strikes of a blade.

A heavy blanket of doom drapes over my entire body as the fighting begins. Nerves prickle over the lining of my stomach. A near-painful chill burrows under my skin.

There are too many.

We've been trained. But we aren't anywhere close to the legend of my father. It was said he could handle this many assailants. More, in fact. And in this moment, watching a storm of armed men rush us all at once, I wish my father was here now.

A throwing knife snags the side of my hip as I fight off two grown men, whacking their swords from opposite directions. I scream as a small chunk of flesh and blood is ripped from my upper thigh.

"Sapphire?!" Niklaus shouts over the chaotic noise of clanking metal.

"I'm okay!" Fuck no, I'm not. But the adrenaline powers through me, numbing my entire quad.

Niklaus grunts and falls to his knees as he's kicked in the lower back. I make the mistake of looking back to check on him, and the hard knuckles of an assailant to my left cracks into my cheekbone. My vision blurs, and I blink furiously to relieve myself of watery eyes.

That's when I see it. A man standing off in the foggy distance, watching the carnage from an elevated hill in the forest.

There's something about him. It sets a sensation deep in my bones, bred of umbra, oppression, and death infused together. From just a glimpse amid the chaos, I see he's about my height with a black pinstripe three-piece suit and a bowler hat.

His black stare spears through the shadows and mist. And it's that look alone that doesn't feel right. I rip my gaze away from him to block another blow to my face—but it's too late. The stormy night edges creep into my sight, sucking my soul into that timeless pit. A vicious force of nausea burns through my gut, spiraling up my esophagus. It's where I feel Dellilian's comforting presence. The hooks of time sink deep into my chest, drawing the breath from my lungs.

It's then I see DaiSzek leap through the air, jaws unhinged, eerily quiet as he obliterates the men attacking us.

My heart completely stops.

DaiSzek came back for me. The way he's done for my mother.

But the cosmic pit of stars and darkness swallows me whole, and we travel again.

11. The Sunshine Has Gone

I sit in a bed of soft grass and small wildflowers, picking the weeds while I pout silently.

We are not home. It was winter when we first left. It is spring here. I count my blessings though. We are not in Vexamen, just the Bear Traps. Not a bad turnout. The weather is lovely. We aren't being attacked.

Niklaus sits up next to me. The cocky smile I'm used to seeing on his face has been gone for a while now. There's only brooding, scowling, and silent seething.

"I don't know," I say with a sigh.

I steal another glance at his face, but I'm surprised when I don't see an expression full of relief that we're no longer outnumbered and being attacked. He looks tired and pissed off. The vein in his neck twitches as those tendons tighten and flex. And there's a phantom heat pouring off his skin, as if from the anger boiling just under his surface.

The silence that hangs between us is overtaxing because my nerves can taste the bitter sample of an explosion peeking over his last reserves of calm.

"Let's find out where we are now," he says stiffly.

I stand up with him, adding pressure to the cut on my thigh.

"Out with it then," I reply, stepping around a boulder to face him.

"Say what you want to say."

Coward.

Niklaus lowers his slightly downturned eyes to meet mine. The irises go pale under the blazing sun, and he just stares at me without blinking as a line forms between his eyebrows.

"I have nothing to say to you."

I raise an eyebrow. "Oh, no? You're fucking welcome for saving you and getting us away from that ambush!"

"*Saved* us?" There's a cruel tilting of his lips, and his deep laugh has an icy core. "You think you've saved us?"

"Of course, I did." But it feels like I've answered a question that is rigged to make me feel small and ashamed.

"You've fucked us, Sapphire! Look around. We're so goddamned far from home. Are you really that deranged in the head?"

What bothers me the most isn't his words. I know he's wrong. But it's the way he's taking steps toward me, invading my personal space with his overbearing height. It's meant to intimidate me. Scare me. What kind of a man does that? And to top it off, he says the word deranged with a certain weight to it. *Deranged. Deranged. Deranged.* A word that he's used to describe my father all our lives. Sick. Disturbed. Unstable.

Heat meets my cheeks in a violent flare of anger.

"Is your penis really that small? The need to get in my face and attempt to scare me is that compelling, huh?" I shove at his chest once to get him to step back an inch. "You really can't help it, can you? No wonder you hate your dad so much. You'll never measure up to Uncle Niles, and you know it! Everyone loves him, and he's twice the man you are!"

The white-hot flames of my ire are quickly extinguished by my unforgivable words. I went too far. Because there's a lot of truth to that statement. Everyone loves Uncle Niles. Too many people in our lives have asked him why he isn't more like his dad.

Niklaus's jaw tics, and the cruel, dangerous smirk returns with a vengeance.

"Niles isn't my real father." Another furious step closer. "And you're one to talk, aren't you? Your father fucked your mom with the weak semen that created you. Then he fell asleep for the *entirety* of your life. Why do you think that is, Spitfire? Is it because God knew Patient Thirteen would have killed you for being a shameful mistake that should have died in the womb? Or because he's the pathetic one who lies in a bed and leaves your mother and his children to rot alone in the woods like a family of psychopaths who belong in that asylum."

And with those venomous words, Niklaus hooks his hands around my ribcage, throwing me into the creek. "Your father is as good as dead. And you've all but killed us too, you evil bitch."

Cold, murky water splashes around me in a small explosion of mud, algae, and mushy grime. I spit out the small amount that splatters into my mouth, gasping as goose bumps run ramped over my chilly skin. I squint against the blaring streams of sunlight, panting in shock as his haunting figure stands over me.

My eyes fill with tears, hot and fast with a lump swelling in my throat. Impossible to ignore or hide. I swore he'd never make me cry again after last time!

I inhale sharply through my nose but am unable to stop the tears from burning miserable pathways down my cold cheeks. The cry is pressurized in my chest, threatening to cause those obnoxious, embarrassing hiccups.

Why am I crying?

Those insults about my father don't hurt me anymore.

They don't hurt me.

They don't hurt me.

He's lying in a bed. Alone in his own mind. Left my mother. Left me. Left Krimson. Left DaiSzek. Left his family. Not by choice. I never knew him. Will never know him.

My mind spirals uncontrollably with fury and grief. *Stop crying!* I don't care about Patient Thirteen. I'm not a child anymore. I'm a grown woman. But the well of tears are heavy, slow, and that of a wounded little girl as they drop into the foggy creek.

Niklaus's cheek and brow twitches, but then morphs back into the careless, ruthless, soulless expression he loves to wear so proudly.

Patient Thirteen means nothing to me… He can't hurt me. Those words can't hurt—

"Whoa, everything okay here?" a man calls out from just over the hill behind Niklaus.

Shit.

"We're fine here," Niklaus shouts back, but doesn't take his punishing eyes away from mine.

"I know a lover's quarrel when I see one." The man's strange voice gets closer. "You okay, little miss?"

Those buttery summer beams blasting from the afternoon sky take my breath away as they land on a young man. His sun-kissed skin and golden hair shimmer before me. Though he's missing the aged smile lines and minor hint of crow's feet around his eyes from laughing every day…there is no mistaking the man who has approached us.

It's my Uncle Niles.

At least twenty years younger than the man I know from my time.

I nearly shout his name, exasperated and speechless. More tears blur my vision as I recall my last encounter with Uncle Niles. We left him behind. I don't even know when! I have no concept of the year, day, or time he is lost in right now. All I know is he's in Vexamen. *Before* Aunt Ruth took the throne and ended the Meat Carnivals. When it was a federal offense to be from the shining Chandelier City.

He must be so confused. So lost.

We left him behind.

The ache and hollowness of guilt dissolve into my chest, pinching my lungs together in a tight fist that won't unclench.

I can't breathe.

"Oh, fuck…" Niklaus loses his sinister glare. It falls so quickly as he stumbles back a step, gawking at his dad.

My eyes bounce between the elevated tension and shock emanating off the two men standing in front of me. I shiver in the ice-cold running water as they stare wordlessly at each other.

"That's no way to treat a beautiful young lady, friend…" Uncle Niles says with a smile.

He reaches down and holds his hand out to help me get to my feet. The action is all so familiar. It's as if he hasn't changed at all from the many times he picked me up off the ground when I scraped my knee playing. How he'd kiss my forehead when I'd cry, tell me he'd always take good care of me—that he loved my father dearly. That when he found out he'd fallen asleep and can't wake back up, he promised him he'd love me as much as he loved their friendship.

Yet even though he looks much younger as he greets me with that warmhearted grin, I catch a strange flicker in his dilating pupils. They stretch wide then small then wide again, nearly consuming his blue-green irises. Even at the age I currently know him, his eyes don't look this tired and sunken in shadows.

Something about him seems sick.

"Are you okay?" I ask.

Young Uncle Niles laughs. "I'm not the one drenched in mucky creek water, darling girl."

Uh-huh. Fair enough.

Niklaus is an immovable, mute statue.

"Come on, let's get you two inside. There's a night dawper on the loose on this side of the Bear Traps. Folks have been staying indoors until the mangy thing sulks back deeper into the forest."

We follow Uncle Niles to a small, ratty cabin along the stream. The black shingles are patchy and destroyed from years of wear and tear and storms carrying strong winds. His traditional smoky stained oak front door is hanging crooked on its hinges. The windows cracked and covered in a gray grime. The wooden porch is a walking hazard, with broken boards that have probably sprained and broken numerous ankles, house many rodents, and act as a current cesspool for moldy debris. And it smells. It makes my nose sting as it spoils the air with its acrid, dead odor. Past the decay and subtle undertone of fish, the atmosphere is hard to describe. It's the embodiment of loneliness and a slow poison hanging in the air for years, living on long after the dead have turned to dust.

It's not Uncle Niles.

His home with Aunt Marilynn has always smelled of freshly baked cookies, warm vanilla sugar, and a gentle stream of sunlight twinkling through the curtains.

This house is not the kind of house I'd ever imagine he lived in.

"This is your house?" I ask as we step onto the creaky porch with soft, unstable wood.

Niklaus shoots me a dark glance, but I can tell he's cautious of the same upsetting thoughts. Whether he has a good relationship with his dad or not…this is not the man he was raised by.

"Home sweet home," Young Uncle Niles replies with open arms wafting to his crumbling abode.

A sinister chill trickles down my spine.

As we follow behind my uncle, I can't help but gawk at the poor condition of his home. The dusty old furniture covered in grime and dirt. Walls speckled with chipping paint, holes, and crooked paintings. Pictures on the walls of his family. A man's face blacked out of the photographs. Flickering sconces and stained floors.

If we were following *anyone* else into this house, I'd turn my ass around and walk out of here. But I'd trust this man with my life. Even if he's been living in a rough spot.

We sit down at an old dining table. The chairs groan under our weight.

"Tea and sandwiches?" young Uncle Niles asks.

I gulp forcefully. Though I'm starving and would love a meal that hasn't been previously hunted…

"You sure we're not going to catch a disease by eating in here?"

Niklaus poisons that stale ambiance with his punitive words.

I pinch my lips together and widen my eyes, throwing a dirty napkin at his chest in horror. "*Shut. The. Fuck. Up,*" I mouth.

He shrugs and signals to our surroundings.

My uncle chuckles. "Maybe just a mild infection. Malaria… Tetanus. Polio." He glances back at us from over his shoulder. "Streptococcus?"

I laugh, letting my shoulders sag in relief. Humor remains intact.

Uncle Niles sets a tray down in front of us. Two pink teacups with steaming amber tea. A small porcelain plate with finger sandwiches. Though the lettuce is wilted and old, I could devour them with how hungry I am.

"Thank you," I tell him, sipping the hot tea that tastes like raspberries and licorice.

Niklaus nods at his father without making eye contact.

I toss my manners out the window and snatch as many sandwiches as I can from Niklaus's grasp, cramming them in my mouth. I leave him two and chomp down on four with a shit-eating grin on my face.

Niklaus lets out a long sigh, eating his food as he watches me with bored disgust.

"So, what was the lover's quarrel about?" My uncle walks around the table to sit on the filthy countertop, swinging his legs in amusement.

"Just a quarrel. Not lovers." Niklaus cannot hide his disdain.

"Oh. Relatives?" my uncle asks with a slight quiver in his voice.

I let out a happy sigh as I lick my fingers. "Nope. I just don't date eunuchs."

"Eunuch?" Uncle Niles raises his eyebrows at his son, then glances down at his crotch.

Niklaus's face falls, and his eyes narrow on me. "My dick is very much still intact."

"Is it?" I sip on my tea with a pinky up. But the taste hits wrong—too bitter, too heavy. "I hear the ladies in town can never find it when they go looking for it."

The right corner of his mouth tilts upward.

"Quite the treasure hunt with little to no reward." I wink at Uncle Niles but am confused as my eyes start to roll in the back of my head.

The room tilts.

A heaviness collapses on top of me.

"Well, you two certainly don't like each other very—"

12. "He Who Shared My Bread Has Turned Against Me."

I can still taste the bitter tea on my tongue.
A touch of drafty air drags me out of a waterlogged state.
And for the briefest of moments, I have forgotten I exist at all.

The floating sensation is followed by drowning, spinning, falling, choking…

Can't breathe.

Bitter taste.

Can't breathe.

My survival instincts flicker on groggily, and I drudge myself out of the weighted fever dream, breaking through an invisible lake of deep sleep to tilt my head to the side, and allow a river of sour contents to spew from my parted mouth. The splash hits the floor followed by a groan that must be my own because my numb chest tingles and vibrates from the effort.

Are my eyes open? Closed?

Am I on a boat? Am I alive?

Floating, spinning, falling, tilting off the side of the earth and…

My mouth gapes open as more of my stomach is emptied. This

time, the thick splatter echoes against walls. A floor. A ceiling.

I breathe in through my nose, filling my lungs with a stale smell, like wet earth trapped in a moldy box. It's familiar yet warped and off-putting. A cold, fungal breath that rises from the walls and whispers, *You don't belong here.*

No, I don't. *Where am I?*

The vile rank of my own vomit wafts back up to my face. I roll my head back to center, recognizing the feel of a creaky mattress under my head. *What the hell?*

Against the blanket of sleep that holds down my eyelids, I blink slowly to try and wake myself up. It's like wading through a pool of sludge. I blink again, unsure if I'm actually doing it or just imagining I am.

Pitch black. No difference if my eyes are closed or not.

I could have my hand in front of my face and see nothing. An absence of light, of space. As if the visceral darkness has a set of teeth, and it's grinning at me for being blind and helpless and now *scared.*

Because I can't wave my hand in front of my face. Even if I tried. Something scrapes against my wrists as I try to tug my left hand free.

The daunting sound of my own breath is too loud, too human, too isolated.

"Hello?" I whisper with a burning dry throat and mouth.

The silence that follows stretches wide across the still atmosphere, abundant with the possibility of movement. Of another heartbeat.

"This must be hell." A deep, groggy voice punctures the smothering blackness.

The desire to flinch recoils as I recognize the man behind the sound.

"Niklaus." I exhale. My tongue sticks to the roof of my mouth. I need water.

"Are your wrists bound?"

I take a deep breath in, then tug my arms in toward my chest, straining against the resistance keeping them splayed on either side of the mattress. A material cuffing my wrists, tough and smooth? Not metal but not rope either. Maybe leather?

I nod in response to his question.

Silence.

He can't see me. Stupid.

"Yes."

His breath is calm and patient, yet tense as we sit and think.

"I didn't travel," I blurt out in a whisper. At least, I don't think I did. "There are *feelings* I get when it happens. It didn't. I just—"

"Blacked out."

"Mmm-hmm."

Niklaus's calming breaths continue.

"Oh god…do you think Uncle Niles is okay? We must have been attacked…"

"No one attacked us, Spitfire," Niklaus says spitefully.

My pupils strain to catch even a speckle of light, returning some sanity back to my brain. He's just an isolated voice in this gloomy, chilled atmosphere. Maybe this *is* hell.

"Then…" I narrow my eyes. "What's going on? You know something."

He doesn't respond for what feels like several minutes. I wonder if I'm hallucinating his voice so my brain can cope with the isolation.

"Are you the—"

"Has your mother ever told you about my dad's past?" he asks quietly.

I relax my head against the firm mattress. "Like their time in the prison?"

"No."

"Then no."

"He was an asylum patient, Spitfire." *Embarrassment.* I don't think I've ever heard Niklaus Demechnef embarrassed in our whole lives.

"For what?"

"He was undergoing Mind Phantom experiments. I think it caused him to abduct people."

Oh shit.

"No…" I do remember Krimson mentioning Uncle Niles being subjected to these experiments at one point.

"How are you positioned right now?" he asks.

"Uhh—" I readjust my legs splayed out, toes wiggling as my bare feet are kissed by the abyss of frosty air. "I'm lying down on a mattress I think. My arms are spread wide with some kind of leather cuffs around my wrists."

He sighs.

"And you?" I ask.

"I'm on a hard chair with similar restraints on my wrists against a cold, stone wall and ankles bound to the legs of the chair." He pauses, and his breath is uneven. "I still have my pants on, but not my shirt."

I look down, even though I can't see my own body. I don't know how I didn't notice before. Pins and needles bite into the pebbled skin across my chest and stomach. I only feel tight fabric across my breasts and pelvis.

My head drops down to the mattress, causing a sharp creak.

"What?" Niklaus adjusts in his chair. A low groan of old wood.

I gulp and roll my eyes. "I don't have any clothes on. Well, I have a brassiere and underwear. That's it."

The room gets so quiet, I can't even hear him breathing anymore.

"*Goddammit*, we need to get out of here," he growls, straining against something, possibly his own manacles.

"I'm so sorry, my friend." A sliver of bright, blinding light bolts down from the far-right corner of my periphery. "No one is going anywhere for a while."

My eyes water as I strain to see a door open, and a man take shape.

My Uncle Niles stands at the top of a staircase, glaring down at us in his…

Basement.

13. Sweet Cupid

"What the fuck have you done?" Niklaus grits through his clenched teeth. He's not speaking to the young man who essentially has no idea who we really are.

Niklaus is talking directly to his father. Betrayal stains his cheeks a soft ruby red.

The glaring sterile light spills over his pale chest. Strands of black hair hang tangled and damp across his eyes, bloodshot and half-crest with rage. Weathered, old leather manacles bite into his wrists binding him to the gritty concrete wall behind him. A light sheen of sweat glistens across the dark hair on his chest. And with that deep brow line carving into his forehead—I can taste the fury bleeding off him, as thick and palpable as the sour rot clinging to the air.

"I'm not crazy," Uncle Niles says quickly.

What's happening? My gut twists and churns with the slow creeping understanding that this man I've grown up trusting with my life and the lives of everyone I love…is now a serious threat to my existence.

"It's just… No. No, I really can't explain." Uncle Niles bangs his fist on the wall as he takes careful, performative steps down the stairs. "You two are going to be my houseguests for a while."

"What's—*wrong* with you?" I blurt out in horror. "Please, let us go. You're a good man. I know you're a good man."

Hold it together, Sapphire.

I swallow that sticky lump in my throat.

Uncle Niles races down the last few steps to kneel at my side. The industrial light behind his head paints his face with gruesome shadows.

"Of course, I'm good!" He smiles and nods with unfocused eyes. "That's why I'm doing this. It won't seem like it for a while…"

"Then let us go," I whisper dreadfully.

At this, his gaze focuses on mine, and it's like he's considering it.

Moving my hair out of my face, he says, "You have strange eyes."

My sluggish heart cracks down the middle. He looks so sad. Confused. Drained of that golden sunshine light. Every ounce of warmth inside him has faded into a restless fog.

"Striking. Beautiful. But strange," he adds to himself.

"I get them from my parents." Something in my words feels like a threat. One I don't even understand yet.

"If you let us go, I'll spare you," Niklaus grunts, yanking his restraints hard and fast.

Uncle Niles shifts on his heels, still watching me thoughtfully. "I'm afraid you're not really in a position to be making threats, my friend."

"I am not your friend."

My uncle stands, twisting to the side to pop his back, sighing at the sound cracking along his lower spine.

"Maybe in a few months, you'll think differently…"

"A few months?" I shriek.

The complete stranger in front of me backs away a few steps, while looking right through me. He offers a small, pathetic wave goodbye.

"I'll have friends coming over soon to meet you two," he says his parting words and jogs back up the stairs, shutting the door behind him. A few clicks and there's movement of cogs and bolts. We're locked in.

And I will no longer refer to him as Uncle Niles.

I have to separate the two. For the respect I have for the uncle who helped raise me and for my own unraveling sanity.

He isn't Uncle Niles at this point in time.

He's just Niles.

14. Generational Curses

"Sapphire! Sapphire! Where are you?"

My hands claw at a cluster of roots tangled on the edge of a cliff. The grand mountain winds roar in my ears, whistling through my hair and attempting to pry my sweaty grip from the lifeline of a very old oak tree.

"I'm here!" I scream against the frigid storm of rain that has almost transitioned to snow.

With a sky full of charcoal angry storm clouds, a dancing aurora borealis, and a gentle dusting of cosmic stars—I try to distract myself from my impending death. A plummet down to a rocky terrain. I have to say goodbye! I have to tell my mother I love her!

"Sapphire! I'm coming! Do you hear me? I'm coming for you!"

That voice is so familiar. I'd recognize it anywhere. It's a warm, comforting blanket at midnight. It's the words of reason when my temper runs rampant. It's my brother's voice.

My twin.

"Krimson!"

"By all means, scream for him louder. They'll definitely hear us now…"

My eyelids stick as I blink away the reality I was in moments ago.

I heard Krimson…

I heard my brother.

"You are drawing attention to us," Niklaus says. Bored. Cruel. Pissed. "Like an idiot."

Up until now, I'd forgotten how much I hate him. How deep that hatred is embedded into my skin and bones and fibers after what he said by the creek. Pushing me to the ground like a coward. And sadly, that's not even the worst he's done to hurt me.

"What're you talking about?"

Footsteps creak above our heads. Muffled voices. A hushed conversation.

"He said he was bringing friends to meet us," Niklaus says quietly. "I don't think it's in our favor."

I try to stretch out my stiff arms and legs, take deep breaths to ground myself, and shake the sleep out of my head. The heavy aroma of a leaky drainpipe sticks to the inside of my nose, though it seems the smell has become worse since the last time I was awake—like something curled up in the corner of the room and surrendered to death long ago.

"Get us to travel again," my insufferable cellmate commands.

The locks clink and shift on the door at the top of the stairs. The muffled voices are silenced at a quick *shhh*.

"Now."

I squeeze my eyes shut, trying to summon those strange feelings I get right before that cosmic ecosystem swallows me up. The disruption of my equilibrium. The stardust and pure, endless shadow of nightfall.

"Spitfire, this is one thing you can do to start repenting and not be entirely useless. Get us out of here!" Niklaus growls under his breath.

The urge to put any more effort into trying to leave this place is as good as dead, even though I don't want to find out what our captor has planned.

"You sure you want to talk to me like that? Considering I could just leave without you," I reply, trying to stay calm and focused.

Niklaus goes quiet.

"Don't be rude to our guests. They came a long way to meet the two of you," Niles announces from the top of the stairs. He whispers to someone behind him. "I told you they were at each other's throats. Thank goodness I found them when I did."

Three figures walk down the stairs carefully, holding golden globes that illuminate the room with flickering firelight. Antique lanterns to reveal Niklaus and I restrained and unclothed.

Behind Niles, there's a woman taking shape. Short, half his size, poor posture with a hunched back, and a low bun on the back of her head. Her black mourning dress has drooping sleeves, a corseted throat, and a solemn old-world elegance. The cinched waist and rough sash remind me of the pictures of the lady-doll regimen in our history books.

She's an old woman judging by her shaky descent down the steps, and the deep-set wrinkles on her face, coming to life as she gets closer.

The spindly man trailing behind her is two inches shorter than Niles with long, thin arms and legs. As the light ignites the room, his gaunt features are made vivid. Spidery shadows casting across his long nose and pointy chin. The prominent freckles splattered across his face. The carrot-red hair slicked back…

What the fuck is that?

In the low, glimmering light, the bones of his face jut out—and his forehead screams at us, pleading for our sole focus to fall on the writing. The pink scars. The *name*.

Dessin.

My father's name is carved into his flesh. We learned about this growing up… About the grandmother and her son who helped run the experimentations on my father. How they tortured him to split new alters to protect himself. How they abducted my mother and tried to run similar tormenting tests on her.

"This the girl?" the old woman asks, voice hard and callous yet raspy with age.

She takes rigid steps up to my mattress and metal bedframe, examining my body with a judgmental, scorning glare. The corners of her mouth pulled downward with a sneer of disapproval and disgust.

"Does she think she's above the law? Not keeping up with the Lady-Doll Regimen?" The old crone jabs at my ribs. "She's *fat*."

Fat?!

First of all, my breasts are above average in size. My thighs are slightly thicker, and I have a little bit of squish on my lower belly…but I'm tall, lean, and my body is far from fat. Does this old bitch want me to look like her? Knobby shoulders, bladed collarbones, and a stomach so starved you can practically see the outline of her vital organs?

I hiss as she jabs me again.

"Now, now, isn't that regimen an outdated concept? This young lady is a true vision of beauty! Would you look at those different colored eyes?" Niles chimes, presenting me like a show pony up for sale.

The quick swing of her arm cracks like a whip. Those old, gnarled, arthritic knuckles backhand Niles's cheekbone, making him gasp and cower in shame.

"Bite your tongue, *boy*! That regimen is the law. Think of where this city would be without it. We'd live in squalor with anarchistic lands and fat, ugly women." She chuffs, glaring back down at me. "They'd look like *this* ungodly cow."

At that last bit, I choke out a laugh.

An ungodly cow.

Cow.

I really oughta write these down. My vault of insults for Mabel Rose will be elite and top tier when we return home.

The brittle impact of her bony fist shatters my laugh mid-breath, leaving the bitter taste of copper on my tongue. My jaw ricochets with pain, and I groan and squeeze my eyes shut.

Through the ringing in my ears, I swear I hear Niklaus yell something.

"Disrespect!" The old woman's arthritic fingers snatch my chin in an iron grip. "You *dare* mock me, girl? Is something funny? Have I told a joke?"

A small fire ignites in my belly.

Oh, my quick wit is going to get me killed.

"Ungodly cow," I respond through clenched teeth as she pinches my chin tighter.

"Was that not meant to be a joke?"

A small shock buzzes behind her milky-sheened eyes.

"If not, I have a joke that might rectify that… You're looking a little plump and chunky around the hips yourself. If you want some advice to lose twenty pounds of ugly weight, this one will work wonders for you… Cut. Off. Your. Fucking Head. You disease ridden *swine*!"

My words hang in the air like a sword over my head. I smile politely as she seems to be frozen, staring at me with an unreadable expression pinching her craggy face.

"*Grandmother…*" the man with my father's name on his forehead finally speaks up in warning.

The old woman passes her gas lamp to Niles. The silence grows heavy. Her fists curl so hard I can see the blue veins protruding on the backs of her hands. Her attack happens all at once. A blur of the black material from her dress, weathered pale skin, and spittle from the corners of her mouth as she shrieks, wet and throaty.

Those knuckles looked so brittle, but I yelp as they pummel my cheeks. A white light explodes behind my eyes. Again and again, she beats on my face, my jaw, the soft spots under my eyes. And with her second wind, she takes to my gut like a rabid banshee, hurling her frail body at me, summoning all her energy into battle. Her fists strike my stomach, sharp and deep, as if she's trying to reach behind my ribs.

The air whooshes from my lungs in a strangled gasp.

Niklaus says furious words behind the commotion. But I can't make out what they are.

The insurmountable pain blooms around the bone structure of my face, within my spleen, kidneys, and stomach. My vision is consumed by black and scarlet red, blurring from involuntary tears. My groans come out choppy and hoarse, grunting against each guttural impact.

I continue waiting for her to grow tired. To exhaust herself to the point of fainting. But I'm stunned by her stamina. Her blatant ability to power through her arms which must be on fire with soreness. The cold sweat dripping down her temples and neck.

My ears ring like church bells, chiming in with her continuous wails of ferocity.

Christ! When does it end?!

"Krimson…" I sputter blood as consciousness pulls me in and out of this basement.

Each strike is a message. Correctional punishment. The bite of my nails into the mattress slowly releases as I fade into the agony swallowing me whole.

Krimson, where are you?

A raging fire eats at my pulsing eyes and cheeks. Is my nose broken? I can't breathe through it. I open my mouth to gasp. My attacker busts my lip.

Krimson. Help me.

My eyes roll back into my head.

Krimson.

15. Correction and Abuse

"…can be quite cruel, can't she?"

I've been staring at the ceiling for what feels like hours.

My mind is lost in a thick web of fog and spinning. It's as though I've survived a natural disaster. Mass casualties. My body thrown around in a tornado. Swallowed into a hurricane. Tossed back out to fall to the earth and shatter all my bones in one fell swoop.

"You are so quiet."

Red spots splotch my vision, runny and warm, but I make out that shiny forehead with my father's name as a raised, pink scar.

I've heard the stories. We all have.

"My name is Abbott," he says as if I should already know this. "A rather accomplished correctional savant. And you met my grandmother, Agatha."

No. These are not your names.

My eyes stretch wider.

Abbott. Agatha. I commit this to memory, even in my incoherent state. I don't want to mess up and say who they really are.

"And what is yours? It's polite to speak when spoken to," *Abbott* adds with a speculative tilt to his head.

We're using fake names, then?

"Audrina."

Abbott smiles. The tug of thin, chapped lips snags my attention. More scars. That of sewing someone's mouth shut. Good God, my father really did that. Not rumors. Those stories were true.

"What an elegant name."

I hadn't noticed before, but Abbott is blotting at my bloody, swollen face with a wet rag. His other hand is twirling a strand of my long copper hair, holding it close to his nose. I can't tell if he's been smelling it or not.

"You smell delightful, dear child."

That answers that.

"Are you going to tell us why we're here? Or is it still a fun little surprise?" *Niklaus*. He sounds calm and bored, but I know him better than that. His words are edgy. Agitated. Silently boiling.

My eyes, though blurry and throbbing, shoot over to his chair against the wall. His cold, stormy blue eyes meet mine. He doesn't seem concerned for me. More like he's cataloging my weaknesses. Not sure what I was expecting. The evil fucker probably enjoyed the show.

Abbott inhales sharply through his nose. "And what's your travel companion's name, Audrina?"

I slide my gaze between the two men thoughtfully. Did the old woman beat the humor out of me? *Mmm, no*. I remember the tutor Niklaus woefully despised for telling our class he had a speech impediment when we were six. He smelled like onions and his thin hair would stand straight up without any effort at all.

What was his name?

"Barnaby." I smile then wince. My cheeks are broken. My face is inflamed and pulsating with an unbearable ache.

Niklaus lets out a small, irritated chuckle.

"Please tell *Barnaby*, it is not polite to speak when no one was speaking to him."

"What do you want with us?!" Niklaus roars, yanking on his restraints.

I flinch at the sudden outburst.

But Abbott does not acknowledge him. He simply continues to

blot the blood on my face, gazing at my features with wistful eyes. The invasion of space is starting to make my skin crawl, especially as he leans his face in, and I'm reminded of how close my father once was to embed those deep scars into Abbott's milky white skin.

"You're probably wondering how I received these scars, hmm?" he asks.

I dart my eyes away. Is that a trick question? Is he not embarrassed by them?

"Don't be shy. You may ask. I love educating meek, frail young women," Abbott adds.

Niklaus barks out a laugh. "Meek."

"How did you get the scars?" I ask cautiously.

"My grandmother and I are tasked with a very crucial line of work. Correctional, if you will. Reform…" He taps his chin and looks off to the corner of the room. "Experimental conditioning. We take what is already in the mind and rearrange it. Repurpose it. Find new heights it can climb. New wires to cross."

Yes, so I've read.

"I had a subject who grew quite weary of this process. That is the trouble with lesser minds, you see. He wasn't fond of my greater calling to educate those who are found lacking in intellect." Abbott has stopped blotting my face. Now, he caresses my cheek. I do my best not to shudder under his clammy touch.

"So, your subject was unintellectual then?" Niklaus sounds amused. We both know he's talking about my father. A man who was a genius. Could outsmart anyone.

Abbott ignores him. "This young man was deeply disturbed. A sadistic monster, even at such a young age. All I ever tried to do was help him. Explain his conditioning. Explain the crippling hallucinations. The inflicted night terrors. But I suppose that's where I went wrong. One day, like a wild animal, the sick individual strapped me down and carved his name into my forehead with a dirty knife, then sewed my mouth shut."

"Dessin," I read the name out loud.

My throat seizes mid-breath as a long, skeletal hand hooks around it—fingernails like splinters biting into the sides of my neck as it chokes me. Air and sound are cut off in one crushing grip.

"Listen here, meek girl." Abbott gets in my face, pointing his spindly finger at me. "Don't you ever say that ugly name. I give it no life!"

"Hey!" Niklaus barks, losing his amused tone and gaining a tenor that is alert and gruff.

"You hear me? Never! That name is grotesque! Vile! I *hate* that name. No one speaks that name." He seems to catch himself at a moment of dishevelment. "There now. Even scholars have limits."

My ears ring over the sound of Niklaus shouting.

"Do I make myself clear, young lady?"

Abbott's complexion has flushed from a sickly pale to a blotchy, boiling red. His freckles are nearly swallowed by the bloom of color spreading fast.

I nod against his tight hold. My vision fades at the edges. Splashes of white light blinding me. My sore body thrashes on the mattress, convulsing for air.

He releases me reluctantly.

"Are you all right?" Abbott clucks his tongue and sighs. "Ah, that's certainly going to leave a bruise. Shame. Very pretty neck too, isn't it?"

Who the fuck are you talking to?

I want to go home. I wish I could control whatever is going on with me. If only I could summon that dark energy that moved us through time. How does it work? I thought pain or fear triggered the jump. But here I am, in pain and pretty damn scared. Why isn't it working? Why aren't we leaving this god-awful place?

I cough out a laugh. "Gorgeous neck, yes. But bruised trachea? Adds a little spice, don't you think?"

There's a breath of silence before Niklaus sighs. "Christ."

Though it sounds like a laugh.

Abbott stares at me with a blank expression. "Would you like me to read to you tomorrow?"

"I'd rather your grandmother beat me again."

"Sarcasm." He laughs, shaking his head. "Grandmother hates sarcasm."

Before long, Abbott reaches the door at the top of the stairs and closes it quietly behind him. The locks clicking into place echo in my ears like a funeral hymn.

I finally loosen my grip on the mattress, relaxing against the hard springs, and accepting the pitch-black basement to be a foundation of comfort against that man's incessant talking.

"Is anything broken?" Niklaus asks. His deep voice is oddly and unnervingly soothing to me right now. It's familiar. The silky baritone reminding me of home. I must be feverish or delusional.

"Just my dignity," I answer with severe hoarseness.

"At least your sense of humor is still intact."

"Yes. That is true."

Though I don't let him hear it in my voice as tears leak from the corners of my eyes, past my swollen temples, and onto the stained bed underneath me.

16. Devil's Words Dying

"Please tell me calling out your twin brother's name in your sleep isn't incestuous," Niklaus says, voice the epitome of severe exhaustion.

Has he slept at all?

"I keep having the same dream." I clear my throat. My voice is terrifying, like I've been gargling broken glass. "I hear Krimson calling for me while I'm hanging off a cliff, about to fall."

Niklaus processes this.

"It feels so real."

"Well, that's…creepy," he sighs.

I attempt a shrug. *Yeah.*

I almost ask him how he's holding up over there. That chair must be uncomfortable and I'm certain he's probably going mad with hunger and thirst. But what the hell do I care? I replay the look in his eyes as he shoved me into the creek. His unforgivable words. And to make matters worse, I'm the one taking a beating! So, he gets to sit in a chair that is making his ass fall asleep. Am I really going to check on the well-being on his numb backside when I'm currently a human pile of bruises, swollen throbbing flesh, and possibly some internal bleeding? *Nope*.

"We need to come up with a plan to get out of here," Niklaus says, breaking the deafening silence with the intrusiveness of his voice. It's clipped and low, like he can't be bothered to speak but is unable to stay silent either.

I pause to think. "I'm coming up empty."

"He seems to like you…"

"I see where you're going with this."

"And?"

"And no."

"Why not?"

I close my eyes. "I'm pretty sure he liked my mother too. You think if she could have batted her eyelashes and gotten him to free her, she would have tried that?"

"It was a different time then," Niklaus responds, though he's skeptical.

"It won't work."

"You're one of the most manipulative human beings I've ever met. You're not even going to try?"

"I—wow—that's so sweet." I raise my eyebrows.

"Wasn't a compliment."

"Look, I'll give it my best shot. But only if you have another plan *when* that one fails."

Niklaus exhales slowly. "I'm working on getting my left wrist out of this restraint."

I pause.

"Hmm." I blink slowly. "So, basically, if I fail at flirting with the captor my father permanently *maimed*, we're dying in this basement."

"Correct," he says.

The basement door swings open, cracking into the cement wall with a boom.

"—and that girl will learn!" Agatha hollers.

Yep, that's me. That girl.

A flood of light swarms the gloomy basement. But in this awful scenario, light bleeding into the darkness is never good. It brings terror and tormentors in its wake.

With more speed and aggression than an elderly woman should

be capable of, Agatha bustles down the stairs. A bucket of water sloshes and spills as she stomps down each step with old penny loafers on her feet and a caddy of rags and sponges in her left hand.

"Oh my, I bloodied you up good, didn't I?" Agatha stares at my face, collarbone, and ribs from a few feet away. For a moment, her thin lips pinch together, and I think she might be experiencing a touch of remorse…

"Next time, that small elven nose of yours breaks. Yes?" She shakes her bony fist at me.

"Understood," I reply blankly.

My face is getting so swollen, I'm having a hard time showing any facial expressions at all, which can only be a good thing for me right now. It would hurt to roll my eyes, scowl, smile mockingly, or any other movement that would showcase my rebellious, pain-in-the-ass personality.

"Good. Now open your mouth. Young ladies should be put to death for using the vocabulary you displayed to me. But I won't do that. I'm just going to scrub that filth from your oral orifice."

My eyes widen. "Uh, no thanks."

"No?" Agatha lifts her chin in surprise.

"I draw the line at anything to do with my oral orifice."

Her slow chuckle is unnatural and off-putting. The powdery lines along her cheeks deepen, but that sickened smile of annoyance does not touch her eyes. They glare at me with a challenge. A deep-rooted need to break me.

"I don't remember asking," she says, timeworn voice like rotting carcasses in a barren, winter desert.

"I don't remember begging."

If Niklaus ever makes it home, I hope he'll tell Krimson I went out swinging—not running my big mouth.

Agatha rolls up the black, flowy sleeves of her dress after setting her bucket and caddy on the floor. Her arthritic hands dig through the caddy, sorting through bars of soaps and amber bottles of solution. But she yanks out a dull, metal contraption. It's has bolts and clamps and a round opening.

Damn.

I shift my wary gaze to Niklaus. He doesn't meet my eyes but raises his brows at the tool that's now hovering over my mouth.

"Wait. You're not going to pick on *him* at all?" I stammer nervously.

Agatha glances at him in disgust. "Oh, that boy's penance is coming. He's got the devil in him too."

"But his mouth and vocabulary are way filthier than mine!" I yank on my restraints, unraveling as the tip of metal grazes my lips. I don't even care that I'm trying to sell him out. My body is a lightning storm of bruises and burst blood vessels. *That thing is not prying my mouth open!*

"I'm flattered," Niklaus says with a bored expression. "But I think everyone agrees you take the cake, Sa—Audrina."

I whimper as Agatha dips a piece of wool that looks like sandpaper in the bucket of soap, water, and God knows what else…

"But maybe she's right, old woman." Niklaus's eyes flicker to me with only the briefest flash of uncertainty beneath that deep water in his irises. His jaw flexes. "My mouth needs cleansing. You'd blush if only you knew where my tongue has been."

Agatha hisses as if his words and the visual that is entering her mind has burned her.

Is he…is he trying to take the heat off me?

"Shut it, boy!" The foul old woman pries my teeth apart with the metal tool. "I'll deal with you later."

Jesus, deal with him now! Please!

Despite my greatest efforts, my jaw is stretched wide open. The force is beyond my own strength without the threat of breaking a tooth. I even try to thrash my head back and forth, but Agatha has put a strap over my forehead to hold me in place.

"I usually use this device for force-feedings," she muses, wringing out the wool sponge. "But it does what I need it to for this."

I pinch my eyes shut and squeal in distress, unwilling to watch those gray, frail hands shove anything into my mouth. The odor is acrid and sharp, like wound antiseptic gone sour or a tin bucket left in the sun. The scraping motion starts on my inner cheek with the wet, scratchy material scrubbing the soft tissue raw. My tongue darts around to avoid the putrid taste of soap and old coins soaked in vinegar. A chemical. A chalky paste.

It's as gross as having your mouth washed out with soap can be—

Wait.

The pins and needles of the rough gravelly sponge sting, yes. But it changes so swiftly, biting into my gums and tongue with a wild, mind-numbingly painful burn. It's not heat, but a shriveling, tightening, stabbing sensation on the most sensitive flesh I have. It's as if each taste bud is curling in on itself, retreating from whatever chemical is doing this to me. My teeth ache and grind against the metal clamp, causing my nerves to scream.

"Here we are," Agatha grumbles, stretching the corners of my mouth wider.

And it hits like I've been lit on fire without a flame.

The moisture in my mouth evaporates in seconds. My tongue, cheeks, uvula, and throat stick together as if all my mucosal membranes have shrunken and died. My saliva glands simply stop producing.

I scream and gargle the chalky soap.

That deadly sponge drags across my tongue like it's trying to steal my voice.

"You feel that, girl?"

Tears well from my eyes even though I squeeze them shut, blocking out the image of Agatha's scornful, craggy face.

"That's the devil's words in your mouth dying one by one."

I swallow involuntarily, immediately seizing as the soap and chemicals slither down my throat. My body bucks against the mattress, choking and coughing up nothing. I'm going to die. I'm going to choke. My throat is closing. I'm dying.

Krimson! Please! Can you hear me? Help!

Niklaus

That fucking sponge is drawing blood.

My shoulders sear with pain as I flex my back in anticipation. How long is this going to last? How much longer can she stand this?

Sapphire whimpers and chokes. The muscles on her stomach coil tightly together. Every time Agatha scrubs at a new spot in her mouth, that sponge is like a live wire. It sends volts of agony through her body that are palpable to everyone in this room.

She's had enough.

Agatha pauses to dip the wool sponge back into the bucket of whatever that shit is, and Sapphire looks at me once. A spark of eye contact. Bloodshot corneas. Swollen, black and blue skin. She's in bad shape. That quick glance isn't a pleading look for help or mercy, it's a mere acknowledgment that I'm seeing her as low as it can get.

I almost call out her name.

But my teeth are wired shut.

My breathing is heavy, labored, and my pulse kicks when she gags.

"Try not to swallow it," Agatha instructs, bearing down against Sapphire's feeble attempts to whip her head away from this evil fucking baptism.

That slight twinge of guilt hooks into my chest because it's her getting the beating again. Not me. *Her*. It makes my stomach twist and turn sour. But she brought this on herself by running that mouth again. These are the consequences of her actions. I'm not responsible for her if she decides to be an idiot in a dire situation that could cost her life. It doesn't matter that we grew up together. That my mother would wring my neck for not protecting Aunt Skylenna's daughter. This girl means nothing to me.

Sapphire tries to scream again, but the sound gurgles and is abruptly blocked by the old woman's hand. I nearly peel the skin off my wrists by straining violently against these restraints.

Finally, Agatha tugs the strap off Sapphire's head and steps away. Sapphire convulses, flopping her head to the side to spew vomit to the floor. It splashes to the ground as saliva and clear liquid, certainly because we haven't been given food or water. She attempts to say something, curse probably, but only whines and moans come out. It seems she has cottonmouth, or her tongue is severely injured. Both are likely.

She got herself into this. She got herself into this. She got herself into this.

That heavy mop of sweaty, honey-copper hair hangs off the side of the mattress. She's speechless. Awake but eyes lost somewhere deep in her own mind, glazed over and out of focus. I've never seen her this way before. It's… disturbing.

The old woman turns and studies me like an insect on display.

I maintain a dead expression. Though a murderous impulse dances behind my eyes, and I let her see it. Unblinking. Unflinching. I could break her neck. All she would have to do is free me.

Agatha scoffs like this isn't the first time someone looked at her with homicidal thoughts. And I remember how her demise turns out. I know it comes from the hands of Skylenna's father. I can imagine she'll see this glare again from him.

"Don't look at me like that, young man." She walks toward me, a little wobbly from the exertion she put into Sapphire's *cleansing*. "I'm doing you a favor."

I stare at her long enough to make her shift on her feet.

"Oh?"

"You see that mouth?" She points a gnarled finger.

My gaze slides to Sapphire's swollen lips quickly, uncaringly, then I shoot it back to the old woman with boredom forced over my features. Every part of me hides how I had to hold my breath when I looked at her.

"I do."

"By the time I am finished with her, that mouth won't be of a whore. It will be of a wife."

Oh god.

Sapphire's dry gasps and wretches distract me for a moment, and I have to hold my breath again.

"Yeah. Not at all interested," I respond to Agatha.

"Well, not now, no." The old woman gives me a once-over. "I have work to do on you as well, boy. You don't think God sees all? Even when you touch your penis to the sight of this girl?"

I stare blankly.

"It'll take some time, but I'm going to build you in *His* image. To be a respectable husband. Train and maintain your wife. Discipline. Coitus for reproduction only," she states.

A small crack fractures my cold exterior. I can't help it. Laughter falls from my mouth abruptly. "I'm sorry, what?"

Agatha pulls her shoulders back, attempting to hide a layer of insecurity.

"Oh," I say, lifting my chin. "I get it. I get it. You haven't been fucked in a while, huh?"

I am just as stupid as Sapphire. But fuck, that felt good to say.

Her charged descent to my chair is unsettling. Pinched lips. Wide eyes. Sweat dripping down her temple. A frizzy, gray strand of hair pulled free from her tight bun. Agatha jabs out her hand and grabs me by the balls. I hiss through clenched teeth as she squeezes.

"You will respect me, boy! I could cut these off with a pair of old sewing scissors for using that language on me. Is that what you want?" Her yellow nails bite into my sensitive skin through my drawers as she tightens her grip.

Mmm-hmm. That gets my attention. Consider me reformed like Sapphire.

"No, I'm good," I grit.

The world goes black around the edges as her fingers script a cruel sermon into my crotch. The nerves across my groin misfire, and my stomach lurches. I've lost the motor functions in my arms and hands to continue attempting an escape.

"I couldn't quite hear you. What was that, boy?"

A thunderous gong claps inside my spine. Her bony hand twists deliberately—not enough to cause serious damage, but enough get the reaction she's looking for.

I growl like a wild animal as my molars grind together.

Fuck!

I refrain from cursing in her face. Calling her the many insults populating in my brain at a rapid rate. I hold back the adjective I want to use. The foul, grotesque threats. The crude, downright evil taunts.

I might as well kiss my balls goodbye if I give in to those

impulses.

"No, that is *not* what I want," I growl.

Agatha smirks. "I thought so. You men are all the same. What a pathetic weak spot."

Don't you fucking say what you're thinking, Niklaus.

That rigid hand unclenches, and I sag in both agony and relief. My thighs tremble as the pain flares wide, cascading into my gut, laying down a heavy, potent wave of nausea for me to sit with. My groin contains a slow, throbbing explosion. The anguish deep in my pelvis makes it feel like something vital has been permanently severed. But I know I have to wait. *Breathe. Wait. Breathe.*

Agatha glances back at Sapphire. Fuck, she looks bad. Open mouth. Half-crest eyes. Skin oily and practically a sick shade of green.

"I'll leave you two to talk," she announces smugly.

Agatha's absence is a huge fucking relief, yet dread settles into my chest as I wait for Sapphire to fire off a string of profanities and complaints. I'd welcome it actually. Anything to relieve this tension.

But she doesn't say a word.

17. The Offering

Niklaus

I have no concept of time.

Is it day or night?

Sapphire only tries to speak once. I ask her if she's all right. If she's dying. Her response is an incoherent guttural sound. It's as if her mouth has been sucked of all moisture, and she's unable to even peel her tongue from the roof of her mouth. I flinch. Not at the noise, but at what it means. Words have always been her way of fighting back.

And now she cannot speak.

"I know I said you didn't save us last time when you traveled us out of that fight, but I'm really going to need you to do it again," I say, my request dying into the silence the moment it touches the dark room.

Sapphire doesn't move. I'm not even sure if she's breathing anymore.

An unwanted sting of guilt penetrates my chest. She's getting this a lot worse than I am. Obviously, if she could travel—even if it's to save herself from this torment, she would. But is it a matter of whether she can control it? Or is it limited?

The basement door creaks open slowly, allowing a blinding light to split the dark like a knife. My eyes water and squint to adjust, searching the room for Sapphire. Is she still alive? I land on her bare stomach first. Thinning out. Ribs slightly protruding with each shallow breath.

How long have we been down here? I can imagine it's only been several hours, not days. But I'm getting increasingly anxious for basic human needs. For instance, I have to piss like a racehorse, and I'm strapped to this massively uncomfortable chair. I'm sure Sapphire does too—if she hasn't pissed herself already.

Those strange eyes open, slow blinking at the ceiling.

"Open your mouth, boy."

I flinch at the aged, hardened voice next to me.

Agatha moves like she's stepped off a church pedestal, self-righteous and pious. Face a caricature of a villain. She stands to my right, holding a small canteen and a plate with a slice of sourdough bread. Her weather-worn face has creepy shadows cast across her wrinkles. And in this light, I'm unsure if it's a hallucination or not.

"You deaf? I said open your mouth," Agatha snaps.

I eye the contents in her hands again, then slide my gaze back to Sapphire's swollen lips.

I shake my head. "I'd prefer not to ingest whatever you washed her mouth with."

Agatha kicks my ankle, but I don't react.

"Don't get smart with me. This is water and bread. If you'd rather starve…" She turns on her heels to head back to the stairs.

"Wait," I say abruptly, suddenly realizing how dry my mouth is. My stomach aches for even a bite or two of food. "All right. Yes."

Agatha smirks to herself, taking smug steps back to me.

"But she needs it too." I jerk my chin in Sapphire's direction.

"Yes, of course. Dear?" Agatha glances over her shoulder. "Would you like some water?"

Sapphire tries to part her lips. Groans faintly.

"What's that?" Agatha taps her ear condescendingly.

"She can't respond. Her mouth is…" I have to look away from the sight of Sapphire's lips, cracked like dry riverbeds. "Her mouth is raw."

And that dooming silence is louder than a scream.

"If you can be obedient and answer me, I'll give you food and water," Agatha challenges.

That small, rebellious flame sparks once again in Sapphire's red-rimmed eyes. Her jaw quivers at the hesitant opening of her mouth, but only a strangled, frustrated breath blows out. It's raspy and rough then abruptly turns angry and loud. A moaning, dying, suffering animal.

I stare at the ground, as if that gives her privacy. As if it spares her even a little bit of dignity. Yes, she got herself into this, but I'm not a monster. This is inhumane torture.

"That isn't intelligible, stupid girl." Agatha's sneer is venom.

Sapphire chokes. It sounds like her throat is made of sandpaper and glass.

"*I-can't-hear-you!*" Agatha shrieks and sings at the same time, pushing her creepy old lady voice to a new octave. "Speak, girl!"

Christ, make this end.

I attempt to go somewhere else in my head. The pond I'd go fishing at as a boy. The rope attached to a great cypress tree I used to swing off in the hot summer months. But nothing quite drowns out the agonizing sounds of the copper-headed young woman I grew up with… groaning and gagging as she fights to say clear words to this old hag.

"Not a word? Not even for a sip of water to coat your dry, blistering mouth?"

Well, you can't say this bitch didn't deserve what she got when Sapphire's father broke her spine in four places. She's an actual sadistic psychopath.

Agatha twists back to me. "Open."

I think about denying it if Sapphire can't have some too. But that thought disappears as quickly as it popped up in my head. What good am I to her if I'm too weak to crawl?

I accept Agatha's food and water without sparing a single glance at the girl who got us into this mess. I avoid her defeated, miserable glare as I drink down the water and chew the bread as quickly as I can.

And I continue to stare at the floor, even as Agatha returns upstairs. Even as the room is draped in darkness once more. I stare at nothingness, listening to Sapphire's breaths grow heavy with sleep.

I offer no apologies. No explanations.

I just stare.

18. Maimed Knight

Sapphire

I am in hell, I'M sure of it.

This is not a basement. It is not a pit of darkness under the house of my uncle. This has to be hell. The fiery cavity of misery and incomprehensible pain. My mouth is swollen, battered, throbbing, raw, and caked in sores and an all-consuming sting that won't go away.

I can't stop thinking about it.

Even if I fall asleep and achieve the sweet relief of a dream, the agony seems to permeate the walls of my mind, poisoning that beautiful hallucination I get to drown myself in to escape my own body. It sours every detail, every fictional sound and image I create.

I wake moments after drifting off. The reality slams into me like an uncontrollable, derailing train. I inhale sharply through my nose, only to find that my sinuses are inflamed and closed off.

Breathing through my parted lips is the damning equivalent of licking a hot fire poker then gargling a pile of splinters as a palate cleanser.

I am in hell.

I am in hell.

I am in hell.

"I think it's potassium alum." Niklaus takes a breath as if he's been holding it. "And lye soap. Maybe salt."

I lie perfectly still. If I move my head, I can feel the movement against the sores in my mouth like a thousand tiny daggers running me through. If he thinks I'm going to respond, he's as stupid as he is ugly.

"Whatever she washed your mouth with," he adds in a low, deep voice.

Why the fuck do you care?

"I read that Demechnef used that combination in training and conditioning subjects to obey without question or talking back."

Hmm. What a wholesome family you come from. Read that in one of Daddy's diaries, did we?

Niklaus shockingly reads my mind. "Yes. I realize you're making many comments about my father in your head. I realize how fucked it is now…seeing it happen in person."

Is that guilt I hear?

"But you brought this on yourself. Running that mouth is going to get us killed," he adds gruffly.

I stand corrected.

I drift in and out for what feels like another hour of torture. I don't even notice the door open or that anyone has descended the steps.

I don't notice until I feel him exhale against my cheek.

"Grandmother is not very tolerant," Abbott says.

Just kill me.

The man smells of a cut lawn, sweat, and boiled potatoes. No sense of personal boundaries. No concept of the obvious social cue I'm giving him by cringing away.

"Cold water will help." Abbott tips a canteen against my chapped lips, letting out a slow trickle of water to wet the dry, throbbing sores and tissue in my mouth.

It's still painful, but I can't help but groan in relief.

I let the cold water soak and swish against my tongue for a while, allowing my throat to soften and expand enough to swallow.

"That purity wash is performed on Emerald Wives often. Did you know that? Of course not. Your skin has—what are those—freckles? Sun damage?" He gently taps my right hand. "Your fingernails have dirt under them. Calloused palms. Dry knuckles…"

Abbott trails off, zoning out as he traces my fingers in thought.

"You must have lived a sheltered life on the outside of the Chandelier City. Your poor skin probably has never seen the Lady-Doll Regimen. How deeply unfortunate for someone of your beauty."

From across the room, I hear Niklaus taking quick shallow breaths through his nose.

"Nevertheless, Emerald Wives accept this treatment all the time, really," Abbott says.

"W-why?" The nerves in my mouth scream from the little movement it takes to utter a single word. It escapes from my lips in a ragged, harsh whisper.

Abbott's sparse, orange eyebrows lift in silent excitement.

"A number of reasons. Lying, talking back to their husbands, or infidelity. It's important to wash away any lingering remnants from another man. Or even diseases carried by a man's penis." Those intrusive, beady eyes watch me for a reaction.

I don't give him one. Even though that sentiment is grotesque. Talking back? Well, I guess it's safe to say that this purity mouth washing bullshit would be a part of my daily routine if I was born in this time period.

"More?" Abbott taps my bottom lip with the canteen.

I nod.

After a few slow drips, I close my eyes at the subtle coating of relief. It's not significant. The inside of my mouth stays dry as if it can't absorb enough water to fully soften. But the amount I got down helped me over that deliriously painful hump.

"I see that you're also cold," Abbott announces mechanically.

I didn't notice. The muscles along my abdomen are coiled tightly together, vibrating as I take unsteady breaths. But yes, I'm cold. I'm lying here in my undergarments. No blanket. No layers. This basement is drafty with a murky chill in the air. There's nothing more uncomfortable than being constantly cold but having no way to curl into a ball to stay warm. No blanket to wrap around myself. It might be the only thing I want more than water or a bathroom break.

I nod again.

Please, bring me a blanket.

Abbott hesitates a moment, taking abnormally loud breaths as he stares down at me. He bobs his head a few times, a nod in reverse, like he's trying to convince himself of something.

Is he going to get in trouble with his grandmother if he covers me up?

"Y-you don't—have to—listen t-to her," I whisper, trying to wet my mouth again between each word.

Abbott eyes me like I'm a lesser species that doesn't understand the meaning of my own words. "She's my grandmother."

With a quick glance back at the basement door, Abbott nods to himself again, then climbs on top of the mattress, on top of *me*…

"Wait…" I gasp, grunting against his weight. "No."

The distressed noises that come out of me through my raw throat aren't recognizable. I buck and squirm under his bony frame, angling my face as far away from his as I can get.

"Hold still!" His hot breath brushes my cheek.

This vile, red-headed, narcissistic man with my father's name carved into his forehead hugs my body tightly.

"I'll keep you warm." He's panting. And I wince at the sheer excitement in his voice. The acne on his chin rubs against my cheekbone. His sharp hip bones pin me down. I suffocate in his stale, unhygienic aroma.

"No," I rasp again. "*No*."

The uninvited invasiveness is worse than the cold. It is the worst kind of discomfort. Intrusive. Non-consensual. Revolting. My skin crawls under his weight, itching with the unbearable need to get him off me.

"I suppose no one has ever told you how the human anatomy works. Especially a woman's anatomy? I can share the warmth of my body with you. Did you know that?" Abbott sighs against my face. "Rhetorical question. Females often lack the understanding of science."

I squirm and whimper under his weight.

"No, shhh, don't worry. The average female isn't capable of holding that sort of knowledge. You're too busy preparing your womb for childbearing purposes. It's the sole reason for your existence."

Please, God, make this end.

"It's probably all you think about, isn't it? Reproducing and—*mmm*, your hair smells sweet."

"Get off her. Now."

I'm not sure I've ever heard such quiet, bottled anger in Niklaus's voice before. It's a deep, authoritative boom in this silent basement.

Every bit of Abbott's frame tenses with annoyance.

"Please tell your travel companion he will wake Grandmother."

I flick my gaze to Niklaus in a panic. Please, not her again. Anyone but her.

I'm not surprised to see a lack of empathy as he slides his cool, downturned eyes to meet mine. His stare is merely surgical. Measured. Calculated. Observant of a situation he knows he must step up in if he has any decency as a human being at all.

I try to communicate with my eye contact. I beg him to put his hatred of me aside for one minute. Just one.

There's a brief hesitation in his expression. For a single heartbeat, his focus loses its lethal precision. That glare isn't so familiar anymore. It isn't warm, not ever, but it's lingering. No blinking. Just pausing like he's surprised with himself for hesitating. Like he's holding his breath for my situation to get much worse.

"Let her wake then," Niklaus finally barks back, breaking our unusual streak of eye contact. That once hesitant stare lands back on Abbott. A slow dissection of an already dead animal. "I'm excited to see what that pious hag thinks of her grandson, groping a young woman. What do you think she'll call you? Perverted predator? Insidious? Spawn? Desperate *virgin*?"

Abbott's face blooms with a flush of scarlet red, spreading all the way to his collarbone.

"TELL YOUR TRAVEL COMPANION TO BE QUIET!" he whisper-yells in my face.

I flinch and close my eyes again the outburst.

"Shall I call her down here?" Niklaus's voice is smooth, but it doesn't soften, it steadies.

Abbott puckers his lips as he considers this with beads of sweat forming around the raised pink scars on his forehead.

"Or is your small penis soft now imagining your grandmother witnessing your sad, pathetic, *deeply* unattractive assault?"

I forget to breathe.

Abbott tumbles off of me, squirming, huffing, and wiping his forehead clean of the trickles of sweat. He looks down at me with a soured expression, balling his fists at his sides.

"I see my good intentions as a gentleman are not appreciated."

The agonizing chills returns to my skin, crawling under my flesh and settling into my bones. But it doesn't matter. I'd rather freeze to death than have that sad, weasel of a man lay on top of me.

The door closes quietly despite that Abbott probably wanted to slam it behind him, leaving us in the dooming darkness once again.

Once the light disappears, I relax back against the mattress, squeezing my eyes shut to attempt blocking that memory for good. If only I hadn't made my situation that much worse by wetting the bed from the mere terror of that interaction.

"Thank you…" I mutter, though the sound barely lives on past my lips.

Niklaus is so quiet, I'm not sure if he heard me. But there's a shift in weight on his chair.

"Your mother would have killed me if I didn't step in," he says.

There's a thick layer of defeat and exhaustion in his tone. That cold, cruelness in his intonation has lost some of its frost. That bite isn't as damaging as it was before.

Yes, my mother would have killed him. But she isn't here. Will I ever see her again? What if we're locked down here for the rest of our lives? What if we don't have much longer to live?

"Your mother would have too," I add hoarsely.

"Yes," he agrees, sounding so drained. "You can thank me by getting us out of here. By getting us home."

What's the point of having this ability if I can't control? Come and go as I please? I'm not special like my parents. They would have figured out how to dominate this great imposition. My father would have escaped from this small slice of hell within moments of being captured.

"I'll try."

Letter #1,007

Skylenna

Dear Kane,

Little Niklaus was abducted. Luckily, DaiSzek and Warrose tracked him down and dealt with his captors before any of us could even act.

But it got me thinking. What if that had been Krimson or Sapphire? No one would have gotten there faster than you.

I will protect our children, but it should be you, baby.

I know you would take a nation down to protect your family.

I love you still.

Sincerely,

Your Soulmate,
Skylenna

19. Umbra Abulia

Sapphire

"You've upset my grandson."

That horrible, awful, sickening voice jolts me awake. The light burns my eyes, but I can still make out her hunched posture and frizzy bun.

To my surprise and relief, Agatha is not talking to me.

"Wake up, boy!"

A hard slap to the face wakes him up. The sound of his distinct, sharp inhale is laced with violent rage. I wish it was strong enough to break through his restraints to break this woman's neck.

"Now I have to deal with you! I thought that girl was going to be my only problem!"

Oh fuck, is she going to scrub his mouth out too?!

"What did your grandson tell you?" That controlled voice is smoke over coals.

Agatha grips his chin and digs her yellow nails into his flesh.

"Don't talk back to me, boy." Her crow's feet deepen as she

studies Niklaus from head to toe. “These will be your names from now on. Boy and Girl. And you’ll refer to me as Grandmother. When I address you, you’ll answer ‘*Yes, Grandmother.*’ Understood?”

Right when I think this experience can’t get any worse.

“I’ll drop dead first,” Niklaus says.

The back of her hand whipping across his cheek is expected.

Agatha pinches her lips into an aggravated smile. Like she was hoping there would be some defiance left before she beats it out of us.

Without warning, the old woman sticks his arm with a syringe, pressing her thumb down on the plunger until the white liquid disappears.

“Fuck,” Niklaus mutters under his breath. His eyes lift to meet mine before they grow heavy.

Agatha begins whispering in his ear, pointing aggressively and pausing as if waiting for him to respond. He winces away from her hot breath at first, then blinks slowly, feeling the effects of whatever she injected him with.

“I blacked it out,” he finally answers, lost behind those tired blue eyes.

Agatha whispers again, harsh and bitter.

“A group of extremists took me,” he replies.

Oh no.

“I kept asking for my father.”

Do I want to hear this? He’s never spoken about that time. It feels like a private moment I shouldn’t be forced to listen to. Sometimes I forget it happened at all.

“They made me stare at… gruesome photographs. Only given water when I’d say what they wanted me to say.” His jaw is tight, but there’s an eerie pain behind his blank stare.

Agatha whispers a question.

“They hurt me if I tried to leave. I had to lie in a grave if I cried.”

What the fuck?

His body flexes, chest lifting as he bears down. A long groan drags out of his lungs, muffled behind clenched teeth.

“Is your name Boy?” Agatha asks after influencing the hazy, delusional state he’s in with the thoughts she whispered to him so fervently.

"Yes, Grandmother," he answers.

Niklaus flexes his arms against the restraints, hardening his entire body as he squeezes is eyes shut to escape the cluster of memories invading his mind.

I want to call out to him. Remind him of where he is. But in the same breath, I feel like an idiot for wanting to help him. Especially after his horrific words at the creek replay in my head.

After another hour of this, Agatha finally takes her exit, leaving me to watch Niklaus fall in and out of sleep. When he's awake, he stares blankly at the floor, seeming to process the demons in his mind.

The decent human part of me has that nagging urge to comfort him. But there's another side of me that's so tired. My body aches and trembles from the beating and the drafty basement. The roof of my mouth and the inside of my cheeks are jagged with sores. All I want is to fall asleep and escape.

My eyes grow heavy, staring up at the ceiling in hopelessness.

What if I can never travel again? What if it was a fluke?

I'll never see my brother again.

A warm breeze of breakfast tea and oatmeal brush over my upper lip.

I wrinkle my nose at the heat it brings, then at the sudden pressure over my mouth. I have no memory of dozing off, but as I'm pulled out of a dim, dreamless sleep—I jolt awake at the forceful pair of lips being smashed against my mouth.

A soft, whimpering groan vibrates against my face, and a slimy tongue pokes between my lips and into my mouth.

Every muscle becomes stone, flexing to the point of searing pain.

A pair of hands cup my breasts. Warm, damp, clammy, and kneading into my brassiere. The weight of his body. The scent of his grassy, sweaty body odor. It makes me seize under his bony figure pinning me to a mattress.

I jerk my mouth away from his and scream hysterically. The

tears come as I thrash my face back and forth, fighting to breathe any air that hasn't already been claimed by him.

Torn wallpaper. A grimy window with blurry streaks of rain pelting over the rolling hills of bright green grass and slanted trees swaying in the storm's ferocious wind.

"Shhh! You don't have to be afraid of that insect. He's still in the basement," Abbott shushes against my lips, panting in excitement.

I want to go home. I want to go home. I want to go home.

"We can be together in here without him watching, okay?" Abbott's scars are glaring at me, screaming my father's name in raised pink flesh on his forehead. I wonder if I scream his name, would he come? Would my father come to save me the way he found my mother with this monster?

"Please, how about we take things slow?"

I want to be smart about this despite the way my heart gallops in my chest, sending floods of adrenaline into my bloodstream to fight until I'm dead. To kill rather than be violated. But I'm still shackled. Still restrained from defending myself. What good were years of training to fight if I'm helpless here? There were so many stories of women and the history of lady-doll oppression back when my mother was my age. They had to accept assault as if it were a part of their weekly routine.

I never thought…

"Please," I choke out again.

"You feel it too," Abbott assures me. And his lips jam against mine, this time with urgent, forceful pecks. With a freckled, shaky hand, he unzips his pants and lays his small, hard penis on my pelvic bone. The curly, carrot-red hair spiraling in a bush around its base.

I have no patience or self-control to try and be smart about this. I always thought I would be able to fake a bond with a captor. To make them like me and win their favor before I escape or kill them. But being here is different than the stories I've read. Being here is drowning and trying to remain calm. Being here is lying perfectly still while someone sets my clothes on fire.

I scream again, this time far more panicked and desperate. The scream carries a cry I haven't heard come out of myself before. The sound is raw, visceral, and heartbreaking.

It's the cry of a woman about to be raped.

20. Call of The Revenant

Niklaus

Sapphire's absence yanks me out of my nightmare with a vicious whiplash.

The basement is empty. How did I miss this? Where has he taken her?

She's gone.

Sapphire is gone!

I search the darkness. But there is no breath stammering from her weak lungs. There is no heartbeat. It's just me here.

Did I black out?!

One minute Abbott was fucking assaulting her and the next no one is here at all. This momentary lapse makes me feel like I am not a goddamned man at all. How could I not protect a helpless woman from this evil?

Agatha's injection is making me lose time!

I was stuck in a loop of those hollow days in that abandoned cottage. The flashbacks of lying in a grave while I tried to stop crying.

The dirt underneath my fingernails. The smell of wet earth burning into my memory.

I cried for my father, for Niles, to come save me.

I was so young.

How long has it been since I relived those days? Yet Agatha summoned my demons with swift ease and pleasure.

But the absence of Sapphire's steady breathing became terrifyingly loud.

I am alone in this cellar now. The stained mattress is bare. I scour the room in a haze with drooping eyes. It's all empty.

I feel so fucked up in the head from Agatha's injection that I begin to worry that Sapphire Valdawell was a figment of my drugged-induced imagination. What if she was never real? What if my reality was fabricated? That's what Mind Phantoms do, isn't it? What if I never time traveled, and I'm really from this time?

There's a black hole forming in my chest. It's not heavy like a weight. It's a howling wind. The thought of being alone here in this era of old ways and sadism. Even the slightest bit of doubt that the Mind Phantoms invented this idea of *her*…

Sapphire Valdawell.

Did I make her up?

Doubt flourishes in the sea of my mind.

Each short breath I take sends echoes through the mausoleum built for someone no one else remembers. But what about that vivid memory of her climbing to the top of the Red Oak trees when we were children? Or the time I teased her for the light dusting of freckles over the bridge of her nose? Those strange different colored eyes…

I've hated her most of my life. But what if she isn't real? I'll never leave this place. I'm stuck here—

That scream finds its way under the crack of the basement door in fragments. It jolts me upright, blasting a hum of panic and relief through my bones. It wakes up that foggy part of my brain that's been asleep, trapped in a loop of questioning my reality. I know her voice but have not heard that fear in it before. That scream is one Sapphire wouldn't make unless…

I twist my right wrist in my shackle again, using my thumbnail to carve into the leather.

"Come on, you son of a bitch," I growl at the restraints.

Sapphire screams again.

"Fuck!" I hiss.

I twist so hard the skin on my wrists begin to peel off.

"Niles!" I shout after hearing another deadly shriek whip through the air. I swear to God if she travels and I'm not with her, I'll fucking kill myself.

Maybe there's one redeeming quality in my father during his complete loss of morals and sanity during this time of his life. Maybe I can talk to him. Reach that part of him who raised me. The man who was kind to strangers and made it his mission to make his wife laugh. Is he still in there?

"Niklaus!" she screams my name from somewhere in the house, and it sounds like she's being choked, or her mouth is being muffled.

"Niles! I swear to fucking God!" I roar as blood trickles down my elbow. Skin curling around the restraints like pencil shavings. I almost have it…

"He isn't coming."

Agatha stands at the top of the stairs, holding a gas lamp, and shuts the door behind her.

21. Seraph's Left Hand

Sapphire

Tears drip down my temples like drops of blood from a deep wound.

"Don't do this. Please, don't do this!" The panic is suffocating as this mad man reaches his quivering hand into my panties. He rubs at my sensitive skin angrily, the same way you'd scrub a dirty dish.

"Why aren't you wet?!" The offense in his voice is shocking.

I can't respond because I can't stop screaming now. It burns through my chest alongside choppy hiccups. My brain doesn't know how to rationalize what's about to happen. I can't seem to process the fact that my arms and legs are incapable of moving to defend myself, though I jerk and heave anyway.

"Stop moving!" He slams his mouth over mine again, this time it's less of a kiss and more an angry attempt to get me to shut up.

Krimson! Please, help me!

The sweaty man tugs my underwear down, angling his penis to my lips.

Oh god, no!

As I squeeze my eyes shut, a pair of sparkling black eyes stare back at me in the void. It's a debilitating flash of the empty cosmic space that now brings me comfort. Grabbing my attention and pulling it away from what's about to happen.

"*Use what you know, Miss Sapphire!*" Dellilian's voice erupts in my mind.

My heart stutters in my chest.

Those words ring in my ears, and it takes less than a second to understand what that means. In a situation like this, I need to use any advantage I have. And in this case, it's knowing more than the man who believes he's a divine educator of women. And I *do* know more. I've studied the history around his actions and experiments. His family's lineage. His last name that held weight with the Demechnef family.

With a few steadying breaths, I stop crying and screaming and fighting. I go perfectly still, looking down at his attempt to penetrate me.

"I wouldn't do that if I were you," I tell him quietly.

"*Shhh*!" He struggles to hold up his own weight with skinny arms shaking as he tries to focus on assaulting me.

I take another steadying breath, masking my face into an expression of cold cruelty.

"Do you like wearing Dessin's name on your forehead…" I pause as mentioning my father causes him to completely freeze. "…Albatross?"

His head snaps up, revealing the sweat forming over his pink scars.

"What?"

I watch him with a neutral expression. "He did enjoy each mark he made on your body, didn't he? Finding your screams a song he would play in his head on repeat."

"How do you know my name?" Albatross asks in horror.

I'm not sure why his identity is a secret. Perhaps, it has something to do with the protection he has within the safety of Demechnef headquarters. Maybe he's too frightened of my father finding him out in the open without his protection.

"Albatross Ivast. Grandson of Crow Ivast. Known for your sadistic experiments on innocent children and young adults. You had a brother named Rook. And you accidentally killed him when you locked him in an isolation tank and left him in there for two nights. You said your first words at the age of four, spent most of your life as a vegetarian because watching your grandmother force-feed victims raw meat and eggs gave you such a strong aversion you are unable to stomach it."

I stop to take a breath. To take in his rattled expression.

My mother used to tell us that part of our dad's greatest gift was he knew his enemies as well as he knew himself. Down to the finest details and traits. I used to tell Krimson that it was such a waste of time. Why would he need to know what age they broke their wrist from falling out of a tree? Or which side of the bed their cat sleeps on?

Now I know I was wrong.

Albatross blinks twice, shuffling through several phases of confusion. Those small eyes narrow at me, thoughts flickering through explanations to how I would knew any of this. Who am I really? Why have I targeted him? Is it a supernatural occurrence?

"Is something wrong, Albatross? Is it difficult to assault a woman who was sent from hell to hunt you down?"

There.

That confusion shifts behind his gaze to a quiet terror. It's a creeping frostbite that spreads slowly, keeping him unmoving over me.

"How—"

"How could I possibly know such intimate details about you?" I finish for him.

Albatross holds his breath.

"I know so much more than your indiscretions. About your extensive records of experimentations of women too sickly from the Lady-Doll Regimen to fight back. Conditioning them to obey you with Mind Phantoms. Yes, I've seen those files too." I smile patiently.

We all have seen those records. Savants have studied them. Coming to the conclusion that Albatross had malignant narcissistic personality disorder, antisocial personality disorder, and heavy sadistic traits. Through possible years of religious abuse from his grandmother or at least witnessing that abuse inflicted upon his younger sister who was drowned during a baptism by the grandmother's hand when she was six years old.

"You thrive on a woman being so helpless that she's forced

through abuse to depend on you, right? Well, what if I told you I know how you're going to die?"

Albatross blinks rapidly.

This man was raised to associate control with righteousness, making him far more punitive when his authority is challenged.

"No one can know when a man is to die," he says, though doubt and doom are paling his features.

"You will be killed publicly…by a *woman*." I've never felt prouder of this known fact in history. In my *family* history. "That woman will force you to crawl to a platform where you will be tied to a post and burned alive for all to see."

Albatross is sitting upright, forcing himself to create distance from me. With his religious background, I know that he is deeply afraid of burning in hell. And on top of that, he is very superstitious. And god, I want to say her name so badly. I want to tell him that one day he will torture a victim who will one day burn him alive.

Her name is Skylenna.

"A divine justice for all you have done to women and children, don't you think? But that isn't all…"

He looks like he wants to backhand me across the face or leave the room and never come back.

"Years before your agonizing fate to perish in fire, the man you fear the most will cut off your genitals and shove them down your throat while your grandmother watches."

22. Momento Mori

Niklaus

"Are you going to apologize to me for yelling and disturbing my peace, *Boy*?" Agatha walks down the steps with a pinched face and clenched fists.

I swallow down the hate forming a hard knot in my throat. Sapphire's screams rupture the stone walls again—Agatha pauses mid-step, then smirks at the shrill sound.

"I am sorry…*Grandmother*."

"Hmm." She narrows her eyes. "My grandson is having his way with the harlot upstairs. Men have gruesome, primitive needs. Is that what you were yelling about?"

My blood runs black and cold.

"What?" I spit out.

She screams again. A long, panicked shriek that is heavily saturated with her tears.

My chest caves in.

Assaulted. Sapphire is being *assaulted*.

I have been dipped in a vat of oil, then set on fire. Yet I remain perfectly still, watching the old woman with a calm and collected mask that aches so deeply I can hardly breathe.

"I was calling for Niles because I need to relieve myself," I say.

Agatha raises an eyebrow.

"I need the toilet," I explain. *You stupid, illiterate bitch.*

The old woman nods her head in understanding, examining the restraints keeping me chained to the wall. Plucking a key from the pocket of her dress, she waives it in my face.

"If I give you a longer leash, you'll be a good boy and do your business when I pass you off to Niles without any trouble?"

I want to spit in her face.

"Yes, Grandmother."

I avoid looking into her smug glare because she's doing exactly what I need her to do. Unlike Sapphire, I can control my anger. I can channel it into a weapon. And in this case, I desperately need Agatha to change the position of my overextended arms. They're stretched so far, my shoulder sockets might be permanently damaged and that tight extension won't allow me to free my wrist.

"Now, if I see any funny business…" The old woman tucks a longer strand of black hair behind my ear, stroking my head like a pet. "I'll inject you again, and we can go back to that cottage together, understood?"

I nod. *I'm going to skin her alive.*

But even the mere mention of that cottage and the men who took me when I was so young fill my brain with images I've long since suppressed. They flood the area behind my eyes and ears with the sound of their voices.

FUCK!

Agatha clucks her tongue, knowing the physical reaction she has summoned. Her gnarled fingers jiggle the old key around my restraints, clicking the locks to unlatch around my ankles, then moving to release my restraints from the walls.

I moan in relief as my arms fall behind my back, going slack as she carries the chains like my own personal leash.

"Let's go, Boy."

I do as I'm told and rise, towering above her mangled height.

Agatha notices my hesitation to walk forward, so she pokes my back with something sharp. "One wrong move and this goes in your arm. I'll let you piss your pants while you go back to that cottage!"

I inhale sharply and smile.

This is the exact position I needed her to put me in. My wrist wiggles under the leather, swelling up my hand from the pressure.

"I understand, *Absinthe*."

I know Sapphire and I silently agreed not to let them know we know their true identities. We can't be sure how that will affect the future. But the whimpers of the woman I've known my entire life seep through the cracks of these old, condemned walls. And this is the only plan I have.

A stillness takes the old woman behind me. As I turn to peer back at her, I see that hunched frame stiffen. Unnatural, like a marionette without strings. Her pinched mouth goes slack the way a bell goes silent after its last toll. And as the air lets out past her lips, so does an appalled hiss.

"What did you just call me, Boy?"

That powdered, preserved face wrinkles in the light from the open basement door.

"Are you deaf or just stupid, Absinthe?" I jerk the chain she holds like a leash, whipping it to knock the syringe out of her hand. "Did you really think I haven't known who you were this entire time?"

Absinthe shrieks from the snapping of chains across her knuckles, holding her hand to her chest as if she's just been bit by a dog. She takes three steps away from me. I might as well be waving around a knife.

"Who sent you, Boy?"

I just laugh. "If I tell you, will you show mercy on me?"

"I might." She lifts that pointed chin.

I smile as I remember she is a highly religious woman. In fact, Aunt Skylenna told us about Sapphire's father splitting a persecuting alter, based on Absinthe who inflicted religious torture on them.

"Abaddon sent me."

There's a dense pause.

"Abaddon," she repeats in a low whisper.

"Yes."

Abaddon. The angel of the bottomless pit. King over the locusts. A holy tormentor of God sent to target those left behind in Revelation. He is unleashed during the fifth trumpet to make the unrepentant wish they were dead for five months with his army of entities described as warhorses with human faces, lion's teeth, and scorpion tails.

And I know Absinthe knows of this part of the Bible.

"God sees all, Absinthe. He sees those who use his name to inflict pain on the innocent."

The old hag's eyes dart across the room, searching to explain her horrific ways. And I fight to hide my surprised smile. She's actually buying it. The pious hag is digesting the possibility of an old, powerful angel sending me to be her undoing.

"I am a loyal servant of God! His right hand!" she justifies with a huff. "Youth need to be punished and treated for their wickedness. Children are born evil, and it's my divine destiny to beat it out of them!"

I sigh. "And with that logic, you *will* go to hell."

The peeling of skin is horrendous. I grunt as I pull my right hand the rest of the way through my restraint. A wet trickle lubricates the exit, but still, that flesh curls as it's skinned from my hand.

Absinthe's neck is squishy and fragile under my hold as I lift her off her feet. Her penny loafers dangle just above the ground. I grit my teeth and watch her struggle to breathe, swatting at my arm to drop her.

"I'd kill you here if your punishment in the future wasn't so satisfying," I growl.

Dessin broke her back and paralyzed her when he saved Aunt Skylenna. Then many years later, Aunt Skylenna hunted her down and burned her at a stake next to her grandson.

The back of Absinthe's head smacks against the stone wall after throwing her light body away from me. I don't have time to inflict the pain that would make me feel better after what she did to fuck with my head. I've never experienced Mind Phantoms before, but I used to defend their concept as my birth father used them to get ahead in war.

Now, I can't imagine who could ever sanction something so horrific.

Sapphire's scream is cut off, and I run for the door. Gripping the rusty handle and swinging it open, I stop in the doorway. Toe-to-toe with my father, Niles.

23. A Message Through Time

Niklaus

"Easy." Young Niles holds his hands up to calm me down. "Look, I don't like the sound of what he's doing to her up there either." I stare at him in disbelief.

"…But we're not finished here yet."

My head begins to shake as I scoff, and blink to process what I'm seeing. This is so far from the man I grew up with. This is a delusional lunatic. From his pupils the size of cosmic black holes, eating up those blue-green irises, to the malnutrition thinning his skin and hollowing his cheeks. He's fucking insane and demented. How long have they been experimenting on him with Mind Phantoms? How was he allowed to raise me?!

"Just head back down to your chair, and I promise your friend will be brought back to the basement soon." My father tries to guide me by the elbow to the stairs.

The fury is too much to contain my rapid movements. I twist his arm around, nearly hard enough to snap a bone. Sapphire's sudden silence blisters under my skin, and I fucking lose it. With my hands gripping the collar of his shirt, I charge my father into the kitchen, throwing his body into the cabinets.

"Wait!"

I snatch a dagger from a half-sliced apple on a cutting board and align it perfectly with his throat. The fast beating of his pulse makes the blade tremble as he gasps.

"I know what's been done to you to turn you into…*this*," I say, fighting to swallow down the lump in my throat. "But I don't care. I don't."

Niles opens and closes his mouth, unsure how to respond.

I ignore the sudden flashbacks of the man who compassionately raised me. Ignore the deep, throbbing wound in my chest that sings at the sight of his withering appearance and tortured, glazed-over look behind his eyes.

"Now you get to live the rest of your life knowing you weren't as strong as Charles. Don't ever forget my words. Because I'll never forget what you've done here."

I shove my father to the side and race to find the woman who is my ticket home.

If he somehow remembers what I've said to him in his recovery, my words will haunt him forever.

24. Anachronism

Sapphire

Albatross releases a scream, a string of garbled scripture, fused by the spittle forming on this inside of his lips, and uncontrollable anger.

A rush of bruising, veiny maroon saturates his neck and face from the sudden outburst. He shrieks at me like a frightened priest exorcising a poltergeist. As if he is about to search for holy water to throw in my face. For a cluster of rosary beads to wrap around my neck.

"You are a disgusting, stupid, blasphemous woman!" Albatross curls his fingers around the air in a fit. "I almost took pity on you! I nearly impregnated you with my seed and blessed you with my offspring!"

The word impregnated makes me want to dry heave until blood splatters from my raw throat.

"No, *I* pitied *you*. Look at that hideous face. You will forever be Dessin's *bitch*. It's just a shame you didn't leave your mouth stitched close." I glare into his scarred face. "Do all women a favor and hide in the shadows for the rest of your life, you pathetic, ugly piece of shit."

That signed my death certificate.

Albatross snaps, throwing his upper body in my direction in a fit of rage. His skinny arms flail, pummeling my face, chest, and stomach. And I tighten my muscles as much as I can to protect vital organs, squeezing my eyes shut, and baring my teeth as the blows drill rounds of pain through my clenched frame.

There's a distant pounding that fades in the background behind Albatross's furious grunts. Then he grows tired, and his hands lock around my neck.

What the fuck is it going to take for me to travel again?

His hands squeeze so tightly, a real set of panic takes hold of me. He's going to crush my trachea. He's going to kill me. I didn't get to say goodbye to Krimson. To my mom. I didn't get to hold my father's hand one last time. To sit with DaiSzek in the summer rain, watching the sunset across the ruby-red trees in the horizon.

He's going to kill me.

My eyes involuntarily flood with tears. My face swells and blood vessels burst under the throbbing pressure. And all I can do is buck and thrash under his psychotic hold, unable to even scream or cry—my vocal cords have been smashed down. My airway flattened. I have nothing left. Nothing.

"*There he is!*" That voice. Soft. Sweet. Innocent. It smears across the chaos exploding in the back of my head.

Something rips the weight off my body. The knobby knees jabbing into my sides are gone. The heavy breathing, grunting, and whining is now across the room. A gust of wind replaces his presence. A coughing fit secures my survival, wheezing and gasping as his hands have been torn away from cutting off my air supply, though I can still feel the sting from where his fingernails cut into my neck.

I fight to blink away the tears and blinding blurriness, but it won't go away. All I hear is what sounds like the smashing of fruits. Over and over again. Splatters of liquid. Grunts. Moans.

I turn my head to see black hair. Five o'clock shadow. A shirtless back. Bloody knuckles and forearms. Albatross lying on the floor like a sack of raw meat.

The relief shoots through me like an arrow directly into my gut.

I fight to breathe. To keep my eyes open. To swallow down my surprise. It's euphoric. He broke out. He found me. He saved—

The familiar sensation floods my senses. The dusting of stars across my vision. The hook that pierces my gut and tugs me into a black hole. Oh god, this is it…

"Niklaus!" The sound is a garbled rasp at best. It hardly touches my own ears much less his. My vocal cords are destroyed and mangled in my throat. "Niklaus!"

The man I've known my entire life turns to look at me. Blood streaked across his jaw and left cheek. Eyes dazed and furious.

"Niklaus—leaving…"

His eyebrows shoot up, and he jolts forward, throwing himself over me. His hands are careful not to touch the places that are bloodied, blossoming with black bruises, or visibly injured. Carefully, Niklaus grabs my shackled hand. Even though we haven't needed to be touching when I travel, I accept the touch.

Even though it's him, I sigh with relief. It's the first bit of human contact that hasn't been nonconsenting, predatory, or abusive since we got here. It's a silent action that waves a white flag for a moment.

The room trembles and darkens as that hole wraps around us, tugging me backward. Falling. Floating. Tumbling. And Niklaus simply rests his temple against my wrist, allowing it to take him too. Relinquishing control and closing his eyes.

"I'm sorry," he whispers.

And this time blinks from existence.

Letter #2,076

Skylenna

Dear Dessin,

Today I went back. A memory in the void I haven't visited yet.

The night Aurick hit me.

I can picture you shaking your head and getting angry, wondering why the hell I would ever want to relive that night. I couldn't even bring it up around you without watching those beautiful eyes turn from a warm brown to pitch black.

After Aurick hit me, I left. He passed out drunk.

That should have been the end of it, right?

It wasn't.

Why didn't you ever tell me you were there that night? Watching? Waiting until I left to get your revenge? It was small, sure, but it was you. I just know it.

I peeked back into the void to wander the halls of that mansion. Remembering what it felt like to be in the beginning stages of falling in love with you again. To go to sleep the night before I feel that thrill of exhilaration because I'd get to see you in the asylum the next day.

But when I passed Aurick's room, I saw the wall adjacent to his bed. Next to the window, it read:

Aurick

Demechnef
Hits
Women.

Blood was used as ink, and it dripped down the wallpaper like thick tears.

My heart throbbed when I saw it. I knew it was you. But why have you loved me through so many memories and never told me about this one?

Thank you for always watching over me. I love you more than life.

Your Soulmate,

Skylenna

25. The Greenhouse

Sapphire

The glowing streetlamps illuminate our naked bodies.

The cold, wet cobblestone street presses into my back and thighs, and dampens my ratty hair. The fog and light misting shimmer across the twinkling night sky, casting a blanket of white shadows across the Chandelier Main Street.

"I should have killed him," Niklaus mutters next to me. His deep, groggy voice is worn and beat down.

It feels like we haven't slept in weeks. From being naked in a blizzard cave to being naked in Uncle Niles basement, strapped to a dirty mattress—I've aged one hundred years.

"No." *Fuck.* My throat is in shreds, funneling a sea of sand and gravel. "His end is too satisfying to mess up."

Niklaus sits up next to me, scanning the empty street, then grimacing down at me. And although I'm in nothing but undergarments, I don't fucking care. My skin is probably unrecognizable. Black and blue. Streaks of gushing red.

"You sound like hell," he comments, eyes dropping to the shiny cobblestone. "Did he…"

There's a long pause before I shake my head, fighting to keep myself from sobbing over the idea of how close he came. How if I didn't bide my time, scare him with what I know of his future and past, he absolutely would have assaulted me.

Niklaus glances up at the stars, sighing. "How bad did he hurt you?"

I roll my shoulders, arch my back, stretch my arms and legs, and wince at the long beam of pain radiating through my nervous system.

"No broken bones," I rasp, then caress my fingertips at the fire eating away at my throat from Albatross's strangulation.

"He beat you before he tried to choke you to death?"

I nod.

A few gentlemen turn the corner across the street, cigars in hand. They adjust their bowler hats to get a better look at us. Niklaus and I come to the same realization as we shift and attempt to scramble to our feet. He pops right up. I nearly faint from the effort.

"We're going to get thrown into that fucking asylum if we don't find somewhere to hide. I'm guessing by their outfits that we aren't back home yet," Niklaus whispers.

I prop myself on my elbows, panting with trembling muscles.

"Don't fight me on this." Niklaus lifts me off the ground, cradling my body to his chest and abdomen.

I want to laugh at his comment. I'm not stubborn enough to refuse help right now, even if it is from him.

Each step is a fight not to scream or groan through my teeth, my bones protesting as they grind and smoosh against my wounds. My body doesn't feel like mine anymore. It's a distraught collection of bruises and inflammation. But even through the jostling of his brisk walk down the midnight main street, I *am* stubborn enough not to rest my head against his shoulder. I hold the muscles in upper back pin straight, putting myself through agony to maintain my posture.

"Just do it," Niklaus says.

No.

But the weight of the night, the pain, the ongoing thumping steps loosens the grip I have on my position. I slump in his arms, dropping the side of my head to his chest.

We take a deep breath in unison.

His bare skin is warm despite the chilled breath of foggy air swarming our nearly nude bodies. It's soothing against my cheek. Calming. Making it easy to drift—

"Son of a bitch!"

Ice-cold hands touch my bare stomach.

Liquid rolls of my skin.

I'm on the mattress again. My arms restrained, my legs—

"Relax," Niklaus growls. "I'm cleaning you up. You'll get an infection and die. Then I'll really be stuck here."

Moonlight pours through frosted glass, casting a green glow over the sheer ceiling. Vines. Flowers. Shrubs. Potted plants. The earthy scent of wet soil and moth balls. This room is a cocoon of warmth, yet I shiver violently.

"We're in my father's greenhouse," Niklaus explains reluctantly.

My back flexes and goes stiff.

"We have to get away from him…" I choke, barely able to get volume above a scratchy whisper.

"Not Niles. My birth father."

I look around awkwardly. *Oh.*

"I don't think he ever came out to his greenhouse much. Just his gardener. We should be safe for now."

I have been in this greenhouse before. This great big house is where Aunt Ruth and Uncle Warrose used to stay when they would visit, until Niklaus moved in when he turned eighteen.

Krimson and I would hide in here when we'd mischievously hide Uncle Warrose's weapon's belt so he couldn't leave. Then he'd find it, and we'd fill his boots with rocks to slow him down.

He'd find us camping out in this greenhouse and call us the twins from hell. He'd say that this was our father's way of laughing at him from his coma. All the while, I could swear his hazel eyes would glisten with tears as he'd say goodbye to us.

"Any idea"—I clear the gravel in my throat—"of where in time we are?"

Niklaus wrings out a blood-stained sponge in a metallic bowl of bloody water. He pauses as russet drops drips from his hands.

"I saw your mother walk into the house. In a navy-blue conformist's dress."

A ghost without a name presses its cold forehead to mine, and my soul flinches at the sudden realization that we are *here*. In the era my parents first met, so close to the infamous asylum that has been dissected and over-analyzed by savants.

"Really?" I hold my breath.

Niklaus glances at me in response, gently dabbing at a spot on my ribs with the sponge. His large hands are calloused but careful, treating this act of service like a task rather than a kindness. And with even, controlled breath, he tears off a piece of gauze with his teeth.

"Where did you get the supplies?" I ask.

I watch his black lashes lower as he presses medical tape into my skin.

"I snuck into his house."

I lift my chin. I suppose that wasn't too hard for him to do, considering he knows the estate better than anyone at this point.

"Did you see him?" I press.

"No."

I take in a deep breath through my nose as he cleans the wounds on my right cheekbone. The garden air is humid, heavy with the scent of wet soil and fallen flower petals. As he mimics my deep breath, I can tell the scent soothes him.

"Do you want to talk about what happened with Uncle Niles?"

His eyes snap up to meet mine, darkening like a tide pulling back before a violent wave.

"Do you think this is social hour?" he says slowly, with condescending lethal precision.

My eyebrows raise. "What the fuck have I done to make you hate me so much?"

"I don't hate you, Spitfire." His dark eyebrows pull together in concentration, applying a last bit of ointment to my temples. “I just really don’t give a damn about you.”

The ointment seems to have strong, medicinal properties as the throbbing pain in every section of my upper body dissolves into a low, thrumming irritation.

I sigh, stretching out my sore limbs as I’m able to get off the mossy stone floor, standing in a flowy, ivory nightgown. I tug at the satin ribbon around the empire waist. The fabric smells of vintage lavender. He must have stolen it from the house.

“Glad we cleared that up,” I say, nodding once then turning to exit. “Then you won’t mind if I return to our time without you.”

26. Rose Colored Glasses

Niklaus

"Hell no," I mutter under my breath.

I jog after Sapphire, tripping over a cluster of sharp vines on my way out.

The panic of being left behind could make me do many things in this moment. I'll lie. I'll steal. I'll easily kill to make sure I'm not stuck in this fucked up part of history. If she left me, I swear on my life, I'd find a way to make sure she was never born.

But as I sprint to catch up, I find her standing in the middle of the garden, cloaked in midnight, staring at the second floor of my estate—my father's estate.

"Hmm?" I follow her line of sight to a large window, glowing with candlelight. A tall figure pacing with a bottle in hand. The raven-black hair is easy to make out from this distance.

Sapphire exchanges a look with me.

"Let's go back," she suggests cautiously.

I ignore her, staring at the window with an irresistible urge building in my system. How often do people get to go back in time and see their dead parents? When will I ever get the chance again to watch the great Aurick Demechnef in real life? Not in history books. Not in stories I hear from his peers.

Right now, he's so close.

I glance down at Sapphire again, then take off running.

I scale the side of the mansion with ease. The vines are thick like waxy ropes, and I know each and every nook and crevice to place my feet in to get leverage. Sapphire isn't far behind me, wincing and hissing as she tries to climb without further aggravating her injuries.

"Go back to the greenhouse!" I whisper down to her, though I reluctantly hold my hand out to help her up to the balcony.

Sapphire's entire body trembles in a misty, cool night air. Her face, usually a glass portrait of flawless symmetry, is bludgeoned. A deep scarlet and plum splotches her swollen cheekbones, increasing to a level of puffiness that nearly hides those striking heterochromatic irises.

I turn my head as her posture droops in pain.

"Let's go back. We can't risk changing any—"

I cut her off. "So, we can see your parents, but God forbid I get to see my dead father."

At the sound of a muffled voice, Sapphire and I duck, crouching low to the black iron balcony floor. Sapphire shoots me a scornful glare as I slowly inch the door open so I can hear what's being said.

The female voice is soft, gentle, and a little higher than what I'm used to. Over the years, my Aunt Skylenna's voice has lowered. But she's around our age here, and her tone resembles the lightness of a wind chime.

I've never heard my father's voice before now. I've imagined what it sounds like. I've daydreamed about what kind of parent he would have been to me. But hearing it now has my stomach in knots.

"...do you find me attractive?" Aurick asks Skylenna in a lazy slur.

Sapphire straightens next to me.

"I—you said we were friends."

My father barks out a cruel laugh. And my eyes trail up his tall, drunk frame as he stumbles in Aunt Skylenna's direction.

"Because I didn't want you to feel uncomfortable staying with me!"

"We should go…" Sapphire rasps with a scratchy throat.

I hold my hand up to shush her so I can listen.

"*Please*!" she hisses again.

But I have to hear this. Like any man who has lost a parent, I believed I'd go the rest of my life without hearing my father's voice. Without seeing how he is in person. And through a disastrous phenomenon, I have been thrown back in time before he was killed in the Great War of the Dralutheran and RottWeilen. Back when he ruled this country from the shadows.

"Aurick…"

Aunt Skylenna's voice draws me to pay closer attention.

"It's been torturing me to live under the same roof as you—knowing you're undressing just across the hall—but I've been patient, waiting for *you* to make the first move. Show me you want me."

"*What the fuck?*" I mutter under my breath.

My birth father gets closer to Sapphire's mother, cornering her.

"Not once. You're my *friend*," Skylenna says.

"No. I'm a man, and you're a woman. A woman living with me. A woman who has to obey me. Care for me. Touch me."

Sapphire stops trying to tug me away from this scene. Her attempts go completely silent as she stares with a gaping mouth at the horror we're both shocked by.

"Did you know?" I whisper to her.

She shakes her head.

My stomach fills with bile at the sight of my aunt quivering in terror. I've never seen her like this. Fearful. Small. Fragile. Aunt Skylenna has always had this primeval look in her eyes. A force sleeping behind her kind gaze. A dragon hibernating until it must fly and breathe fire once more.

But this young woman isn't my aunt. She's scared to death of my birth father.

"Don't you dare walk away from me when I am speaking to you!" Aurick roars in a slur.

The back of his hand making contact with Aunt Skylenna's cheek sends me into a brief state of shock. I jerk at the impact, watching her fall backward as she yelps.

Sapphire throws her hand over her mouth, gasping at the sight of her mother being *hit*.

And cowering.

Crawling backward.

Cowering.

I never thought I'd see that woman look so helpless. So scared. So weak and gentle.

A cold creeping rage pours into my chest, stuffing my hands into hard fists. The edges of my vision are lined with tendrils of red and black smoke as my eyes go dry and scratchy from not blinking.

He hit her?

I lunge forward, prepared to throw open the balcony door and step in front of Aunt Skylenna. I'll wring his neck. I don't give a shit that he's my birth father, and I've spent most of my life looking up to his memory. He hit her.

Something hooks around the inside of my elbow.

"Don't," Sapphire says quietly.

I crank my neck to get a better look at her, unable to hide the surprise and betrayal darkening my glare.

Sapphire lifts her chin in defiance. A sad stoicism captures her swollen features in the cloudy moonlight. She shakes her head at me. No reasoning. No scolding. No convincing me why messing with time in this moment may alter our very existence forever.

No, because somewhere deep inside her, she's fighting her own battle. She's reminding herself that this needed to happen to help her mother become the legend we've all heard of. Yet it's just as difficult for her to watch as it is for me to process that my father hit her.

I lower my head and wait for their confrontation to end, breathing a sigh of relief when Aunt Skylenna picks herself off the floor and leaves the room.

I lift my head to watch Aurick Demechnef pass out drunk on his bedroom floor.

I waited for Sapphire to fall asleep in the greenhouse to do this.

I've never moved so quietly in my life, painting the last couple of letters with the sponge. Streaks of red and pink soak the cream wallpaper, dripping to the floor.

My movements are vigilant, careful not to knock anything over in my anger, not to make any loud noises to wake him up.

The letter N is last.

Watery blood trickles down to my elbow.

Why is this triggering me so much? I've heard about the horrendous things that were done in the name of Demechnef for the war. But hitting Aunt Skylenna…

I drop the sponge to the floor, glowering down at my father. His pale skin, sweat stains, shiny charcoal hair…

What a colossal disappointment.

I wonder what he'll think when he wakes up. When he sees my work of art on this wall. Will he remember hitting her? Will a small part of him know, deep down, that he disappointed me? His future son and heir of Demechnef?

Glancing back at the words written from a dirty bucket of Sapphire's bloody water, I exhale and read it again.

Aurick
Demechnef
Hits
Women.

27. "Hello There, My New Friends."

Sapphire

Niklaus stares out the window covered in condensation, crossing his arms and zoning out.

He just lost so much respect for the father who raised him and the father who died before he was born. Both devastating, but Aurick Demechnef being physically abusive to my mom shoved an invisible sword a little deeper through his heart. After seeing what Uncle Niles has done in the past, I think he was hoping to see his birth father in a better light.

I chew on my apple slices slowly as the sun begins to rise from the top of the Demechnef estate. Honey rays of light are amplified through the water droplets collecting over the glass that surrounds us, warming the air like a small furnace.

"Do you think—"

"I don't want to talk about it," Niklaus cuts me off. "I just want to go home."

Me and you both.

I set my apple down in the gravel, tapping the tips of my fingers together in thought.

"I'm so scared I'll never be able to control this," I whisper in defeat.

The muscles in Niklaus's jaw tighten, but he doesn't turn around to look at me. It's as if he's searching the land he will own one day for answers. Wondering how he could have been so wrong about Aurick Demechnef.

"You know, Uncle Niles was only the way he was because of the Mind Phantom experiments your birth father issued on—"

"Stop. Talking."

Niklaus turns his head slowly to peer down at me with bloodshot eyes.

I avert my gaze back down to my hands, nodding at his request.

"Just work harder on getting us out of…" Niklaus trails off, cranking his neck forward to look out of the window, narrowing his eyes in small slits to get a better look.

"What is it?"

Niklaus shushes me with a hand in the air. He tilts his head and glances down at me in surprise.

"There's no fucking way," he utters.

Before I can respond, the shift in the air is faint. So faint in fact, I almost miss it. The minuscule added pressure behind my eyes. My fingertips are numb. And there is a weight leaning on my lungs, like breathing in old dust from another century.

"What?!" I groan and huff through the sharp bursts of pain, pulling myself up to face the window with him. "Oh."

I instantly shudder at the man standing in the center of the garden, boots sinking in mud, and hands clasped together below his waist.

It takes me a heartbeat to connect this figure with the one who stood among the carnage in our ambush with the Vexamen Breed back in the woods.

Dressed in a funeral's finest—coal pinstripes, polished shoes, and a bowler hat shadowing that terrifying display of paint on his face. It's a dirty, off-white, gray, and yellow painted into a skeletal face. And how could I forget those eyes? Black and precise, stretching out to haunt me, like relics behind a protective sheet of glass.

"That's the man behind the last attack," I say quietly.

Niklaus doesn't respond.

"How could he have possibly followed us here? We traveled through time…" I add.

This doesn't make sense. It's not like we moved from one forest to another on foot. We were yanked through the fabric of time and thrown into another year altogether.

The man whistles a tune that sounds like an old nursery rhyme, and he just…stares at us.

"I'm going to talk to him," Niklaus finally says.

"Wait." I tug at his wrist. "Let's think about this for a second."

"Mmm, yes, okay. Let's think. This disturbing skinny man dressed like a gravedigger or dead funeral director might have been following us through time. *Time*. But maybe we should try and sneak out and hope he isn't capable of following us from this greenhouse to the main street. Have we thought it through?"

I drop my head. "Proceed."

Niklaus studies my beaten, swollen, and bruised face once before offering a curt nod. He steps around me, brushing his shoulder against mine as his determined footsteps stomp through the greenhouse gravel.

The stranger is hard to look at in the glow of the sunrise. The paint crusted around the edges of his chin and jaw. The stringy mousy-brown hair hanging from around his bowler hat. The way his coat flutters though there isn't any wind.

He's an eerie painting no one remembers hanging.

"Why're you following us?" Niklaus asks calmly, though his stomping footsteps through the wet grass say otherwise. They begin to drag the closer we get.

And I see why. There's a faint warmth building at the base of my throat now, the kind that precedes a fever. Does he feel that too? It's aberrant. Invasive. A slow creeping, foreign germ clawing into my pores.

The man tilts his head, blinking quickly, studying us like an equation gone wrong. Like our very existence disturbs the rules he lives by.

"Why weren't you covered in blood when you...*moved*?" the man asks.

I cringe at the way he speaks.

Each syllable is annunciated with surgical care. Slow. Unnatural. His voice is a foreign sound to him. It's as if he's forcing his tone to be higher, like when one would read a character out of a book for a child.

"What?" Niklaus blurts out.

"You breathe like your mother," Strange Man adds. "Same lungs, I expect."

What the fuck?

"Are you going to answer his question or not?" I cut in.

The stranger moves his head to me slowly, woodenly, like the hand of a clock ticking to the next hour. Those black, shifty eyes inspect me as his cheek twitches. Unblinking stare travels down to my feet, then back up again.

"Do you hear voices like your father did?" Stranger takes a step closer to me, blinking like a reptile.

"No," I answer coldly.

"Hmm." He nods, seemingly disappointed. "I don't either, even though my father also heard them."

Who the hell is this man?!

"And who is your father?" Niklaus asks.

Bowler Hat Man considers the questions, tapping his index to his thumb as he thinks. I wonder if he's contemplating lying to us or not.

"I believe your father referred to him as Val. But his full name was Vallíticus Bear Edison. And my name is Vrath."

Val. My blood stops pumping.

"Vrath," Niklaus repeats.

A sticky dizziness curls around the edges of my vision like a shadow.

"I do not have a last name."

Val.

"Was your mother's name..." I hesitate. "Vinaley?"

I didn't notice it before, but Vrath winces in my direction, though it is subtle through the paint on his face. He's either disgusted by me or spooked.

"Yes," he responds. He taps his fingers again. "Did you kill your mother, Sapphire S. Valdawell?"

"What? No?"

"You can obviously time travel too, otherwise you wouldn't have been able to follow us," Niklaus interrupts.

I'm still reeling from this new information. This man is Val and Vinaley's son. The two experiments who came before my parents. The murder-suicide subjects. My mother didn't tell me they had a child.

Vrath cracks his neck. "Yes, evidently."

"Can you help us get home?"

I want to pull Niklaus to the side to tell him what I know. My gut tells me Vrath isn't here to help us. That we shouldn't show him our cards, or even that I don't know how to control this yet.

"Why would I do that?" Vrath steps closer, boots mushing through the mud. "I am still observing."

Niklaus straightens back and lifts his chin, catching on to the conclusion I've already arrived at. He clears his throat and attempts to swallow like it's painful to do so.

"You're observing us."

"I don't understand you. How have you not infected anyone? How—" Vrath peers down at me with that disgust wrinkling the corners of his eyes again. "That strand of hair is touching your collarbone. And the right isn't."

He points to the stray hairs closest to my face. I tuck them behind my ears.

"How have you not taken ill? Been soaked in blood? Disease ridden?" Vrath continues.

Niklaus exchanges a look with me. One that says, *this man is fucking crazy.*

"Is that what happens to you when you travel?" I ask.

Vrath exhales in annoyance, smearing the paint over his eyes in the agitated way a toddler would do when they are overtired. Charcoal smudges over the backs of his hands, blending with cream and yellow colors down his cheekbones and eyelids. It's in this moment I come closer to identifying his age. Vrath is at least ten years older than us. Maybe more.

"You left doors open for me, you know," he tells us, still

harboring that agitated tone.

"Doors?"

"Yes. I slip through and have to search for you. But you leave none of the usual signs. I see no blood, no maps, no symbols, no evidence of infections. How have you come and gone? How are you moving without them?"

Niklaus glances down at me again before huffing. "We have no fucking idea what you are saying. Do you hear yourself?"

An aged tiredness coils in my bones. And as I bring my hand to my chest, Vrath notes the movement with his eyes. As if he knows all too well the sensations that are unwinding in my body.

"Do. Not. Curse. At. Me." Vrath's thin lip twitches.

"How are you traveling, Vrath?" I interrupt before someone's temper is set off.

The tall, slinky man shrugs a shoulder. "The same way I did at early birth. A mother's blood is the only way I've come across."

Sorry, what's that now?

"I advanced faster than you, Sapphire S. Valdawell. I traveled for the first time while I was still in my mother's womb. Third trimester."

Niklaus parts his lips, flickering his stunned gaze at me, then back for Vrath.

"Can't seem to return to the exact moment in time I belong." Thumb to index finger, he taps then rubs them together. "And I can't really change anything, yet I spoil and infect myself and others."

"Spoil and infect?" I ask.

Vrath's deep frown curdles the air between us. The particles to which he exhales into the air are out of place, toxic and deadly.

"I am often quite ill with infections. Possibly because I don't belong here."

"And what about others?"

"I infect them too. Sometimes before I am sickly at all."

"How?"

His calm yet annoyed stare seems centuries old. "Because I don't belong in these timelines. Anywhere I travel, I'm a cancerous parasite that infects anyone close to me. It's as though the universe is allergic to my presence."

That's why I can feel myself aching and wilting the moment we moved closer to him. I take a step back, and look down at my hands, wondering if I've noticed myself infecting anyone too. Not that I can recall. Although, I almost wish I had that ability when Albatross was on top of me, or when Absinthe was pummeling me with her bony fists.

"But I don't understand why you haven't taken ill," Vrath adds thoughtfully. "I've watched you. Those you have interacted with are left in perfect condition."

"That's a shame," Niklaus says, clearly following my train of thought.

"Is there a reason you wear the paint on your face?" I ask.

Vrath instinctually lifts his hand, hovering gloved fingers over his cheekbone.

"Yes, there is a reason."

We wait for him to explain, but he merely stares at us blankly.

I try again. "You said I left a door open?"

Part of me is cautious of picking this man's brain. He doesn't seem mentally stable. His eyes twitch and go empty. His thought process is warped and choppy. But I don't have a choice. We need to get home, and right now, he's the only person alive who might be able to help.

Vrath nods so slowly, I wonder if he's having a stroke. "You leave footprints through time. They scream into the darkness. I heard them from a thousand years away."

"Can you control where you come and go?"

"And travel on command?" Niklaus adds.

"Somewhat."

"How do you do it?"

Vrath pinches his lips in frustration. "Did you use your mother's blood? Yes, or no?"

"I seriously don't know what you're talking about," I say.

"I do not like liars."

"Use my mother's blood for what? To travel? I wasn't even within a three-mile radius of my mother. I just did it!"

"*You just did it.*" That monotone slithers under my skin.

"We were attacked, and it happened. I don't know anything other than that."

"Are you certain that is all you know? Or are you a liar?" he presses.

"Liar?! We're trying to get your help because all we want is to go home! If you know how I traveled, please tell me! I'm all ears!" My temper flares to the surface, smoldering in my chest like a wildfire.

Vrath adjust his stance, uneasy as he locks eyes with me.

"I made eye contact with your father once. In the Vexamen Prison."

My temper swims away, though still warm to the touch.

"He was on stage with your mother, being whipped to accept another inmate's fate. Your father broke free to stop the boy from bludgeoning your mother. And he looked up at me."

Those wide-set eyes zone out, getting lost through a confusing string of memories that aren't really his.

"It's the same look you just gave me. You may have different colored eyes unlike him, but your fury is his. It's uncanny."

"How long have you been watching my parents?" I ask.

"Too long to put a number on."

I sigh. "Look, I don't care to know your fascination with them. I just want to control this thing so I can return home. Can you please help us?"

Though I know the answer, I still have to try.

"I want to know what else you can do," Vrath says with that disturbing tone that has no inflection or cadence.

"And then you'll help us?" Niklaus asks.

Vrath pauses. "I cannot lie."

The sun unfolds over the clouds, and it begins to rain softly, pattering gentle against the black shingles of the roof.

"Then don't…" I offer.

"I am not certain you'll still be alive when I get what I want." The strange man rubs at the paint along his jaw. "I could start by seeing your blood."

Well, fuck.

"Hand me your wrist, please," he requests, holding his gloved palm out to me.

"*Bad man! Bad man! Bad man!*" Dellilian's, small, frightened voice shrieks through my mind. And judging based on Niklaus's slight widening of his eyes, he heard it too.

The sickness isn't so subtle anymore. It's as if my body is aging prematurely. It crawls down my throat, melting into my bloodstream, and rots away my white blood cells.

I didn't need to hear our gentle friend's warning to feel the dooming strike of fear rattle my bones. It isn't exactly what Vrath says, it's how *still* he is when he says it. He's been dead a long time, yet his body just isn't aware of it yet. It's that the knowledge behind his eyes is centuries old. He's the kind of figure in an evil nursery rhyme that was told to children to keep them obedient and terrified of the dark. But not evil in a traditional sense, the kind that is without shape or pleasure. The kind that peels the wings off a butterfly out of pure curiosity.

Never have I had this strong of a gut instinct to stay far away from someone.

Because he's right. His blood, his skin, the air he breathes—it all sings with an incurable plague, infection, ancient disease no one's heard of.

And as he jerks my hand closer to his chest like an animal getting ready to bite, I am *terrified.* With the good sense to scream, and Niklaus yanking me away from him…

The night captures us in the middle of the brightening morning sunrise.

And it doesn't hurt as much this time.

Letter #8

Skylenna

Dear Dessin,

I attended a harvest ball in the woods with our friends. I watched them dance and kiss, and although I was happy for them, I wanted to die inside.

It reminded me of when I danced with you for the first time at the Dellilian Castle. You weren't even supposed to be there. But you made a point to attend after you saw the black eye Aurick gave me. Do you remember when I collided into your body after switching partners? When you held my waist and pulled me close? I never told you then, but I was mad for you. I knew my feelings were inappropriate because I was your conformist. So I tried to bury them. I tried so hard. But seeing you in a suit you stole from Aurick's closet (Ha!), wearing that mischievous look in those dark brown eyes...

I was all yours. You had to of known that didn't you? I've always belonged to Kane—since I was a little girl. He was my first love. And then I had forgotten those memories.

But in that asylum and in that ballroom, my heart would sing again.

I wish I could tell you this with your eyes open. I wish I could bring you back to that memory in the void and relive it with you all over again.

After the ball, I returned to our home in the Red Oaks and sobbed at the foot of your bed. I begged for you to wake up. Although Chekiss was in the next room, he pretended to be asleep. There are times he knows to get up and comfort me. And there are times he leaves me to cry for you all on my own. This was one of those times.

And now I'm sitting on the front porch, looking up at the stars, and writing you this letter.

I pray to God you get to read them one day. I'll write thousands if it means you have reading material for the rest of your waking life.

I love you. I want to share a dance again. Maybe at our wedding?

Your soulmate,

Skylenna

28. Alpha

Sapphire

"Up you go."

I grunt as I'm thrown over Niklaus's shoulder, making a focused effort not to vomit as his joint digs into my soft underbelly.

"Fuck, Spitfire. You're freezing."

I'm a sweaty, aching, bruised, swollen block of ice. Is it when I travel? Does it make me cold? Didn't my mother mention her trips to the void would leave her in hypothermic levels?

"I'm—fine." I tap the coiled muscle on his back. "Let's just—rest a minute."

Everything hurts. I'm still suffering the aftermath from our time in my uncle's basement. And traveling isn't exactly making a full recovery that much easier.

"I read your mother would undergo hypothermia when she fucked with someone's mind in the void. Do you think that's what's happening?" Niklaus asks.

Flashes of green whirl past me as he walks quickly through what looks like the Emerald Lake Forest.

"I bet that's why your swelling went down. Hypothermia reduces inflammation."

"Please. Put me down. Cold. *Tired.*"

"Vrath just said he can follow us through doors you leave open. We aren't staying put. We're half a mile away from the castle. Let's hide out there and regroup."

I groan again.

Shouldn't we go deeper into the forest? Put as much distance between us and Vrath as possible? I don't want any more run-ins with him. That psychopath is going to harvest my organs and cut off my hair.

After a short while, Niklaus is able to set me down, and we slip into the cellar of the small castle. We sleep for hours but eventually wake with the symphony of noise occurring above us.

Footsteps clack across the ceiling. Violins and cellos are tuned and practiced, muffled over our heads. The room we rest in is dusty, carpeted, and lit by old chandeliers that swing and creak as people move around above us.

"Isn't this exactly where Vrath would think to look first? I think there's a ball tonight. Tons of people are going to be here," I say.

Niklaus shakes his head. "Exactly. He knows we're trying to be inconspicuous. He saw us hiding in the greenhouse. I guarantee his first thought will be to go deeper into the forest."

Makes sense.

A soft tune bleeds through the crown molding ceiling and flows past us. I watch Niklaus massage his temples.

"What'd you think about what Vrath had to say about traveling?" he mumbles through his hand.

"I think he kills mothers in order to travel. That's why he doesn't catch up to us very quickly." Maybe he even came to that conclusion when he traveled from his mother's womb. Wearing a coating of her fluids and blood. I slide my gaze to Niklaus. "I don't ever want to be near him again."

"Yeah."

"Did your mother ever tell you about Val and Vinaley?" I know it's a long shot, since I'm pretty sure the only person my father told about them was my mother.

"She did," he replies, resting his chin on his fist. "She was there when they were being experimented on."

"Wait, what?"

"*Demechforth*, remember? Her family was a part of the trials too."

"Did she know them?"

Niklaus nods. "She said she was there for the miscarriage. Though they assumed Vinaley terminated the pregnancy herself. The baby wasn't in the womb anymore."

I can't believe how many dark secrets there are within the confines of our families.

"My mom said Vinaley was so depressed, she fell into an unresponsive, catatonic state. Val ended up killing her and then himself."

I look away. "That's so sad."

"I don't remember anything other than that."

"Since I can travel *without* the blood of mothers…he wants to know what else I can do that he can't." My stomach turns sour at the memory of the paint crusting over Vrath's face. "I bet traveling and killing to try and return back to his timeline has made him insane."

"And that little detail about how sick he gets because he doesn't belong anywhere."

The music grows louder, and the footsteps jingle the glass ornaments on the swinging chandeliers.

"Where do you think we are in time?" I ask.

Niklaus stands himself up, and strides to a giant wardrobe in the corner of the room. Even in our time, they've always kept suits and dresses of all sizes and colors in there. There were days when Mabel Rose and I would sneak in here, get all dressed up, then Krimson would tease me for stuffing the chest area with tissues.

"You…you want to go to the ball?"

Niklaus flicks his gaze to me, then back to the assortment of tuxes he flips through.

"Shouldn't we just stay hidden in here?" I yawn, stretching my sore arms over my head.

"No."

"Why not?"

"You don't travel when you're calm," he says, laying out the tux he likes. "You travel when we're in danger, I think."

My eyes fall shut. Why can't I control this?

"There isn't danger at a ball," I sigh.

"No, but there are food and drinks."

At the thought of hot appetizers, finger foods, and buckets of champagne—my stomach claws at itself, echoing with a long, dragged-out growl of hunger. Lately, I'm damn near at the brink of death with starvation constantly. Every time we move to a new time, my mouth waters, and my stomach twists for the next meal.

Niklaus sighs reluctantly. "Get drunk with me?"

For a sliver of A moment, I felt relatively normal while we got ready for the ball. The makeup, the gown that is a little loose around my shoulders, and the curlers I put in my hair.

We took our time, found a half-empty bottle of bourbon and took two shots each.

I spent most of the time blotting away at the discoloration and bruises on my face and neck with heavy makeup.

Now, at the top of the grand staircase, we stand to take it all in. The great dome ceiling painted with fluffy pink clouds, majestic beasts, family and portraits, and giant honey chandeliers sparkling over the ballroom of spinning, twirling, laughing, dancing men and women.

Niklaus and I have been to many balls before. But this is the first we attend from an era before we were born. The Lady-Doll Regimen era. It doesn't take long to recognize the clear signs of eating disorders, starvation, and pallid skin that has seen very little sun. I've never see such sharp, protruding collar bones or pointy shoulder caps. The corsets around each waist make me want to faint from lack of oxygen.

Niklaus clears his throat, holding an arm out to me.

Being here, in this ballroom, seeing his cold eyes and sharp jawline—it all brings me back to the time he made me cry the most when I was fifteen.

Niklaus read my diary after I mistakenly left it out on my bed during one of the Sunday's everyone came over for family dinner. Inside of the many humiliating thoughts I wrote down, one of them was that I wanted my first kiss to be at the annual ball. I wanted to dance with my crush, Dorn Leviat, and share my first kiss under the chandeliers.

And it all came true.

Niklaus Demechnef made sure of it.

Dorn asked me to the ball, danced with me, kissed me to the last song of the night. It was a masquerade ball. The orchestrated dance required us to switch partners a few times. Dorn found his way back to me after a few rounds, and when the music slowed, he stopped our dancing, held my face, and dipped down to kiss me.

It was, unfortunately, the best kiss I've ever had. Soft at first, testing the waters, then his kiss took me by storm. Like he had been waiting as long as I had to have this kiss under the pink clouds of the ballroom ceiling. Like there were romantic, lustful, passionate feelings pent up in his chest, shaken in a bottle—then released into this kiss.

When it was over, Dorn pulled off his mask and grinned at me.

Though it wasn't Dorn.

It was Niklaus Demechnef.

He proceeded to recite a few lines from my diary from memory, lean in, and whisper, "Every second of tonight belonged to me. You just didn't know it. I bet Dorn and the rest of the boys that you'd kiss me back. That you wouldn't even notice it wasn't your precious crush kissing you. Thanks for making me a few gold coins, Spitfire."

That night, as I left in tears, my brother beat the living hell out of Niklaus. He has always been superior in hand-to-hand combat like our father. Krimson doesn't show it off often, but that night his vicious temper that stays practically invisible to the public eye came out on full display. And after Niklaus was beaten unconscious, my brother tied him up in the pig's pen, covered in mud and blood with a message on his chest.

Female Swine.

Then told Aunt Marilynn and Uncle Niles about his indiscretion. To which they kicked him out of the house for three weeks after he gave me a bullshit, half-assed apology.

I shake the memory off and slide my hand into the crook of Niklaus's arm. Our descent down the staircase is slow as we both silently scan the crowd for any sign of that disgusting painted face and black hat. But we seem to be in the clear.

As we make it to the last step, the few eyes that were on us flip above our heads to the top of the white marble staircase. Their eyebrows raise, lips part, and whispers gently flow from person to person.

I let go of Niklaus's arm to turn around, gawking up at my mother standing in a satin, bloodred dress, holding the arm of Aurick Demechnef. I nearly lose my balance at the sight of her. Long, flowing golden curls that hang below her breasts. The low v-neck covered in sheer fabric and dazzling red jewels. Tall red heels. Rosy, glossy, plump lips.

"Oh shit," I mutter under my breath.

"Come on."

Niklaus tugs me off to the side where the violinists practice and tune their instruments. And we stare in silence, watching my mother whisper to Aurick uncomfortably. The tension, the hushed tones, the daggers he gives her. The way he storms off after a quick, scolding word.

I have to grip Niklaus's forearm to keep him from doing something stupid.

"We should go. We can't risk being seen by them," Niklaus tells me in a low, haunted voice. Something about watching his father mingle with the men and women that make up different factions and boards of Demechnef releases a quiet, simmering frustration inside him.

"Yes," I agree, nodding while I search for a waiter. "But only after we chug champagne and dance."

Niklaus gives me a reluctant sidelong glance, though his shoulders lose their stiffness.

"I'm not dancing with you," he says coldly, but still plucks to champagne flute glasses from a tray and clinks his with mine.

We down a few of them until the glow of the lights are soft and fuzzy around the edges, and my mood is significantly lighter and happier. I lift the heavy skirt of my raven-black ball gown and do a little twirl. Dancing sounds good. I want to dance.

But Niklaus continues to brood and watch my mother speak to

Aunt Ruth in the corner.

I gasp. "Aunt Ruth!"

Niklaus puts his big hands on my shoulder to keep me from racing over to her.

"Goddamn, drinking was a bad idea," he growls.

"You think I'm an imbecile? I wasn't going to say anything to her. Just going to watch them interact!"

Niklaus chuckles. "You were just going to stand in front of them and stare like a stalker."

"Yes, that's right."

The musicians introduce a new dance. The room shuffles into brief, graceful chaos. Women clacking across the glittering golden tiles to find their partners. Two ovals and men and women, side by side in the center of the ballroom.

I raise my eyebrows at Niklaus expectantly.

"No," he says.

"We've known this dance since we were kids!" I squeal, stomping my heel.

"Hmm. True. I don't care."

"Well, if he won't, I will…"

Niklaus looks over my shoulder, glaring at the man's voice behind me. I drunkenly spin around, coming face-to-face with a six-foot, blond-haired, brown-eyed *looker.*

"Ooof." I grin up at him.

"Oh god," Niklaus grunts.

The man has a tousled halo of sun-bleached curls, with a flicker of mischief in his caramel eyes. The misleading look of a cathedral angel. He smiles back at me confidently.

"When a man won't dance with you, it's because he can't dance, sweetie. I don't have any problems in that department," the blond man says.

I laugh. Unfortunately, not being able to dance isn't Niklaus's problem. He's just a dud.

"Terrible dancer!" I agree, taking the stranger's hand to dance. "I'd rather have a man to lead me."

Niklaus scoffs, but humor doesn't come anywhere near to lightening his gaze.

"I'm Hawthorne."

"Audrina," I reply, deciding to stick with my fake name.

As Hawthorne guides me to the beginning of the star-crossed couples dance, I give Niklaus a cute little wave and wink. The clap of heels and shoes stomping to the floor with the first step has me scrambling to get into position, taking the tips of Hawthorne's fingers and letting him guide me into the synchronized movements of the other dancers.

"If you don't know the steps, just follow me," he whispers in my ear.

I smile. "I know them."

And I get lost in the sweet swaying and stepping and turning to one of my favorite string quartet pieces. Hawthorne pouts as he twirls me to my next partner, giving my fingers a tight squeeze between twirling me away from his hold.

My next partner is an older gentleman, then another, and then the next lets me take a quick swig from his flask.

I inhale the sweet scent of roses and baby powder, catching a soft breeze from the swishing and wafting of ruffled gowns sweeping the floors.

"Come find me later, pretty girl." The man with the flask twirls me away, and he returns to his wife like the shithead he is.

And as I spin on my tiptoes, careful not to bump into the other women around me, my movements are a little too quick. I land in the arms of my next partner, grunting into his hard chest and subtle aromatic cloud of aquatic wood. The muscles in his arms turn to stone as I'm pulled in close, my stomach pressing against his.

Those downturned, lethal blue eyes are weaponized as they glare down at me. His jaw ticks once, the kind of detailed gesture I wouldn't have noticed without being this close. And I can't help but breathe him in again as I inhale sharply. Niklaus Demechnef smells like a distant memory. Cold metal, winter air, and those nervous feelings you get at a great height.

"You—you said no to dancing," I say exasperatedly.

"You said I was a terrible dancer." That stare narrows just enough to feel angry and cold, yet it falters—briefly lowering to my lips. The sudden minute detail makes my stomach dip.

"That's right," I respond, flickering my eyes down to his lips out of pure curiosity. I've never taken much time to notice them. At his five o' clock shadow. And the tightly coiled masseter muscles in his jaw.

"Hmm." He nods.

I'd be blind not to notice the way he effortlessly weaves through the many different clusters of dance partners, some easily coordinated, and others fighting their two left feet. Niklaus has been a natural since we were children. Not just with dancing, but everything we do. Much like Krimson, he either adapts quickly to perfection or obsesses over what he's not good at until he excels past his peers.

I, on the other hand, had to spend years fumbling and conditioning myself to move around my two left feet. Twenty-one years old, and I'm a champion at these balls.

Unfortunately, Niklaus is a fucking prodigy. The man glides on clouds, walks on water, and moves with an unnatural grace to his steps.

Rigid arms tighten around my waist, and his hand drops to my lower back. My skin prickles under his hold, and for some reason, as his long fingers knead against the base of my spine—I feel it in my toes.

"And what about now?"

"Not the worst," I choke out.

"But still pretty terrible."

I nod. His eyelashes are so long. What a ridiculous detail to notice. I shift my gaze away from the way his throat shifts as he swallows.

"And now?" Niklaus dips me backward, lowering my weight with effortless ease.

And I let my head fall back with the blood rushing to my face. It feels way too good to let his hand arch my lower back like this. Why the hell does it feel that good?

I'm brought back slowly, meeting his eyes as he holds me a breath away.

"Good," I say, and I swear, if I breathe a little heavier, my lips will touch his. That small movement would bring me into this grasp.

"Better."

I'm twirled around once, but instead of sending me to the next partner, Niklaus tugs me into his chest again, skipping the swap with a possessiveness I haven't seen in him before.

"Why did you do it?" I blurt out. Maybe it's the alcohol. Maybe it's the familiarity of this setting that's giving me flashbacks.

"Do what?"

"Kiss me."

"Hmm?"

"You took my first kiss." I hold my breath. "I didn't give it to you. You took it from me."

"I remember," he says.

"Well, why did you do it?! I wanted Dorn to be my first kiss! I spent hours getting ready for that ball. HOURS!" I look around in embarrassment after raising my voice. "How could you do that to me?"

Not that he hasn't done worse. But that one stung. That one left me sobbing all night, still in my ballgown.

Niklaus darts his eyes away, unable to look at me. He raises his eyebrows and nods for me to look over at the couple next to us.

"Answer m—"

The voice to my right cuts me off. Cuts off my thoughts. Cuts off my oxygen.

"I guess it's finally time for Aurick and me to get acquainted, hmm?" my father says in a low voice, hovering his mouth close to my mother's cheek.

He attended this ball? How? He was a patient…

"*Nooooo*, absolutely not," my mother responds, trying to block his view of Niklaus's father.

Patient Thirteen twirls her around his finger. "You think I'm going to cause a scene?"

My father is dressed in an expensive, charcoal tuxedo that looks too tight around the arms and shoulders. And I have to pause, hold my breath, blink away the drunkenness clouding my eyes. Because the way he looks at my mother is a confused mix of a ferocious restraint not to fall for her and a devastating hopelessness because he knows it's too late.

He's fallen.

Though he's trying hard to hide it, it's blatantly obvious.

My father's eyes are so dark, so cruel, they're almost *evil.* Murder, torture, an eagerness to inflict pain in creative ways…yet there is a tenderness as they rest on her face, studying her concerned expression. A silent, yearning to touch her. A hesitation to show her how black his soul really is.

Something about it all makes me want to cry.

"Let's go." Niklaus leads us away from my parents.

"No, please…" I'm at a loss for words. I need to see him just a moment longer. I need see how he treats her. If he is everything they said he was. I need to know…

"Now, Spitfire!"

The room blurs and sways as I stumble on my heels further and further away. My father steps toward Aurick in a dominant confrontational stance. And I want to scream for him. Tell him who I am. Ask him if he ever wanted children. If he would have wanted a daughter. If he truly loved our mother. I want to beg him not to fall into the coma.

I just want him to know me!

"*Bad man back!*" Dellilian's urgency floods my veins with a spark of soberness.

Even with a queasy stomach, drooping eyes, and unstable balance—I spot him in the back of the ballroom. Among the curtained shadows, hidden from the golden honey lights. But he can't hide that hideous face, even if this castle is full of women wearing enough paint on their lips and cheeks to paint a masterpiece in the grand hall.

"Shit!" I sputter, turning to sprint behind Niklaus.

"Yeah, shit," he agrees.

As we bump into drunk couples, bursting through the backdoors of the castle, I throw off my shoes and run as fast as I can. We don't have weapons on us. No knives, swords, or ways of getting rid of this psychopath.

But do we really need them? Niklaus and I have been training damn near our entire lives for this kind of crisis, right? Why can't we fight him off ourselves?

"*No fight! Must run!*" Dellilian shouts in her fairy-light voice.

Evergreen branches whips across my skin. The night sky beams with sparkling stars and a waxing crescent moon. A charge of chilly gusts of wind whirl around us.

"Shit!" My feet crunch over twigs and roots, collecting splinters by the dozens.

"Don't slow down!" Niklaus whispers-shouts over his shoulder.

"We can fight him though!"

Niklaus slows down to get a better look at me. He considers this.

"Yeah, I've thought about that too…"

"There's two of us and one of him."

"But—"

"But nothing. Are we really going to let him hunt us like this?"

"She's right, Niklaus Demechnef. Are you really that frightened of me?" A storm of goose bumps, nausea, and disgust roll under my skin like a flesh-eating disease.

How Vrath managed to catch up to us, I don't know. But there is a layer of betrayal in his eyes that we had the audacity to run at all.

"No, not frightened." Niklaus takes a bold step toward him. "Your face does turn my stomach though."

Vrath reaches for his face before freezing in place. Those giant eyes slipping to the shadows behind us, jumping back and forth in soundless astonishment.

"You are *cheating*!" he hisses in disgust, a rare sight of explosive emotion. Two steps back. Vrath sticks out his plump bottom lip, appearing so much younger all at once. His inner child clawing its way to the surface.

"What?" I ask, whirling around to search for whatever he just saw in the shadows.

"I know what that is!" Is he hyperventilating? "You think I don't know what you've brought to this world?"

Niklaus's only reaction is a slow, bored blink. There's an understanding in his posture that neither of us know what Vrath's talking about, so there is no point in getting worked up with him.

"Stay back!" Vrath yanks out a black, gooey tree branch strapped to his back. "How could you…"

Not a tree branch. An antler. A sharp, spiked antler glazed and crusted in blood. He points it at the shadows behind us with a shaky hand, huffing and panting in great distress.

At this, Niklaus and I look back to the shadows under a dying tree. Nothing, I see noth—

"Back!" Vrath howls.

Dellilian emerges, crouched low with speckled paws lifted and stepping slowly, preying on the man in front of us as if he is some insignificant rodent she's hunting for game. A fine mist of coal and glimmers of amethyst light orbit the small, black wolf. A charred cloud of night and an eerie quiet that eats away at the natural sound of the forest.

He's scared of Dellilian?

Abruptly, Vrath reaches into his coat pocket in a burst of energy—fumbling with something wet and the color of a pale peach. It's spread like a starfish, dripping, shining with a single piece of jewelry.

Oh my god, it's a severed hand!

A woman's hand!

I shriek as he squeezes what's left of the chopped wrist until a small drizzle of dark cherry blood drenches his antler. Vrath quickly marks the dirt with his deranged weapon coated in a woman's blood. And in a contained explosion of winter air, umbral clouds, and ink that breathes over us before we have a chance to run—he travels.

It isn't like the few times I've triggered the ability. My moments seem to suck me in like a tornado. This way of traveling doesn't feel right in any sense. It feels like the cold side of eternity has a gaping wound that Vrath invades like a virus. A place where light goes to rot.

And before I know it, that infectious ink blasts over us, dragging me into that festering wound without any opportunity to resist. My hands find Niklaus's elbow, and I latch on until my knuckles turn white. I can't risk the possibility of me leaving him behind since I'm not the one calling the shots.

"Think of where you want to go, Spitfire! Think of somewhere you'll feel safe!"

29. Krimson Arthur Valdawell

The dream comes again.

The cliffs. The storm. My brother screaming my name.

It's more vivid and ethereal than any dream I've ever had. The jagged, glass-like rocks cut into my palms, extracting thick streams of blood to rain down my arms and into my shirt. And the sting of my skin peeling from my hands as I begin to lose my grip from the downpour, shaking my head to fling the water and wet hair out of my eyes.

"Krimson! I'm over here!" The louder I yell, the weaker my voice becomes.

"Sapphire! I'm here! I'm coming!"

I cry out as white and pink lightning crack across the gray sky.

I'm going to fall! I can't hold on much longer!

Tears burn my eyes. I can hear those heavy footsteps splashing through the mud.

He's close. He knows where I am. He's going to find me. He's going to save me!

"I'm slipping, Krimson! Please don't let me fall!"

Skylenna

It feels like I haven't had much sleep in twenty-one years.

Tonight, though, I blame my restlessness on the fact that Krimson and Sapphire have yet to return home from their night out on Main Street. It's not that I'm worried about them—I've made sure to raise them strong. Both physically and mentally. It's what Kane and Dessin would have wanted. But I think it's the loneliness that keeps me awake these days. Chekiss goes to sleep fairly early after helping me clean up after dinner. And after that, I usually do some reading on the front porch swing while the sun goes down. So often I would imagine Kane sitting there with me, reading out loud while I rest my head on his lap and let his soothing voice caress me to sleep.

But after so many years, those thoughts have made me unbearably sad. Even though I try to hide my sadness from my children, they are too smart to fool. They have his brilliant mind, and I've known I'd have trouble getting anything past them since they were born.

Tonight, I tried to fall asleep alone in my bed. But something about the soft sheets rubbing against my legs made me cold. It triggered a memory of the nights in the forest, on the run, Kane would let me tuck my cold toes into the backs of his knees. I'd shiver against his warm back and nuzzle the icy tip of my nose against his hot neck. It always made him chuckle no matter how exhausted he was.

A couple of hours lying in the darkness, I got out of bed, put on my robe, and went to Dessin's room. I massage his legs, move his arms to prevent muscle atrophy, and kiss his hands while I pray for God to bring him back to me. Most of the time, taking care of his body in this coma is a ritual that keeps me sane. I'll change his clothes, brush his hair, and ensure he has clean sheets. How could I not? He's my soulmate. The love of my life. I will take care of him until the day I die. There will never be anyone else.

I know in my heart that if the roles were reversed, Dessin and all of his alters would never give up on me. Not ever. They would take care of my body and protect me until their dying breath.

It's well past midnight, so I make myself cup of chamomile and lavender tea, sitting at Dessin's bedside while I read to him.

"Mom."

I lift my head from the book, locking eyes with Krimson in the doorway. He has his father's height, build, and eye shape. Nearly all of his qualities except for his one emerald-green eye on the left.

"You're back," I say with a sleepy smile.

"Mom…" he says again, this time I catch the tension in his voice, the static in the air.

"What's wrong?"

"Sapphire left the tavern with Niklaus."

I raise my eyebrows. "Do I really want to hear this?"

They've hated each other their entire lives. But I don't want to know what my daughter is up to when she's drunk.

"I can't find them anywhere."

I almost suggest that maybe she doesn't want to be found. But there's an alertness in his eyes. A piercing expression that's trying to tell me something else. Something out of fear.

"You already know what my response is going to be. That maybe they don't want to be found right now because they went back to Niklaus's house. But there's something you're not saying…"

Krimson nods, pressing his fist over his mouth with wide eyes.

"I have this feeling," he says in a deep, low voice. "She's in danger."

"Is she hurt?!" I toss my book to the ground and rush over to him. "What're we still doing here? Get Aunt Marilynn and Uncle Niles up. Let's go look for them."

My blood is charged and generating bursts of adrenaline. The sleepiness that once hung over my eyes is now completely gone.

I go over a million different scenarios in my head before I can blink again.

"No. It's…fuck, I don't know how to explain this." Krimson tightens his jaw and looks to his father's bed for answers.

"*Try*," I say through my teeth.

"There is no point in searching for her here."

I wave my hand in a circular motion for him to get to the point before my anxiety really takes over.

"Sapphire isn't here. No where we can look."

"WHERE THEN?!" God, I feel like Dessin's temper has taken over my senses. I never snap at Krimson like this.

"I-I don't know, Mom. It's as if she blinked from existence." He crosses his arms and shakes his head. "She went somewhere we can't reach at all. I know that doesn't make sense. But I swear to God, Mom, I can feel it in my gut. Sapphire needs me. I can practically hear her calling out to me."

My mouth falls open, and I'm at a loss for words.

"Fuck. I sound crazy!" Tears glaze over his piercing stare. "It doesn't make any sense, I know! But something happened to her!"

"Stop. No. I believe you. You're not crazy."

I pace the room, drumming my fingers against my mouth in thought. The void would have alerted me to find my daughter. But it didn't. That must mean she's outside of my reach, wherever she is.

When Krimson and Sapphire were little, I wondered if they would have any special traits like Dessin and me. I wondered if I kept them away from any traumatic experiences, which I did, would they have unexplained abilities.

After this long, I assumed those questions were silly. That my children would lead normal lives. That the afflictions or abilities that I've come to manage would die with me.

This changes everything.

It has to.

"Mom! What do we do?!"

I snap out of my train of thought and look at him.

"Now I'm the one who's going to sound crazy." With two long strides, I take his hands. "I'm going to show you how to do something…"

"What?"

"I don't think I have access to find her, Krimson. But you're her twin. If I teach you how to go into the void, you can find her. You can bring her home."

30. Somewhere Safe

Sapphire

"You brought us about a hundred yards from the Red Oaks."

I look up at the ceiling of stars twinkling over our heads.

"I'm willing to forgive you if we're back in our own time," Niklaus adds.

I huff, pounding my fists into the dirt. "I can't control it."

It doesn't feel right, this era of time we've landed in. It doesn't feel like home. Yet when Niklaus told me to go somewhere I feel safe, I thought of my parents, I thought of our house.

"Do you think Vrath came with us?" I ask. Although, I know the answer. When we fell into that pit of moving time with him, I could sense the separation as he ejected himself to a time far from Dellilian. There was a popping sensation, and he vanished.

"*Phew. That was scary.*"

I whip my head to the left to see Dellilian sitting upright and proper, waiting for us to notice her existence as she blends in with the midnight air and grim shadows.

"Hey!" I beam at her, adjusting myself to sit crisscrossed in front of her. "He's afraid of you! Vrath's scared of you!"

Niklaus crosses his arms, glaring down at her.

"But why is he scared of her? Are we too stupid not to have the good sense to be afraid?"

I fix my gaze back on the curious creature, blinking at me patiently. I don't know my own logic behind this…but with every fiber in my body, I can tell Dellilian is here to help us.

"*Bad man hates Dellilian,*" she expresses melodiously.

"But why?" Niklaus presses.

Dellilian paws at the dirt sheepishly.

"Don't act like you don't know."

"*Bad Man has seen Short-Haired Windilas many times in the Nightlung before.*"

"What's a Nightlung?" I ask.

Dellilian blinks and chuffs. "*Dark place. Time.*"

Niklaus raises an eyebrow at me.

"She means that empty black pit we get sucked into when we travel," I explain and let out a long, exhausted sigh. "And Dellilian is a Morphing Onyx Short-Haired Windila…which means she's saying her kind have run into Vrath before when time traveling."

Dellilian chuffs again in confirmation. A quick stomp of her speckled paw in the dirt.

"Does that mean your kind is dangerous? They must have made an impression on Vrath."

The Short-Haired Windila nods once.

"Should we be afraid of you?"

Dellilian paws at the dirt again. A jolting shake of her head.

"Why not?"

"*Dellilian scared a lot.*"

"And your kind normally isn't afraid?"

She shakes her head again.

"Huh. Well, what did the others do to him to make him so scared? Did they hurt him?"

"*Windilas hunt in packs. Windilas chased Bad Man into scary timelines. Windilas corner Bad Man and make him sicker.*"

I laugh. "So, they bully him."

Niklaus looks pleased.

"Reminds me of something Krimson once told me about the ocean. That dolphins bully sharks." I laugh again, patting Dellilian on the head. "How come you don't bully us?"

Before Dellilian can respond, I think back to the first conversation I had with her.

"You said you were sent to help me. Protect me…" I tilt my head and narrow my eyes at her. "Who sent you, Dellilian?"

"*Can't say.*"

"Goddamn," Niklaus grunts.

"You said they would one day ask for my help," I add.

Dellilian nods, wagging her tail.

I pause. "You also said Vrath is scary."

Niklaus growls. "This is a waste of ti—"

"Shut the fuck up. If you can't be nice to her, then walk off a cliff," I snap. An uncontrollable anger wraps around my limbs like vines that have a mind of their own. I've grown up loving and respecting animals. DaiSzek has always been an extension of our family, so hearing the disdain pour off Niklaus toward our unique, gentle animal companion is blinding me with the need to slap him.

"*Scary, scary!*"

"But if your species is so dangerous, why are you afraid of Vrath?" I ask.

Dellilian's ears go floppy, one pointing to the sky, and the other sticking straight out. She levels her body as something beyond the midnight tree line catches her attention. The only warning we get is her sharp gasp rattle through our thoughts before a rift in the Nightlung opens, breathes, and she disappears. Like a dead star imploding on itself.

"What happened?" Niklaus asks.

But I hold my breath. Her sudden fearful gasp and vanishment can only mean one thing.

"Niklaus!" I whisper, jumping to my feet. "We have to run!"

He told me to picture somewhere I felt safe. But what if I'm not taking us to locations exactly? What if I'm moving us in a gravitational pull to the people I love? Uncle Niles. My mom and dad. What if they are my beacons?

We head north, jogging over dead trees, thorned vines, and crunchy foliage. My vision is cloudy, and it constantly feels like I'm falling. I need at least three days of rest. Lots of water. Food. Something to combat this hangover.

"He doesn't *belong* to anyone."

A low, thundering voice shatters the peaceful forest ambiance. Interrupting the rustling of leaves, hooting of owls, and symphony of crickets. I heard that voice at the ball. At the hunter's trap in the woods. I don't know it well, but my mother does. And it is unforgettable.

"Fuck," I utter, bringing Niklaus and I to a complete stop.

Two stags looking down the length of an arrow.

And we've come face-to-face with my parents. Wet hair. Conformist's dress. White patient uniform. The moonlight glimmers in a halo over Mom's golden, wavy hair. They hesitate in front of us, pausing their strides to examine our sudden appearance in front of them.

I can't believe it's them! I'm standing in front of my parents over two decades in the past. It's really them. They're looking at me. He's looking at me. Dark brown eyes bounce between Niklaus and I, shifting to study our appearances, and only taking half a second to come to his own conclusion.

As his eyes land on me again, a weight sinks in my chest. A feeling that ages me backward fifteen years. It both makes me want to cry for hours or grow hot with anger. I could scream in his face, cower, or bring my hand over my mouth and sob at the sight of him.

His attention landing on me, then Niklaus, then back to me again is something I've dreamed about. A happening that I would wonder how it would make me feel. But I didn't expect to feel so small, so powerless. A terrifying ache in my blood as he glowers down at me like an insect that must be stepped on.

"What's your business here, friend?" my father asks, directing his attention to Niklaus.

There's a violence in his stillness as he waits for a response.

Niklaus looks to me for help, but I have no words for him. I'm stunned into silence. I'm hanging on to the small mannerisms of my father's presence. The way he stares without blinking. His confident stance. How he stands in front of my mother out of a natural instinct to protect.

A lump forms in my throat and my chest burns.

"Going for a late-night hike, sir. How about the two of you?" If Niklaus is scared, you wouldn't be able to tell from his tone.

But Niklaus grew up with the same stories, legends, and lore that I did. He's heard the gruesome stories of the things Patient Thirteen has done to protect those he loves. And right now, we pose an immediate threat to the love of his life.

He thinks we've been following them.

My father's stern glare drowns us with suspicion. It dawns on me that Niklaus says we were out for a hike…dressed like this.

"Mmm-hmm, yes, I can see that. Tell me, is hiking in a ball gown and tuxedo a new trend I'm unaware of?" Patient Thirteen asks, eyes cold and hard in the trickle of moonlight spilling through the trees.

I dart my eyes to my mother for help. Because, well, how the fuck are we going to get out of this one? But Mom looks just as suspicious of that statement.

In my periphery, I see Niklaus glance to me for assistance. Before I can come up with a response to help save our asses, my father jerks forward, snatching Niklaus by the throat and lifting him off the ground with ease. I'm stunned into silence as a gasp gets lost in my throat. Niklaus is by no means light. He's not as broad and muscular as my father, but he comes pretty close.

"Who are you?!" Patient Thirteen growls, pinning Niklaus to a tree.

Niklaus tries to speak, but his words are masked by the sounds of choking. My father curls his finger into a space by Niklaus's carotid artery appearing to be his vagus nerve. It causes a sudden drop in heart rate, loss of muscle control, and disorientation. Otherwise, Niklaus wouldn't so easily be overpowered like this.

But again, this is Patient Thirteen.

And he is living up to his name.

After a few long, agonizing seconds of listening to Niklaus fight for his life, for a single gasp of breath, I know my father is absolutely capable of killing him. Unless I act quickly.

"We came to have sex in the woods!" I scream, panting against the anxiety attack rattling loose in my chest. My eyes swell with a warm flood of tears. It takes me biting my tongue and cutting my fingernails into my palms to keep the urge to cry at bay. “Leave him alone! We just wanted privacy away from my parents!”

My father slides his murderous gaze down to me. The weight it carries crushes my insides. And all I want to do is hug him. Tell him it’s me. His daughter.

Reluctantly, Patient Thirteen lowers Niklaus to the ground, but his eyes don’t lose their fire. The suspicious hesitation tells me he thinks we’re spies from Demechnef.

“You’re too young to get caught up in this world,” Dessin says, turning to me with a warning in his tone. “I will spare your lives once. Do not run into me a second time.”

31. "He Didn't Know Me."

Sapphire

My father didn't spare me another glance as he left with my mother on the back of his motorcycle. But lingering effects of the incident left me cold to the touch and numb…until it didn't.

"I was almost just murdered by your dad," Niklaus comments, though there is a sliver of humor in his tone. "*Murdered,*" he annunciates dramatically.

My limbs tremble as we walk in the general direction of the city.

"He hit a spot on my throat. No idea how he did it, but I couldn't fucking move." Niklaus runs a hand over his bruised throat and laughs. "He fucking manhandled me like a ragdoll."

If only my dad knew of the horrendous things Niklaus has said in his name. Would he have let him go? Would he have seriously hurt him if he knew how Niklaus has spent our youth tormenting me?

My chest coils in on itself. Lungs pause too long before taking in another breath. A thick blanket of tears forms a protective shell over my eyes, until they fall endlessly down my cheeks. I can't erase the image of my father's measured, executioner's stare from my mind.

He didn't know me.

All the years I dreamed about what it would be like to meet him, to watch him open his eyes and look at me. Really look at me. For my mom to say the words, this is your daughter, Sapphire.

It is unnatural how many tears slip from my hold, splashing against my chest. I'm not sure if I've ever cried this effortlessly. This quietly.

"We've heard stories about how Patient Thirteen could—" Niklaus pauses, stops walking, snatches my chin with two fingers. "—are you crying?!"

I blink up at him through swollen eyes and red cheeks, then jerk my face out of his hold.

He resumes walking behind me. "You're crying because that was your first time meeting him."

That reality put into words from a man I despise clenches a fist around my heart. The ache is so severe, it could bring me to my knees.

He didn't know me.

He didn't know me.

He didn't know me.

Niklaus walks next to me in complete silence for a while. I'm not sure which direction we're going in, or if we've been walking in a circle. I spend the majority of my time dissociating from what just happened. Detaching from the little girl that lives in the bed of my soul, so excited to come face-to-face with her daddy.

After a while, we make camp under a vast opening of trees, gather firewood, and lie under the stars. At some point, Dellilian appears to my right, curled in a ball fast asleep. Her black, moist nose nuzzles into my side. The subtle affection reminds me of DaiSzek. Any time I was sick, he'd know it before anyone else.

When I was six, I woke up to DaiSzek sniffing my face. I had a high fever, and he knew it immediately. After alerting my mom, he would snuggle up next to me—burrowing against the side of my body and draping his huge head on my shoulder to make sure he could keep track of my racing pulse. Somehow, I also felt so much better when he did this.

Dellilian's snuggles make me miss home so much.

I miss walking past my dad's room and seeing my mom take care of him. Change his sheets. Talk to him. Say prayers while she held his hands. I miss seeing him sleep and deep down choosing to believe he would have loved me.

I turn away from Niklaus to sob in complete silence. The only thing that gives me away is the shaking of my upper body.

"Absinthe made me go back to the abandoned cottage in the woods," Niklaus says, breaking the silence. I'm not even sure if he's speaking directly to me or not. His velvety voice is a deep hum under the night's breeze, rustling of leaves, and owls cooing.

My sobs lessen but don't stop.

"The Mind Phantoms. She used Mind Phantoms." Niklaus covers my upper body with his tuxedo jacket. "Remember when I went missing when I was five? Uncle Warrose and DaiSzek found me?"

I don't have to respond. He knows we all remember that day.

"Absinthe made me relive it. It gave me flashbacks to things the Demechnef extremists were trying to teach me. Trying to have me believe."

I breathe in the warm aroma of his jacket. It smells so good. No fancy colognes or fragrances. No heavy body butters or oils. Just the slight whiff of fresh citrus and aquatic wood seeped into the warmth of his skin.

"I was in a state of shock after they killed my friend and his family on that hunting trip. They didn't just kill them, either. They—"

The silence lasts seconds too long. I peek over my shoulder to see him staring at the starry sky as he remembers.

"They cut them into pieces with dirty hunting knives. My friend's hands tossed in front of me while the other parts of him were scattered across our camping site."

My stomach churns because I see it so clearly. And in no way can I imagine a five-year old witnessing this.

"They told me horrible things about my mother. And what a great man my birth father was. They had horrible things to say about your parents. About the Valdawell family. They made me lie in a grave I had to dig for myself if I cried for my mother. To teach me that a man should never depend on a woman." He sighs then chuckles at that last part. "I was supposed to stay there for years…I don't think they took in to account that DaiSzek and Uncle Warrose are complete savages who could find a snowflake in a blizzard."

No, I suppose they didn't. If they knew, maybe Niklaus would have been spared out of fear. Maybe he wouldn't have been influenced to hate me so much.

"I watched DaiSzek burst through the front doors first. I remember pieces of wood exploding from the hinges as his huge form annihilated it. I remember there was no hesitation in his eyes either. He didn't wait to investigate the scene. He didn't give my captors a chance to run. DaiSzek…"

My eyes fill with more tears. I squeeze them shut to release the pressure.

"DaiSzek ripped their skin off and let them suffer first. I heard their screams in my head for years after that. Uncle Warrose came about thirty minutes after DaiSzek began carving out their organs." Niklaus pauses, crossing his arms against a stiff wind. "Uncle Warrose had to carry me out of that massacre with his hand over my eyes."

I watch a tear splash on the dirt below me. My breathing is shallow through my mouth. If I inhale through my nose, I'll have to sniffle. Somehow, that makes me feel so weak as he shares the story I've been desperate to hear since I was a little girl.

"I'm glad you got to see him with his eyes open," Niklaus rasps. And his foot touches my leg faintly. Too casual to be deliberate, but also too lingering to be accidental. If it were anyone else, I would be certain it was an accident.

He's never been an affectionate person. In fact, he's always been downright evil. Not even accepting a hug from Uncle Niles. He's never enjoyed sharing affection with women either, unless it's in bed, so I hear.

Between his body heat, Dellilian's cuddles, and his tuxedo jacket—I drift off to sleep without being touched by the chilly midnight breeze.

And I forget that my father looked into my eyes and didn't know who I was.

32. Eclipse at Noon

Sapphire

I am sitting in the woods, wearing an expensive black ball gown, eating pheasant and blackberry sauce next to the man I grew up hating.

Yet I woke up this morning to a hot meal, served on a rock. Dellilian was hovering over it, politely waiting for me to wake up and grant her access to some of my food. Not shockingly, Niklaus was an asshole and didn't make her anything to eat.

I eye him suspiciously as Dellilian and I finish off my plate. Blackberry sauce is my favorite. I eat it with most of my dinners at home. So much so, Krimson used to tease me and say my insides were just goopy blackberry sauce.

"We need to figure out your triggers for traveling," Niklaus says, putting out the fire.

I dust off my dress and pat Dellilian on the head, smiling down at her little mouth covered in blackberry sauce.

"I know."

"So, let's make our way to the city and talk about it."

Ah, so that's why he made me breakfast. Trying to butter me up so we can figure out a way to go home. Can I really blame him though?

"We've traveled, what, six or seven times so far?"

I hang my head as we walk. This feels like we're discussing the symptoms to a shameful disease I have. "Yes."

"What's been the trigger?" Niklaus flicks his gaze to Dellilian, dillydallying behind us. "I thought it was when you were scared. But unless you weren't afraid of Absinthe and that bar of soap, I don't think that's it."

My fingers are drawn to pat my lips as I fight those sick images that want to suck me back into the memory. The taste of that soap and acid is seared into my taste buds, like pouring vinegar into a deep, festering wound.

"Yeah. I definitely would have traveled if it meant I could have gotten away from that punishment."

"And when Absinthe attacked you," Niklaus adds.

I'm still not healed from that. "We don't have to rehash these incidences."

"So, what do you feel right before it happens?"

I think back to the attack in the woods. The fighting. The clashing of swords. I can practically see the dark cosmic smoke of the Nightlung breathing me in and closing in on me as it throws us into a new time. I take a deep breath.

"Fear. Panic. Adrenaline…" I shrug.

Niklaus stops, perking his head up. "Adrenaline?"

I nod.

But Niklaus looks past me, and I follow his glower. Dellilian kicks at dirt, nodding with me like she agrees with this assessment of my travel triggers.

"You know something, Dellilian?" Niklaus barks, causing her to flinch.

The black wolf with starry eyes backs away as if she's being cornered, darting her eyes between the two of us in distress.

"Hey! If you know how to fix this and get us home, and you're choosing *not* to say something, I swear to God—"

I shove at his broad, stone chest. "Leave her alone!"

But the asshole advances, pushing his chest back into my hands, and pointing an interrogating finger down at the frightened wolf.

"No! She knows how to get us home! Look at her!" His voice is a beat of thunder that rolls beneath the earth.

I make the mistake of glancing down at Dellilian. She trembles at the sight of Niklaus's anger. And that does it for me. Watching a sweet creature like that cower in fear at a man I grew up hating is all it takes.

Krimson taught me this.

He made me practice it with him twice a day.

He made sure I'd get so good at it, not even my own brother would see it coming or be able to stop me.

I drop down into a squat, swing my leg out and like a blade it cuts through his stance. Niklaus falls backward, hitting the dirt with a grunt as I jump on him, straddling his waist, and pinning his hands to the ground with my feet. With my forearm pressed to his throat, I let him see my stare. That in this moment of rage, I have the intent to kill. If he hurts her, I'll break his neck.

"What kind of man enjoys intimidating something smaller than him?" I grit through my teeth.

Niklaus blinks up at me in surprise, peeking down at my legs spread over his torso. The muscles along his stomach coil tightly together, forming hard squares under my seated position. And I'll be fucking damned if he doesn't look…aroused.

"I am not trying to intimidate her, Spitfire. I am trying to get answers out of her," he says, though his voice is too calm, too sensual for someone with an elbow to his throat.

"Don't care. I've had enough of your attitude toward her."

Niklaus relaxes under my grip, like he's getting comfortable. Like he has no intention of fighting his way out of my grip.

"I realize you seem to hate animals. Even though my DaiSzek saved your life as a child, you still hate creatures like him—but I don't! They're better than humans. Understand?" I huff in his face.

His relaxed gaze bounces from my green eye to my brown eye.

"Understood."

"Very good. Apologize to Dellilian."

The asshole narrows his eyes at me with a curious glint that I haven't seen before, and his smirk is faint, almost unrecognizable.

"I'm sorry, *Dellilian*."

I look over my shoulder to see the mystical black wolf sitting upright, watching us meekly. "*It okay, Mr. Niklaus.*"

The sound of her voice in our heads is so precious, so innocent, so childlike—I turn back to Niklaus, sticking my bottom lip out with round, gushing eyes at how cute she is.

"God," he groans, but his smile bleeds through his annoyance.

"So sweet!" I prattle. But as I peer back again, the small black wolf is gone. Vanished in a puff of black sand, back into the Nightlung.

"*Mmm-hmm.* Are you going to take off your dress for me and finish what you started or are we going to keep moving?"

Even though that statement sends a rush of unwanted heat between my legs, I practically levitate off of him.

"We need to get new clothes. We draw too much attention like this," he says, as if his suggestion moments before didn't punch me in the gut.

But I agree quietly, replaying him asking me to remove my dress with disgust at myself for allowing my toes to curl at the thought of that ever happening.

Our walk to the city is agonizing. This dress is comfortable and light…until you walk miles wearing it. My bare feet are covered in splinters and sliced with thorns. The corset waist is cutting off the circulation to my ribs and stomach. And fuck, it's so heavy I might collapse.

But the amber glow of the streetlamps peek over the horizon. And the world of the Chandelier City returns in full view. The scent of essential oils, buggy exhaust, freshly laundered cotton, and newspaper ink. Feminine clusters of laughter, heels clacking against the cobblestone, and the hollow ring of a church bell.

It's all familiar, except…

"Is that…?" Niklaus trails off in shock.

He sees what I see. It's hard not to. We're standing in its shadow. A piece of architecture that we've only ever seen in history books. It's bigger than I imagined. A monolith of human suffering. And this shadow, this cloud of eerie stillness away from the sun—long and unyielding, like it has a mind of its own. Like it's decided it wants to claim me too.

Niklaus and I hold our breath, crank our necks, and stare up at the towers piercing the stormy clouds. We have no words. No commentary. No way to express the feelings that fall over us.

Because we are standing in the shadow of…

The Emerald Lake Asylum.

33. Folded Between Decades

Niles

Twenty-One Years in the Past

Timeline: The Year of Dessin and Skylenna's Vexamen Imprisonment

I know better than to speak in my native tongue.

The language of Old Alkadonian is being used everywhere. The Vexamen Breed uniforms are here. The Meat Carnivals are back. And there is no sign Ruth has ever laid claim to her right to rule this country.

I can only guess Sapphire finally came into her own.

She claimed an ability like her parents.

I am collateral damage.

I have been left back in time, haven't I?

The other captives call this place Draèmth Voryth. The boy next to me speaks my language and says it is called the Blackspire Ward of the North. It's not associated with the Vexamen Prison. It's an in-between. It's a holding cell until they figure out where to put you. Prison, or working in servitude for life. It's a waiting room of quiet despair to be sorted like livestock.

I sit on the cold granite floor, speckled with brown, black, and the occasion stain of blood. My back rests against an onyx pillar connected to a rib vault ceiling. There are nooses up there. It's one of the first things I've noticed after arriving. *Nooses*. I counted them my first night. Thirteen. The boy told me they leave them up there to scare us. To show us that is the only means of escape.

Yes, nooses and cobwebs.

Crusted blood splatters.

Oddly the occasional claw marks.

The air in these barracks is too warm to sleep, thick enough to chew. A breezeless atmosphere infused with the nauseating scent of body odor, rusty metal, and sawdust. I've grown weary of the second layer of sweat that greases my skin and makes it rather irritating to work.

Work.

What else will we do while we wait?

I sort articles of clothing that need mending or need to be burned from the terrible stains of bodily fluids that will be too difficult to get out. Useless chores until the wardens call lights out, and we sleep in a gathering of sweaty bodies, waiting to wake up and start work again.

"Do you miss your family?" Renly asks.

The boy, Renly, has been here longer than me. He is eight years old with dark skin, dimples, and eyes so round and kind—he's more likely to dissolve in a place like this than to survive it. Renly has no sharp edges, no hardened gaze. Not a mean bone in his body. He tried to offer me his small portion of bread when I got here.

Obviously, I'd never accept a child's food.

Ever.

However, I did risk getting my head cut off by stealing a piece of chocolate from a soldier's satchel. Renly hummed for an hour after his first bite as it was his first taste of chocolate.

On my second day here, I watched Renly's eyes go wide and fill with tears as a guard purposefully stepped on his barefoot to be mean. This little boy's bottom lip jutted out, and the potent fear and disbelief that someone could hurt him intentionally shoved a sword through my chest. He has no instinct for cruelty. The kind of child who would build a small leaf fortress over an ant pile to keep them from drowning during a storm.

"Yes, I miss my family." I close my eyes at the memory of my wife's beautiful face. Of the way my son waters her garden and speaks to flowers to help them grow when no one is looking.

I miss them so much.

"Do you miss yours? Or are you happy to have a little break from them?" I ask, nudging his shoulder with my elbow getting him to crack a smile. I don't know if that joke is appropriate or not. But I'm just trying to make this disgusting place a little less stressful for him. He's only a child. I hope I can make him smile more.

"I miss catching minnows with my father," he says in a whisper, like it's a secret I must keep extra safe.

I nod. "Minnows are hard to catch."

"Not for us," Renly sighs. "We are very good swimmers."

"Not me, Ren Ren. I've got dense bones, I think. I sink like a rock."

Renly laughs but quickly covers his mouth with a dirty palm, so his single moment of joy isn't heard by the wardens. A fist clutches my heart at the sight of those dimples fading.

"Don't worry. You'll catch buckets of minnows soon. Just you see."

We pause to keep sorting through rags and uniforms as two wardens approach to breathe down our necks and review our work.

Unbeknownst to me, Renly is in charge of sewing rags that are torn. Perhaps they saw my scarred hands and decided I'm too old to keep up with extensive needlework.

"*Ceveizst, souvixst!*"

Crooked, boy!

I've picked up some Old Alkadonian in my days helping Ruth reform Vexamen.

The warden with a slanted nose and blisters on his lips kicks the rag out of the boy's hands. And I jump to my feet. Blood firing like a thousand arrows through my arteries.

I backhand the man across the face. I know it won't harm him too much. But I'm not aiming for physical pain. I'm aiming to make his ego *bleed.*

"*Veit leixcsz né gexex! Quécx heicv wiuox loovez!*" I hiss in the warden's face.

Half the room gasps before bursting into laughter.

I said: *Get out of my face, bitch! Your breath smells like poop!*

At some point, I'm not sure when, the wardens dog-piled me. They kick me in the ribs until I'm certain I'll die before I can catch my breath. The air is knocked out of me. I can't pant. I can't gasp.

I *can* think of my wife. I can think of Niklaus as a little boy, the same age as Renly.

"Renly," I choke out. "Close your eyes, son! Think of the minnows!"

Renly nods frantically, throwing his little hands over his face as he sobs. And with a furrowed brow, he goes somewhere else in his head. Somewhere with cold creek water, his father, and the minnows.

34. The Emerald Lake Asylum

Niklaus

I used to wake up in the middle of the night to my dad screaming for help.

Peeking through my parents' door, I'd watch my mother hold him in tears. Telling him that the asylum is gone. He'll never see the inside of those walls again. She'd kiss his temples and remind him of good memories. Remind him that Meridei is gone. Remind him that the hose they would use to spray him with cold water is gone.

Aunt Skylenna burned it all to the ground.

But as I stand here in the shade of this spring afternoon, that is no longer true.

The Emerald Lake Asylum is a living, breathing vessel. An evil conduit of torture to the mentally ill. And it mocks our generation by standing here, gawking down at us like insects.

My lungs feel heavier as I study the backside of the architecture.

Haunted. Gothic. Deadly. Sinister. *Evil*.

It's like looking into the abyss of the ocean. The asylum is looking back at me. It recognizes me.

Vines crawl up its pillars. The garden is well-watered. The gray statues and fountains are blotted with moss and slimy algae. Lily pads in the pond. Rose bushes. A perfectly cut lawn.

"I don't want to be anywhere close to this place," Sapphire mumbles, mesmerized by the same scenery I can't look away from.

"We're fine." Though I don't believe my own words.

Sapphire pins me with two daggers, scorching me with those heterochromatic eyes.

"Do you see my body?! I'm not skinny like the women here! I'll get thrown into the female ward for not keeping up with the dietary standards!" Genuine disbelief at my naïveté parts her lips.

I can't help my gaze trailing down her curves. Even in that black ballgown, her breasts swell over the top, her hips and ass are full and…

I turn away, grinding my molars together.

"You look a hell of a lot better than forcing women to achieve the skeletal look," I say.

Sapphire narrows her eyes at me, blinking in surprise, wondering if I just complimented her. Did I? My gaze falls to her breasts again.

Fuck.

"They'd take me in a heartbeat."

A spike of anger hits my lungs. *I know they would.*

Curtains fly shut in a window on the third floor. I lean against the black iron gate to watch that window for movement again.

"What is it?" Sapphire asks.

I watch the back of the asylum for additional movement. None.

"I thought I saw something."

"And I thought I saw Adam and Eve standing in the garden of Eden at the sight of you two." My eyes shoot to a man sitting on a stone bench under a tree to our far left. "But I suppose that's what happens when I read Genesis 3:1-24 for the sixth time today."

"Not good," Sapphire whispers.

"Not good?" The man in all black walks toward us with a Bible in one hand and rosary in the other. "Only sinners are nervous in front of a high priest."

An aching fever suddenly tumbles over me. Chills. A throbbing sore throat. Head splitting wide open. It's the kind of fever that heats up my eyeballs, singeing the inside of my lids.

Sapphire moans softly, placing a hand over her throat.

Sickness.

Infection.

Vrath.

He's close. He's close but hidden. He wants us to get caught.

"Let's go." I grab Sapphire by the wrist, turning to put as much distance between us and this institution as possible.

"I can't let you leave with that girl, kind sir," the high priest calls.

Several orderlies emerge from behind trees, approaching us in no hurry at all. They saw us coming. We must have been spotted in our ballroom attire. Vrath must have tipped someone off.

"And why is that, Father?" I ask, my voice slightly altered by the swollen tonsils in my throat.

The high priest leans against the iron gate, casually, hanging his hands over the railing and pursing his lips.

"Refusing to sustain the standard weight and follow the guidelines of the Lady-Doll Regimen is a federal offense. Isn't that why you're on the run?" The high priest taps his Bible against his fingertips. "And I hear you suffer from delusions, my dear boy. Delusions are given to those who are too weak to fend off the devil."

"What kind of delusions do I suffer from?" My stomach jolts with nausea. I can hardly swallow without a sudden need to gag.

How does this work? The high priest and the other orderlies aren't affected by Vrath? Shouldn't they be if he's close enough to infect us with his presence? Can he control it? Can he influence who gets hit first?

"You believe you're a descendant of the Demechnef name. Niklaus Demechnef." He chuckles, shaking his head. "The name flows nicely for a ruler of a nation. I'll give you that."

Fuck, Vrath told them my goddamned name?!

"That is not my name," I say, low and deadly.

"Do not lie to a high priest, dear boy. God allows us to see only truth. And I could see it in your delirious gaze that you truly believe that is who you are." The high priest scratches at his blond and gray beard, giving me a look of pity.

"Hmm." I stare at him through hot, watery eyes. "Fuck you. We're leaving."

I reach for Sapphire's waist as I'm being bear-hugged from behind. Multiple arms are around me. Multiple hands are fighting me into submission. And this wouldn't normally be a problem. For me or Sapphire.

But this fever has knitted itself into my lungs and bit into my bones. All I want to do is sleep in a warm bed. Not just warm, but hot. A thick blanket with a hot pan of coals. And a fireplace. I'm so cold.

The last words I hear are a prayer from the high priest.

My hand slips from Sapphire's waist.

35. Lady-Doll Correctional Rehabilitation

Sapphire

My name is Sapphire S. Valdawell.

If I die in here, know that this time isn't where I have originated from. Know that I am from a time where you don't need to starve yourself because men told you to. You don't need to bathe in oils and rose water in order to be beautiful.

Men will fuck anything.

Men will fuck anything.

Men will fuck anything.

Men will fuck anything.

Men—

I startle awake at the sound of a door clicking open. Fuck, did I really hallucinate writing on a wall in the asylum?

"Welcome to the Emerald Lake Asylum." A heavy door drags across the floor.

High heels clack.

A voice like wind chimes brushes over the room.

My eyes are closed, but I'm becoming more and more aware that there are eyes on me. Multiple sets. Judging. Glaring. Waiting impatiently for me to wake up.

The insides of my eyelids are bright red from light trying to burn its way into my retinas. And I completely reject the idea of opening them to witness what I'm hoping is a fever nightmare. It comes back to me in flashes. The high priest. The orderlies. The sickness that swept over me in a single breath.

The tall, haunting asylum.

Not burned to the ground.

I've read about the horrors of being one of Absinthe and Albatross's subjects…but ending up in the Emerald Lake Asylum or the Vexamen Prison has been an irrational fear of mine since I read about them in school. I used to wake my mom up in tears, telling her I didn't want to be committed to the asylum.

And here I am.

"We will have to wake her up," that high feminine voice says. "She was acting funny when they found her. Possibly from all the food she's been unnaturally consuming."

My eyes pop open.

No one is waking me up. I can only imagine a bucket of ice-cold water to the face.

I scan the ceiling, the bright sconces on the walls, the metal bedframe, the tall woman hovering over my bed. She swipes away a loose blonde curl from her left eye and offers a porcelain fake smile.

"Hello, Miss Sapphire S. Valdawell," the tall conformist says.

I know this woman, don't I?

The white collar with her conformist dress is the dead giveaway. Head conformist. Council member.

"My name is Suseas Parlomon."

Oh, goddamn it.

Three orderlies stand back and let Suseas have the first introduction with me. I flinch at the nun standing in the corner of the room with her head bowed in prayer, muttering to herself.

"You were *almost* committed to the women's ward for your inability to keep up with your Lady-Doll Regimen." She trails a sharp, unpolished fingernail over my lower belly, clucking her tongue.

"Almost."

She pauses to smile down at me with a glint of confusion clouding her eyes.

"You look so familiar, Miss Valdawell. So very familiar."

I should hold my tongue. I should have learned my lesson about speaking out at a time like this. "I believe you know my parents."

I believe you tortured my parents.

I believe my mother boiled you alive in the scalding bath treatment before she burned this place to the ground.

"Hmm." She places a finger on her pointed chin. "I have attended many parties with my husband. We meet quite a few faces."

None like my parents.

"That must be it," I respond without blinking.

"Well, I'd ask you to give them my best, but you are in here after all for the time being."

A burst of hope fills my lungs. I wonder…could they be here right now? Where in history are we? Is my father a patient? Is my mother a conformist?

"We have decided not to commit you to the female ward after receiving new information." Suseas nods at the nun still praying in the corner. "I understand you believe you can time travel."

Vrath, you stupid, conniving fucker.

I nearly bark out a laugh. But this isn't funny. Not at all. It's one thing to be committed for eating too much. Yes, the treatments are fucked up to get a woman to comply with surviving off of fucking breadcrumbs to lose weight, but it's all nothing compared to being committed to that one special wing of the asylum…

"Welcome to the Intricate Section. We bring very, very special cases here to rehabilitation."

I am swallowed by a collapsing black tide of terror, my body suspended in its violent current with no shore in sight. No hand to pull me from the stormy waves. Though this ward is silent now, the screams that have echoed down these halls have been absorbed into the shadows of each room. And I am locked away, between these walls that breath like ribcages, getting smaller and smaller as it sucks the air out of the room.

"I…I don't think I can time travel," I sputter out frantically.

"You received false information."

Suseas looks down at me with pity. "I don't believe we did."

"No, really. This is so silly, Suseas. My…*husband* and I attracted the attention of a terribly ill stalker! He has been spreading horrible lies about us." I sigh and shake my head dramatically. "It's a shame, really. My biggest crime I will admit to is, of course, eating too much."

Forcing myself to say that last bit is the aftertaste of vomit.

"That is for certain." Suseas giggles behind her hand.

Oh, fuck you.

"Will you just send me to the female ward, then?" I ask, then look around. "Wait, where is Ni—my husband?"

It's frowned upon to gallivant around with a man who is not your husband in this time period. I'll gain more respect if people think I am married to Niklaus.

"Out of moral precautions, we cannot send you to the female ward until we are certain your mind is no longer possessed with these notions of traveling through time." She giggles to herself again. "Your husband has been committed to this section as well. He is in room three."

Only a slight glimmer of relief. At least we're both here in case I travel again.

"Moral precautions," I repeat.

"Yes." Suseas nods.

"You think it is moral to hold a woman against her will for eating until she is full?" *I—I have a death wish.*

"Excuse me?" The head conformist tilts her head.

I drop my head. "I'm sorry."

Suseas narrows her eyes and stares at me until I lift my gaze to meet hers again. Even though I've been to many different moments in time as of late, looking into the face of the head conformist of the Emerald Lake Asylum is looking into the face of the past. She has the blood of the asylum written all over her. Every inch. Her lengthy figure. Elongated face. Makeup so pristine she looks like a mannequin in the main street boutiques.

"I'm prescribing you a strict diet for the next three weeks, then we will reassess." Suseas turns to the orderlies as she scribbles on her clipboard. "Six a.m. she will have three raw eggs and a glass of water to wash it down. Lunch will be rolled oats and two laxatives. Dinner a glass of water and a tablespoon of cod liver oil."

My mouth falls open.

"Sundays are fasting. Wednesdays administer an enema in the morning and at night." Suseas peeks over her clipboard, eyeing my physique one more time. "Let's add an emetic purge as well. Ipecac syrup with some water. I've seen gorgeous transformations from this weekly. Oh, and on Fridays, she will be weighed in front of the female ward with the others."

Weighed? Publicly?

"If she gains even an ounce, increase the enema and emetic purge to twice a week. Although, I doubt that'll be the case." Suseas finishes scribbling as the orderlies nod in agreement.

The clipboard is handed to the orderly closest to the door, and he disappears. My entire body trembles from the cold air and wondering if he left so quickly to prepare my food.

"Now, onto more pressing matters. Your delusional disorder." The psychotic woman tsk-tsks. "I'm a bit understaffed, but I want my best and most hardworking conformist on your case. Since your husband has a similar delusional disorder, we can do dual treatments to save time and resources. I'm thinking electroshock therapy, the isolation tank, and the bloodletting treatment should do nicely. But your conformist may adjust strategies based on your needs."

I squeeze my eyes shut and try to fucking travel. If it's adrenaline, I'm good to go. Adrenaline marches through my veins and chants a war song. I am not sticking around to survive the full presidential asylum experience. No. Hell no. Goodbye. Thank you. Happy holidays.

"In fact, additional treatments to correct his enablement of your eating habits could have significant benefits to your recovery and your marriage." Suseas taps her chin in thought.

Divorce. She better mean divorce.

"Have you been pleasing your husband daily, dear?" she asks.

"I—I don't recall."

"Ah. It can be an easy trap to fall into…not performing your marital duties, but let me assure you, Miss Valdawell. Oral sex will do wonders for maintaining your physique. *And* semen has unforeseen nutritional value."

God, you can take me right now.

She laughs. "I know, I know. What does this have to do with my treatment? Well, we recently started experimenting with a new marital exposure treatment called The Matrimony Method. Your husband pleases you sexually if you resist food. If not, you'll be given a potent dose of wormwood concentrate. Those terrible stomach cramps will stop when you perform exceptional marital duties on your husband. It's a full circle therapy that I have absolutely fallen in love with."

I realize I'm staring at Suseas with bulging eyes and a gaping mouth. I shut them both to concentrate on traveling again.

"I don't think that will be necessary," I spit out.

Suseas does that condescending little head tilt again. "It's not really up to you, is it?"

I slice into my own tongue with my two front teeth. I'll be damned if I let my mouth run me into the ground again. I have to act this out just right. They value a submissive woman in this era. Quiet. Meek. Obedient. Polite.

All of the things that I am not.

But am I going to be smart or am I going to be stubborn?

"Whatever you think is best, Suseas. I trust your educated judgment." I bow my head, noticing the shackles.

I couldn't fight my way out of here, even if I wanted to.

"Delightful. Any other questions before your daily regimen begins, young lady?" Suseas asks, clasping her hands together.

I shake my head, then consider something I am dreading even bringing up. There is only one positive outcome to this. It's a long shot.

"Who will my conformist be?" I ask.

Please, say Skylenna. Please, God.

"That would be me."

The door opens, squeaking as I realize that voice is not my mother's.

The woman in the doorway, arms crossed, much shorter than Suseas stares as me from her position of power. White pantyhose, protruding collarbones, a powdery face with a perfect smile. And I mean, a perfect smile. Her teeth look so white, so shiny, so straight—I could be convinced that she endured some kind of cosmetic procedure for them.

But that smile does not touch her eyes. Black as a starless sky. And nothing behind them. Dead, even. She hasn't even blinked yet.

I've seen her photographs in the history books.

An oblong face shape. Narrow nose. Skinny eyebrows.

And that signature raven-black hair.

It's Meridei.

Meridei is my conformist.

36. Senior Conformist

Niklaus

Report Filed: Staff Misconduct - Dismissed/No Action Required

This room has been scrubbed clean recently.

The stone is still wet. The fumes from the chemicals still potent and hanging in the air. But they didn't quite get everything, did they? The right corner of the room has a puddle stain of urine. And there are marks on the wall by my head. Human fingernails that scraped and clawed and bled to get out. I stare at it until Suseas stops fucking talking and leaves.

An hour, I think, passes by me before the door opens again. My new conformist stands in the doorway for a long moment before finally getting bored of her own grand entrance and stomping in. I don't care to look at her. I'm choosing to spend all my time planning an escape for me and Sapphire. I can't imagine what they're going to put her through for not following these fucked up rules of beauty.

Her name is Meridei.

I silently mourn that slight bit of hope Aunt Skylenna would be my conformist when she first started. She was said to have compassion and kindness for her patients. That is decidedly *not* the case for the other asylum workers.

And to my horror, if I remember correctly, Meridei was by far the worst one.

The sadistic woman folds herself into a neat, seated position with crossed legs on the edge of my shitty bed. "Are you scared of me, Patient Three? Is that why you won't talk to me?"

She twiddles the white sheet resting over my legs with the tip of her index finger.

I blink slowly, then find her black eyes dissecting me. They're two saucers that burn holes into my skull. And they're empty. Blank. Isolated. Like screaming into a cave and never getting a response. I can picture most patients shuddering and avoiding her pointed attention. And maybe she enjoys that effect she has on people.

But I simply stare back in utter boredom.

"Do I look scared of you?" I ask.

Meridei straightens, and she lights up in surprise. "You do not."

"There you go."

"Suseas tells me you're married," she muses, eyeing my arms and the many scarred tattoos that cover them.

Oh, yeah. She said something about that. It was smart of Sapphire to throw that detail in there. Without it, she would be labeled a paid whore for wandering around the woods with a man, unmarried and completely alone. Who knows what they would have put her through if that were the case.

"I am," I say.

"And she's an asylum patient?" There's a degrading insult laced within her tone.

"We both are."

Meridei uses her pinky to smooth out her lip gloss.

"Yes, certainly. But…never mind, I shouldn't say that." She blushes into her hand. I pay even closer attention to her very deliberate mannerisms. I can't imagine this woman gained such a notorious reputation for being this sheepish and shy.

"But you'll say it anyway," I say.

"I mean, I must, right? What kind of woman would I be for not speaking up on such a topic that has probably cost you years of suffering!"

I raise an eyebrow.

"Your wife has not been upholding her wifely duties to you, has she? Look. At. Her. Those plump hips and backside are far from meeting any seamstress's measurement requirements! How could you want to penetrate her with your penis? How could you want a woman like that to bear your children or…" Meridei glances away submissively. "For recreational purposes, *swallow* your seed."

For fuck's sake, I clench my jaw to keep from laughing. I'm no fan of Sapphire's, but my god, that woman has the sexiest body I've ever fucking seen. Her hips? Her ass? I immediately get hard when she bends over. She is not overweight. She is not underweight. Her body is every man's dream. Why does everyone give her so much shit here?!

I can't hold back the first remark that pops into my head.

"It's hard to notice the size of her backside when her big tits are bouncing in my face."

Meridei's sweet expression slips into a brief mask of shock.

Sapphire would have a wicked death glare for me right now. We've never had sex. But I would be lying if I hadn't thought about it.

"And I bet that's your delusional disorder talking. Not the real you, hmm?" Her voice maintains that syrupy sweet tone. And she begins massaging my foot over the sheet.

I glance down at her pale hand, stroking and kneading my heel, ankle, then calf.

"A woman who follows her dietary regimen and nightly beauty routines has a softer touch. Like *this*. Does this feel good?" Meridei rubs her palm against the inside of my knee. "A woman such as myself would massage your penis every day. Isn't that something you want?"

I'm momentarily hypnotized. My body reacts to this unexpected approach of her coming onto me. My heart races. And my bloodstream shoots down to my groin.

"You are so handsome. And you poor thing, you've probably built up so much married to that awful woman. You must need to ejaculate so badly…" Meridei's voice slips into a dangerous sensual place. Like a siren calling to me.

And that small hand slips over my hardening cock under the white sheets. She uses the palm of her hand to massage my shaft, up and down, up and down.

"Does that feel good?" Meridei lowers her lids and stares up at me through thin eyelashes. They aren't long, full, and wispy like Sapphire's.

That's all it takes.

There's an unfamiliar feeling that rises like steam in my chest. A deep, unprovoked yearning over the thought of Sapphire, the girl I've known my entire life, suffering a barbaric treatment right now.

My erection vanishes.

And a burning pit forms in my belly. A well of fury at this woman thinking she can manipulate me while my wife is being tortured. No, not really my wife. But Meridei doesn't know that. She thinks I'm like any man who enters these doors. She thinks I'd betray my wife for her. Is that part of her fucked up psychosis? Simply knowing she can harm someone or make them do whatever she wants by any means necessary?

Christ, I almost fell for it.

Meridei notices my dick go limp under her touch. There's a brief flicker of panic as she tries to summon it back. I grin at the failed effort.

"I am so sorry, Meridei. You're just not nearly as stunning as my wife." I sit up as much as my shackles will allow. "And not to mention, you must have contracted so many sexually transmitted diseases by doing this to your patients. I'd rather not catch whatever you have brewing down there. But please, I'd like to report a highly inappropriate misconduct for what you just attempted. Add it to my chart."

Meridei stares at me long enough for that submissive mask to fall off. Long enough to show me the demon who made a lasting impression on my father and Aunt Skylenna.

I lean closer, refusing to break eye contact with this new version of her.

"I'd like to see my wife now."

37. Famine Without End

Sapphire

Patient Two expected to respond favorably to correctional Lady-Doll Regimen within three weeks. Temporal Displacement Fixation (Time Traveling Delusions) requires further investigation and rigorous treatments pending compliance.

The raw eggs weren't that bad.

But the oats and laxatives had me spending most of my day in the washroom.

"Were your meals as tasty as you hoped they would be?" Meridei pulls up a small metal chair. I was hoping she was too busy for my case. That I could slide on by without attracting anymore of her attention.

"They were fine. Thank you." I face away from her on my bed, strapped down after the washroom trips finally stopped.

"Fine? I'm sure they are nothing compared to your feasts of crumpets and cookies, yes?"

Ah, I see what we're doing now.

"They were even better. I feel cleansed and well nourished," I say in a level, controlled voice.

Meridei is quiet for a little too long, though I don't dare turn around to see if she's left or not. I know better.

"You sure you aren't craving cake? Perhaps a bite of chocolate? I could sneak some in for you, if you'd like?" Meridei slips into a friendly mask with a hushed volume to her questions. If I didn't know who she really is, I might have fallen for her olive branch.

"Oh, no thank you. I am dedicated to the carefully planned regimen you have arranged for me."

"How…womanly of you to fully immerse yourself in this experience, Miss Valdawell."

I can feel her eyes bore into me.

"When will I get to see my husband again?" I change the subject, hoping she'll stop baiting, stop attempting to catch me slipping up.

"Tomorrow. At your first dual treatment." She pauses, sighs like she has something to get off her chest. "I am so sorry, Miss Valdawell, I know he asked me not to tell you about what happened earlier…"

I perk up but still refuse to face her. "What happened?"

"I would just hate for this to affect your rehabilitation. Especially with how *committed* you are."

"What is it?"

Meridei sighs again as if she might cry. "Part of your husband's affliction is caused by how pent up he is…sexually."

I blink at the stone wall, then turn to look her in the eye. "Huh?"

"I know it's a sin, but it's my duty as a conformist to help him recover and relieve him of these obstacles."

Is she still talking about Niklaus?

"I performed oral sex on him, Miss Valdawell. I am so deeply sorry. I offered to take that burden off him, since you've been failing your marital duties and participating in overconsumption of sweets and pastries. He was so desperate for my mouth to swallow his semen. I had to uphold my vow to help those who can't help themselves as a senior conformist of this asylum."

Meridei stands to move a loose strand of hair away from my left eye.

"Between us girls, his cum tastes *wonderful.*" She uses her thumb to wipe her bottom lip, then sucks it clean. "Maybe if you spent less time stuffing your trap with sugar, you'd remember how delectable his cock tastes."

It's not hard to keep my face emotionless because I don't care what he does. He isn't really my husband. I have no romantic attachment to him. But I'm trying to understand why my chest pulls taught, like someone is pulling a string and tightening the fabric that keeps me together. My skin prickles as I examine her mouth, her lips curling into an innocent smile.

The thought of her mouth on him…

My stomach knots. A stack of coals smolders and smokes under my ribs.

Am I angry that she thinks this would hurt me, and she's clearly hoping for a big reaction? Am I burning on the inside out of disgust? I don't want to know what kind of explicit activities Niklaus takes part in! I don't want to think about his hands woven into her hair as she…

"H—he asked you to do this?" I stammer then clear my throat.

The image of him on a patient bed while she pleases him…that image refuses to loosen its grip on me.

"Yes," she says, watching my reaction closely.

You think I care?! How do I keep from laughing in your smug little face? I don't give a shit about Niklaus. You can have him!

But that resounding ache blooms in my gut as my thoughts refuse to go quiet.

"Thank you for doing what you need to do to help him," I respond submissively, bowing my head in gratitude.

No, I will not give you the satisfaction of a reaction. I'm sure that's what you're used to getting. And what happens after that, Meridei? You probably punish your patients with gruesome treatments for lashing out.

Meridei's perfectly serene face flinches at my lack of a desired response. A quick twitch in her cheek and the fake look of remorse and feigned innocence is gone.

"Good." She turns to the door, walking on her tiptoes with her hands behind her back like a disciplined ballerina. "You will get your glass of water for supper, then I will see you and your husband first thing in the morning for dual treatments."

I unclench my fists and rest my head back on the bed as the door scrapes open.

Meridei pauses at the threshold.

"I do hope it's not awkward for the three of us tomorrow."

One orderly escorts me to a treatment room with a circuit board and two white reclining chairs I've only ever sat in for a dental checkup.

Meridei stands behind the circuit board, examining her cuticles as I'm seated, strapped in, and told to wait.

Nerves whoosh in out of my lungs, though I refuse to let her see it, so I keep my bored gaze trained on the white shoes of my orderly stationed at the door. The only thing that breaks my trance is watching *three* orderlies escort Niklaus into this room.

His walk is confident and unbothered. Why? Probably because he just got his cock sucked. While I'm digesting laxatives, he's probably getting his choice of which conformists he gets to bury his dick into.

Bare feet stand next to the shoes I'm choosing to focus on. I won't look up. I swear to God, I won't lock eyes with him.

"How terribly uncomfortable." Meridei pats the top of my head. "We're all in the same room together after last night."

Niklaus laughs, but the sound is unnerving. It has a sharp edge to it that is unexpected. Somewhat cruel. Somewhat angry.

"Here." My orderly holds a glass out to me. Three raw eggs swirl in a slimy puddle. *Awe, and here I thought I wasn't getting breakfast today.*

"I think I'll skip it," I say.

I have a twisty feeling inside that this treatment is going to upset my stomach. And it's already seriously unhappy with me after yesterday. After the ninety-seven trips to the toilet.

"Drink it!" Meridei orders with a little less patience she's had yesterday.

My eyes flash up to Niklaus, watching me in his white uniform and dark hair hanging in his face. Those hardened deep blue eyes have lost their usual unamused look. They're wider. They're…alarmed.

I gulp down the raw eggs, ignoring the slimy lumps as they pass over my tongue. *It's just raw eggs. It's just raw eggs.* But that convulsing urge to gag is definitely there, however I would rather drop dead then let either of them see it.

Niklaus waits for me to finish. That subtle grimace flashes from existence, and in its place he smirks. "Hello, darling wife."

I let my eyes roam over his face before redirecting my attention to the orderly.

"Thank you," I say as he takes the empty glass away.

Niklaus's orderlies connect his shackles to the reclined chair, ensuring he can't do anything to break free.

"That's good. I can strap him in myself," Meridei commands, heels clacking as she rounds the circuit board to join Niklaus.

The orderlies nod like mindless soldiers, exiting the room to leave the three of us alone. And the silence leads to an image that sneaks past my best mental guard. An image that pierces a hole in the cold, emotionless state I've decided to meditate in.

The image of these two together. Her mouth on him. On her knees. Niklaus looking down at her with stormy eyes.

Why would he want her? Knowing everything he knows about her from what we've read? Her disturbing proclivity for tormenting her patients? What my mother did to her? What Meridei put my parents through?

I didn't have much respect for him to begin with, but this tanks whatever remained.

Still, the burn in my chest grows as I watch her touch his chest, tighten the straps over his stomach, and lingering for a moment too long. That uneasiness sends my nerves into a frenzy.

"Is that too tight?" Meridei asks, making circles with her thumb over his wrist.

My stomach falls.

"No."

"Mmm," Meridei moans. "And here?" She runs both her hands over the straps on his upper thighs.

I turn away, trying to summon that numb sensation that lets me dissociate from the ache that's curling around my lungs like a venomous snake. It's hard to retract into myself though, to go somewhere deep into the forest of my mind. They're right next to me. Our chairs are pushed against each other. I tighten my elbow against my body to keep from touching his.

Niklaus laughs again. "I see what you're doing."

I'm filled to the brim with hard shards of ice.

Breathe.

"You're awfully quiet over there, Miss Valdawell," Meridei taunts.

I keep my mouth plastered shut. If I speak, I might cry.

"Sapphire S. Valdawell. That's what your file says. What does the S stand for?" She waits, but I remain unmoving. "Or could your parents just not decide?"

"My mother couldn't decide." *That's only half true.*

"And she didn't realize you'd get made fun of for that I bet."

I slide my glare to Niklaus. Because she's right, what my mother didn't anticipate was that Niklaus Demechnef would be that person to find any little thing to tear me down with.

Even my middle name.

"We're starting out with Electroconvulsive Therapy, due to the nature of your delusional disorders. This helps to reset your disturbed neuropathways. Your illnesses are a combination of your nervous system misfiring and being weak-minded, which allows the devil to influence your thoughts."

I'd laugh if I wasn't so terrified.

"And how will we feel after this?" I ask.

"Memory gaps. Disoriented. Docile. But the confusion you feel will help break up the scaffolding of delusions."

Memory gaps? I look to Niklaus with a surge of panic rupturing through my calm, meditative state.

"We could lose our memory?" Niklaus glances back to me without moving his head.

"Why?" There's a smile in Meridei's taunting voice. "Are you afraid you'll forget about the lack of intimacy in your marriage?"

My breathing comes hard and fast.

We can't forget! I can't afford to lose any memories of where we're really from!

"How bad are the memory gaps?" I say breathlessly.

"I've seen wives forget their husbands. I've seen mothers forget their children." Meridei adjusts her circuit board, taking great interest in my sudden rise in panic.

My eyes dart to Niklaus again as they fill up with tears.

Krimson. DaiSzek. Grandpa. Mom. My father. Uncle Warrose. Aunt Ruth. Aunt Marilynn. Uncle—

I gasp, suffocating on the tears. "Uncle Niles!"

Niklaus stiffens.

"We can't forget him! Oh god, we can't leave him there!" I'm blubbering now. Unable to focus on a plan to get the hell out of this mess. Unable to calm myself long enough to think of a way out. The sobs rack my body uncontrollably. I'm scared like a child left alone in the dark. I'm in a small boat, drifting into a cloud of fog and mist over the sea, knowing I'll never return to shore again.

"Spitfire…" Niklaus whispers.

Doesn't he care?! Doesn't he want to save his dad from Vexamen before Aunt Ruth made it a better place?

"Patient Two exhibiting severe hysteria. Check menstrual cycle," Meridei says as she takes notes on a clipboard.

"Just wait a second, please! I don't want to forget!" I try my best to shake my head and clear my eyes of the rush of tears. "Please, I'll do *any* other treatment. Please!"

Krimson, please don't let me forget you! I can't forget my twin.

I gather the memories like a trove of sacred gems in my mind. I see the rabbit Krimson got for his fourth birthday. I threw a fit when I saw him hug that white rabbit, and all I got was a silly porcelain doll. Uncle Warrose made a white rabbit for me, and Aunt Ruth stitched my name into its lucky foot.

I remember the day I fell on the cobblestone street and cut open my knee trying to keep up in a race between Krimson and Niklaus. I dropped my head back and screamed. Uncle Niles scooped me up before I could have a full meltdown. He cleaned my knee in a nearby boutique, patched me up, and kissed the bandage. I wrapped my arms around his neck, and he held me until I fell asleep. His shirt smelled like soap and candles.

I read my mother's journal once after I told her I wished she was in the coma instead of my dad. The page was stained with tears. She told my dad in her letter to him how much she loved me, and she knew I didn't mean what I said…but my words still cut her so deeply.

"Please, please, ple—" A folded cloth is shoved into my mouth. My screams are muted. The room spins. The sconces flicker. Tears gush down my temples. And I see her face, the black eyebrows, pursed lips, powdery white face as she glowers down at me. Prongs slide along the sides of my head. And even though I buck like a wild stallion, I don't move through time.

I'm stuck here.

We're stuck here.

And because of me, I could lose the most precious moments in my life. I could forget my home. We might never make it out. We might stay here until the place burns down.

"…two, three!" Meridei counts down, flipping a switch that cuts my thoughts off.

I see the room in flashes as the world erupts in white. Blackouts occur in pulses. A sharp iron rod impales me, from my skull, through my spine, down to my toes. I'm levitating off the chair, back arching, neck curling backward. My veins bulge into my throat, pumping something thicker than blood back to my arteries.

It feels like hours.

Neverending.

No oxygen coming in and out.

Indescribable pain.

I'm turned to stone on a bed of hot coals in this humming, buzzing, quaking room around me. A fierce web of lightning threads itself into my brain, burning through my thoughts, feelings, memories, *soul*.

I am a puppet convulsing under unseen strings.

And as my spine bows upward a little harder, I worry my ribs will snap under the strain—that cage of bones cracking clean apart.

"Very good!" Meridei purrs.

Emptiness. The lighting flickers off in my brain. The noise falls flat. And I collapse against the chair in a sweaty, heaving, aching mess of copper hair and a white gown.

Faintly, over my own heavy breathing, I can hear Niklaus grunt next to me.

"I'll give you a few minutes to rest," Meidei says, walking toward the door. She pauses and looks back at Niklaus. "Unless you'd like to me stay and help you recover?"

I don't have it in me to feel the rage I felt before. I'm exhausted. I'm petrified. I'm completely empty and confused.

"No," he grits out.

"Very well." The door opens, and she steps out.

As I close my eyes, I attempt to summon the last few minutes. But there's nothing there besides the bolts of white sparks that ricocheted across my skull. I focus on my limbs straining against the leather straps digging into my skin. Where was I before I sat in this spot? Who was I just talking to?

I want to remember. I know that much. But what was I trying so hard not to forget?

A pair of fingers tickle my knuckles.

"Tell me your name," a deep, scratchy male voice commands.

It's muscle memory. "Sapphire."

"Your *full* name."

"Sapphire S Valdawell."

"And I'm Niklaus Charles Demechnef."

A tear falls from my cheek. Every nerve is fried. I can't tell if I'm asleep or awake. Dying or alive. Swimming or sinking.

"It hurts," I rasp.

My jaw throbs and swells as claws sink into my back. I want the pain to go away. I can't remember why, but I know I've been in physical pain for days on end. Why?

"I don't want to fucking hear that," he growls. "Now, say it again."

I sniffle. "My name is Sapphire S Valdawell."

"Niklaus Charles Demechnef."

"I'm so scared," I admit.

He exhales through his nose, trying to gather the patience.

"Again."

"I am Sapphire S Valdawell."

"I am Niklaus Charles Demechnef."

"Do you think she'll do it again when she comes back?" I ask, voice wavering from holding back tears. I am so unbearably tired.

"Tell me the names of your parents," Niklaus instructs sternly.

"Okay." Deep breath. One, two, three, four. "Skylenna Ambrose. Kane Valdawell."

"Marilynn Blackforth. Aurick Demechnef."

In the pit of my stomach a mix of sadness and hatred spill out everywhere.

"No. Say his name," I say through grinding teeth and labored breathing. "Don't you *dare* forget him."

The only sounds that can be heard in this deathly quiet room are Niklaus's wrists twisting in his leather restraints and shackles.

"Niles Offborth."

"Niles Offborth," I repeat.

His knuckle brushes mine once more. It's oddly the only bit of comfort I can find.

"Tell me—all your father's alters," Niklaus pants.

"There are too many. I don't know them all." I push my brain to see past the fog and draining exhaustion. "My mother doesn't even know them all."

"That's okay. Name as many as you can."

It takes everything in me not to close my eyes and drift off to sleep. I want to, fuck I want to so badly. Even to escape for a short amount of time.

"Dessin, Kane, Greystone…" I pause, *come on, come on, come on…* "Bloom, Aquarus, Kalidus, Sophia, Young Kane, Dai."

My eyes droop shut. Every breath sinks deeper, lulling me further away.

"You know more than that," his deep voice booms into my throbbing brain.

"…Syfer. Fuck, I don't know. What were we talking about?"

"Which alter would you want to meet the most?" He's going to fall asleep too. His voice is normally so sharp and direct. But right now, it's sluggish, warm, thick.

"Kane."

"Why?"

"My mom told us she grew up with him. He was her best friend. He's the one who's kind and patient. She was closest with him and…Dessin."

"Kane isn't the one you want to meet the most," he argues.

This wakes me up. "What?"

"You want to meet the infamous Patient Thirteen the most."

"No, actually, I don't."

"Not as a stranger, but as his daughter. You want him to know you."

I'm too tired to feel the full force of rage pressurizing in my chest, but I know it's there. Who the fuck does he think he is? Telling me which one of my father's alters I want to know the most? The vicious psychopath? No, I want to meet the kind man who has loved my mother since she was a small child.

"You don't know anything about what I want," I rasp.

The circuit board hums back to life. And the door locks clank and click as it slides open.

"No," I utter. *Please, let this be over. Please!*

Meridei closes the door behind her, leaning against the door with a thoughtful look. "I know it must feel like I'm leaving the electrical current on for a long period of time, but I'm not."

Despite the trembling in my bones, I am unable to keep myself from dozing in and out.

"I trigger a strong electrical current. The pain you experience after that is seizures. Or, as the high priest believes, the convulsions are the demons leaving your body. It only lasts about sixty seconds."

In no way does this make me feel better.

"Does this conclude our session?" Niklaus asks.

Meridei smirks, walking to the foot of his reclined chair, massaging his bare feet without breaking eye contact. "Ready for me to walk you back to your bed already?"

I close my eyes.

"*Or* you could walk me back to my wife's bed," Niklaus, though his inflection is weak and slow, maintains his cold edge.

She stares at him, long and aggravated. Her eyes are the essence of a grand, gothic, haunted estate. A compound of massacres, gore, and insidious intention.

"I think you both need one more round. Resisting a woman's hot, soaking cunt to have a dry fuck of a wife is surely more delusional than I originally thought." She speed-walks to the circuit board behind us.

And my eyes snap open.

Meridei shoves the clothes back in our mouths as I scream.

She's seriously punishing us because he won't fuck her? Desperation claws at me to find a way out of this. Can I travel again in this weakened state? Can I open that unpredictable Nightlung to send us home?

Prongs on my temples. Electrodes smear the jelly on my skin. And a white blinding heat fills my head. I have no control over the thrashing that comes next. Against the restraints, I jerk like a wild animal. There is no time. It's gone. Dissolved. Blackened from a wretched moment of eternity where this suffering never ends.

Then a crushing emptiness fills the burn.

My bladder empties, saturating my gown with a spreading heat. The raw eggs bursts from my esophagus, spewing from my lips with a faint mixture of bile. I gasp and release a surge of fresh tears.

All that's left is confusion.

As they take us away, I can hear Niklaus whisper, "Tell me your name."

Sapphire S Valdawell.

But there isn't much else. I'm surrounded by locked doors, checkerboard floors, and screams that erupt violently across this vicinity. Drool hangs from my lips and chin. How did I get here? Why am I in so much pain?

Tell me your name.

I am Sapphire S Valdawell.

I am Sapphire S Valdawell.

I am Sapphire S Valdawell.

Someone...please help me.

38. Mother May I

Sapphire

There are so many gaps. Too many to keep track of. But there are two things I'm certain of.

I have lost a significant amount of weight in the last two weeks. Between the laxatives and eggs yolks, I'm merely a husk of the woman I was. It can't be healthy to lose weight this quickly. In fact, I can tell a difference in the weight of my bones, the thickness of my hair, and the glow to my skin. Everything is dull. Cloudy. Grim and gray.

We've endured the electroconvulsive therapy two more times. I can't recall anything. If it's morning or night, if I've had my raw eggs or not. It's all a terrifying blur of information.

The wall next to my head bangs once. I knock back.

Niklaus started doing this after his first escape attempt, I think. They had to start sedating him. Not me though. The malnutrition, seizures, and frequent fainting spells keep me from having any energy at all to be a problem for them. In fact, and I don't know this for sure, the combination of these symptoms has left me feeling detached from the Nightlung. Not that I necessarily felt connected to it before this, but there's a loss there. It used to feel like I was able to run my fingers along the windowsill, the glass panes, I just couldn't figure out how to undo the latch.

Now, there's no window. No exit. No seeping darkness that lingers, dragging behind me like a long cloak.

I bet my father would laugh in my face. Oh, how disappointed he would be in my inability to be like him at all. To escape whenever he pleased.

"Up you go," Meridei instructs, lifting her eyes from the clipboard to study the scale I'm stepping onto. "Oh. Look at you."

I look down at the number. A visceral sickness purges from my stomach into my throat. *My god, I'd have to be missing actual organs to lose this much weight.*

"I am *very* impressed," Meridei says, though she jots on her clipboard with a flat, bored expression. "Are you famished? I have seen women perish from losing this much weight… Maybe an extra bowl of oats this morning?"

I am obscenely hungry. But the thought of shoveling food in my mouth makes me want to gag. The bland oats with their lumpy texture, the runny yolks, the sour aftertaste of vomit that has singed the back of my throat. *I never want to eat anything again.*

I step off the scale with shaky knees. Each movement feels like I'm dragging chains. Like I'm wading through tubs of oil.

Meridei examines my wilted stance with clinical eyes. "We'll skip the enema today as well."

Thank goodness.

I've been violated, cleansed until I'm raw and empty. The enemas now have the ability to send me spiraling into panic attacks before they're inserted. It's the anticipation—the burn, the humiliating position of being on all fours with my gown lifted and my panties at my ankles. And, of course, after it's removed—I'm drained of the fluids that kept me moving at all.

"Would you like to rest today?" Meridei asks, a rare sensitivity to her voice.

I nod. "Yes."

I'd like to rest for days. I'd like an extra blanket because I'm so cold all the time. I'd like more water. I'd like music to drown out the sounds of the screaming and sobbing coming from the other rooms.

I want to know if my mother and father are here.

I want to scream for Patient Thirteen to free me. To save me. I want to call out for my dad and tell him who I am. Tell him what they've done to me in here. I want to know that he'll avenge me the way he'd avenge my mother.

"Maybe tomorrow." Meridei brushes my hair away from my face. "Today is your next dual treatment."

"No." The air deflates from my lungs. "Please. No more shock therapy…"

Sometimes my body still convulses when I'm alone. Right before I fall asleep, the phantom of an aftershock hits me before I can escape to my dreams. My memory already comes in pieces lately. I've lost entire days. Conversations end before I even realize they've begun. It's as if someone has taken a blade to my thoughts, poking holes and tearing them to unrecognizable shreds. I'm not myself anymore. I'm all alone. I don't even remember the last time I saw Niklaus.

"And what will you give me if I postpone your electroconvulsive therapy for a while?" She tilts her head curiously.

"Anything." I have to keep whatever is left of my memories.

"Hmm." Meridei shrugs, knocking on the asylum door to let in the orderlies. "Today is your Matrimony Method therapy. I'm rather excited for it."

My shoulders sag, and I let the orderlies guide me away from the scale and out of the room. With my elbows pointed outwards, they're practically carrying me to the treatment room as I have no strength to walk myself on my quivering legs for too long.

"Also, have I told you we'll have a special guest observing today?" Meridei asks me as she smooths the shiny black hair on top of her head.

"No," I say.

"I don't allow guests to observe often, but I trust you and your husband implicitly," she replies with a smile that only effects the bottom half of her face.

And I really don't care.

But the energy I have to tell her that is nonexistent.

The orderlies set me down on a metal chair located in the center of the white treatment room. My shackles cuffed to the metal arms, which is silly. Do they not know that I'm not even close to being strong enough to fight back?

I glance to my right at the tall pole next to me. A skinny needle connected to a tube is poked into the inside of my elbow. Meridei tsk-tsks. "*Oof.* I almost couldn't find a vein. You're quite dehydrated."

Something clean and cold flushes past my nose and face, internally.

"A bit of saline," Meridei narrates.

The door opens again, and her head pops up. "Did you lower his dose of sedation to what I added in his chart?"

The orderlies nod.

"Good. I want him a little more alert for this, but still not strong enough to attempt another escape."

I lock eyes with those deep, bottomless blue irises I've spent my entire life hating. Though this ward reeks of despair, loneliness, and antiseptic—his eyes cut through it all. He's clouded and sleepy, but still sharp and aware.

The orderlies cuff him to his chair, though there are extensions to give him extra slack and room to move.

There's a beat of silence as he adjusts in his seat. And we've never locked eyes this long. Something shakes loose in my chest. A sense of relief. Familiarity. Comfort. A flicker of hope at the way he looks pained to see me this way. I know it can't be a pretty sight. I looked into my own reflection once, yesterday, I think…and I was horrorstruck by the sight of my hollowed cheeks, pale skin, and brittle hair. I was witnessing my body transform from healthy to a corpse.

There's something dehumanizing about it. Letting someone control my nutritional intake, dangling me right over the brink of death.

"I am so glad we have finally made it to this treatment," Meridei announces proudly.

But he's still looking at me. There's an apology in his gaze. A message for me to unravel. That he tried to escape. He tried to break me out before it got this bad.

I breathe through the blinding emotion that he's triggering in my soul. It's forming a lump in my throat and burning my eyes.

"Hey!" Meridei snaps her fingers in front of Niklaus's face.

He blinks, then drags his focus to her scolding expression. If looks could kill…

"When I speak, I want all eyes on *me*. I know you're impressed with my work now that your wife is suddenly so thin, but we still have an unreasonable amount of work to do. Understood?"

Niklaus glares at Meridei long enough to make her shift on her feet.

"*Continue*," he says coldly.

Meridei crosses her arms. "Before we begin this special exposure therapy, I have a special guest that I want you both to be on your best behavior for."

A woman steps into the room wearing not only a white patient gown, but a robe and slippers to match. My eyes fixate on her hair before her face. It's the most gorgeous head of hair I've ever seen. Thick, long, blue-black hair down to her lower back. Large, wavy curls that unwind in loose spirals down past her ribs.

"My mother will be released from the female ward in a few days. It's been really more of a retreat and a lady-doll refresher for her since being checked-in. I thought this would be the perfect way to cheer her up!" Meridei holds her hand out to her mother, waving for her to stand by her side.

The woman strides over to her daughter, short, bony, and so pale I can see her blue veins as if her skin is see-through. She has Meridei's face too.

The mother grabs her daughter's hand lovingly, eyeing Niklaus a little too long.

"Hello, I'm Meridei's mother!" She gives me a disgusted glance, then gazes adoringly back at Niklaus, tapping her finger to his bicep.

I sag in my chair and roll my eyes.

"My name is Apple May."

39. The Matrimony Method

Niklaus

Where have I heard that name before?

"Fairly simple guidelines here. Mrs. Valdawell, if you're pulse and saliva production increase at these photographs of delicious meals, there will be very unpleasant consequences from this IV I've hooked you up to. If not, your husband may pleasure you how *I* see fit," Meridei explains, still holding her mother's hand.

My stomach drops.

"What?" Sapphire's dark, sleepy eyes widen.

"Don't get too eager! Most patients have difficulty getting past the initial stage of correction from the excitement of food."

What the fuck?!

My world is lagged from the days of sedatives Meridei has kept me on. I've slept so much, eaten very little, and fought endless to try and escape to find Sapphire. But I wasn't prepared to see her look like this. And now Meridei wants me to do what to her? *Pleasure* her?

"This treatment…" Sapphire clears her throat, blinking as if her eyeballs are covered in glue. "This treatment is not necessary. I swear I will never eat those foods again."

There's a hint of truth to her statement. And there's something agonizing about that.

Apple May chuckles pretentiously, patting her daughter's shoulder with the back of her hand.

"Be that as it may, Mrs. Valdawell. But your lack of intimacy with your husband is a separate issue altogether. Your gluttonous ways have caused you to neglect your wifely duties. That alone has given both of you intense delusional disorders. We can't let that go untreated."

The fucking logic passing through her brain is comical!

Sapphire locks eyes with erratic nerves splintering her composure.

"I will be a good wife to him, I promise. I will perform all of my wifely duties. Won't I, darling?" Sapphire's eyes start to water as she looks to me for support.

I glare back at Meridei. "Sapphire is a wonderful wife. She—she already pleases me daily. This is pointless."

Apple May clucks her tongue. "Look at him! He doesn't know what he's saying. Positively feverish. Probably built up with too much semen."

Jesus Christ.

"This is all a misunderstanding," I say to Meridei, ignoring her idiot mother.

Meridei shifts on her heels, considering my appeal. At first glance, she seems so level-headed, so well-balanced, but deep down—I know she feasts on our desperation like the manipulative, sadistic psychopath she really is.

My attempt was a losing battle. But I had to try, for Sapphire's sake.

"Let's begin." Meridei grins.

Apple May takes a seat in the corner of the room as Meridei holds out a photograph with one hand and feels Sapphire's pulse with the other.

Sapphire becomes a statue, lowering her eyes to the photograph without showing any kind of physical response.

Come on, Spitfire. You've got this.

"Pulse went up," Meridei comments, then swiftly sticks her fingers in Sapphire's mouth, index finger jabbing under her tongue. "Salivating."

Sapphire squeezes her eyes shut in defeat and my heart twists in my chest.

"What an unreliable method," I growl.

Meridei shoots her dark eyes to me. "Reliable enough."

Well-rehearsed fingers inject a syringe into the IV tube, and I have to hold my breath. She said there will be unpleasant consequences. I've seen Sapphire suffer during our time with Absinthe and Albatross. I really don't want to bear witness to this again. I don't have the strength to see her cry.

"Oh god." Sapphire doubles over in her chair, hands clutching her stomach as she winces in pain. Her whimpers are all I hear as they flow freely from her lips. "Make it stop. *Please!*"

"I want you to associate those intense stomach cramps with—"

Meridei is cut off as she rushes to place the metal pail in front of Sapphire as she heaves into it, emptying her stomach of the only meal she's had. Raw eggs.

I look away and grind my teeth so hard, I almost crack into my enamel.

Two splashes hit the bottom of the bucket.

"There it is." Meridei coos, holding Sapphire's hair out of her face. "Get it out."

Sapphire whines through a tearless sob.

"Wormwood concentrate. It's not fun, is it, Mrs. Valdawell?" Meridei adds.

I'll fucking slit her throat for this.

Apple May claps her hands from the corner of the room, bouncing off her seat. "Now for my favorite part!"

My rage eats through the sedatives coursing through my veins.

"Patient Three, you may please your wife now, and the pain will stop." Meridei readies another syringe.

I blink three times with my mouth open. "What?"

"Finger her. *Now*."

An orderly shoves me to my feet. I whip my head to look at him, shocked that I was unaware any men were in this room. He extends my shackles like an elongated leash for a dog.

I look down at Sapphire who is wincing in agony, possibly unaware that this command is even being made of me.

"No," I respond, balling my fists in front of me. "She isn't well."

Meridei's demented eyes light up from the challenge.

"She'll be even worse for much longer if you refuse your marital obligations."

I shoot my stare down to Sapphire, so small and frail in her chair, wrapping her thin arms around her stomach as she dry heaves again. For a few long seconds, I wait for her to tell me what to do. I wait for consent. For anything that tells me what the right thing is to do.

"Alrighty! Next dose of wormwood coming up!" Meridei fills another syringe from a glass vial.

"No!" I shout, fighting the vertigo caused by the sedatives that sways my standing position. "Okay. What do you want me to do?"

Apple May and Meridei laugh in unison. "Haven't you ever fingered your wife?"

I'm going straight to hell.

With cautious steps toward the woman I grew up tormenting, I approach as if she'll tell me to stop. I pause between each movement toward her, hoping she'll ease my indecisiveness. I thought about what it would be like to touch her so many times. I've fantasized about her against my better judgment. I've hated myself for picturing what her body would look like without clothes. And now? I can't stomach doing this. But I also couldn't forgive myself for letting her writhe in pain for God knows how long.

"Slide her panties down to her ankles first," Meridei sing-songs condescendingly. Apple May giggles behind me.

What do you think, Spitfire? Would it turn you on more if I snapped Meridei's neck in front of you?

Sapphire's knuckles turn white as she bites her palms into the edge of the waste bucket. A thin layer of sweat glistens over her forehead, soaking into her strawberry-blonde hairline. Her groan echoes into the sloshing pail.

I feel like a monster for this.

I am so sorry, Spitfire.

My shackles clank to the floor as I kneel in front of her chair.

"I'm going to make the pain stop, okay?" I murmur to her gently, placing a warm hand over her chilled ankle to get her attention.

Those piercing heterochromatic eyes blink up at me through a wall of tears. Pleading. Begging. Praying for my words to be true. She nods her head.

I lean closer to whisper. "You can hate me for a lot of things, Spitfire, but please don't hate me for this."

Sapphire nods again, grasping her core as she writhes again.

Goddamn it.

My breath grows heavy and loud as I slide my hand up the inside of her thigh, my fingertips meeting her panties. *Just do it. Don't think about it. It's a task you have to complete. It's an assignment. That's all.*

With my knuckle, I shift the fabric to the side. And not surprising in the slightest, I discover she isn't anywhere close to being wet. I sigh, feeling like a pig for what I'm about to do. I push two fingers in my mouth, wetting the skin and returning them back between her legs. I won't do this to her dryly. It'll hurt and be uncomfortable. Regardless, I'm nauseated by the act. Doesn't matter if I'm relieving her pain. Doesn't matter if she nodded her head. This is fucked up.

As I push my middle finger inside her, the warmth rushes around my skin, sending tingles up my arm. In my periphery, I watch Meridei slowly inject another syringe, to which Sapphire lowers her bucket to the floor, sliding it away from her chain.

Her entire body softens, and she drops her head back as I curl and uncurl my finger.

Sapphire permits a rush of air to leak from her lungs.

"Make her feel good or this happens again," Meridei barks.

I clench my jaw, gazing up at Sapphire to tell her something with my eyes. Tell her I'm sorry for having to do this. Tell her to relax and enjoy what I'm about to do so Meridei refrains from giving her more of that wormwood concentrate crap.

She blinks once, tilting her hips up for me to get a better angle. And I let my thumb slip over her clit, massaging in small circles until I hear a small, sweet whimper. Her cunt clenches and unclenches around my knuckle. A brief pulse, so I keep going, fighting the dark sensation of my own pleasure growing as her pulse hammers into my hand.

"Good. Let's start again," Meridei exclaims, snapping her

fingers for the orderly to yank me back to my chair.

With my fingers still wet, I clench my hand into a fist and glare under lowered lids, trying to catch my breath.

Meridei props Sapphire's weak body upright. "Another photograph. Then if you don't have a reaction—"

"You said if I pleased her, she wouldn't have to do that again!" I raise my voice, wrapping my hands around my restraints and jerking them in frustration. The chain leash claps the floor behind me, causing the orderly to stumble forward.

"I said no such thing." Meridei glances over at her mother in amusement. And to my horror, Apple May has just finished touching herself.

"She's had *enough*," I growl.

Meridei watches me for several seconds, unearthing my patience with a twitch of her lips.

"And I think we are just getting started," she says harmoniously.

I can't watch her go through that again. I'll lose my mind. I'll get us both in trouble by having a meltdown and picking a fight in this drunken, sedated state with the orderlies. *Think, Niklaus, think! You aren't from this time. That has to be some kind of an advantage, right? Think!*

I fumble through sluggish thoughts as she refills another syringe. And it hits me…

"You inject her again, and I'm going to have to tell Patient Thirteen what you've done," I say in a low, threatening tone.

Meridei's head snaps up, and she leans forward, wondering if she heard me right. That's definitely a reaction I was looking for.

"I beg your pardon?"

"Patient Thirteen," I repeat.

"You don't know what your talking about. The current resident of that room is Skylenna Ambrose." Meridei laughs humorlessly. "You know nothing about Patient Thirteen. No one does!"

"His name is Dessin. Did you know that?" I taunt.

Sapphire's tired gaze bounces from me to Meridei, probably praying I can buy her more time with this bit.

"How could you possibly know that?" A vicious edge laces her words.

"I know more than you think. And unfortunately, I'm going to have to tell him if you make my wife sick again."

Meridei lowers the syringe. "A pathetic bluff pretending like you know him personally."

"You don't think I do?" I raise an eyebrow. "Darling wife, hasn't Dessin been saying how much he enjoyed poisoning Meridei at her dining party that one time?"

Sapphire's eyes awaken slightly. She nods once.

"You remember that don't you, Meridei? Spewing vomit across your dining room floor? Swimming in your fellow conformists' bodily fluids all night?"

Apple May jumps to her feet. "Does he really know that awful, crazy man, Meridei?"

But Meridei is speechless. Meridei drops the glass vial of wormwood concentrate. Meridei looks from wall to wall of this gruesome treatment room for a solution to this current predicament she's found herself in. Because I have found her nerve, exposed and isolated, and I have struck it.

"Even if this was all true, you are a patient now. You don't have the capability to send Patient Thirteen a message!" Meridei shouts, stomping her foot with a face that's pinched and flushing pink.

I mentally flip through the Emerald Lake Asylum textbooks we were assigned to read in my teenage years. I used to find the information so useless, so redundant. Now, I'm grateful for the knowledge I wield against this bitch.

"The orderly behind me? His name is Jeremiah. His wife calls him Jere-Jere. He can't go more than an hour without sneaking a sip from his flask of vodka. Two years ago, he caught you standing over a patient you drowned in a treatment, right? He helped you resuscitate him and never told Suseas that you had no intention of bringing him back."

I stare at her as a cluster of emotions strengthens my voice.

"That patient's name was *Chekiss*. How would I know that if I didn't have an entire network of employees here that would happily give a message to Patient Thirteen for me? Go ahead. Call my bluff."

"We have to continue—the treatment." Meridei gulps.

"Hmm. You see, I don't think we do. That unreasonable fear

that's been twisting around inside your head lately? That Patient Thirteen will do something this horrific all over again? That fear isn't so unreasonable after all. Why? Because you and I both know that Dessin has escaped."

I stand despite the orderlies clawing at my back to sit back down. But I can't. I have to get this last part out. I have to plant the seed. I have to get Sapphire out of here.

"And. He. Knows. Where. You. Live."

Meridei shudders before she slams her hands down on the tray of vials and syringes behind Sapphire's head. "Fine! They sleep in here tonight. Think about the threats you've made and how it keeps you from a warm, comfortable bed tonight!" she screams at me.

With a furious swipe of her hands, the glass and needles hit the floor.

And they're gone. No more orderlies. No more Apple May. No more Meridei.

It's me and Sapphire.

We are finally alone.

40. "I am not Skylenna Ambrose."

Niklaus

I'm up before the door can click shut. Quickly surveying the IV bag, her arm, the shackles around her wrist.

"I'm going to leave the IV in, okay? It's giving you fluids you need," I tell her.

But as Sapphire nods, I'm frozen in place by her features. The dark shadows under her cheekbones. The bruised-look around her eyes. Skin dry and ashen.

With one finger, I lift her chin to get a better look.

There are still tiny drops of tears clinging to her eyelashes. And that look she's giving me. Fuck, that *look*. It's a crucifixion within my chest. An inexorable ache that spills through me like a slow bleed. She's so sad, so hopeless, so disappointed in herself.

"What'd they do to you, Spitfire?" My voice breaks.

Sapphire

Niklaus is kneeling in front of me again, holding my chin up, and surveying the hideous aftermath of my correctional treatments over the last two weeks.

Genuine concern is a rare sight for him.

I must be dying.

But it's his question that rips something vital out of me. What'd they do to you? Because in this moment, as I try to recall everything that's happened, the memory gaps cloud my thoughts. It's a biblical fog that cloaks my suffering.

My bottom lip trembles. "I—I can't remember."

My forehead drops to Niklaus's shoulder, and I sob against his white shirt. To my surprise, he loops his hands over my head as he is restricted by the shackles. His arms wrap around my shivering body, pulling me as tight to his body as his restraints will allow. The warmth from his embrace surrounds me, it settles under my cold skin and spreads to the tip of my icy nose. This hug is so fucking comforting, it shatters me quietly.

"Come on, Spitfire, you're breaking my heart."

"I'm so scared!" I sob into his neck, words muffled. "I am so weak. I can't feel the Nightlung anymore. I'm having trouble remembering anything. I don't even know how long we've been in this place!"

It's been an eternity!

"Two weeks, I think." His big hand strokes my hair.

I shake my head. "I'm fucked up, Niklaus."

"You've always been fucked up. It's part of your charm," he murmurs with a smile.

"This is all my fault. I don't know how to get us home. My dad would have been able to figure this out. I'm just a damaged result of my parents." A thought populates in my head. "If you manage to break out of here, just leave. Don't risk your freedom to get me out!"

Niklaus pulls me an inch away by my shoulders. "If I leave, we leave. And I don't want to hear you suggest that bullshit alternative again."

With a shaky hand, I attempt to wipe my face clear of the tears.

"Besides, we haven't been using our greatest weapon in a place like this." Carefully, Niklaus massages my wrists under the shackles. "Your father manipulated the entire staff with what he knew about them. Spitfire, we are *decades* ahead of these people. We're at a huge advantage here. It's time we stop tippy toeing around trying not to make detrimental changes to the future."

I nod, but even that movement sends shooting pains through my spine.

"My head is so cloudy all the time, though. I can't think."

Niklaus slides his warm hand to the back of my neck, kneading his fingers along the places it aches. "Leave it to me, then. I swear to God I'm going to get you out of here, okay?"

The curling of his fingers sends both of our eyes locking again. Remembering what they made us do. Remembering what we had to do to save me from that hell.

"Sapphire…" He looks ashamed. Niklaus Demechnef looks *ashamed.*

"Don't."

"No, listen—"

"If you didn't do it, she was going to kill me. I know, I know that sounds dramatic—but Niklaus, I don't have any nutrition in my body. I am dying from what she's been putting me through. That woman is a psychopath. She would have pumped me with that shit until I dropped dead!" I grab the spaces on his wrist that are not covered by shackles. "You did nothing wrong. You *saved* me. You had my consent."

My words only slightly ease the tension in his furrowed brow. But not by much. I can see it in his eyes… He's going to hate himself for this for a long time. There isn't enough reassurance in the world I could give him to change that.

"Can we pick a corner of the room to lie down? I'm so tired," I say. *I'm always so tired.*

I try to stand, nodding my head in the direction of the left corner of the room.

"No. Not that one."

I pause. "What? Why?"

He shakes his head.

"Tell me," I push.

"Apple May was masturbating in that corner," he says, staring up at the ceiling.

I choke on a gasp. "I'm sorry?"

"Don't make me say it again."

I fixate on the corner and make a sour face. How did I not notice that was going on? I mean, thank God I missed that disgusting detail.

"Are you sure that's what she was doing?" I ask. His annoyed and repulsed expression is bringing back a little bit of joy to my soul.

He glares down at me. "Yep."

"Because she could have been adjusting in her seat…"

"No, she was masturbating," he says again confidently.

I laugh, draining myself of energy from the small sound. But it's worth it. Nothing beats seeing Niklaus feeling uncomfortable by a woman publicly touching herself. Especially someone's mother.

"Laugh it up."

I can't help my grin as he drags our chairs, connected to our restraints to the corner of the room. We lie on the floor and look up at the ceiling.

"It's not adrenaline," I say in a volume barely above a whisper.

Niklaus listens patiently.

"I don't know what it is… Pain? No. Fear? No. Does it happen at random? I don't know! I've been trying so hard to remember what was going on in my head before each occurrence since we've been in here. But it's all disappearing. I can't even recall the first time we traveled." I'm out of breath, and my hands shake from the exertion. But Niklaus keeps listening.

"All my life people have spoken so highly of my parents. They've told stories of their greatness. My mother ended a war with her mind. And look at me?" I ignore the tears. "I am not Skylenna Ambrose. I cannot go into the void and rewire a person's brain. I cannot drag their psyche to hell. I *can* fall through time and get stuck!"

I'm lightheaded, hungry, and angry with myself. My hands cover face as I shake uncontrollably. It's all so bad. It's all too much. I'm never going home. I'm never—

"What're you doing?" I ask.

Niklaus removes his white shirt and opens his arms to me.

"Come here."

"What?" I turn my head to get a better look at him.

"You're freezing."

I glance down at his bare chest. The symbols of tattoos. The scattering of black hair on his pecks. And he's staring down at me with that furrowed brow, not out of anger, but another complicated emotion that's laboring his breathing.

"Yes, and you're going to freeze with your shirt off," I object.

Niklaus sighs. "No, I won't. The sedatives make my skin hot."

I study his invitation cautiously, while trembling like my body is made of a block of ice. He stays perfectly still, waiting while I decide if I should lower my mental guard to accept his kindness.

"I promise not to insult you if you get over here and fall asleep on me, Spitfire."

I prop myself up on an elbow, watching my long hair drape over his arm.

"Then say my name, Niklaus," I say.

His eyebrows raise briefly. Jaw tightens. He exhales.

"Let me hold you, Sapphire."

This one sentence…it unlaces me. It leaves my lungs in a stutter. I must have been heavily armored against him this entire time. But the emotion creasing his forehead and stiffening his muscles—it makes my bones go slack, like the very frame of me could collapse in his arms. My hatred, normally so robust and volatile, is paper-thin and hollow. I should remind him of the vicious things he's said to me. The many occasions he's made me sob to my brother.

But all I can manage is a silence so vast, so fragile, it trembles between us.

"Okay," I reply.

And I tell myself it's because I am far too weak to fight with him. I'm far too beaten down to remain stubborn and sleep on the cold hard floor without a blanket. But right now, I can admit to myself that

Niklaus is more than just physical warmth in this intimate dwelling of hell on earth. He's a piece of home I've brought with me. He's a bit of comfort in this nightmare.

I curl against the man I once hated more than anything.

I fall asleep in the arms of the man who is now my refuge in this asylum.

41. The Disciple of Silver

Sapphire

I wake to Niklaus stroking my hair. The tickling sensation feels so nice, I smile and hum as chills sprinkle across my upper back. It's hard to tell if he's fiddling with my hair in his sleep or not. His fingers are precise and tender as they're utterly careful not to comb through the tangles and hurt me. A feathery light touch that sends my mind drifting in and out of euphoric sleep.

I pay close attention to the soothing rhythm of his breath. His heartbeat that thuds against my cheek. The permeating heat of his skin that forms a protective cocoon around me.

It could be the middle of the night or early morning. There would be no way to tell without windows. But I feel well-rested. Or at least, as well rested as I can be on the asylum floor, in shackles, starved, and suffering the aftereffects of extensive electroconvulsive therapy.

"I don't want to wake up," I whisper, unwilling to open my eyes and possibly remember what happened last night. Another memory gap. It's there somewhere under the surface of my scattered, worn-down thoughts. But just out of reach. Like a dream that begins to slip away from recognition after you finally wake up.

"I know," Niklaus responds in a hoarse morning voice. "We can stay asleep."

But he isn't fooling me. I can sense his lingering discomfort from this position. We're lying on the cold hard floor. Our backs are stiff and aching. Necks rigid. Muscles taut. I thought the mattress in my room was uncomfortable, but its firm build is nothing compared to this. Though he won't admit that he's in agony, will he?

"I don't remember why we're in here," I admit, small and wounded.

"Not remembering is probably for the best."

Niklaus flexes and adjusts his arm underneath me. I realize it's most likely numb, so I roll onto my side, snagging his left hand and tugging it with me so he'll roll too.

"What're you doing?" he asks.

"Readjusting so your arm can wake back up."

"Oh."

Niklaus is hesitant with where to place his other arm. He hovers it over my side, studying my shape and wondering where he belongs against me. I don't guide him or offer an appropriate placement. I wait.

After a moment, he hooks his arm around my waist, sliding his hand up my stomach between my breasts, and over my chest to pull me tighter to his body. The act is too intimate to be normal for either of us. It buzzes down to my toes as he buries his face into my hair and takes a long, dramatic breath.

The fluttering sensation reels through my fingertips. His nose nuzzling in the back of my neck dissembles me.

I may have forgotten small moments in here, but I remember who Niklaus is to me. I remember the horrors I've endured at his hands growing up. So, I must be deeply fucked in the head to be shamelessly experiencing these intense feelings from his touch.

"We're delirious, I think," I mutter, closing my eyes as the feverish bliss of being held takes hold of me.

"Why do you say that?"

"I—because." *What was the question?*

"Mmm-hmm?" He holds me closer.

"Because—I want to keep feeling this…"

Niklaus breathes against my hair, slow deliberate breaths. He thinks about this for a long moment. It's seconds longer than I anticipate, making me think I've broken the spell for him.

"It's all I've been thinking about," he finally admits.

My heart stops. I can't even take a breath.

And the door opens, disarming us of this moment, breaking my train of thought and probably losing it forever. As the orderlies collect us to return us back to our rooms, I think about how I should be relieved. Niklaus is the last person in the whole world I'd ever want to be forced into this ominous situation with. Cuddling? Traumatized? No.

But as they pull me away from him, gripping my elbows and forcing me upright like a used-up marionette, Niklaus snaps forward, restrained, the muscles in his jawline pulled tight, and a look of desperation and panic written in cursive across his face.

I'm used to that expression of boredom and annoyance toward me.

This…this isn't that.

It's a glimpse of protectiveness.

And he's never looked at me like this before.

The storm in him stirs as their hands bruise my elbows, and I'm dragged away from him like a prisoner being paraded and stoned in the streets. It's the edge of possessiveness that I'm unsure if I'm seeing right. Like these orderlies are touching something that is *his*.

In the hallway, steps away from my room—I can tell it's too early for the Intricate Section to be bustling with busy conformists and crying patients. The sun is probably just noticing the sky as it peeks over the horizon, and yet there he is.

At the end of the hall, a man I recognize immediately.

Light strands of silver on the sides of his slicked jet-black hair. A cleft chin. Five o'clock shadow. A tweed three-piece suit.

The man studies a patient file vigorously, flipping through papers and biting his lip in unshakable concentration.

My orderly fidgets with my clipboard as he takes his time unlocking my door.

My vision is blotchy with sleep and the blur of my neuropathways being distorted, yet I know him. Maybe I haven't had as many interactions with him like Niklaus in the future…but I know him. And I know he knows me.

From what I was told, he was a savant of the Crimson Kres Colony—studying the words and stories of the prophecy like a vital piece of scripture. He's Aunt Marilynn's brother and knows just as much as she does. Could that mean he will know that Niklaus and I are time travelers? Does he know and is unwilling to help us?

"Let's go," my orderlies commands, heaving my arm like a dog on a leash.

The man's head snaps up, and our eyes collide.

"Judas!" I cry out, pulling forward to reach him. "Judas! Do you know who I am?"

Judas's gaze flips back and forth between my different colored eyes—he raises his eyebrows and drops the stack of papers he was holding. And the recognition is there almost instantly. But that spark of acknowledgment quickly morphs into a look of horror.

"You know me!" I gasp, breathing hysterically, as I pull harder from my orderly, using every bit of strength I can summon without fainting. "Please, Judas! You have to help us!"

But something terribly strange takes place. Something shocking and unforgivable.

Judas quickly shakes his head at me. He kneels to gather the patient file he dropped and tries not to make eye contact.

"No," I mutter, confused, betrayed, astonished.

Is he…running from me?

"Look what they're doing to me!" I yell at him, whimpering as my orderly snatches a handful of hair, cutting into my scalp with his overgrown nails. "LOOK AT ME!"

Judas glares up at me from his kneeling position on the floor. And I can't quite tell if his eyes are watering or if it's a trick of the light.

"How…" My voice cracks. "How could you let them do this to women? Would you care if it was your sister?"

Marilynn, I whisper to him with my eyes. *If you're doubting yourself for even a second, just know that I know your family. Something I'm sure you're used to going undetected.*

"Would you care if it was your mother? Your daughter? Your wife?" Blood rushes to my head like a catastrophic dustbowl. And I have to suck in a deep breath to keep going. "Look at me, Judas! They're starving me! They're strapping me down and are forcing seizures! How much do they pay you to look away? How much will they pay you to look away from our children after us? Our grandchildren?"

Arms around my brittle ribs. A hand attempting to cover my mouth. But I scream. I give it everything I have because he's walking away. Judas is leaving. He's leaving me here!

"Goddamn it, please, *please* don't leave us here! Judas! Please, God! You know me. I'm someone's daughter." I buck and thrash, but he keeps walking, and they're dragging me away, back into my room. "Every time you look at one of those patient files, every time you witness these treatments—you are just as guilty as the hands that have held me down since I got here!"

Just as I give into my orderly and another that arrived from the screaming, I hear someone snapping their fingers. And just as I look up through my hysterical sobbing, Judas steps into my room's doorway. He holds a hand up to the men restraining me, and takes three steps over to me, leaning over to my cheek and whispers in my ear.

"Your mother is here," he says, far too quietly for an orderly to hear. "I'm so sorry. But it won't be long now."

42. Mother of Thy Serpent

Sapphire

I'm still thinking about Judas's words into the night while I crouch on the washroom floor to lather healing ointment on myself. The most recent enema and round of laxatives have left me raw and in constant throbbing pain. I hike up my panties once I'm done, and remain lying on the washroom floor, closing my eyes as the iron cools my cheek.

This room smells heavily of rust, urine, and drain grime. It echoes with groaning and jutting old pipes. And often the screams bleed through my vents, bouncing off the walls and waking me from a dead sleep.

But right now, it's quiet. Its cold floor is soothing my warm cheeks. And I'm left alone for the time being. Left to analyze my thoughts and go over my memories to ensure I'm not missing any.

"You look rather ungrateful to be here."

A woman's voice jolts me from my semi-peaceful meditation on the floor. I shoot my head up to a pair of white socks and a white patient gown and robe. The long, gorgeous black hair sends a new set of stomach cramps gurgling in my gut.

"How did you get into my room?" I ask, wincing as I try to sit up.

Apple May holds her hand over her chest, taking great offense.

"I am the Senior Conformist's *mother*."

"That's nice. Please leave."

"You're not enthusiastic to have my company?" she asks genuinely.

"No."

Her thin, nearly hairless eyebrow goes up. "My daughter was right. You are an ungrateful little bitch."

I prop myself up against the stone wall adjacent to my sink, never taking my eyes off this unhinged woman who has shown a twisted interest in me. She remains in the doorway, staring at herself in the mirror, fluffing the waves of her hair.

"What can I do for you, Apple May?" I want to argue with her so badly. It's in my nature to run my mouth until it gets me into trouble. But I used up the last of my energy on Judas, which didn't do much. I slept for hours after that encounter. And for what?

"I am bored," she says, still combing through her thick hair in the mirror.

"My condolences."

"And I am quite horny," she adds.

I drop my head against the wall with a thump. "I cannot help you with that."

"I enjoy looking at your husband."

Goodie.

"Those eyes? His hair? How do you ever stop looking at him?" she asks with a devious smile.

Easy. Niklaus says something unforgiveable to me. I'm repulsed by him. And then I can't stand the sight of him. Nothing to it.

"I was incredibly horny watching him finger you actually. It was rather arousing." She snickers into her hand, then smooths out her smile lines quickly. "Oh dear. I'm getting wet thinking about it now."

That immediate sense of danger prickles my fingertips.

"I'm trying to enjoy the post-enema bliss. Perhaps you could come back another time?" I suggest sarcastically.

But Apple May looks me up and down with thoughts circling her mind like vultures. Thoughts that should stay hidden in her head.

"Could you tell me what it felt like? His fingers inside of you?"

I shake my head.

"In *immense* detail, please."

I shake my head again.

Yet her request summons that muddled memory swimming in the murky waters of my brain. It was so confusing being in agony one moment, then instantly replacing it with powerful pleasure. I blink away the feelings that return with an upsurge of warmth between my legs.

"You know, if I were you, I'd be very nice to me," she purrs.

"Why is that?"

I wonder what would happen if I screamed for help. Would an orderly barge in and haul Apple May out of my washroom? Would they punish her for roaming the halls at night? Or does being Meridei's mother hold as much weight as she claims?

"Because I can put in a good word with my daughter. I can assuage her to, hmm—oh, I don't know—off the top of my head? Give you a break from your least favorite treatment?" Apple May twirls a wavy lock of black hair around her finger.

My eyes open wider. Electroconvulsive treatment.

"My daughter tells me you are a little scaredy cat when it comes to the shock therapy. Is that right?" She pauses, then smirks. "That's what I thought. But…if you'd rather let me suffer without giving me the proper mental images I request to absolve the crazed arousal I'm experiencing—I suppose I could tell her to *increase* your therapy."

"No!" The word half-explodes out of me.

Apple May's smugness blinds me with rage.

"Go on then. I'm waiting."

I drop my head. "His fingers were long and felt good. Okay? Good? Can I go to sleep now?"

"*Pfft*!" She throws her arms to her sides in frustration. "You could never write literature with such a lack of descriptive words! Make me feel what you felt, Patient Two, or I swear…"

"He started off pushing my panties to the side," I say with a heavy sigh. "I wasn't wet because the injection had me so nauseas. But he wet his fingers in his mouth, then slid the pads of his index and middle finger over my clit before…penetrating me."

"Oh my." Apple May slides down the washroom door, one hand on her stomach, the other massaging the back of her neck. "Continue."

I wish to God I had the strength to break one of her bones right now, but I can barely hold my own head up.

"Nik—my husband pushed his fingers in and out of me slowly, curling and gently pulsating inside me until I was very close to having an orgasm."

"*Mmmm*. Mmm-hmm, yes, *oh*." Meridei's fucking creepy mother touches herself right in front of me, on my washroom floor. Her hand moves fast and hard, like she's naturally so comfortable with masturbating in front of a perfect stranger.

Do it so you don't have to lose anymore memories, Sapphire. Please. You can do this.

"I got so wet—I was spilling around his fingers. I couldn't stop thinking about what would happen if he finished me off. If he licked my clit and…" I trail off.

Apple May's lustful eyes snap open. "And what?!"

"Nothing. Your daughter stopped him before anything could happen."

Her veiny fists pound the floor in a small tantrum. "That stupid, awful girl! I didn't raise her to be so selfish!"

I slump against the wall, relieved that Apple May's grotesque session of harassing me is over and that I won't have to keep suffering through Electroconvulsive Therapy anymore. Yes, what I had to say to this disturbed woman might haunt my nightmares like a cursed apparition for the rest of my life…but at least I'll stop fucking up my memory.

"Get up!" Apple May snatches my elbow and with shocking strength, tugs me to my feet. "Move! I do not have all night for this."

"Where are we going?"

Symptoms that could only be compared to the influenza slam into my body like a train as I stumble out of the washroom and to the exit of my room. I ache from head to toe. I'm out of breath. My eyes throb with heat. My spine is being held together by a string of pins. I look back at my hard bed longingly, desperately wishing I could crawl into it and sleep for the next twelve hours without interruption.

"Your husband's room!" Apple May knocks twice and an orderly opens the door to let us out.

"Found yourself some fresh meat tonight, Apple Sweetie?" The orderly asks in a nasally, congested voice.

Apple May feigns a gasp. "Shame on you! I'm just a delicate, Godly woman!"

"Right, right." They laugh together. "You want into Room Three?"

"Yes. Is he sedated?"

The orderly nods, stepping around us to unlock Niklaus's door.

"Asleep?" Apple May presses.

"I don't think so. We've had to keep increasing his doses over the last few days. The man builds a tolerance quickly, and it takes five of us to hold him down."

God, Niklaus.

A swell of pride briefly replaces the ache in my bones. I should have known he'd keep fighting back. No matter how much they sedate him, Niklaus Demechnef is a fucking killer through and through. For once in my life, I'm thankful to have him on my side.

"But he should be fairly easy for me to play with?" She pokes the orderly's side with a sheepish giggle.

"Yes, dear. He should be a good little toy for you to ride tonight."

The door opens, and I'm drilled with the instinct to protect Niklaus. To cause this woman irreversible pain. Does she plan on assaulting him? Is she going to make me watch? A stroke of irate flames licks the inside of my chest as Apple May shoves me into his room.

The door clicks shut behind us.

Niklaus doesn't say anything as he sits up from his bed. And my stomach turns sour as I note that he's restrained to the bed. But as his alert gaze shifts from Apple May to me, he only seems concerned as to why her nails are digging into my arm.

"I can only imagine my daughter did not let you two finish what you started because she's been so overworked dealing with that woman she used to work with in the thirteenth room. Sky-something!" Apple May releases her vicious grip on my elbow and kicks me in the back toward Niklaus. I land on my knees in front of his bed, hissing at the zap of pain that crackles up my femurs. Niklaus tries to stand to catch me, tendons corded under his chin as the leather straps cut into his wrists. A guttural sound rumbles in his throat. He snaps his head up to stare at Apple May, and it's as if the room shrinks to nothing but the deep, endless violence in his stormy blue eyes.

"Now, your wife pushed me right to the edge of my orgasm with the vivid description of your fingers inside of her. It was exquisite, but I wasn't able to reach my climax because you two were robbed! *Argh*! My stupid, imbecile of a daughter!"

I drop my eyes to the floor feeling the weight of Niklaus now staring down at me.

"I'm sorry, you had my wife do what now?!" Niklaus remains calm, but each syllable is clipped as if he might explode if he lets his words out too fast.

The word snags in my chest. *Wife*.

"I had her give me a detailed recount of you performing your marital duties to finger her. It was just what I needed," Apple May explains.

"Why?" Niklaus is quiet. He doesn't yell, but that's because fury lives in the weight of his tone.

Apple May blinks a few times. "I couldn't sleep."

I'd laugh if this weren't so fucked up.

"You are fucking crazy," Niklaus says.

"Pot kettle, baby." Meridei's mother flips her hair over her shoulder. "Back to business. I need you two to finish so that I might be able to finish. Understand?"

I scramble toward the bed, scared and desperate to reach Niklaus. I have a bad feeling. This insane woman has something up her sleeve, and I need to tell him this before it's too late.

My weak hands find Niklaus's shoulders, and I pull my lips to his ear.

"Whatever she forces us to do, you have my consent, okay? Whatever we need to do to survive this—you have it, okay?" I whisper frantically, eyes growing misty as he stares back at me. I'd never hold any of this against him. We're in a place we've only ever read about like a scary folklore story.

The Emerald Lake Asylum has come back to life.

And it's claimed us as it's forgotten son and daughter. Anything that happens in this place—anything we have to do—it's for survival. Nothing more.

Niklaus stares back into my eyes. "You've always had mine."

I'm stung in the side of the neck. The bite is small, pointy, sharp. It's a poke that stays in place for several seconds before a sudden release.

I wince, and Niklaus's face darkens before his focus cuts to a space over my shoulder.

"What did you do to her?" Niklaus snarls.

"Oh relax, gorgeous. She's going to thank me for this modest boost in a moment," Apple May chimes, clapping her hands together in a manic uproar of excitement.

I sink to the floor, but Niklaus extends himself as much as he can to keep me close to him. With a few blinks, I almost smile at him in respite. I don't feel anything. Was it supposed to be poison? Something to make me sick again?

"Spitfire?"

"I'm okay. I'm fi—"

A blast of heat spreads from my lower belly to the sensitive space between my legs before I can finish my sentence. I feel betrayed by my own body. It leaves my legs trembling and my back arching.

"Hey. Look at me." Niklaus dips his head to get my attention. "Talk to me. What's going on?"

My mouth falls slack, and I wage a war in my head to regain control. To ignore that flutter, that bizarre stirring inside me to be touched. To touch him.

I can't hide it either. My breathing is heavy and loud. My thighs pinch together as I begin rolling my hips and undulating around air. It feels so good to chase this feeling, to squirm and grip the sheets on Niklaus's bed.

"I—"

My pulse stammers as I finally look up at him through heavy lids. And *fuck*, how did I not see it before? How did I not realize how handsome he is? That serious look on his face. The way his scorching, infinitely blue eyes track my every move. I reach out and touch his facial hair. The prickly texture charges me with a typhoon of electricity. *Oh god!* I want to feel it against my lips. I want to kiss his cheek, his jaw…

"Your eyes are saucers, Sapphire." Niklaus goes pin straight and stares at Meridei's mother with ferocious distain. "Give her something to make this stop!"

"You should be thanking me, ungrateful man," Apple May hisses.

I whimper pathetically, running my hands up and down my thighs as I try to relieve the downpour of arousal being pumped into every cell of my body.

Niklaus glances down at me, pinching his eyebrows together, and exhaling loudly through his nose.

Is he angry with me? I don't want to upset him. Have I done something wrong?

"Niklaus, I'm sorry…" I pant, continuing to grind against nothing.

"You're sorry?"

"You're mad at me. Please, tell me how to make you feel good. Don't be mad. Please!" I'm desperate. Hungry. And I haven't an ounce of dignity to keep me from begging.

"I'm not mad at *you*." He looks down at me again as I wedge myself between his knees. His gaze darkens once more, and he curses.

Apple May is suddenly kneeling next to me. "Didn't it feel good when he fingered you, Mrs. Valdawell?"

I nod like an eager puppy, bouncing up and down.

"Mmm-hmm, I thought so. Don't you want to touch him now? Make your husband feel *so* good too?"

"*Yes!*" I moan excitedly. "Yes, I want to make my husband feel good."

"Prove it to him. Touch a place on his body you've been dying to feel all day," Apple May suggests.

My eyes redirect to Niklaus's stomach. Without another thought, I do as she says. My hands slip under his white shirt, and I run my fingers over his warm skin. I moan loudly as his strong abdominal muscles flex and harden.

Desire floods my veins and makes my vision vibrant and vivid.

"Christ," Niklaus says. His knuckles turn white, and I can't tell if he's holding his breath or just not moving.

"How does that feel?" Apple May asks.

"So warm. I want him so badly."

I flash my pleading gaze up to Niklaus, and every emotion whirls through me. His stare unearths me. It's my safe place. My home. I never want to stop looking at him.

"Apple May." My husband raises his chin in defiance. "I am *begging* you. Please, don't make her do this. You want me? Fine. Control me. Not her."

Apple May taps her fingers to her chin. "I'll tell you what. Mrs. Valdawell? Why don't you run your hands over your husband's cock? While his pants are still on of course. If he isn't hard for you, I'll put an end to this right now. When I inject you with a special counter drug, you won't feel this strange burning desire anymore. Okay? Fair enough?"

My heart rate picks up as I feel terror at the idea of this ending. Of Niklaus not being hard for me. Not experiencing any type of arousal to my touch, to my waist pressing between his knees. But as my attention falls to his pants, my mouth begins to water.

"That. Isn't. Fair," Niklaus whispers in a gravelly, unwell voice.

I'm no longer listening, because as my quivering hand lowers, I make contact with his hard cock. It twitches under the light weight of my hand. A new burst of endorphins explodes in my veins because he groans with me, enveloped in this shared euphoria.

"*Ahhh*. Wouldn't his cock feel so nice in your mouth, Mrs. Valdawell?"

"Yes. Oh, yes." I hardly notice Apple May touching herself as I fumble to unzip his pants.

"Wait. *Fuck*, Spitfire…" Niklaus wraps his hands around mine, momentarily stopping me in my tracks.

"He's right, eager little girl. You can't just have whatever you want. You need to tell him how badly you want it. Beg your husband for his cock."

It takes several moments for her words to reach my brain. Because his hands are holding mine. The delicious warmth from his palms spreads into my ice-cold fingers. I want to kiss them, I want them under my gown, feeling my breasts.

"Mrs. Valdawell!" Apple May scolds irritably. "Beg your husband to lick his cock."

"Please, baby. Please, *God*, I need you to fill my mouth!" I rock back and forth impatiently, a little surprised at myself because I've never called him that before. "I'll be so good for you. I'll swallow and take all of you. I promise. Please I'll make you feel so good!"

"So help me God, Spitfire…" Niklaus groans, dropping his head back with an aggravated exhale. "Yes. Okay. Fuck."

Bliss fires through every pathway in my brain, and I unzip his pants, nearly crying in delight as his long cock stands up for me. I act on instinct, running my tongue from base to tip, savoring the taste of his skin.

Niklaus's pulse races and so does his breathing.

This spurs me on. I lick again and again, making a mess as I begin to drool from the hunger building. I'm insatiable, ravenous, *feral*. Each move he makes from the pleasure of my touch is another concentrated dose of ecstasy for me. It's as if his reactions control my puppet strings. He moves, I move. He moans, I moan.

"You are so beautiful," Niklaus murmurs as if he's in pain. "I am so sorry, Spitfire."

"Enough teasing! I want to see you suck it." Apple May snaps her fingers.

I look up at Niklaus from under my eyelashes and slide my mouth over the tip of his cock, desperate to do this however he wants it done. I want to please him so badly, I could come without being touched if he comes in my mouth.

Niklaus growls, and I know I've summoned the animal in him. Despite the war waging behind his eyes, he wants this. He's given in to how good my wet mouth feels as I suck more and more of him past my lips.

"Oh yes! Atta girl. This is far more erotic than the patients I've done this to in the infirmary!" Apple May's voice gets higher as she shakes her hand faster, getting closer to climax.

…than the patients in the infirmary.

Wait. I know this woman, don't I?

Hey, Ruthie, didn't you have a run-in with her mother?

It was a conversation at our last family dinner.

Apple May, yes.

You did?

At the infirmary during my recovery. She really had it out for me.

The cosmic darkness that used to rest under my thoughts like a sleeping giant, resurfaces at this memory. The part of me that can travel through time. I thought it died from the torture and electroconvulsive therapy. But it stretches its wings, and slowly, it begins to eat away at whatever Apple May injected me with. I remove my mouth from Niklaus to get a better look at her.

"I did not say you could stop!" she gasps.

"You've been a patient at the infirmary…"

She tormented me a few times, said Aunt Ruth.

The family dinner conversation ricochets around my head.

Aunt Ruth clawed Apple May's eyes out with her thumbs.

With a new pulse of energy, I'm able to care again. To feel the venomous fangs of anger.

A black, boundless flame burns away the rest of the drug coursing through my system. It manifests into an entity that possesses me, full of hatred and the unbearable need to protect those I love. And I gain tunnel vision right on Apple May.

"I think I've had enough," I tell her. Cold. Expressionless. Empty.

"You want him, Patient Two! You *need* him!" Apple May shrieks, revving herself up into a childish tantrum. "Please your husband! It is your duty!"

The air in the room is sucked from existence as the quietness grows loud.

"One day, many years from now, you're going to hurt someone I love."

Beside me, Niklaus covers himself, straightening his back. I can sense he put the pieces together just as I have.

"You insane little girl! You're more delusional than I once thought! My daughter would love to hear how disobedient you have been, and how your mental diseases have completely overtaken your mind!"

I rise to my feet. "You should spend as much time with your daughter as you can, Apple May."

"I beg your pardon?" She stands, not coming anywhere close to my height, but trying her best to stand tall to intimidate me.

"Her days are numbered," I say, detached, dissociated, disconnected from the weakness my body has known for so long now.

Before this psychotic mother can open her mouth again. I take a vulturine step toward her. "Somehow, I don't think Meridei's fate will harm you as much as you deserve."

I remember the pain in Aunt Ruth's eyes as she recalled the time she spent with Apple May. The way she spoke about the aftermath of the war. How she clearly didn't want to tell my mother what happened to her in that infirmary. She didn't want Mom to hold the guilt of not being there for her best friend.

"The injection should have lasted another hour!" Apple May holds a stern finger up to me. "My daughter will make you *bleed* for approaching me with such disrespect. I am an Emerald Wife. You'll wish you were dead when she's through with you."

"You made me do intimate acts with a man I've known my entire life," I whisper. And for some reason, it's as if I'm attempting to convince myself to not unleash something so dark, so sinister, so positively ferocious…it goes far beyond feminine rage. A beast whose hunger won't end once it's tasted freedom—because I know that once it's been released from its cage, there will never again be a world untouched by what comes crawling out.

She was an incredibly vain woman, Aunt Ruth recalled.

The breath between us curdles into earsplitting silence. And Apple May takes a step back, her confident sneer faltering as she sees something sacrilegious, hideous, blasphemous, petrifying spread like a contagion—a black fog from my pupils.

And Niklaus sees it too. "Spitfire…"

"Her name is Ruth. I want you to remember that name."

She was an incredibly vain woman.

She was an incredibly vain woman.

She was an incredibly vain woman.

She was an incredibly vain woman.

She was an incredibly vain woman.

She was an incredibly vain woman.

The Nightlung crackles from my fingertips as I heave forward, sinking my nails into Apple May's scalp until I'm certain the moisture touching my skin is her blood. That dark, stunning head of flawless hair shines to me like a beacon. Her screams sing to me, serenading me with that precious tune of terror. I don't care that her arms punch and flail hard enough to leave bruises across my entire upper body. I can't even feel it.

And as I drink in her vanity, her constant habits of devilish sins, I let that bond between the Nightlung and the void blast through every pore, every cell, every nerve until it burrows into one targeted area. Apple May's beautiful black hair.

Just as the Nightlung gives me the path to travel forward or backward through time, it also gives me another vessel to explore. It gives me a magnifying glass to turn the clock forward or backward on anyone or anything.

And I choose *this*.

A catastrophic hurricane of power engulfs me, stitching into each hair folic, every pour and imperfection of her scalp. And I fast-forward *her* clock…

…by sixty years.

The black hair shortens and shrivels, becomes white brittle straw before our eyes. And as patches of her scalp become clear, that skin withers too. Sunspots, sores, and a horrid smell of decay. I push those years, magnifying all the focus on that hair until it's gone.

Nothing but white cottony clumps.

Nothing but her decaying, sun damaged scalp.

The rest of her remains young. But that hair? That scalp?

That hideous top of her head is now that of an old woman who has lived past the age of a century.

43. Calm Before the Storm

Niklaus

Son of a bitch...

I watch in shock as Sapphire's toes barely touch the ground. Her body levitates as a charge or charcoal-coated electricity plummets into Apple May's head. And she burns every strand of hair into nasty tufts of white and gray fuzz.

Apple May's screams aren't just heard throughout the asylum.

They are felt.

The cavernous, yearning, agonizing realization that the part of her body she favored the most, she spent hours a day on perfecting—is now nothing more than the head of a hag. And her pain is visceral. It's a mother mourning her dead baby. It's raw and shrill, hammering into every eardrum within a hundred yards of this room.

I want to laugh. My smile has my thoughts of amusement and glee written all over my face. But it's also all so paralyzing to witness. I can hardly breathe as I see Sapphire morph into this ethereal being. Is she still herself? Is she an entity lost to a constellation of darkness?

The urge to break free of my restraints to hold her is gutting me.

"You… you…" Apple May sobs hysterically into her hand as she screams at the fuzz tickling her fingers. "You've maimed me!"

That bald hag is crawling backward, gawking at Sapphire like she's just come face-to-face with the devil and must pay for her sins.

Sapphire goes completely still before clutching her stomach, then chest, and stumbling back. She falls into my lap, and I wrap my arms around her shivering body. Her skin is stone and a perfect sculpture of ice.

Hypothermia.

Just like her mother.

"Stay with me," I whisper, squeezing her tighter. "I'll keep you warm."

The seizures come hard and fast, curling into her spine and shaking her from the inside out. It all happens as the orderlies storm my room. They coddle Apple May as she cries and covers her head in the corner of the room. They rip Sapphire from my arms as she continues seizing.

"Wait!" I roar, reaching for them to bring her back to me. "Let her get through the seizure first. Please, God, don't move her!"

The orderlies are not gentle as they drag Sapphire from my room, leaving me alone in the dark. Leaving me with nothing but my thoughts and the memories of tonight cycling through me until they drive me insane.

Sapphire

Hours of lying in a blizzard without clothes. Without a blanket. Without any warmth at all.

It takes hours for heat to return to my limbs. For the trembling, chattering, violent jolting to finally stop. My memory stutters, stops, and restarts again. I fall in and out of sleep, accompanied by nightmares about never escaping a cage. I daydream about seeing Krimson again. About hugging my mother. About sitting next to my father's bed and telling him that it was me…I'm the one he met in that forest. I finally saw him with his eyes open.

I can't be sure, but I think everyone forgot about me in this room. Either that or I'm being punished. How long has it been since I did what I did to Apple May? Can I even be sure that actually happened and wasn't a fever dream?

They haven't brought me any food or water, so the brief periods I feel strong enough, I crawl to my washroom and drink from the faucet, cupping the running water with my hand and slurping it down.

After two or three days, I start to lose hope that I'm sane anymore.

What if this is all in my head?

What if I've been locked away for actually being mad?

What if these are all delusions of grandeur, and I've been placed in isolation?

"Krimson," I cry to myself in the corner. "Krimson, I'm so scared. I don't know what's real anymore. This place is so dark and cold. And I—I can't remember anything."

I ball my hands up and tap my knuckles against my forehead in frustration.

"Please, get Mom. You have to find me. Help me return home."

I use my patient gown to wipe my tears as I rock back and forth in the corner of the room. And the screams and racket outside my door are proof I've lost my mind completely. It's unlike the screeches I'm used to hearing through these thick walls. The noise is scattered down the Intricate Section. And the yelps are short-lived, as if someone cuts off their air supply before they've had a chance to sound an alarm. There are frantic footsteps and doors slamming so hard, I can feel the prolonged vibrations against my back.

Whispers.

Strangled breaths.

Gurgling.

A female voice screams, crying, begging. More just like that to follow after each voice fades. And one set of footsteps that is unhurried, unlike the rest that pass my door. My room is abruptly so soundless, I can tell the feet are bare. They frequently pause midstride, and within their hesitation, a *drip drip drip* fills the empty space.

The doors open.

44. The Original Puppeteer

Sapphire

One by one, all thirteen rooms unlatch.

The patients scatter.

There are a few who say thank you. There are a few who gasp and run.

I watch from my corner as their white gowns and uniforms flash across my doorway in a blur. And yet, I still can't tell if this is real or not. A trap? Meridei's way of punishing me? My hands shake uncontrollably as I wage back and forth with what I should do. Leave? Stay? Grab Niklaus and sneak out?

Krimson, I'm so fucked up. Is this real?

In my periphery, a shadow lurks in my doorway. One step, then another, and I can see the set of bare feet covered in splattered blood. The moment I see it, I am not afraid. My eyes trail up the tan feminine legs drizzled in dark blood to the white patient gown. Stringy, wet blonde hair hanging just under her ribs.

I raise my head to meet my mother's scarlet bloodshot eyes.

It takes every last drop of restraint I have not to start sobbing. Not to crawl to her. Not to hug her waist and tell her who I am. Beg my mother to bring me home. For every time she's picked me up when I've fallen out of a tree, fallen ill, or had my heartbroken—I've always been held close by my mother. I've been kissed on the head, told how loved I am, told how beautiful and strong I will always be.

And today, when I need her most, I can't do that.

"Do you remember me?" Mom asks. Her voice is low and gentle in her approach, as if she's trying not to frighten me.

My eyes fill with tears. I nod once.

Yes, Mama. I remember you.

"You've had some bad luck lately." Mom glances around my room.

I trail my eyes over her bloody patient gown. The sight slams my heart away in a metal coffin because I know what this is. The portion of her story she never liked to talk about. This is the era of her life that—

"I've had a lot of bad luck too," she says, holding out her hands that are dripping with Meridei's blood. "I guess this is my way of getting even…for all of the bad luck I've received."

She's trying to soften her voice, keep her mannerisms non-threatening to me. Though, I can see why someone might fear looking upon her face right now. From the splattered blood soaking through her gown, staining her like a grotesque baptism, to the whites of her eyes spidered with veins and the enlarged pupils, a hollowed galaxy of horrors.

But I don't care about any of these. She's still Mom.

And I don't feel that shocking sense of fear that most would.

Seeing her like this just makes me sad.

"What happened to you?" I ask, afraid to hear her say it…

The corners of her mouth twitch as if she wants to smile, to maintain the attempt not to frighten me. But her face remains stoic and detached.

"I've lost the only man I've ever loved," my mother says.

And there it is. My heart crinkles around the edges and folds in on itself. I've known this. I've read about this. But seeing her, like a villain in a massacre, step into a room I was never supposed to enter—it kills me.

She thinks my dad is dead.

And I can't even tell her otherwise. Because guess what? One day, he'll be as good as dead. He'll be in a coma my entire life. How much better does that sound?

I lift my head in understanding and the acceptance to keep my mouth shut. And before I can muster a response from my fried brain, Niklaus appears behind my mother. The whites of his eyes are pink, surrounded with heavy shadows, and his black shoulder-length hair is wavy and unkept. He looks as exhausted as I feel.

"*Shit*," Niklaus says through a breath. "Are you what happened to the hallway?"

My mother has to look up at him to meet his eyes. She doesn't answer. Doesn't even nod. Her stare is carrying so many emotions, so much heartbreak, I can feel it crushing her insides.

Niklaus flexes his jaw and turns to me, approaching my corner with caution. He kneels to get a better look at me. "Hey, Spitfire. Ready to get the hell out of here?"

I try to hold it in. I try to be strong like *her*. But the fact is, I am not like my mother. She took this entire place down and never looked back. I am about to witness it firsthand. My eyes water, and I nod my head with a quivering chin and bottom lip. But Niklaus doesn't let me fall apart here, not now. He scoops me against my chest, and I throw my arms around his neck.

"Can we leave?" Niklaus asks Mom, standing me upright.

"Yes." My mother steps out of my room. "But you should run. This place won't be standing for much longer."

Without another word, a goodbye, a second glance—Skylenna Winter Ambrose is gone, releasing an asylum of patients back into the world.

Standing is unnaturally painful. It's like trying to reshape or bend a slab of hardened concrete. I'm sore and stiff, and the thought of running down flights of stairs, out of this giant rat maze is inconceivable.

"Can you stand?" he asks, as the sound of the Emerald Lake Asylum becomes an inaudible tomb. Perfectly still. Hollow yet still breathing. Still holding the years and years of anguished memories from those who have died here. Who didn't have a mother like mine who could free them before it was too late.

Niklaus assesses my hunched stance and lack of answer. He lifts me off the ground and sprints down the hallway, like he has all the energy in the world to move us to safety. Like he was never abused with sedatives since we got here.

The stale air of the asylum blows through my hair as we descend down to the lobby. The patients have all escaped. Papers and files are scattered across the floor. Orderlies hang like puppets from the archways. Drops of blood puddle like spilled ink across the white marble floors. And moments after we reach the cool weather with smoky clouds and bustling winds, Niklaus and I hide in the tree line to watch the asylum explode into flames and a black mushroom cloud overhead.

"You said you were not Skylenna Ambrose," Niklaus says, breaking the silence with his scratchy baritone. "You said you aren't like your mother at all. You can't do what she'd done."

I take a deep breath as we take in the view of bright yellows and orange and floating snowflakes of ash.

"And you're right," Niklaus adds, tightening his hold on me. "You are not like your mother. You do not have a halo, Sapphire Valdawell. You have horns. I've never seen so much power."

I sigh and rest my head on Niklaus's shoulder. Before I can respond, one last patient exits the asylum.

My mother doesn't seem to care about her appearance drenched in blood as she walks away from the catastrophe of a crumbling landmark. Her bloody bare feet leave ominous footprints in the damp soil and wet grass as she fades into the shadows of the Emerald Lake Forest.

The sight of it tickles the tangible veil of the Nightlung. It flickers behind my eyes. First, a crisp image of daylight that blinds me. The sound of a woman screaming. The crashing of ocean waves over the top of each other. Clanking metal. Pikes of flames. Clouds of sand spraying through the briny air.

"It's him…"

Through the flashes, Vrath walks through tall grass in a horizon of evening fog. He's wearing a new painted face with fresh creases forming from his frown.

Niklaus falters in stance while holding me to his chest. The sickness creeps into my lungs, causing a slight wheeze as I suck in a deep breath.

But it doesn't stop the world from wavering to that beach, as if something in the Nightlung is seizing too. I'm not strong enough to have a showdown with Vrath here, and I'm not sure Niklaus is either.

"Del—" I can't breathe. The air dissolves from my lungs too quickly. "De—"

Niklaus looks down at me, pinching his eyes together. And then it clicks.

"Dellilian!" he roars, then clears his throat in discomfort.

Dellilian, please!

A black vein tears through the air in front of us and out comes a small implosion of fusain dust followed by a fierce Short-Haired Windila charging through the air. A show of white sharp teeth on display.

"Niklaus…" I croak. "Something—something's happening."

The vertigo is unbearable. I'm neither here nor there. The world tilts and sways like a ship on rough waters.

"Are we traveling again?" he asks.

But I can't answer. The sensation of moving into an invisible current is as hard to resist as sneezing. It's a relief to give in to the pull. I taste the salty air and am swallowed up by the sound of seagulls and the soft lapping of water.

I grip Niklaus's shirt as the darkness of the Nightlung spills over us. The terror of ever leaving him behind claws a wound into my chest more than any other time.

"Don't let go." My last words as we land in the tree line of a stage I have never wanted to see nor hear about.

My father's death.

45. "On His Head a Golden Crown, and in His Hand a Sharp Sickle."

- Revelation 14:14-16

Sapphire

From the tree line, I have the best seat in the house for my father's murder.

There is the dull roar of the ocean. The clashing of metal. And then, silence. My father's silence. On his knees. Bent forward. A sickle cracking into his spine, sinking into his right lung.

They say his mind protected itself by splitting new personalities when he was just a child. Trauma is enough to kill a person, especially when we are little. As I watch the head of my family cut down at the edge of the sea, I wonder if I'm going to split too. This has to be it. Nothing on this earth can be worse than this.

I think Niklaus says my name. Wraps his arms around my upper body.

I think my eyes dry out from not blinking.

My world goes mute as I watch my mother scream, dropping to her knees and cradling my father in her lap. How could there be so much blood? It's a river pouring over her legs.

My body shakes uncontrollably as Uncle Niles rolls through the sand and rushing water to put out his body swathed in flames. Niklaus goes tight around me. DaiSzek slaughters the soldiers still fighting. My mother never lets go of my father.

Her screams are forever. They'll survive through new eras of destruction. That pain will never go away. It will outlive us all.

"Help him! Save him!"

I'm so dehydrated. I don't know how tears have managed to wet my cheeks and drip down to my collarbone.

"I'll love you until hell freezes over."

My knees buckle. There is just—so much blood.

And it all happens so fast. They carry Niles's writhing, burned body away. My father stops breathing, stop moving. My mother listens for his heartbeat in denial. Everyone watches. Their faces twist with pity and horror. Her hands are bloody, and she stares at them as if her mind simply can't process the color. DaiSzek guards my father's body, howling like a wounded puppy.

My mother says so many things that gut me.

Things like, "Bring him back to me! We hardly had any time. His body is still warm! Please, don't be dead!"

I've never seen her like this. She's always so well put together, so poised and composed. I can't remember if I've ever seen her cry. Maybe a little sad? But she's hid it so well for her children. We've never tasted this level of anguish she's known. How has she been able to keep this from me for so long?

And eventually my Uncle Warrose comes to her side, careful not to get too close to DaiSzek. He's the only one who cracks that hard exterior, getting through her heartbreak and panic.

"I don't know how to let him go."

My uncle holds her close.

They carry my father's body away.

That patch of sand is stained in ruby red. The puddle of it seeps into the sand. And I can't look away as we stay hidden far enough away to remain undetected.

I turn to Niklaus, hiding my face in his chest like a child frightened of the monsters hidden in the shadows of her closet. I can't unhear her voice screaming. My Uncle Niles being burned alive. DaiSzek's growls. My father's body going limp.

I know it was all a setup.

But I never imagined it was so gruesome. So absolutely devastating. And my mother endured it all.

The Nightlung pulses behind my eyes, reeling me back into a sliver of an opening to another time.

And Niklaus falls with me.

46. The Executioners Game

Niles

We are forced to watch an execution once a week.

It keeps us in line. It keeps escape attempts to a minimum. It keeps trust from brewing, because too many captives are eager to tattle and receive a sweet treat for their loyalty.

My small friend, Renly, has perfected our routine at this point. He stays by my side and counts the number of times I tap my forearm with my index finger. I never actually keep track, but every time I stop and glance down at him, he mouths the number, and I make my best surprised face. Renly always smiles big, so proud of himself for always counting the right number.

And then when it's time for our fellow captive to step off the block and hang with a broken neck or long, drawn out strangulation…Renly turns into my arm and hides his face, reciting the nursery rhyme native to his colony so he doesn't hear the sound of bone snapping.

I do something similar. I go somewhere else. To a time when

Dessin invented a best friend handshake with me for my birthday. The blatant annoyance on his face can still make me smile to this day. How he kept glancing at Skylenna for moral support. I remember the sense of victory when I had to slowly gain his respect and friendship while in that prison.

"It's over, Mr. Niles," Renly whispers, tugging on my shirt.

I scan the tall onyx pillars, leafless trees nearby, and the hanging body from the executioner's block. A man, not much younger than me, with chestnut brown hair, deep smile lines, and kind eyes.

It's warm day with a lightning storm looming above. Clouds so dark, they could pass for blasts of smoke and ash from an explosion.

"Did you look?" I ask Renly.

He shakes his head.

"Good man." I pat him on the head. "Now, it's nearly time for the big finale…"

Renly's dark brown eyes light up with mischief. He smiles with determination, flashing me his dimples on either cheek.

"The villagers will throw magical rocks at us and yell enchanted spells. What do we do when this happens again?" I inquire.

Renly leans in so the guards won't hear. "We put on our invisible shields and crouch low in the middle of the crowd, so we don't get blasted with their magical rocks!"

Somehow, this part is much worse than turning away from the execution. As we pass the horizon of the East Vexello Mountains, there is a swarm of villagers who wait for us to pass in our dirty gray rags, huddled in a tight group because we all know what's coming. How do I explain that to a child? These men and women are going to throw rocks at us now. Why? Because hurting us, humiliating us, it makes them all very happy. No, you didn't do anything wrong. These are just evil, soulless people.

No. I'm going to make a game out of it to distract him.

Funneling through one of the villages, we come close to entering the well-guarded walls of the Blackspire Ward of The North. But just before we get to the onyx pikes dancing with lit torches, the villagers throw the stones. Renly and I huddle in the center of the other captives, crouching low as our eardrums are filled with grunts, moans, and shrieks from the downpour of rocks hitting bone. There's a group of taller, muscular men and women who rotate every week to form an outer shell around the women, children and elderly.

I offered to take a turn on the outside, but they considered me elderly to which I *tried* not to take offense at.

Although, I'm grateful now as I can play this sad game with Renly. He huddles between the mashed, sweaty bodies around us, careful to stay wedged and protected as we shuffle out way past the threshold. Renly hugs my waist as per our routine. I don't want him to see the other captives with bloody gashes on their heads or knocked out teeth.

"Did I do good?" Renly mumbles into my shirt.

My throat is tight, but I don't let him hear that I'm so close to tears, it hurts. So, I nod and say, "Mmm-hmm."

"You too."

We're left alone to ruminate on the previous events of the execution and hateful, bloodthirsty villagers. It's their way of letting our new reality sink it. Not all will we be killed if we try to escape, the villagers might do it for us. I've tried asking why they are so hungry to hurt the men and women in the first place, but the answers are unclear.

"Do you still think someone's coming to rescue us?" Renly sits in our corner, tugging open a loose brick to snack on a small piece of bread. I told him I'm allergic, so he'd finish the little loaf himself and stop offering it to me.

"I do."

"Why?"

I smile. The "why" stage was always my favorite when Niklaus was this age. Every explanation I gave always resulted in him asking why again. Marilynn would try to distract him to put a stop to the endless loop of questions. But I loved it. I'd give elaborate answers that would fuel his curiosity.

"Because…it just so happens, I have the strongest, most powerful family in the whole world." I cross my arms proudly and lean against the wall. "They'd find me across time, Ren Ren."

"Are they royalty?"

My cheeks warm at the image of Ruth's pretty face popping into my head. Her upturned little nose and freckles.

"Some of them," I say.

"Wow! What about the others? Who is most powerful?"

"My sister, I think. Though, it's arguable the big-headed mastermind, Dessin."

"Why?" Renly asks with a mouth full of bread.

"Well, my sister, Skylenna, has magical powers. She—hmm, how do I put this? Take that fat warden over there, see him?" I lift my chin to point to the shittiest guard here. "She could jump into his brain, scramble things around, and lock him up in a dark prison so he can never hurt anyone ever again."

"You are serious?" Renly gawks at me in wonder and joy.

"Yes. And the mastermind, Dessin? He could outfight any warden here. No one would be able to take him down."

Except his brother and Masten.

"And what's your magical power, Mr. Niles?"

"Making them laugh. Being eccentric. Annoying everyone."

Renly scrunched his nose as he giggles. "You have magical powers too."

I think on this. "I am very good at picking locks."

And pockets, but I'll leave that out.

Renly throws his fist in the air. "Mr. Niles is the most powerful at escaping!"

I bunch my lips to the side, tempted to take on that title, but my old friend would kick my ass for stealing the thing he was known for.

"Actually, big-headed Dessin would take the cake on that one. He is a master escape artist. He used to be locked up in the Emerald Lake Asylum. Escaped loads of times."

"Oh. Not a good place." Renly pops his head up, facing falling.

"You know it?" Have they really heard of it from smaller villages in Vexamen?

Renly nods solemnly. "I live next to it."

My eyes narrow. "What?"

"Right next to the two mountains behind it."

"Hold on…" I suddenly can't hear anyone around us having background conversations. "Renly, you're from the Chandelier City?"

He shakes his head. "No. I'm from the Naiadales."

"The Emerald Lake ancient colony?"

Renly nods. And abruptly, I realize why his face looks so

familiar to me. Why I've been drawn to protect him the moment I was thrown in this penitentiary.

"What is your father's name?"

I hold my breath.

"Rydran." The young boy looks away sadly. "I think he'll come for me too."

The wet leaves he put on my burns. Golden hair braided down his back. Vines and moss covering his dark skin. Rydran. He stayed by my bedside while I recovered. He took care of me and is the entire reason I didn't go completely insane from the intense pain of those burns.

Rydran told Ruth that one day, I'd help relieve his pain just as much as he's relieved mine, according to their prophecy.

Renly is Rydran's little boy, and he's a captive in fucking *Vexamen* during its worst, most barbarous years.

"I know your father," I utter to this sweet, brave boy in disbelief.

"You do?!"

Determination fills my blood in a spike of adrenaline so powerful, nothing on earth could stop me.

"I'm going to get you out of here, Ren Ren. I'm bringing you home to your dad."

47. Wrong Place, Wrong Time

Sapphire

We are dumped into a pile of snow in the North Sapphrine Forest.

Flecks of ice melt over my eyelids. Crunchy snow is mashed into my scalp. I blink sleepily at the pine trees crisscrossing over the winter sky.

Winter.

Ice.

Snow.

I'm barefoot, in a white patient gown. At least Niklaus has pants.

I hiss through clenched teeth and coil my sore, aching body into a tight ball as the snow melts into my back. Lifting my head, I hug my knees to my chest.

"H-h-holy shit…" I stammer. "I'm s-s-sorry. I—"

A cold hand covers my mouth. I look up at Niklaus, on his knees behind my head, eyes bolting from one side of the forest to the other. And I catch on that we are not alone.

My eyes follow his. To my left, there are men in dark camouflage clothing, blending into the bark of the pine trees. To my right, there are those that blend into the snow. They are everywhere, spying on someone. Or at least, they *were* spying on someone. Slowly, they nudge each other, pointing us out. And Christ, there are so many of them. Twenty-five? Thirty?

My eyes water at the doom of it all. I just want this to be over. I'm so tired of fighting. So tired of running. Why must I keep traveling to places that put me in harm's way? Why can't we just go home?

If they attack us, I don't have the energy to fight back.

"Do you think you can do it again?" Niklaus whispers.

Whispers in Old Alkadonian become apparent. Vexamen Breed.

"Do what?"

"What you did to Apple May. Do you know how you did it?"

I shake my head. "I'm so weak."

Useless.

After everything we've been through, we can't die here. We can't! I need to get Niklaus home. I don't care if he hates me for this forever. I don't care about all the shitty things he's said to me over the years. I need to get him home.

They move in on us. The slow steps are like watching your own public hanging. The noose. The audience. The slow walk to an old wooden stage. The truth of it is, if these soldiers don't kill us—sitting here in the snow will.

I grab Niklaus's wrist and squeeze, though my fingers are hard and numb.

More hushed conversations go on in Old Alkadonian. A debate. It's a back and forth. They point to us as we shiver in silence, holding on to each other.

Krimson, you've protected me my entire life. Where are you now? Have I lost you forever? Has moving through time severed our connection?

A word keeps getting tossed around as the soldiers move closer.

"*Bliétzvìz.*"

Bait.

My name is not Krimson.

I blink in surprise at the unnatural intrusion in my thoughts. It echoes through what I *believe* is the void, though I could be wrong. The voice is low, a faint scrape beneath a calm tone. Low and controlled. Male. Each vowel ending in cursive. And an authority that seems infinitely undisputed.

The soldiers whisper-yell at us, pointing and demanding answers to their questions we don't understand.

"We do not speak Old Alkadonian," Niklaus responds.

How have you come to enter this mind? The voice pushes into my thoughts with more aggression this time. *Are you a threat to our system?*

Are you... are you a Short-Haired Windila too? I ask, feeling like I'm going completely mad. But perhaps he is like Dellilian. A guide?

The voice goes quiet.

"*Ȅupzx! Ȅupzx!*" The soldiers snap their fingers at us.

Up! Up!

Before we can protest, our wrists are bound, and we're shoved through the snow to an open area. The Vexamen Breed look over their shoulders in loud, obvious paranoia.

They say things like *scream, bait, hurry, the great beast is with them.*

Ah, you must be a fictive alter. Though, that doesn't seem right either, does it? The voice returns.

Alter? I think on this. There's no way. Unless I've been driven to real, debilitating delusions from the electroshock therapy. *Which alter are* you?

Cricket, the gatekeeper.

My eyes go wide.

Do you have two alters named Dessin and Kane?

How could you know that? How have you invaded this mind?

"Sapphire!" Niklaus reaches for me as I'm thrown to the snow while he is tied to the trunk of a tree.

"Wait!" I say to the soldiers digging a hole next to my head. "P-p-please!"

Cricket! I need your help! I can't explain now, but your system must be close by. The Vexamen Breed is going to... I stare at the grave being dug at an impressively fast rate. *They're going to bury me alive!*

And why should we trust you?

I cough hysterically as my back hits the bottom of the hole, wet dirt and snow sprinkle down into my eyes. Niklaus yells my name through grunts. They're beating him. I smell smoke. I smell an arctic death waiting our arrival.

DaiSzek and Skylenna are my friends. Please!

Cricket pauses. Shovels throw dirt over my body and face. I cough and gasp, thrashing and trying to break free of the ropes around my wrists. I thought I was too weak to do anything, but I was wrong. When you're about to be buried alive, something else takes over.

Scream. He will come for you. Scream.

The choking, gagging scream barrels through my throat, bursting through the piles of falling soil. I keep screaming, desperate to be loud enough to get my father's attention. I simultaneously try to tap into the Nightlung, reaching for it in my mind with a voiceless plea to take us anywhere but here. Take us home. Take us somewhere safe.

But it's as if I'm reaching for the top of a mountain from the ground. Inside, I've lost the spark I need from lack of food, water, and sleep. I'm dying, and now, all I can do is scream.

My teeth grind against the gritty texture of ice and earth. It is scratching my eyes and burning my nostrils. I throw my head side to side, grunting in fury.

Now, calm yourself, strange feminine voice in our head. Cricket instructs.

How?! I'm being buried alive!

I feel the weight of the oncoming piles hit me hard. There is no panic quite like what I'm feeling now.

Breathe through your nose and turn your face to the side. You must create an air pocket.

I pinch my lips together and turn my face, unable to avoid the clouds of dirt wafting into my nose. I choke and screech again.

Can you cover your face?

No! Please! I'm going to die!

Niklaus screaming my name dissolves into the background of the wind scattering the through the crisp tree branches and the grunting of the men killing me.

With a combustion of starlight, a source of heat and dark fur appear next to my head. The animal nuzzles against me, pushing her neck and head over my face.

"*Dellilian protect Miss Sapphire.*"

I gasp in relief, quick to bury my face into her warm chest to avoid inhaling anymore of the dust.

Stay calm. Conserve your air, Cricket reminds me.

I let Dellilian's soothing heat pass over my shot nerves. And as the hole fills up, I remind myself that my parents have to be close by. The Vexamen Breed was targeting them. Watching them from a safe location nearby. My father would have heard my screams.

The weight is suffocating by itself. The blood supply to my hands is cut off as my bound wrists are smashed under my tailbone.

My burial eats up any remaining light.

And Dellilian and I are left to die here alone.

I count the seconds. I recite the lord's prayer. I call for Krimson. I recall brief moments in my childhood that stand out. Uncle Warrose kneeling in front of Aunt Ruth and resting his head in her lap after finding Niklaus when he was taken. My mother telling Krimson funny memories from her time in the prison with our father to make him laugh after crying over never getting to meet him. DaiSzek bringing a dead raccoon into the house and leaving it at Grandpa's bedroom door. DaiSzek carrying the carcass out after we all screamed because Grandpa stepped on it with his bare foot.

"*Don't be scared, Miss Sapphire.*"

I need my dad, I tell her.

Running footsteps are muffled above us. Voices. A fog of lightheadedness. The pocket of oxygen thins. My stomach rolls with a foreign queasiness. And just as my lungs wheeze and my eyes shut, a pair of hands digs the dirt off of me, letting in a stream of bright light.

48. Summoning the Father

Sapphire

Dellilian disappears as a pair of strong, sturdy hands lock around my forearms and pull me out of the grave I'm buried in. Dirt pours off of me like sand. And I cough and gasp, clearing my throat as the pair of hands wipe my face, brushing the debris from my eyes so I can see. So I can look up at the face that saved me.

But before my vision clears, I can sense his presence without the use of my eyes. The warm, giant hands steady my shoulders. The great height can be felt from far away.

I blink away the snow and grime and look upon my father's face. His stern, serious brown eyes. Furrowed brow. Tousled chocolate hair.

It's my dad.

My dad saved me.

"Are you hurt?" he asks.

Nothing could stop me from letting every emotion come detonating from my soul. I whimper with lips pulled behind my teeth.

Thank you, Dad. Thank you for coming for me.

My grief leaks out in sharp, grunting cries behind my teeth. Each racking sob is a call for someone who has never been able to be there when I needed him most. Warm tears cut through the dust on my cheeks, dropping from my jaw onto the slush beneath my numb feet.

My father looks down at me, eyes darting across my face, more surprised at my sudden hysterical outburst than the fact that I've been buried alive. And my face crumples like the little girl inside who has been waiting for her dad for so long and has finally found him. I throw my arms around his neck, despite the knowledge that he could seriously hurt someone for hugging him without permission.

But he's my father.

And moments ago, I just watched him die.

I watched a sickle pierce his chest.

I watched his blood spill over my mother's lap.

My cry is tired, aching, full of the need to tell him everything. I want to warn him, to give him the knowledge he needs to avoid falling into that coma. I want to save him like he has just saved me.

It's me, Dad. I love you. I've missed you my entire life. I wish you knew me. I wish you knew Krimson. I wish you could hold Mom one more time.

My dirty wet face is pressed into the center of his chest, and he touches my back once before keeping his arms hanging in the air around me. If only he knew how badly I need him to hug me back. Just once. But not just any hug. One that means something. One from my dad who knows my name and loves me back.

A hand caresses my back. I peek over at my mother, holding her arms out to me. I nearly choke her neck as I leap into her embrace. Though she doesn't know who I am, or what I will mean to her one day, a hug with my mama is long overdue.

"What happened?" Mom asks.

A hand is placed on my arm. "I don't know if you remember us…but the two of you found us in the woods a few months ago…"

Niklaus's guess of meeting a few months ago is bold. We have absolutely no idea how much time has passed since then. But his voice does not waver in its confidence when speaking to my parents. In everything we've read about Patient Thirteen, identifying any area of weakness is one of his many specialties.

"I remember," my father answers with a heavy tone of judgment. "And you only have a minute to explain before I tie you back to that tree."

No!

I stiffen though the vehement shivering does not stop even as I find intense comfort in Mom's body heat.

"—And before you think about lying, I'll know. I don't like liars. I *burn* liars."

We refrain from speaking at all. If I say anything, I know he'll see right through me. The desire to tell my dad who I really am is too strong right now. I have no urgency to preserve the future after the hell I've seen.

"What's your name?" Mom asks.

I keep my face pressed into her shoulder.

"Niklaus."

At first, I'm surprised he gives them his real name. But then again, Patient Thirteen might have detected the lie quickly.

"How old are you, Niklaus?"

"Twenty-one."

Stand upright, leaning away from Mom to wipe my face and nose. I dig my feet into the dirt to keep them from freezing in the snow. I can see Niklaus doing the same.

My father advances forward before my mom puts a hand up to stop him.

"Niklaus, my friend here has many gifts, but patience isn't one of them. I need you to tell me why this is our second run-in with you two, and I need you to be honest."

I watch the dynamic between my parents with intense curiosity and admiration. How can I be terrified of being caught in a lie and yet still amazed at the way he looks at her with so much respect and tenderness through his rough exterior? I've never seen them interact. I've seen her hold his hand. I've seen her talk to him. But never have I seen them speak to each other.

"We're being chased by people who think we are in cahoots with the two of you. We just broke out of where they were keeping us. They followed us here and you saw what the end result was." Niklaus levels his stare on my mother, careful not to look at my father. He uses an approach I've seen before. It's political. It's poised and sincere. A tactic in his leadership training.

"Why would they think we're affiliated?" my father asks.

Niklaus continues to speak for the two of us. "They said they saw us with you that night. I guess they had eyes on the two of you."

Patient Thirteen walks through the snow to think. "No, that's not right. Demechnef wouldn't have taken people we only had a random interaction with once." Those concentrated, dark brown eyes pin Niklaus in place. He stops walking.

"Because it isn't Demechnef who has been chasing us," Niklaus says, and it's as if a lightbulb goes off. He finds the details he needs to convince my father. "They're called the Vexamen Breed."

"I see." My father's demeanor changes.

"Who are the Vexamen Breed?" Mom asks.

Patient Thirteen shoots his gaze to her, pausing with uncertainty.

"They're children, well, teenagers that the leaders of Vexamen trained to be vicious soldiers from birth. The same men who slaughtered that village." His eyes fall to his boots in thought. "But wait, that doesn't explain why they tied you up and buried her alive."

I search my mind for answers. But the truth is, I'm not all here right now. I couldn't be more thankful that Niklaus has it in him to speak up, to confront my parents head on. If my father chose to interrogate me right now, I'd crumble to pieces.

"Maybe they were trying to draw us out," Mom offers.

But something shifts in my father. He turns to the forest, searching the open planes of pine trees and ice. A quiet panic sets in. "Where's DaiSzek?!"

Oh no…

Niklaus opens his mouth to speak then stops himself. He searches for a way to answer without giving away that we do in fact know who DaiSzek is. "What, the animal? The black wolf? It took off after the Breed left us here."

My father takes off into the woods, leaving us with my mother, Uncle Warrose, Grandpa, Aunt Ruth, and Uncle Niles. We're careful not to interact with any of them as Mom ushers us into the cave they've been camping out in.

At first, we eat in silence away from the others. I chew the warm meat sluggishly, unsure how much will make me sick since I've been conditioned not to consume this much at the asylum.

After we're done, Niklaus and I curl up next to the fire, sitting close together. I scoot dangerously close to the flames. The airy chill is rooted so far within my body, it feels like no amount of fire could warm me up again.

"How did you not inhale the dirt? They didn't shove you in a coffin or anything." Niklaus shakes his head as he stares into the bright crackling orange aura. "You should have died. Even down there for a minute or two. You should have…"

"It was Dellilian," I answer hoarsely. I did inhale enough to cut into my windpipes and make my throat raw though. "She showed up to cover my face and create an air pocket for me to last long enough for my dad to come get me."

"She did?"

"Mmm-hmm."

He rubs a dry, windburned hand over his facial hair, but has nothing to say on that.

After a minute, tears burn the backs of my eyes. "My dad came for me."

"I know."

I can feel Niklaus's eyes on me, examining the tears build over my gaze.

"He saved my life."

"Yes."

"I'm a perfect stranger to him with no emotional ties whatsoever. And he still came for me when he heard me scream knowing it could have been an ambush." A tide breaks in my chest. "DaiSzek was captured because of it."

"Maybe not," he says quietly.

"Maybe not what?"

"Maybe you weren't a perfect stranger to him when he found you."

"Of course, I was." I lower my head. "He doesn't even know who I am in the future."

Niklaus turns his body an inch to get a better look at me. "I know that. But I've seen and heard of impossible things from your family. My mother once told me that your parents are warrior angels sent from God to stop a great evil. She's told me they are soulmates, and their souls would recognize each other in any life. I always thought that was a load of crap meant to build up their lore, but…"

"But what?"

For once, his eyes don't feel like knives. Those storm-dark, oceanic blues pin me in place. It's cold water on my skin and scorching red fire in my chest.

"But I've been thrown back in time by your hand, Spitfire. I've watched you wield time like a weapon and scalp a woman, turning the clock forward on her hair. You and your family have done impossible things. So, what if my mother was right? If your father's soul can recognize your mother's…can it also recognize his own daughter's?"

More tears bully their way in, but I hold them back.

"I hope so," I whisper.

My palms press into my eyes, pushing away the sadness and exhaustion clinging to my skin like a disease.

"You've never been this nice to me. I've known you for twenty-one years," I tell him, sniffling against the back of my hand.

"I'm aware of that."

"Then why?"

Niklaus's demeanor hardens. "We've been through a lot."

"But you've always hated me."

"No, I have not."

"Lie."

"I liked you a lot before I was taken, Spitfire. You were my first crush," Niklaus says.

This wakes me up a little. "Before I…gave you that wood carving?"

I feel a flush of embarrassment bloom across my cheeks at the mention of this. It's a memory I can't look back on without cringing. Five years old, and I confessed my love for him. Five.

"Yes."

"Hmm."

For a moment, we watch Uncle Warrose and my mom talk at the opening of the cave. He's so young here. There is no white in his beard or dark hair. No frown and smile wrinkles creased over select places on his face.

"Can we talk about what happened in the asylum?" Niklaus readjusts his legs next to me.

I shrug.

"I know it's low on our priority list…but I don't know how to act around you after it happened. I'm confused."

I pull a wool blanket tighter around my shoulders. "Which part is confusing you?"

"All of it. The treatments. What Apple May did to us. We did what we had to do, I know that, but fuck…" He clenches his fists and opens his mouth to add something but decides against it as he attempts to tone down his temper.

"We did do what we had to do." I stare back at him without blinking. "And it's a good thing we're no longer patients, because we don't have to pretend to be husband and wife anymore."

Niklaus lifts his chin to look down at me with a gaze showing more confusion than before he decided to bring this topic up. "No, I guess we don't."

"I can forget about touching each other because we were *forced* to if you can…"

His Adam's apple shifts, and he nods while looking away.

"And if you ever use anything that happened in that asylum to humiliate, degrade, or bully me when we finally get home…I'll fucking destroy you." The quick spark of anger and hatred dissolves as soon as I see the hurt burn in his eyes.

"You think I would do that? Sapphire, we were emotionally, physically, and sexually abused in that place. I'd die before I weaponized that." That hurt modifies into shame because he can remember as well as I can why I have to put my guard up so quicky. But as expected, that shame disintegrates into apathy. "We're better off forgetting then."

Mabel Rose.

Wood-carved figurine.

Dorn Leviat.

Disrespecting my father's name.

Pushed in the creek.

Milk dumped down my back.

My father's picture burned on my desk.

Vandalism.

Rumors.

To my surprise, it's almost difficult to recall his sins toward me after everything we've been through. Not just because of the memory gaps from the electroshock therapy. But because there were moments when he's all I had, and I'm all he had. I grasped at anything, any bit of light in the pit of hell. It was Niklaus. He was there. He was a warm body. That's all. I swore I'd never let go of this hate for him. Every time he'd made me cry. I swore it to myself.

But right now, I'm too tired and sick to revel in a grudge.

Right now, I need to sleep. I need an ally. It takes too much energy to hate someone as much as I've hated him. I can resume when I'm feeling like myself again.

"Let's sleep while we have the protection of my parents right now, okay?" I finally say.

Niklaus stares at the fire a moment longer, pushing away his clean plate, and adjusting our pelt of furs to sleep on. As I snuggle into the heavy blankets, the soreness in my muscles can finally melt and skitter away from the constant tension in my bones. My eyes fall shut, throbbing and dry from the large amounts of tears I've shed lately. My breathing stretches and deepens in its soft rhythm.

And I wish I could stay here forever.

The pure and natural state of euphoria from finally being able to sleep in a safe place with trusted loved ones is something I will never take for granted again.

49. What Waits in Sleep

Sapphire

A sandstorm collapses OVER A strange architecture of sandstone walls, onyx pillars, and black iron gates.

I stand in front of it, hair whipping through the gritty winds, watching an eclipse shift over the bright sun.

"Sapphire?"

The hairs on my neck stand. My chest can barely contain my galloping heart. I hold my hand up to block the blizzard of beige sand obstructing my view.

Krimson stands on the other side of the gates. And I fall to my knees with shaking arms wrapping around my torso.

"Krimson!" I scream, holding on to a rock to my left as the bustling winds threaten to knock me over. "Oh god! Krimson, it's me! Is this real? Please, tell me it's real!"

My brother holds onto the iron gate to steady himself, squinting to keep me in his line of sight. And now that I've seen our father, up close with his eyes open, I can confidently say Krimson looks *exactly* like him, but with heterochromatic eyes. Any difference is so minute, you'd have to know them both very well to see it.

"Where are you?" Krimson cups his hands over his mouth, shouting through the storm. "Are you hurt? Tell me how to find you!"

"I'm…alive! We're like our parents, Krimson! We can—"

The sound of a horn cuts me off, and from the storm, an assembly line of men and women in rags huddles together, covering their faces and heading for the entryway to the strange penitentiary surrounded by the iron gates. The large group of people pass between Krimson and I. Among them, dead in the center, our Uncle Niles holds a young boy in his arms, sheltering his face and holding him tight to his chest.

"Uncle Niles!" I yell, but my voice drops like a whisper.

Krimson stares at our uncle in confusion, steps forward to confirm if it's really him, then looks at me.

"We have to save him!" I shout, crawling forward, feeling the burn of the sand and wind make tiny incisions in my face. "They have him! I don't know how to get back!"

"Uncle Niles?" Krimson hollers as the crowd passes us.

He doesn't hear. He can't see us. They shuffle back into the place surrounded by barbed wire and iron spikes. They shove, kick, and hit the captives as they're forced to move faster. The last person stumbles across the threshold. The doors slam shut.

"We—have to save him!" I reach for Krimson, holding my hand out for my twin to take.

Krimson lets go of the iron gate and runs to me, crossing the narrow road of scattered stones and black pavement. But the Nightlung latches on to both of us, as if two different hands reached out from the heavens and tugged us in opposite directions.

Away from each other.

Tumbling through time on another axis entirely.

Krimson

My mother is still holding my hands when I open my eyes and am released from the void.

"You saw her," Mom states hopefully. She remains steady and unshakable despite not knowing what happened to her daughter. She's always been that way. Never letting us see her suffering.

"I…"

Mom's face is unreadable. "Is your sister safe, Krimson?"

I shake my head.

"She's alive." It's not a question. Her bright emerald eyes burn into my eyes, willing that statement to be true.

I nod. "It's not that, Mom."

Even though I'm in the safest house I know, by the hearth of the fire in the living room, sitting next to DaiSzek—all I can see is…

"It's Uncle Niles," I tell her at a loss for breath. "I don't know where they are. It's not here. But Uncle Niles was with them, and he's the one in the most danger right now!"

My mom blinks, trying to process the weakness cracking into my voice. Her full lips part, and she tightens her grip around my wrists.

"Sapphire—she was scared for him, Mom. She was—I don't know—concerned for herself, yes. But there was real panic and terror in her voice for Uncle Niles. We have to—we—"

"What did you see? Do not leave out a single detail." That maternal look on her face changes, transitioning into something cold and professional.

I tell her everything. The scenery we've determined to be Vexamen. But the version before Aunt Ruth took over. My mother doesn't write anything down. She doesn't ask for details to be repeated.

She watches as I retrace my steps in my head, logging every movement Uncle Niles made, every word Sapphire said.

It's all carefully calculated behind her firm gaze.

"DaiSzek, stay with my son," she commands.

He lifts his head in understanding, perking his ears up.

"What? Where are you going?" I ask.

"Keep looking for your sister. I'm getting the rest of the family involved. Now."

50. Prophesy Be Damned

Skylenna

My heels split and crack as I sprint through the woods, into the shallow Emerald Oak River, over fallen trees, and onto the uneven road that leads to Marilynn's hidden house.

Jumping onto the front porch, I pound my fists on their front door. I don't care what time it is. I don't care if they're asleep. My mind pulses and goes up in flames. It's more than the fear of my daughter being lost. It's Niles being left behind too.

"Marilynn! Open the damn door!" I shriek.

My fists boom through the hum of crickets and early morning birds. I'm two seconds from breaking the door down as it flies open.

"Warrose," I say out of breath.

He looms over me with a giant shadow that blots out the light coming from the living room behind him. I almost forgot they were staying with Marilynn and Niles a little longer to draw up new trade agreements.

"What's wrong?" he asks in a raspy, tired yet alert voice.

Ruth appears at Warrose's side, resting her wrists on the arms of her chair.

I look between them, trying not to let myself fall apart. "Where is Marilynn…"

"We had a lot of wine last night. She's passed out," Ruth answers with a yawn.

"Skylenna," Warrose says, narrowing his eyes on me. "What is it?"

My hands clasp together, pressing against my mouth as I shake my head. I can't decide which emotions want to be set free the most. Devastation, because I can feel it…I can feel death and doom and an everlasting ache hanging over us. The void gathers a layer of ice awaiting an apocalypse. Something is coming.

Or am I furious? If something happens to my daughter, I won't forgive Marilynn for knowing and choosing to stay silent.

"Sapphire and Niklaus are missing." I watch their backs straighten and faces fall. "Not here. They're somewhere we can't reach. Krimson believes they've moved through time and can't find their way back to us."

Warrose was seconds away from pushing past me to start looking for them. Until that last bit. He pauses in the doorway, glancing back at Ruth at a complete loss of words.

"They…*time traveled*," Ruth clarifies, staring up at me in thorough disbelief.

"They took—Niles with them," I add. My blood runs cold at the full description Krimson gave me of what he saw.

Warrose shakes his head, placing his hand over his mouth before speaking. "Maybe that's a good thing. Niles won't leave their side. He'll watch out for them. He knows what our world was like before we fixed it."

Tears rush to my eyes at the hope he suddenly has.

"It's true. He'll know how to keep them safe," Ruth agrees.

"No. They—" My voice breaks, and I have to breathe to keep the heartbreak at bay. "They left Niles behind. They *lost* him…in *Vexamen*."

Ruth's face falls. The color leaves her flushed cheeks.

"When…"

"Far enough back when the Blackspire Ward of The North was still around."

Ruth blanches, moving her chair back as she clutches her hand to her chest.

"NO! Tell me he's not in there, Skylenna… Tell me they don't have Niles!"

I look to Warrose, then back at Ruth. "From what Krimson saw, he is currently a captive."

"No! Oh god, no!" Ruth shrieks, crying in her hand.

"God-fucking-damnit!" Warrose shoves past me, stepping off the porch and pacing the tree line with a horde of pent-up energy.

"Where are the kids?! Are they safe?" Ruth is still crying but trying to straighten up enough to hear my response, desperate for some news.

"We don't know yet. All Krimson knows is that they are at least better off than Niles."

"Can Krimson travel too? He must! We need to leave now! We have to—"

I hold my hand up to her. "He's working on it. I've shown him how to search for her in the void, though the place he's going is different. Similar to the void, but a separate entity entirely. I can't follow him there."

"But does he know how to travel like Sapphire did?" she asks.

I shake my head.

"Oh, Skylenna…" Ruth reaches for my hand and tugs me to her. "If Niles is a captive, we have to find a way to get to him now. Most captives there ended up dead or horribly maimed. *Especially* ones from our country."

Warrose places a hand on my upper back. "We have to do something. I can't leave him in that place. Fuck, Dessin would have burned both countries to the ground to get him out."

"Does it look like I'm going to sit around and wait for a miracle? I don't care if it fucking kills me—I will bring my daughter, Niklaus, and my brother home," I say confidently.

The floorboards behind Ruth creak.

"They've traveled back in time, haven't they?"

Down the dark hallway, Marilynn steps forward in her nightgown and slippers.

And I practically float out of body to watch what happens next. Squeezing past Ruth's chair, I charge Marilynn, sinking my fingernails into her throat and slamming her into the wall. Picture frames clatter to the floor. Her head makes a small hole in the wallpaper.

But Marilynn, though perfectly capable, does not fight back.

She stares back at me with those, rich, all-knowing, blue eyes.

"You knew, didn't you?" I shout in her face.

No response.

I slam her head into the wall again, to which Warrose shouts my name.

"Answer me, you fucking bitch!"

Marilynn nods. "Yes."

"FUCK!" I scream in her face until my vocal cords are shredded. "Your son is lost in time, and your fucking husband has been taken captive at the Blackspire Ward in Vexamen! Did you know that?!"

Her eyes give nothing away. Nothing except that constant glint. The one that tells me she has always known how this story was going to end.

"Tell me why! Are you a psychopath? Are you fucking demented? That's my daughter! My little girl!"

A little fight flashes in her gaze. "Don't you think I would have tried to stop it if there was any other way?! I'd give my own life to stop them from having to go through all this if that were an option. You have known me for over two decades, Skylenna. Trust me. This *has* to happen."

I want to hit her. I want to choke the life out of her for knowing my baby was going to be swallowed through time and left in the worst parts of our history. I'd give anything to shelter her from that horror.

"Fuck. You. I don't care if I have to sell my soul to the devil. I am getting them back."

Marilynn shoves me off, taking a threatening step forward.

"It won't come to that. I'm going to teach Krimson how to travel too. How to take you with him to bring everyone home."

51. Collecting Souls

Sapphire

I roll on my side, letting my eyes peel open, and come face-to-face with a woman staring back at me through the rusty bars meant for the cage of a gigantic bird.

The sight of her round brown eyes scares the daylight out of me. I fling myself back, cracking the back of my head into another set of bars behind me. Hissing, I rub my scalp and grit my teeth.

Those curious brown eyes blink timidly, like she didn't mean to frighten me. In fact, my reaction equally scared her. The woman strains to sit herself up, using a scabbed elbow and dirty hand to inch herself up to lean on a set of bars.

"*Skievéz.*"

I'm sorry.

"Fuck me. Old Alkadonian can only mean one thing," I groan, adding pressure to the back of my head.

"She's from Dementia," a man says from a cage next to the woman studying me with an interested gaze.

"I speak your language too," the woman tells me with a smile.

I nod, jerking forward as a hand lands on my upper back.

"It's just me." Niklaus. Groggy. Annoyed.

I twist around to see him lying in the cage to my right, pinching the bridge of his nose as he keeps his hand on me.

It only takes me one or two seconds to know where we've landed. It's a hallway made of brimstone and two columns of oddly shaped cages. Red and yellow bulbs, glitching and pulsating with inconsistent light. A dreary old tune, like that of a vintage carnival—an organ, trumpet, and other instruments I don't recognize. And the scent is exactly as I pictured it. Candied apples and the scum at the bottom of a well.

I lock eyes with Niklaus as he lowers his hand.

"We are in the fucking Vexamen Prison," I exhale. The dread and denial arrive and leave like a puff of smoke. The uncontrollable laughter snuffs any other feelings out. I sit up, covering my mouth with the back of my hand, pinching my eyes closed as a fit of giggles ruptures my lungs.

"Yep," Niklaus adds with zero humor to his tone.

I laugh harder, wheezing with tears in my eyes.

"We must have done something horrible to a saint in a past life," Niklaus continues.

I can't stop laughing.

"Is she okay?" the woman asks.

Niklaus ignores her. "It has to be bad for our health to travel this much."

I'm delirious, shaking my head, and reaching back to pat him on the shoulder. The muscles under my fingers tense and coil tightly together.

"She's in shock," the man two cages down says.

You are damn right, I am.

"The sentinels didn't put them in uniforms."

"White material? Could they be from—"

"No."

"But they wouldn't have just thrown these two in a cage without inspection and—wait, they don't have collars?" The man stands to get a better look at us.

I rest my head against the bars and close my eyes.

"It was a last-minute imprisonment," I sigh.

The cage doors open and the ground rumbles with hurried footsteps.

"Follow us!" the woman is already in the hallway, careful not to get in the way of the inmates jogging past us. The man stands behind her, watching us suspiciously.

I look back at Niklaus, and we exit our cages and follow our neighbors down the long hallway. Men and women aren't dressed how we read in our books. Niklaus notices it too.

The women are barely covered in dark red rags, patches and strings that only cover their private areas. The men only wearing black and red pin striped pants.

"I thought they wore red one pieces like bathing suits, and the men wore black pants?" I whisper to Niklaus.

The man peers back at me with a subtle scowl. "There have never been uniforms like that here."

At a closer look, the man isn't really a man at all. He's a teenager. Younger than me. Short, shiny black hair, and lime green eyes. The woman looks close to his age. Maybe seventeen? Long, chocolate brown hair, tan skin, and gentle sprinkling of freckles on her cheeks and slender shoulders.

"She's thinking of someplace else," Niklaus replies.

And we come to a complete stop. My bare feet tap at the murky water spreading past the entrance of the community showers. There are multiple jagged pipes gaping from the ceiling, hosing gray water onto a compact grouping of naked inmates.

Some howl at the cold water pounding down on their backs torn to ribbons of loose flesh and open meat glistening with blood and other fluids. The beastly results of recent whippings. Others shiver and keep their heads downs until sentinels nod and release them from their shower time.

"Laughter gone?" Niklaus asks, unamused.

"Laughter gone."

I don't look his way as I slip out of my white patient gown, eyes lowered, arms clasped around my chest. As my hands grip my sides, I wince at the rib bones so easily defined to my touch. I can't believe how much weight I've lost. I don't feel like myself anymore at all.

"Walk in front of me," Niklaus orders.

"So you can gawk at my backside? No, thank you."

Niklaus keeps his head angled away from me but stays at my side.

"So I don't have to worry about anyone grabbing you while my back is turned," he responds with tired aggravation.

I take another look around, weighing my options. So many male prisoners staring at me already. Well, not just me. The teenage woman is the target of a lot of attention, but as she enters the showers, she stays locked arms with the young man with bright green eyes.

"Okay."

Reluctantly, I accept his hand, and we step into the angry downpour of water that reeks of rusty pipes and a well full of mold. I wince and bear down as the pins and needles stab my skin. The water is colder than I expected. But I stay in place in front of Niklaus, keeping my head down as my wet hair forms a wet curtain around my face.

…eleven, twelve, thirteen, fourteen, fifteen, sixteen, seventeen.

"*Veitzentuiex! Dé venouis zéxeknéxies!*" A man with long, fuzzy white hair grabs my elbow. He tugs at me once, wearing a big, crooked grin. "*Veitzentuiex, iñexec!*"

The malnutrition in my body is like a drug that won't leave my system. I let go of Niklaus's hand and try to use his weight against him. A maneuver that would normally be effortless, feels like I'm trying to move a mountain. The man laughs angrily, snatching my throat with his other hand to force me into submission.

"*Let her go!*" the young woman yells in Old Alkadonian.

But Niklaus steps to my side, seizing the inmate's wrist, and prying him off my throat. Though he doesn't stop with that downward movement. With a fast twist, I hear the bone in his forearm snap. Then another. The first proximal metacarpal is separated from his radius bone. The inmate is powerless to fight off Niklaus's dominating hold on him. And Niklaus's shadow stretches over the wet stone floor and the whimpering man like a reaping from scripture.

The inmate begs in Old Alkadonian, but Niklaus doesn't respond. His head tilts and his eyes go cold, as if measuring how much more this body can take before breaking entirely.

"All right, that's enough," the young man tells Niklaus. "It's not worth it. Let's go."

"No?" Niklaus glances down at me, mocking the young man with a raised eyebrow. "Breaking the bones in his hand for attempting to sexually assault this woman *isn't* worth it?"

I massage the bruising skin around my throat as I watch another small bone crack. The inmate screams, crumpling under Niklaus's iron grip.

"I think I'd like to break the rest of his hand. Then his forearm. Then his elbow. Then snap each of the tendons that string everything together." Niklaus cracks his neck. "Would that make your throat feel better, darling wife?"

I scan the crowd. The whispers. The men seemingly getting ready for a fight as they move their way to the front of the circle forming.

I shake the water from my eyes and place my hand on his chest. "Let's get out of here."

Niklaus hesitates, eyes dropping to my hand, then giving me a sidelong glance.

"Come on," I coax him.

The young man and woman watch us cautiously, clearly fearing the retribution of other prisoners who are gathering closer.

Niklaus unlocks his hold, blinking down at my assailant flailing on the floor as he clutches his arm to his chest.

I turn away from his naked body, feeling disgusted and so fucking sick of being thrown into the most barbaric, inhumane situations that made up the past where our parents are from. How could this world be so evil? How is it so different than the cushioned life Niklaus and I have lived? I mean…I'm in a goddamned co-ed community shower, being cleaned with rusty drain water and assaulted by middle-aged men with boils and sores on their backside.

The sentinel nods for our next wave of inmates to move forward, changing into clean uniforms. And now that our asylum garbs are disposed of, there will be no other details to stand out with. We are now Vexamen prisoners who committed no crime to end up here.

I slip on the cloth and straps that are made up of scarlet rags—small patches of flax linens, coarsely woven together to give me that scratchy, uneven texture against my skin. First is the brassier, stringy and so small and thin, I can clearly see my hard nipples pressing against the material. The bottoms are a shred of red braided string for my backside, and a tight cloth covering my front.

Niklaus buttons his black-and-red pinstriped pants next to me.

"They're going to make us wear the collars," Niklaus warns me.

"Huh?"

I look up just as a sentinel stomps toward us, an inflamed acne-covered face pinching in a grimace at our appearance. He holds out two iron collars and grumbles something in Old Alkadonian.

I give the faintest dip of my head, bearing no more fight in me.

The walk behind our two neighbors is a blur. My feet ache and sting at the sharp, jagged ground. My stomach grumbles from a piercing hunger that won't go away. And I feel sick all the time.

"Do you know how we got here?" Niklaus asks as we wait in a long line of prisoners for our first meal.

The commissary is loud and echoey, bustling with metal plates dropping, cups clapping against tabletops, and inmates shouting over each other.

"No." I drop my head back and roll it side to side to stretch my sore neck. "Kind of. I had a dream I saw Krimson."

Niklaus lifts his gaze hopefully. "Was it real?"

"I don't know. I think. Maybe. It felt real."

"What happened?"

"He was trying to find me. And—" The rest of the dream pummels into my thoughts with a force so powerful, I lose my breath. "Uncle Niles. I saw him. He was in some kind of imprisonment. Shit, I think he was…"

"What?!" Niklaus turns me to face him, so we're not overheard.

"Do you remember that chapter on the different forms of captivity in Vexamen? During the era of the Mazonist Brothers?"

"Yes."

"What was that one where those captured were forced into physical labor until they were assigned a place in society, like the Vexamen Breed or imminent servitude toward the Meat Carnivals?"

Niklaus focuses his blue eyes over my head as he zones out to think. And that gaze shudders, then darkens as a dreadful realization falls over him.

"What? You remember the name?" I ask.

"The Blackspire Ward of The North."

My insides twist into a tight knot.

I let my chin drop in firm agreement. "That's where I saw him. It looked exactly like the photographs."

The line moves along, our metal trays are filled with a green chunky soup, and metal cups scooped from a porcelain tub of cold water. We follow our neighbors to an empty table. I do my best to avoid eye contact with anyone but can feel their eyes drilling holes down my body.

"Husband and wife, hmm?" the young woman asks. "At least you weren't separated during imprisonment."

I briefly cut a glance to the couple observing us. But I'm too overwhelmed by the food in front of me. Too confused, sickened, hungry, anxious, and conflicted over why I'm starving yet filled with a stomach full of tangled knots. The thought of not eating is nauseating. The thought of eating is nauseating. It all just makes my stomach hurt.

I swallow a small spoonful, unbothered that the soup tastes like grass and sour cream with the gritty texture of undercooked rice and oatmeal.

"How long have you two been married?" the woman tries again.

"Not long," Niklaus and I answer at the same time.

I try another spoonful. Nerves impale me from the inside out. What the fuck did that asylum do to me?

"It is a good thing you two are together. Single maidens and gentlemen don't do well. Assaults happen often."

"Hmm." Niklaus taps his spoon to the tray. "Would either of you happen to know of a group of inmates here? Commander Kaspias would have taken a special interest in them."

The young couple furrow their brows at him. "Who?"

"Kaspias? He's a high-ranking commander. Would have a close relationship with the Mazonist Brothers."

They look confused. "Are you talking about Dr. Ivast?"

Niklaus searches my face, then blinks back to our neighbors. "Crow Ivast?"

I raise my eyebrows at Niklaus's question. Not possible. Crow

Ivast was Albatross's grandfather. The savant who once worked for the Mazonist Brothers but was stolen to work for Demechnef.

They nod.

"Do you know of any prisoners named Dessin, Skylenna, Niles, Warrose, Ruth, or Marilynn?" I ask urgently.

"No, I'm sorry. Do you have family or friends here too?" The young woman pats her neighbor on the shoulder. "We've been here a long time. We know almost everyone's names. Haven't heard of those."

I shrink in my seat and stare at Niklaus with parted lips but no words to spare.

"I thought…"

"I've always traveled to places where there are loved ones. But—"

The young man nudges the woman's arm. "I told you. They have to be from that asylum in Dementia. That white gown? That's why they aren't too frightened by the prison. Most are. And they were either traded or abducted, right?"

"You've solved the mystery," Niklaus mocks, but I hold my hand up to him.

"I didn't get your names," I say cautiously.

The woman smiles warmly, crinkling the freckles on her nose. "My name is Sophia. And this is my friend, Jack."

52. Generational Ties

Sapphire

"Jack…" I struggle to form the name.

Niklaus looks between us, confused.

"Yes?"

"Jack Ambrose?" I clarify.

His bright green eyes scroll over my face, my neck, my hands pausing over my tray. He's trying to figure out if he knows me. Is my face familiar? Have we had encounters before? But he comes up blank.

"I've kept my last name a secret." Jack leans across the table, whispering, but close to losing his temper. "I haven't even told Sophia, my oldest friend."

I sit up, unsure how I should even approach this. I open my mouth, but there aren't any words to articulate how I know him.

"You work for them, don't you?" Jack pounds his fist on the table, then points at me. "The brothers sent you. It's not enough what you psychopaths did to my brother, is it? You had to dig deeper into my family tree, huh? I swear to God, if you go after any of the Ambroses,

I'll—"

"I'm a witch!" I spit out. Not the best lie, but not the worst.

Sophia laughs, then bows her head as she realizes I'm serious.

"A witch," Niklaus repeats, angling himself to face me with a polite smirk. "Do tell."

"I can summon knowledge about people. I am not a spy."

Jack scoffs. "That's a bullshit lie an infiltrator would tell."

I give them both a once-over. I'm so confused. None of this makes any sense. How far back did I go? Are my parents even alive yet?

"I don't understand. I thought you both were born in the Chandelier City." I shake my head, trying to piece together everything I know about my grandparents. Chekiss has been the only grandparent I've ever known. I suppose I've never really given much thought to Jack and Sophia, other than a few brief mentions from my mother.

Sophia and Jack exchange a look, smiling sheepishly.

"We have always dreamed of escaping this place. Traveling to Dementia. Starting a new life. But no one has ever escaped the Vexamen Prison." Sophia shrugs, as if she's accepted her fate.

"And you two haven't married yet?" I ask.

"No. Goodness!" Sophia laughs, taking another spoonful of soup past her lips. "Jack has always been a big brother to me."

"Shouldn't you know that if you're a witch?" Jack challenges, still glaring at me skeptically.

"I didn't mean to each other. I know you will never marry Sophia. But you haven't found a wife?"

Violet. One day, you will marry Violet.

Jack shakes his head.

"Jack is very jaded about the idea of love and marriage," Sophia clarifies.

"And children?" Niklaus says.

Jack looks down to his clasped hands on the table. He shakes his head again without a word.

Hmm. That's interesting. He never wanted to have my mother and Aunt Scarlett?

"And you, Sophia?" I add.

Her high cheeks turn a deep maroon. "I'd love to have children and a loving husband one day. Two boys and a girl. It would be lovely to have the boys first so they can protect the little princess."

My heart throbs.

"So, you two were born here? How long have you been imprisoned? What did you do to get in here?" I can't keep up with the questions producing endlessly in my brain. And most importantly, how will they eventually end up back in the Chandelier City?

Sophia perks up to answer, but Jack places a firm hand on her shoulder.

"Not another word. I'm still not convinced you aren't working for the brothers. Until you prove otherwise, no more questions."

I want to keep pushing, but Niklaus pats my thigh, giving me a reassuring nod.

"Fine. Would you two mind filling us in on how to survive here then?" he says, changing the subject.

Jack lifts a bandage on his forearm, checking to see how it's healing so far. I only catch a glimpse of the wound, but it's deep and bright red. Still fresh.

"There is a House of Jester Night," he says with mock excitement.

"A what?"

Sophia explains patiently, "It's an event for the Vexamen Breed soldiers a couple nights a week. They send the inmates to the grand hall with a stage…and make us do awful things to entertain their twisted army."

Niklaus and I exchange a look.

"You mean Fun House Night?" I ask.

"Never heard of that," Jack replies.

Wow. We've traveled so far back, much has changed.

"Do you know what the theme is tonight?"

Sophia and Jack place their guesses to things I haven't heard of from our parents. Hangman's Sword, Screaming Fortune Wheel, Organ Grinder, Black Widow Show, Marionette Theater.

"What's Marionette Theater?" Niklaus asks.

"They take a female prisoner who has too many strikes against her and place her on the stage alone. A long line of male inmates takes turns performing oral sex on her for the crowd. Whichever man brings her to orgasm gets exempt from the next three House of Jester Nights."

"You're fucking kidding me," I choke.

"It's sickening to watch," Sophia agrees. "If the sentinels aren't looking my way, I usually just place my hands over my ears and pray until it stops."

"Sentinels make you watch?"

"You'll be forced to take her place if you're caught closing your eyes."

I'm going to be sick.

Niklaus pushes his tray away, cursing under his breath in revulsion. I watch the way he traces the lines over his knuckles. A simple gesture he only does when something deeply troubles him or makes him nervous. He does it over and over again as he works something out in his mind with a forehead ridged with tension and clenched jaw.

"*Víentezech püvuiz.*"

Jack and Sophia divert their eyes back down to their trays as a thunderous male voice whooshes over my shoulder. The warm breath is stained with the heady scent of pork and tobacco. I wrinkle my nose and refuse to turn around.

"Or is that not your native tongue?" the rumbling voice speaks again, seeming to command obedience with its baritone.

"Correct," I respond curtly.

"You may look upon me when I speak to both of you."

I turn in my seat before Niklaus does. He takes a long sip of his water, then rotates slowly.

The man before me is a thousand-year-old oak tree. I make eye contact with his belt buckle made of leather and solid gold. His muscles are that of a statue, protruding and made of stone from the finest sculptress. And I have to crank my head to stare straight up at him, at least six feet and eight inches from the ground.

"Up. Now."

I examine the weapons of gold and diamonds hanging around his waist. The man does not wear a shirt. It's all leather straps and weapons cutting off the circulation in his enormous pectoral muscles.

"Have we done something wrong?" I ask.

The man lowers himself to eye level, boring a set of strange, bloodshot eyes on me. Shiny, bronze skin, full red lips, and hair in a stunning display of braids twirled around a metal headdress on his head.

"You tell me. I do not have any documentation of your arrival. It's as if you two have leaked in with a breeze through our ventilation system."

I can't help but have the urge to cower. His voice is a cathedral, low and ominous, rolling over me like a death sentence.

"We should not be here, you are right. We have broken no laws," Niklaus responds.

The brawny, god-like man slides his glare to Niklaus, giving him a judgmental once-over.

"Follow me. Willing or unwilling," he orders.

"Are you letting us go?!" I shove my tray to the side and stand excitedly.

"Now!" he roars, silencing the room.

My adrenaline fires spikes of energy through my spine. Before it's too late, I lean across the table to Jack and Sophia.

"If we do not meet again, please know that you will both marry. You will both have children. They will be twins. And you will love them dearly." I savor that little spark of hope that gleams in their eyes. "It…it was so special for me to meet the two of you."

A hand catches on the inside of my elbow, and I'm towed away from our table. Chains are hooked and latched on our iron collars. Our large friend has an impenetrable grip as he hauls us down the long corridor where the music is louder and the stench of human feces and rusty metal is stronger. I curl my fingers on the inside of my collar, trying to soften the strain as I'm practically dragged across the brimstone floors.

I think about how I'm going to explain to my mom that I met her father in prison. That what she knows about him isn't the whole story. He wasn't born in Dementia. He lived in Vexamen for more than half of his life. And Sophia? I wonder if my father knew where she was really from. I wonder if he ever told my mother.

"You speak if you're spoken to." The man looks down at us from over his shoulder, curling his lip in disgust. "You disobey a command, I rape your woman and chop your body into tiny pieces."

I release a startled breath, sticking my jaw out. He's looking at only Niklaus now, and his expression is unwavering and absolute.

"Yes. Fine. We just want to leave," I say quickly, before Niklaus can piss this guy off.

The doors open, grinding against the ground, and welcoming a gust of dusty air that sends the stray hairs on my face flying back. At first glance, I think the figure greeting us in the grand sitting room is a man based on the same lofty height as our escort, but it is not. The person smirking and nodding at our guard is a rather beautiful woman.

"*Désvou niéz?*" The woman nods to us, batting her wispy, long eyelashes.

"Yes. But they cannot understand you," our escort replies, softening a bit for the woman.

She lowers her pointed chin, scrutinizing me with deep-set eyes, and enlarged pupils. Her manicured fingers caress glossy lips, then they return to her belt of gold daggers.

"Do you want my mate to touch you, scrawny woman?" she asks.

"*Stïevesx*, my love. So jealous." Our escort chuckles, shaking his head.

"No, thank you," I say, biting my tongue.

The woman blocks the door, straightening her back and pushing out her impeccable, large breasts. "Good! My brother does not fuck scrawny short women. Only me. Understand?"

"Brother?!" Niklaus and I blurt out together.

"Let our new guests in, Glinorious." A command from a soft-spoken male voice comes from the corner of the sitting room.

The woman, Glinorious, bows her head in routine submission, stepping aside for us to enter.

We follow our escort inside, quietly observing the room.

"Hello, nameless guests," says a red-headed man, moving a heavy chess piece across a board. A Mazonist Brother.

The room is a windowless tomb. It's dim with a few sputtering flames of tallow candles and the orange spit of a hearth so bright, it makes the granite walls sweat. There are heavy wool tapestries on the walls, and meat rafters on the ceilings blackened from the smoke of the poorly ventilated hearth.

The red-headed man waves his hand for us to pick a moth-eaten high-back chair to sit down in. I walk cautiously to a chair with a little more cushion, but as I lower myself, Glinorious tugs my chain and fastens it to the chair.

"They do look sick, don't you think?" The other Mazonist brother moves a chess piece fashioned from tarnished brass. Some of the pawns appear to be replaced with tiny effigies of prisoners.

"Yes, quite."

I make note of the massive guards taking their positions on either side of the room. The man holds his finger under an iron sconce in the shape of a maniacal jester face, dripping wax onto his skin like drool.

And I catch Niklaus scanning the weapons on their belt once more, probably mapping a way out of this in case it goes south.

"I don't suppose you've ever met the esteemed warriors of the North Vexello Mountains, have you?" One of the brothers lowers his small, circular bifocals to direct his question to Niklaus.

"I have not," Niklaus says.

"This is Glinorious Blood and Tycraniz Blood. A prestigious family of the most skilled fighters and swordsmen you've ever seen. And they are devoted to protecting the Mazonist legacy."

My yawn is unintentionally loud.

"My point is that if either of you deem it fitting to assassinate me or my brother, the Bloods are worshipped like gods for what they do to traitors. Impaled, but not enough to kill immediately. Then skinned gradually, and dissected until their victim dies a slow, excruciating death. Remember that if you reach for a knife."

"Point made," Niklaus says flatly.

"We don't want to assassinate you," I note, meeting the lifeless eyes of the brother on the left. "We are here by mistake and want to be released."

That brother doesn't turn away from me. His stare is lifeless, pinning me to my chair as though he is weighing my value as livestock at a market. I am not a person sitting in a chair. I am a noise in his sitting room that has caught a brief moment of his attention. But I don't avert my eyes. I wait until he understands that I am not here to cower.

"Did you know I have a reputation in this dear country I call home?"

That question is for me.

I shrug.

"My people call me superstitious. And it is true. I am." This Mazonist brother speaks with tone that hangs on the urge to yawn or sigh. He bears a thick, raised scar on his jugular where his own mother tried to kill him when he still lived in Alkadonia.

I am speaking to Maxwell Mazonist.

"My scouts have reported that you are a witch," Maxwell considers aloud.

I resist the reflex to meeting Niklaus's eyes. Our conversations were being spied on? How could they know I just told Jack and Sophia this lie to keep our time travel escapades to myself.

"And you believe them?" I ask.

"Quick tongue, young lady…" Malcolm chuckles, moving another chess pieces with mild interest.

"I believe them."

I have no idea whether or not it would be beneficial for me to confirm or deny. Will being a witch get me burned at a stake here? Will it save our lives and get us kicked out because Maxwell is superstitious?

"We'd like to be released," I point out again.

"Oh, I bet you would. And why would I release prisoners who are so clearly from the prim and proper Chandelier City, who have magically appeared in my prison without so much as a trace of appropriate admittance?"

"Do we have a criminal record?" Niklaus interrupts. He waits mockingly. "Have we broken any laws? Guilty of any offenses against you?"

Malcolm's hand tightens around his queen, hovering over the board.

"Tell us your names and perhaps we may be better suited to answer those questions for you."

"My name is Ophelia Dredmoor, and this is my husband, Mortimer Dredmoor," I announce.

Maxwell offers a faint nod to one of the guardians. The doors open and shut to fact check. Aunt Marilynn read us a bedtime story once. It was about Ophelia and Mortimer, a husband and wife who would walk the streets at night and find evil men to invite in for supper. Mortimer carried a lantern with a black flame. When that flame went out, it meant the Ophelia had cursed another evil soul with plagues unknown to man.

We used to ask for that creepy story every Hallow's Eve.

Niklaus catches on quickly as he goes with it without objection.

"I take it you are aware we are at war with your country, Mrs. Ophelia Dredmoor?" Malcolm lowers his bifocals to inspect my immediate reaction.

"I've heard mentions of it, yes."

"Hmm." Malcolm signals to someone behind us with two fingers. "Drinks for our new guests. And, ah, Crow, I sent for you hours ago."

"I was undergoing trials with a rather difficult subject." A startlingly short man walks into the room, dropping into a crooked chair next to Malcolm. He can't weigh more than one hundred and ten pounds. With a low ashy brown ponytail hanging at the base of his neck, and greasy slicked back hair, he reminds me of a ferret or maybe a gerbil.

"We're having a drink with our newest guests. Undocumented, which is, well, anyway… They are in the cages next to two of your subjects! Don't you find that interesting?" Maxwell clasps his hands together and sits up in his chair, making an animated face at the doctor.

Right on cue, a servant delivers two dull metal cups to Niklaus and I. The liquid has a potent smell. Stronger than alcohol, mixed with an earthy sweetness that smells just like…

My eyes snap over to Niklaus so quickly, I'm sure no one catches it.

Black rose of the well.

The same plant the Mazonist Brothers gave our parents to get the truth out of them. When ingested, it's impossible for anyone to resist spilling every ounce of the truth. But not for us. Thankfully, our mother's put black rose of the well in our food since we were small. Amounts so light, we never even noticed. It had no effect on us, and they made sure we knew it too.

Study that smell, Krimson. If you ever catch that earthy sweetness coming from your food or drink, someone is trying to wrongfully extract information from you. But you've all grown such a wonderful tolerance to it.

Guilt claws at my chest.

I used to call my mother paranoid to Krimson once we were let outside to play. I'd fuss, call her names, and laugh at how obsessive and distrustful she was for no reason.

I was wrong.

"Drink," Malcome urges with an inviting smile.

I hold up my glass and tip my head forward in gratitude, chugging the drink, and resting assured that we are not being poisoned. That would be a colossal waste of black rose of the well.

"Thank you," I say, handing the cup back to the servant.

"Certainly." Malcolm rotates away from his game and steeples his fingers. "How did you say you found yourself in our prison again?"

I run my mouth as if it has a mind of its own. "A few soldiers from your breed were belligerently drunk. They arrested us by accident. I believe they were running after a few individuals who were caught stealing."

"And they simply…threw you into a cage?"

"Yes. Like I said, they were obscenely drunk."

Malcolm pinches his lips together. He knows I'm telling the truth, because the black rose of the well shouldn't give me a choice. But the story is still puzzling him.

"What foul behavior. My Breed is usually very disciplined about drinking while on duty. The punishment is usually steep, ten days of isolation at the bottom of our prison well without any clothing at all."

I give Crow Ivast a once-over. "Jack and Sophia are your test subjects?"

"Indeed."

"Why? They are quite nice."

"To you, I'm sure. They don't particularly like me much after my procedures have effectively ended the lives of their twin siblings," Crow remarks while reflecting on past mistakes the way a librarian would jot down slight imperfections to an old book.

I fall out of character. Twins? Siblings? I don't think Mom knew about that. Grandfather Jack had a twin? So did Grandmother Sophia? And they were killed here? Being tested on by the infamous fucking Crow Ivast?!

"And was it random that the two of you were placed next to such valuable subjects of our esteemed doctor?" Maxwell interrupts.

"You should ask your drunk soldiers that. We were thrown in the cages because two of the soldiers had to stop and take a piss in an empty cage across from Sophia and Jack." Niklaus follows my lead with ease. Speaking at a relaxed, lethargic pace, as if we're around a group of inquisitive friends and not the tyrants of Vexamen.

"And you're from Dementia, judging from your accents and the devastated health of your wife." Maxwell bores his condemnatory frown over my ribs and collarbone.

"Yes. We came here seeking refuge," Niklaus answers.

The Mazonist brothers laugh, exchanging amused glances. Crow snickers into his hand.

"I do not think we have ever received a refugee."

"We've had countless seeking refuge from us, in fact."

They chuckle among themselves again.

"We've heard great things of the impressive work you've done with your country. It puts Demechnef to shame." Niklaus doesn't let his serious expression falter. If only these two tyrants knew the future leader of Demechnef was playing them for a fool.

"Yes, well, who can fault you for that? Demechnef has the government of hormonal menstruating woman," Malcolm muses.

"Orin and Abraham should have been put to death in Alkadon, not for treason, but for having these beliefs that are nothing more than *laughable*," Maxwell agrees.

"You can imagine how difficult it is to desire citizenship from the inside of your prison." Niklaus swishes the last sip of his drink around in his cup, then finishes it off. "Which is why we desire to be released as soon as possible."

The dim, muggy room is a bed of stagnant water as the brothers contemplate the request. They stare at us, silently weighing their options.

"I will give your wife a choice, as she has claimed to be a witch." Maxwell leans forward in his chair. "You can either spend three nights and three days in my bed chamber so that I may sire Mazonist heirs. Your eyes are very interesting. Perhaps if I impregnate you, our children will have similar eyes…" he trails off topic.

Niklaus stands abruptly.

I'm going to hurl. "And the other option?"

"You can spend those three days in my prison, proving you are a real witch. I would release you and your beloved husband from prison and offer you employment." Maxwell shifts his weight and looks to his brother. "I've never had a witch work for me before."

Malcolm lifts his fluffy eyebrows. "Just as you've never impregnated one either."

The three men laugh again, as though I am not sitting in front of them. As though Niklaus isn't standing with balled fists despite the enormous guardian in the room taking cautious steps toward him.

"No one will be impregnating my wife," Niklaus states with a growl.

"Oh? A Mazonist ruler may impregnate whomever he pleases."

Niklaus curls his hand around his collar.

"I'll prove I'm a witch. Three days. That'll work!" I interrupt, rising from my chair to get Niklaus's attention and try to keep him from getting killed.

Maxwell frowns, looking a bit disappointed. He drums his fingers along the table in thought. And I know he's debating whether or not just to choose to have me in his bed, if only to put Niklaus in his place.

"I am barren, so impregnation isn't even an option. But I am a very powerful witch and would be very useful to the Mazonist legacy," I add, but Crow Ivast flips through pages of a book in my periphery, and something buzzes in my core as I recognize the cover.

There has never been much information about Vexamen history in our lessons growing up, but Aunt Ruth and Uncle Warrose shared much of what they knew. They told us all about how Crow Ivast uncovered the original human experiments on twins. How he migrated with the rest of the Mazonist followers from Alkadon and was seen as a psychologically impaired freak there for talking to himself in public and having inherently maniacal ideas to expand the mind.

And there was a book where he wrote down all of his trials, tests, and…chemical warfare archives.

In other words, the injection Masten and Kaspias used to put my father in his coma.

Aunt Ruth found the details of the neurotoxin that was used.

Crow Ivast named it *Díevetz Alkadon* Agent. Which translates to, Death to Alkadon. He planned to use it on the royal families there so that they would be unable to sire any additions to their bloodlines, but fell ill when his son, Cardinal Ivast was just a child. Crow knew how important his book, known as the Ivast Codex, was to his enemies. He burned every page that had an antidote, counteragent, neutralizer, or remedy to his creations.

Aunt Ruth and Uncle Warrose scoured every archive in Vexamen existence.

Crow Ivast had a brilliant mind and ensured those secret remedies would die with him. Ultimately keeping my father in his coma for twenty-one years thus far.

Yet here he is. With that highly sought after book. Right in front of me. Can I live with myself if I leave this room without even attempting to know how to wake my father when I come back?

"But if it appeases you all, I do have a way of proving my powers can collect intimate details on complete strangers. Shall I demonstrate?" My voice shakes. This is a long shot. It holds great potential to break my heart. But I'm going for it.

"Oh, we do love magic tricks," Malcolm hums.

"Crow Ivast, there were spirits whispering your name as we speak. They've shared many secrets. May I share a few?"

Crow sighs, waving his hand for me to continue, as though he finds this entire charade a waste of time.

"Your wife's name is Absinthe. She is an incredibly religious woman."

The men chuckle, looking unimpressed.

"Not a secret," Crow comments with a slow blink. "Anyone who's been in the same room as my bride knows this."

I smile sheepishly. "And that you've had many affairs? Had two bastard children that you had killed? Fell in love with a woman twice your age who mysteriously disappeared? Is that all common knowledge as well?"

I've never been so thankful that I paid attention in this part of our history lessons.

The Mazonist Brothers gape at me in shock, then back to Crow.

"This all true?" they ask.

Crow is positively stunned. His oily brows pull tight together, then lift to his hairline.

"Yes. It is true."

"And I'm also hearing how you created a neurotoxin that can put a person in a coma once they have sexual intercourse. That's impressive." I hold my breath and hope my inquiry isn't too on the nose and obvious that I'm fishing.

Crow's upper lip twitched, then curls into a mocking half-smile.

"I haven't even completed the formula and equations for that yet. It's all theory."

"Well, you will." A twinge of hatred burns my forehead and cheeks. "But…it looks like you always have an antidote, except this one. I suppose this one was too complex for you to form a solution to."

"Absurd!" Crow stands, slicking his stray hairs away from his face nervously. "Yes, it is complex. All of my chemical agents are. But I've already mapped out the only antidote that could reverse the effects of the neurotoxin before it is activated by consummation!"

"The spirits say you don't have a clue, actually."

"Wrong! There is a cluster of trees that only grow in Dementia. The leaves hold rare properties that, if boiled and consumed before intercourse, would prevent the victim from falling into a coma."

My heart races. "And what are these trees called?"

"It's said a great dragon died there. It's called The Red Oaks."

I could drop to my knees in tears. All this time. The answer was among the trees that surrounds our home. The fiery red leaves that would fall around my parents when they were children, sprinkling across the ground they'd play on.

But I must keep my composure.

"Drinking the tea made of red oak leaves would cure such a powerful neurotoxin?" I ask skeptically.

"Yes. You've raised my blood pressure with this debate. It's like explaining astrology to an infant."

"Hmm." I nod with only a sliver of interest in the topic.

Maxwell angles himself to a more comfortable position in his chair. "You two lost me at all of your neuro-nonsense topics. It's a decent start, my beautiful prisoner."

I sigh. "Three days then?"

The brothers come to a firm agreement, then continue conversing and playing chess like we are not there, and then we are sent back to our cages until the House of Jester Night commences.

Niklaus walks the entire way back in silence. Even as we sit against the chipped, dented bars of our cages, he cranks his neck back and closes his eyes.

"There's so much to unpack," I murmur, breaking the ice. Our situation isn't great, but it feels relieving to be away from the other inmates for the day.

"Mmm hmm."

"So, we're what? Over fifty years in the past?" I prompt.

"Sixty or seventy, I'm guessing."

"And we're here distinctly by the anchor of my grandparents."

"Let's go back. You said you dreamed my dad was in The Blackspire Ward of The North?" Niklaus does move, not even to breathe as he waits for my response.

"Yeah."

"And Krimson saw you?"

"I think he was searching for me," I say.

"If he knows you're missing, he would have gotten your mother involved. By now, the rest of the family must know," Niklaus contemplates in a hushed, gravelly voice.

"And he saw where Uncle Niles was. He'd relay that to my mother."

Niklaus nods. "Good."

I peek over at him and can't help but trail over his bare chest and the prominent muscles over his strong arms. Does he want to stop talking and sleep? He's so uninterested, I feel like a grating little pest for wanting to keep talking.

He speaks again. "Three days here, little witch?"

I sigh. "That or I could've gotten comfy in his bed chamber."

Niklaus growls in the base of his throat.

"Of course I'd never do that. I'm a devoted, faithful wife."

"That a fact?" Niklaus smirks but keeps his eyes closed.

"Yes, it is."

"I didn't want you to have to bear being married to me another moment after the situation called for that title *here*…the way it did in the last predicament we were in," he explains.

I shake my head and look down. "It isn't the worst thing."

Although, it sort of is. I can't stand the way my lungs are zapped with excitement when he calls me his wife. If only he knew my body reacts this aggressively. There would never be a day I'd live it down.

"I bet your future wife will hate me for our illegitimate marriage once we make it home." I lean against the bars we share between our cages.

"And is there a man back at home you'll hope to tie the knot with?" he asks, though the boredom layering his tone is heavy today.

"Your best friend, Stark."

Niklaus's eyes snap open. He grimaces at me from the corner of his eye.

I wink.

"He is no longer my best friend."

"Oh, no?"

His angry blue eyes drop to my waist then find their way back to my face. "No."

"Why not?" Am I bored? Do I still crave that vengeance I wanted before we started traveling through time? I don't know. But this feels like a needed distraction.

"Are you still best friends with Mabel Rose?" The question swings into my gut with brutal force.

My molars grate against each other as I stare ahead. I shake my head.

The jokes have ended.

The humor at poking him to get a reaction has ceased to exist.

"Why did you do it?" I ask as I wind my arm around the bars. "Why did you have to fuck my best friend?"

His exasperated breathing becomes heavier. "Mabel Rose had it out for you, Spitfire. She spent many months making advances on me at the tavern while we were intoxicated. On a night she was drunk off her ass, she admitted that she was tired of living in your shadow."

"What?"

"You really never noticed?"

My chest stings with a sudden epiphany.

"You and I had a nasty fight, and you got me suspended from

sword training. That's when I eventually gave in."

"You got yourself suspended for being a piece of shit," I retort.

Niklaus chuckles.

"That fucking killed me, Niklaus." I stare at him until he meets my eyes. "I don't know if I'll ever get over it. That sounds so dense and vapid after everything we've been through. But it's true. You wanted to hurt me, and it worked. Mabel Rose was my best friend. Granted, her being a jealous bitch had nothing to do with you, but she still took you…and you rubbed it in my face to *wound* me."

Niklaus sits up, opening his mouth to argue my point—but I stop him.

"I'm sorry. It's ridiculous to even rehash this now. Jesus, look at me. I just met my dead grandparents in prison. And I'm over here talking about petty drama."

Niklaus watches me closely. Several seconds go by. And I can't tell if he's frozen in his spot because he's still hanging on to my last words about our previous discussion or if he's just pissed at me for changing the subject.

"My mother told me they both met violent ends," he finally says.

I dip my head. "Jack ended his life. And Sophia was sexually assaulted by men from Demechnef in front of my father and—they forced him to murder her with a sickle at the age of six."

"Yeah, I remember something about that."

"My father watched both of them die, actually." The image in my head of him lying in that bed at home jumpstarts my brain. "Holy shit! I have his antidote!"

Niklaus shakes his head. "Not an antidote. Not really. He would have had to drink the red oak leaves in tea before…you know, with your mother in order to be saved."

"Then it's a good thing I can move through time!"

"You can control it now?"

"No."

"Okay then."

"Do you not get how incredible that information is, Niklaus? All I'd have to do is warn him. Just once." My skin tingles from the warmth that is spreading to every inch of my body. "Can you imagine my mom's face? She'd get to see him again. I'd get to bring him back to her. And

Krimson? Oh god, what he wouldn't give to meet our dad. He's Krimson's hero."

"And you?"

"And me."

It took years to bury this blasting river of hope inside my heart. It's been an unwanted guest for so long, knocking softly even when I refused to answer, even when I turned out the lights and pretended not to be home. That swell of hope was always there, praying that I'd meet him one day.

"What if it makes our future worse? Changing something like that?"

"*Future could get worse.*"

A cold, wet snout nudges the back of my arm. Whiskers. Soft fur. I balk at Dellilian looking up at me from her seated posture to my left.

"Dellilian!" I yelp, throwing my arms around her. I nuzzle my face into her black fur and grin. "I didn't get to thank you. Not just for saving us from Vrath, but for keeping me alive and breathing when I was buried!"

The precious little creature starts to purr, leaning into my hug and burrowing into my chest.

"I don't know who sent you, but I'm so happy they did," I tell her.

"You think warning Sapphire's father could harm our timeline, Dellilian?" Niklaus interrupts. His approach toward her isn't nearly as agitated and hostile as it usually is.

Dellilian peeks around me to acknowledge Niklaus.

"*Save lives. Lose lives too.*"

Niklaus and I freeze.

"Tell me that doesn't mean what I think it means," I mutter.

My pulse is heavy in my throat. The strange circus bulbs start to dim.

"*New births. New funerals,*" Dellilian replies vaguely in her childlike voice.

"No, Dellilian. I need a firm yes or no. If we prevent Patient Thirteen from falling into his coma, will someone else have to take his place?" Niklaus sits upright, grabs on to the bars by my face and leans toward us.

"*Yes.*"

"Fuck!" We throw ourselves back against the bars.

"There has to be a way I can warn him!" I slam my hands on the ground.

"Are there any ways around it?" Niklaus asks.

Dellilian takes a few seconds to think. "*Kill.*"

I lock eyes with Niklaus, sharing the same thought. We seem to follow a similar train of thought as his eyes spring between mine at a steady rhythm.

"If we kill Vrath, could it be done?" I ask.

"*Yes. Bad Man.*"

"But there could still be catastrophic consequences to the future we came from, Sapphire."

I scoff. "I doubt it."

"If bringing him out of his coma ensures that your brother dies in fatal attack from one of your father's enemies? Or maybe that his existence triggers another deadly war? Are those seriously outcomes you're willing to risk?"

The disbelief comes simmering off my skin in hot bursts.

"How can you even ask me that?"

His face does not soften. It's as though he found that infuriating expression he used to wear all the time. The one that is uncaring, unfeeling, unbearably cold toward my feelings.

"How can you ask me to let you do this and risk everyone's lives?"

I ignore his question and lie down next to Dellilian, inviting her to curl up next to me. My mouth stays shut. My eyes stay closed. And Niklaus doesn't try to talk about it either. This is something we will never agree on. Is there logic to his concerns? Of course. I don't want anything bad to happen to anyone we love because I changed the future with my warning.

But I have to believe that ensuring my father never falls into that coma would only make our home a better place. If he can't see that, then we have nothing to discuss.

With his help, or without it…

I'm going to warn my dad.

53. House of Jester Night

Niklaus

The dome of soldiers is larger in size than I originally pictured. A colosseum of cheering, laughing, drinking men with few women in uniform, pointing at the stage in front of us and kicking their feet up as they listen to the Ringmaster making demands of the inmates.

Blasts of fire shoot out from the ceilings. Prisoners wait around the stage with mixed emotions wilting their postures or causing them to bounce on their heels in anticipation. The draft in the air wafts the scent of burning coal and filthy soldiers who haven't showered in days. Deep reds, black, and bright yellow illuminate the stage stained with bodily fluids and burn marks.

"Looks like it's the Fighter's Gallows tonight," Sophia shouts to us over the chanting soldiers and roaring flames. "The Ringmaster chooses your weapon, and you fight until someone is injured."

"All of the inmates fight?" I ask.

Jack shakes his head. "They pick us at random."

"Have you ever been chosen, Sophia?" Sapphire asks nervously.

"No. If I were to get chosen, I'd die. I don't know how to fight. Instead, I volunteer to go to the Black Widow's room. It's not offered to every inmate, but they'll definitely take you. We'll raise our hands to have a sentinel escort us before they begin."

"What's the Black Widow's Room?" I ask. I remember a chapter about the different Fun House Nights, but there wasn't too much detail on them.

Sophia shrinks into herself, looking cornered in her own body.

"They give the women a medication and assign them to a room. They lie on a table, naked, and end up—*touching* themselves to relieve the intense arousal in front of a small audience of generals and commanders to view," Jack explains matter-of-factly.

Sophia's neck darkens with redness.

My vision turns red as I slash my gaze in Sapphire's direction.

"I won't need to do that," she says absently, watching the stage get set up with racks of dull, stained weapons.

"I know it doesn't sound very scary, but inmates die here. They lose limbs or are gutted on the spot. We're safer in the Black Widow's Room," Sophia begs, touching Sapphire's elbow.

They do lose limbs here. We know this devasting fact quite well.

"I can defend myself."

Sophia steps back. "You can fight with a weapon?"

"She can do more than defend herself. Sapphire is a skilled fighter," I say, keeping my voice even so the surge of pride stays buried in my chest.

"That's incredible." Jack looks her over with raised eyebrows.

"Sapphire? That's your name? How beautiful." Sophia's warm brown eyes light up. "If I have children one day like you say I will, I do hope they will be skilled fighters too. It's a monstrous world we live in, isn't it? How wonderful that you have learned how to protect yourself."

Sapphire's forehead wrinkles as her eyebrows pull together. Her lips get pulled behind her teeth as she struggles to hold information in.

"Thank you, Sophia."

The Ringmaster's animated voice echoes across the overstimulating colosseum. The inmates quiet down to listen, being shoved together as the last lines of us are jam-packed around the stage.

"Goodluck. I'll see you both back in our cages." Sophia rubs a warm hand on the back of my arm and Sapphire's, smiling reassuringly at us. I don't know how that one smile manages to calm my nerves, but it does.

Sapphire steps toward her, ready to stop her from having to go to the Black Widow Room. But my hand catches the inside of her elbow, and she bulldozes me with the fiery eyes.

"Let her go," I whisper, leaning into her ear so Jack can't hear me. "If that's what she normally does, then we cannot change it. Imagine if we changed the course of her life to end before she can give birth to your father."

Sapphire doesn't move as she plays that scenario out in her head. Then, with a frustrated breath, she pulls away from me and faces the stage again.

"You still mad at me?" My breath flutters a few strands of loose copper hair on the back of her head.

"You still an idiot for saying I can't save my dad?"

I roll my eyes. "Still an idiot."

"Then yes, still mad at you. Still hate you."

Sapphire straightens her upper back as I move so close, my chest grazes her hair.

"Now what if I get called up on that stage to fight and get myself killed?" I taunt.

"I doubt you'd have a mark on you."

I smirk. "Is that a compliment?"

"Absolutely not." She crosses her arms, and the movement pushes her heavy breasts together under those shreds of dark red fabric. "It's just a fact."

I'm fucking confused as hell being this close to her as she compliments me, whether she meant it or not. She has this natural scent at the top of her head that I've always noticed. Every time our parents forced us to hug, I would close my arms around her reluctantly, and even though I would grimace at the insufferable act—I'd always breathe in her scent.

That paired with these muddled, disordered, inexplicable thoughts I've been having toward Sapphire. There are these knots in my stomach that just won't go away when I'm around her. It's a physical exertion not to look at her. Maybe it's a mental illness or trauma response I've developed since being thrown into these fucked up situations with her. Maybe when we return home, I'll be able to look at her and only feel that cool indifference or hatred again—no in-between.

"And if I get hurt? You going to feel sorry for me?" I ask, low and hoarse in her ear. I see the skin on the back of her arms pebble and raise.

"I already feel sorry for you," she bites back.

I grin.

The fighting begins. First, the two inmates chosen are older gentlemen—mid-forties. They're given a set of dull throwing knives and war hammer. The man with the throwing knives had no idea how to properly throw them, so he ended up getting his cheekbone shattered by the war hammer.

And Sophia was absolutely right. Sentinels religiously monitored us to ensure we were watching the blood and gore, not flinching away as the next victor cracks into bone until the inmate is screaming, unconscious, or dead on the platform.

"They aren't trained combatants," Sapphire says under her breath.

"No, they're not."

Servants mops up the stage of the last brutal blow. Chunks of skin are splattered from the impact of a spiked maul. The Ringmaster takes his time searching for the next fighters, only briefly interrupted as a soldier approaches his stand at the corner of the stage. The young man with long braids and fresh scars painting across the left side of his face, cups his hand to the Ringmaster.

And his eyes land on me.

I knew it.

Those electric eyes are glowing with the need to entertain the crowd. He smiles wide like a clown who has just lost his mind. Cheeks pull back unnaturally. And he dips his hat at me, pointing and shouting something I can't understand, eliciting a roar of excitement from the Breed.

Sentinels force their way through the mass of inmates, eyes trained on me.

"You'll be fine," Sapphire says nervously, losing all the icy edge she had for me moments ago. "Get to a sword, okay? I don't care what they assign you. There's a reason they say you could have fought next to my father, Niklaus. You are *that* good."

I was never nervous about having to fight, but it's clear she is. For me.

"I *will* be fine, darling wife. The inmates here aren't trained the way we were."

She nods, exhaling deeply to calm her nerves.

"Good luck." Jack pats me on the back, stepping out of the way of the sentinels that roughly escort me to the front.

I walk up the steps confidently, not letting myself be fazed by the heat of the torches surrounding the stage, stomping soldiers, the screams of profanity, or the ripe smell of blood from under my bare feet.

Since I was a little boy, my mother and I would wake up before sunrise, and we'd duel with every kind of weapon. I learn to throw axes, swing a whip so precisely I could split a grape in half from several feet away, giving Uncle Warrose a run for his money. We'd throw knives at targets, fight with small daggers, wrestle, and of course, swing the sword until my arm was throbbing and numb from the weight of the metal. It's like she knew this was coming for me one day. It's like she planned to prepare me every day so I would survive here.

Even if I'm not assigned a sword, I'll be okay.

And as I scan the mob of prisoners surrounding the stage, there isn't a single man or woman that concerns me. Most of them already have preexisting injuries, probably from prior House of Jester Nights.

Like Sapphire said, I'll be fine.

"*Yiéxc seivész!*" the Ringmaster announces, stomping his cane on the metal platform, clomping a boot with it in excitement.

I choose his wife.

"Wait..." I blink rapidly, watching the sentinels surround Sapphire. "No..."

"That's against the rules!" Jack shouts, repeating himself in their language. "You cannot force man and wife to fight!"

I shake my head as they shove her onto the stage, hard enough to make her crash to her knees. And she looks up at me through a mess of copper waves and untamed curls.

How the fuck could this happen?

"No." I glare up at the Ringmaster, gritting my teeth, and standing my ground. "I will not hurt her."

Sapphire stands to her feet, unsure of what to do with herself as all eyes are on us. And it's all too overstimulating to think straight. To search for a way out of this. To get Sapphire out of this. I will not fight her. I'd never raise a weapon against her.

The prisoners gasp and talk among themselves as the soldiers in the stands throw food and drinks, not hard enough to make it to the center stage, but enough to make Sapphire flinch.

The Ringmaster stares at me again, still grinning.

"They will take it out on your wife if you refuse to fight!" Jack hollers over the noise.

Sapphire and I lock eyes in horror.

We know what happened to Aunt Ruth. They do not take punishments lightly, in fact, it's another added element to their performance. And I'd never forgive myself if Sapphire lost the ability to walk because I refused a challenge.

"We'll put on a good show for them, okay?" I say low enough for only her ears.

Sapphire gulps. "Okay."

A Vexamen slayer sword is tossed to me. Double bladed, heavier than the average but light enough that I can still hold it with one hand. The hilt is wrapped in a red leather, so worn it looks scorched.

Sapphire has a curved scimitar sword, crafted to sever tendons with a single swipe. It's a dancer's weapon, merciless and swift—the kind of sword that was forged in a desert, fought under many days of drought and burning suns.

I sigh in relief as that sword type has been proven to be light enough for her, especially now as she's most likely lost a lot of muscle mass from being starved in the asylum.

The stadium sings a battle cry as I assume the fight is supposed to begin.

We side-step around the ring, testing the weight of our weapons and the balance it takes to maneuver them comfortably. There's a silent agreement that we will make our moves as predictable as possible without alerting the Ringmaster that we're simply putting on a performance for their liking. No one gets hurt. It will just be a damn good duel.

"I guess they really did find the one inmate in this prison who could keep up with me," I comment with an inviting grin.

Sapphire makes a face. "More than keep up."

I move so quickly the first few rows of inmates around the stage go quiet, and normally, I would have caught my opponent completely off guard. This slash of my blade would have created a gaping wound across their collarbone.

But Sapphire is just as fast as she blocks it with such little effort, I can't help but blink in amazement.

Sapphire

Everything. Fucking. Hurts.

The strain on my weak, feeble muscles from blocking his first blow is enough to make me black out. But thankfully, the nerves from fighting on full display gives me a surge of blood pumping into my muscles and joints that I desperately need to keep up with this man.

I've only jousted with a scimitar once, but it was fairly easy to wield. The torchlight catches glimmers along the crescent edge. But Niklaus's sword is built for far more damage. It's a predator's claw against a god's blade.

As the fight begins, I focus on my footwork because each of his calculated strikes drive me backward. Sparks spit where steel collides. And I meet his advances in quick fragments, darting around him like lightning, redirecting and deflecting.

The sharp tip of his weapon zings through the air with obscene precision. I can see it in his eyes. Each move is measured to miss me by an inch. Even if I stopped fighting back, his strikes would never touch my skin. That mastery that so many have praised him for in our years of training…it's all being used to ensure I don't get hurt.

With a speedy glance, I notice the Ringmaster lean forward on his podium, seemingly unimpressed at the lack of gore.

My scimitar slices the air a breath away from his ribs, but my hand falters before I can hurt him. And it all has the audience jeering, spitting, howling for more. For someone to get hurt.

"You're going to have to rough me up a bit, Spitfire," he says in a low enough pitch to avoid any other ears.

I dodge the swing of his double blade as it zooms over my head.

Out of breath with sweat dripping down my back, I say, "No."

"They won't let us stop unless they see some blood."

"No," I cough out, blocking his downward swing and holding his weight above my chest as we meet an inch away from each other.

"I know you're good enough not to actually hurt me too bad. Okay? I'm a big boy. I can take it."

I grunt, shaking my head again.

He gives me an annoyed glare. "Wouldn't you like to nick me just once? Since I'm going to do everything in my power to stop you from changing the future and saving your dad?"

A second wind floods my core, recharging my veins with a lethal rage that blinds me, controls my next movements, and brings tears to my eyes.

"Over my fucking dead body." I throw my weight into my next advance, drawing a nice, clean cut across his bicep.

Niklaus smirks, bowing his head in approval.

"Very good."

I peer up at the Ringmaster, curling his upper lip in disgust. Though he barks something to his audience of restless soldiers, and they fall into a fit of drunk laughter.

"Again," Niklaus orders, following the same context clues I'm piecing together.

Still not enough.

I huff, groan, then side-step his next jab at me. I cut the edge of my foot on his razor edge on purpose as I use my heel to kick it away. With his core vulnerable, I slice into his stomach. The swipe is so fast, so unexpected, Niklaus growls. Both at the sudden sharp pain, but also at the dripping blood coming off my foot and onto the stage floor.

But I need to bleed too. It's an artificial wound meant to give them a scene bloodier than it actually is. The scarlet red smears across the floor, enough to form a noticeable obstacle for me as I keep my feet moving to maintain agility.

I search the sentinels for any sign that someone is going to stop the fight.

But there is no end near.

"You are a selfish little girl, Spitfire." An unnerving amount of blood streams from Niklaus's stomach, pooling over his waistline and saturating the fabric. "You'd jeopardize both of our families' futures just to warn a man who was criminally insane!"

At this point, I cannot tell if he's only saying these things to provoke me. It's enough that his eyes gleam with a hateful truth burning through his pupils. I bite down, tossing my sword from my right hand to the left, and slash at one side of his chest. The attack is harsher than I intended, and he groans at the skin being ripped open.

Those oceanic eyes darken.

Niklaus's attacks are even harder to fend off as I'm out of breath. My lungs burn. My hands tremble. My pulse stutters like a flame being snuffed out.

At some point, I can't keep up with my feet stumbling back. I'm too tired to provide well-orchestrated footwork or agile maneuvers. Each of his strikes hurt my joints and blister into my bones. And I fall back, head thumping against the stage.

Niklaus cages me to the floor with his body, throwing his sword down against mine. I don't even know how I'm managing to hold my weapon to his, with his weight and strength pressurizing against my shaking arms. But here I am. Teeth gritting together. Hands going numb. Eyes welling with tears. Sweat glistening across every inch of skin.

"Are you submitting to me, dear wife?" His deep murmur glazes over my skin.

I'm too beaten down to offer any fight left.

"I can't—I'm so tired."

Drops of blood splatter from Niklaus's arm, chest, and stomach to the floor around me and onto my body huffing and puffing under his hold.

He scans the audience, sweeping over the countless rows of individuals observing us, then to the Ringmaster who has not budged. There's a set of gears that rotate in his head, and for several seconds I adversely feel safe under the security of his body guarding mine. I can breathe. I can catch my breath.

Cheering. Stomping. Clapping.

Niklaus drops his gaze back down to me.

Flames soar behind his head.

And he looks absolutely stripped of words.

"Niklaus…"

"I'm not going to hurt you, Sapphire."

With that, he holds his breath, scoops his hands along the side of my face, and kisses me.

It's careful, restrained, and cautious. But as the noise dies beyond this safe place on the platform, I soften my tired, defensive posture. I open up for him. My legs part, letting his hips lower between my thighs. He pauses to pull away, lifting those dark lashes to get a good look at me. And his head dips down again, taking my lips, my tongue, and melting his frame into my own.

It's like being underwater and caught in a thunderstorm without shelter all at once.

It could be the delirium. The exhaustion. The malnutrition.

But my heart jumps into motion. Warmth washes over my legs and lower belly. Everything is doused with white-hot flames. And I can't imagine wanting anyone else. The taste of his tongue as it slips into my mouth. His familiar scent. The way I'd know the texture of his skin if I were blind and falling into a deep sleep.

We fight to deepen the kiss, pulsing with desire and uncontained lust.

The euphoria is drenching the good sense I have to stop. But I can't. I want him so badly, I'd have sex with him right now, on this stage, in front of everyone. My legs spread wider, and his growl vibrates against my lips.

If Niklaus wasn't on top of me, everyone would see how much I need him. They'd see my red uniform darkened as I grow soaking wet. I writhe against his hard cock, rubbing against my clit.

But a brazen gust of air hits me. An empty space takes Niklaus's place. He's torn from my arms. He's pushed to stand at the edge of the stage.

"I will not hurt my wife!" Niklaus yells, flipping off the Ringmaster.

The inmates combust into a bout of complaints, crying, screaming, begging, trying to run. And the Ringmaster looks downright pleased with this decision. He tips his tall black hat to Niklaus, the crow's feet around his eyes creasing into dark lines as he beams at us.

Jack's voice barely rises above the ongoing commotion.

"They're going to take it out on all of us!" He forms a funnel around his mouth with his hands. "Join Sophia!"

I prop myself up on my elbows, staring at Jack in confusion.

I avert my eyes to the female prisoners scurrying to the sentinels with pleading hands, begging them with tears bulging from their eyes and hysterical voices.

Niklaus loops an arm around my waist and lifts me to my feet. The show shuts down. The fire ceases its explosive fireworks. The strange music scrapes to a stop. And the multitude of inmates are ants trying to outrun a tsunami of rain with nowhere to go.

"What's going on?" I ask.

"Everyone gets punished, I think." He holds me close, strokes my back. "Consequences of not fighting to the death."

"But that's not fair!" I shrink away from the sentinels jabbing us with rods to join the others.

The stadium is drained of its entertainment. Like cattle being herded from one enclosed space to the next, whips are lashing across the backs of stragglers, and bull hooks are poking those who resist.

So, we follow behind Jack who seems to know the best ways to blend in and stay out of trouble.

"Are you angry with me?" Niklaus asks.

"Always."

But I can still taste that kiss. And I'm not sure where it came from. We had that talk in the cave. We were in agreement. I feel so twisted and uneasy over the new desire that draws me into him.

"Good because I meant what I said," he replies coldly.

I flick my gaze to him, sticking out my jaw. "Are you fucking kidding me?"

"I stand by not warning your father."

Even though Niklaus has always shown me his true character, that of an incessant, insecure bully…why did I think things were different now? I am an idiot for even feeling that sting of betrayal.

"Even after kissing me?" I ask. My voice sounds so small. So defeated. And I am ashamed of myself for letting him have any control over these intimate feelings that are quickly being erased.

Niklaus stares ahead. "That kiss didn't change anything for me. I only did it hoping the Ringmaster would find that more entertaining than the fighting."

My thoughts fracture. One section mourning, and the other plotting. My immediate spike of anger isn't loud—it's ice cold. I cut my stare into him with wide eyes. There are absolutely no words to explain to him what that sentiment means to me…

It's humiliation strangled by utter disbelief.

This fury coils low in my stomach, crouching and waiting patiently for the right thing to say. And as Niklaus finally shifts his attention down to me on the long march to our punishment, through the creepy prison halls—he waits for me to reply. Those unfeeling, indifferent blue eyes do a quick examination of my expression, trying to identify what I'm thinking.

But my stillness is deceptive.

I do not give a fuck about him anymore.

And he'll never know that I did.

When we finally get back, I will never speak to him again.

Screams break me out my blood-boiling trance. The sentinels at the back of the herd are burning prisoners with torches to get the line to move faster.

After running and leaping over inmates who have tripped—we arrive at the community showers. The room fills up beyond capacity standards. Jack is separated from us, jostled away from the hysterical group.

"Get to a wall!" he shouts to us.

People begin fighting, punching, kicking, and throwing the weight of their bodies into getting away from the center of the circle. I yelp as an elbow flies into my temple. My feet are being trampled. Shoulders slam into my back. I'm being thrown from side to side by caged animals, stampeding in every direction.

"Sapphire!" Niklaus shouts as he torn away from me. He reaches his hand out, and that's the last I see as a stray fist plows right into my nose. Blood springs free, dripping down my mouth.

"Damnit!" I hiss.

A man tries to use my body to jump over the crowd, taking me to the ground. I land on my back but quickly flip over to protect my vital organs. Feet step on me, kick the back of my head, stomp on my shoulders—and there's nowhere to seek shelter. I can't even lift myself off the ground. It's an endless beat down. My only hope is to crawl through the brief open spaces.

I scurry on my elbows and slither along the damp, scummy floor. Rolling, twisting and shimming through legs, and around jammed areas of fighting inmates.

Get to a wall.

Get to a wall.

Get to a wall.

After getting a knee to the cheekbone, I run my fingertips along the rocky dark gray wall. With a sigh of relief, I claw my way up its jagged terrain to stand up. Men and women shriek and cry to be let out of the center of the showers, but the room is so packed, there is no escape. I'm plastered to the wall, wedged between two younger men who are shielding their faces.

What the fuck is going to happen? Ice water? Poison? Are they going to kill us?

A man and a woman kiss, then hold each other in tears.

No. They're going to kill us, aren't they?!

"Niklaus!" I screech. But I can't see him through the great mass of bodies surrounding me. Tears spring to my eyes. What if this is it? We both die here? Fifty years in the past? And we don't even get to say goodbye?

A Guardian, a member of the Blood family, eclipses the room like a dark curtain pulled over a window, smirking as he toys with a lever.

"*Devietzx né lïevitz quinxcéitz!*"

The room erupts in a nuclear blast of panic and terror.

The lever is pulled.

And just before pipes burst with steaming water, Niklaus shoulders his way through the crowd to me. In a forceful thrust, he throws his body against me, slamming his hands down on the wall of either side of my head. He encloses me in, blocking the sudden downpour that beats down his back and head.

The sounds of the room drastically morph from terror to agony.

But it all blends into the background as Niklaus screams.

And he doesn't stop screaming.

Residual drops and a fine mist scorch my arms and the sides of my calves. Boiling water mixed with something. Not as potent as acid, but a chemical that leaves a mephitic odor and lasting burn.

I squeeze my eyes shut, in misery as I can feel the Nightlung floating closer to the surface. I reach for it. The fingers of my mind curl around nothing. *Please!* I beg for it to take us somewhere safe. *Home. Home. Home. Please bring us back to our families!*

But this mysterious entity is like a black cat, coming and going as it pleases. Losing interest the more I want it to let me near.

I give up on traveling momentarily. Never have I heard such a terrifying sound in my life. Niklaus's screams will echo through my nightmares until my final days.

I watch the skin on his shoulders bubble in horror.

"Niklaus!" I cry. Because, what else can I do? Is this going to kill him and spare me?

Oh god. I try again, reaching for that cosmic mist in the back of my mind, forcing myself to break whatever unwanted barrier or block is restraining me from controlling this.

I slide my hands along his jaw and let him press his forehead against mine. His howls come between his clenched teeth now as he bears down.

"I'm here!" I hold him against me. "Hold on, okay? Hold on!"

People around us drop to their knees, flopping on the floor like bugs being burned by the light from a magnifying glass. But Niklaus holds his position against me, and despite the excruciating pain, he doesn't waver. Not for a second.

54. All My Relics

Vrath

The blood has dried on my hands.

I like when it does that. It makes my palms stiff and shiny. The crimson red stain turns darker, a dull ruddy brown. And while the soldiers around me are dancing and cheering in glee as Sapphire and Niklaus wave their weapons around, twirling and skipping in a choreographed attempt to put on a show without killing each other—I use my yellow thumbnail to scrape at the blood in the crease lines of my left palm. It twists and lifts from my skin in flakes.

I smile adoringly as I blow on the dried blood, watching it scatter in the humid air of the stadium, floating like scarlet butterflies.

The Vexamen Breed are much too easy to infiltrate. When they are off duty, here at House of Jester Nights, they are belligerently drunk and stupid. I fit right in with my clothing and painted face. They don't even notice as I lick my fingers, making the dry blood runny again.

"Why don't you just move to another era, Sapphire S. Valdawell? Why be imprisoned this far in the past?" I tap my stiff fingers against my paint chipping around my lips. "Are you unintelligent?"

I have watched her move through time. I have studied her patterns, though her methods are shocking to me. Does she not need the blood of a mother to come and go? Does she not need relics from their personal belongings? Time equations and a map? And why aren't others affected as she interacts with people that she does not belong with?

No one falls ill around her.

Speaking of, the soldiers around me become increasingly snotty and hoarse the longer I'm nearby. Their perspiring skin loses color by the minute. But of course, they do not notice. They are drunk, moronic men who are fixated on shiny toys fighting to the death before their eyes.

Niklaus Demechnef kisses Sapphire Valdawell.

I tilt my head at the psychorrhagic interaction.

I have never understood the peculiar act of intimate touch. I do not receive the slightest ounce of endorphins or excitement of any kind toward touching another human being gently. Perhaps I feel something when I hear the wretched cries of a mother as I insert a tear in her skin and collect copious amounts of her blood. There really is nothing quite like it. Especially if she is a new mother and pleads for me to spare her infant.

Those are the cries that lead to me doing something God-like.

Now, Sapphire Valdawell is not a mother. But her blood sings to me like a darling sea nymph. It chants and hums a tune that reaches me when she travels. It wants me to bleed her. It could be the answers I've longed for. The only way for me to return to where I truly belong. Perhaps I will no longer be deathly ill? Perhaps I will be worshiped as a divine deity for my time craft?

I will know for certain once I bleed her.

I do not hate Sapphire Valdawell nor Niklaus Demechnef.

But they run from me, and it is not fair. It is not right. Do they not know that I have watched their ways over and over again? I have seen them interact in alternate paths of what is to come. I have seen all. Why resist me?

The two get directed off stage.

"But how can I reach them?" I ponder.

"You talk to yourself," the slurring soldier says next to me in Old

Alkadonian.

I ignore the brute. I have had enough of my potential interactions with him. His mind is sideways and insides are diseased. I do not like the eyebrow with the scar or that he perspires more from his right underarm than his left.

I want no more interactions with Lotus Bludgeon.

"And he is not of the Breed," the soldier next to Lotus comments.

"I do not enjoy chasing her. Those splits in time are getting more difficult to slip through," I continue, assessing my equations. "And that tenebrous creature continues to aid them and taunt me!"

I have upset myself greatly at the thought of the black squalid beast.

"How did he get in here?" another soldier asks.

To acknowledge them is to feed the plague. I will grant no audience to their vermin.

"If I use the World's Dark Twin tree branch to evade the Nightlung vermicide…"

I use the World Dark Twin tree branch sparingly, only when I come across an exuberant amount of those hellish, noctivagant Short-Haired Windilas that ride my coat tail like the obsessive pestilence they are. The sacred tree can be found three seas away, in a small quiet country called Morphollow, and is protected by generationally refined and ritualized murderers. But with my eldritch affliction of moving through time, I may appear right past their walls.

The tree contains elements, minerals, and compounds that are comparable to veins and organs of a living being. Thousands of years ago, a rare crop of black trees grew from the cinders of a war that killed both armies. Months later, a village cultivated nearby, casting out the Ashvine Family of scandal to the outskirts—forced to live in solitude among a cornfield, and the black cinder trees. The Ashvine Family had six children, four boys and two girls. The youngest sisters were not allowed to tend to the crop as they were girls, so they found purpose in caring for the strange crop of black trees. Watering them daily. Singing to their crisp, oily leaves, and praying at the base of their roots.

The village eventually hunted down the Ashvine family, slaughtering them in their sleep on a moonless evening. The Ashvine sisters hid in one of the trees as the surrounding trees were burned to the ground. They were devastated and took their own lives in front of the only tree that survived. They prayed that their sacrifice would manifest ruin and plague on the village for generations until their disgruntled spirits were satisfied.

Following their death, the roots absorbed their decay and blood—a cellular event occurred. Perhaps it was the iron from their blood that reacted with the irradiated soil, hardening the trunk in a vascular mass. Either way, the tree is said to have grown veins and disfigured organs. The bark breathes and pulses in the Nightlung, syphoning very bad people to that village. Serial killers. Rapists. Aristocrats.

It picked each villager off one by one until there was no one left.

And I have stolen a branch.

A beautiful, exquisite, glorious branch.

It summons me to the slender rift Sapphire S Valdawell leaves when she tumbles through time. It acts as a compass, a guide, a lantern in the abysmally dark Nightlung. I have prayed to it just as the Ashvine sisters have, caring and tending for it as if it is a delicate extension of myself. It has brought me joyous feelings that the branch rewards me for such devotion. The black cinder branch sends phantom sounds through the Nightlung when those Short-Haired Windilas are near, mimicking their natural predators, and other beings they fear, such as RottWeilens. I've seen it infect their weaker counterparts, runts of the litter.

"And I still have yet to discover all of its peculiar aptitudes!" I announce.

"We *burn* trespassers," the soldier, Lotus, warns me.

"He speaks to himself. His condition of insanity might be contagious."

I have every intent to let their existence rot within the hollow corners of my disinterest. But Lotus touches me. He *touches* me. His smarmy, cimicidic hand latches onto my inner elbow. That rancid breath humidifies the air I breathe, so I stop inhaling to prevent it from contaminating my lungs.

The world reacts much faster than I can. It spits on the interaction, spreads a miasmic disease that leaks from my pores, through the thin fabric of my shirt, into this flesh. The sickness is highly corrosive, drying up his veins, and carving its way into his lungs. Blood sprays from his sudden coughing fit to my face.

I waste a perfectly good handkerchief to dab at the mess.

"I now appreciate the memory of watching you asphyxiate on your own vomit seventeen years from now," I whisper to Lotus.

The others drop to their knees from the predictable effects of my presence, defiling this timeline with my execrable *wrongness*.

"Now if you will excuse me, I must tend to a troublesome girl, a Valdawell—a mordacious, notorious bloodline. I saw her face many times in the vicious time loop I was trapped in as a child. And now, I am failing to obtain an audience with her."

Even mentioning the time loop gives me pause. When I traveled out of my mother's womb a week before she was due, I moved to an isolated beginning with a congregation that lingered in the swamps of Vexamen. They called themselves caretakers of the "unbound." They tolerated the sickness I brought with me. The fevers. The seizures. The hours where time would stutter around my crib. They did not fear it. They documented it. Measured it. Studied me like proof of prophecy.

They listened when I spoke of the Valdawell family and agreed they were necessary to stabilizing my ability. But at the age of five, I was caught in that time loop. A side effect of attempting to return to the same moment of my mother's pregnancy too many times. It stuttered through my like a seizure. It lasted ages. I stopped reacting like a child because reactions slowed the cycle. I learned to stay still. To observe. To wait.

I watched the same people die dozens of ways. Disease. Drowning. Murder. And the loop was drawn to the Valdawell family. Variations of their time stamps on the world. They were a perfected product of what I am. Their blood was my only hope to end these cycles and rid myself of internal plagues. To never be trapped in that loop again.

I shake off the fog of memories.

I draw my equations on their foreheads with the iridescent vial of mother's blood I've accumulated from my last crusade. And the Nightlung takes my hand, granting my momentary asylum in its haunting darkness as I wait for Sapphire S Valdawell to travel again.

And she will…

I can sense her itching to leave abruptly, even now.

Her powers are begging to implode.

55. The Endless Night

Sapphire

At least half of the prisoners remain on the shower floor. Unresponsive.

Skin bright red with a faint steam permeating off their bodies.

The sight turns my stomach as I remain holding on to Niklaus's deadweight as he falls in and out of consciousness, slumping over me. My body aches and quivers as I find it challenging to hold up his upper body. With his skin still wet, I fumble to get a stable grasp on him.

"You're okay, big guy. I'm not letting you go."

The room, the halls, the prison is a cathedral of moans and guttural cries for help.

But I force myself to tune out the noise. Niklaus is my only focus right now. The raw, blistering skin on his back causes me to slightly dissociate from the shock of it all.

"Sapphire!" Sophia shouts from the shower entrance. "Follow me. Hurry!"

Sophia is dry and unharmed. She slings Jack's arm over her shoulders and move diligently to get him away from the shower area.

"He's too heavy!" I gasp, widening my stance to get a better hold on him.

Niklaus is easily over two hundred and twenty pounds. And I'm the weakest I've ever been in my life. There's no way I can carry him back to our cages. At least, not without dragging him across the floor and further tearing up his skin.

"You have to! The sentinels will be here any minute to start jabbing the remaining inmates with hot pokers!"

Shit!

I whine, losing my slippery grip on his waist. But looking down at his singed back—the boiled skin, hot to the touch and still making a terrible sizzling sound…

It's his scream that still bellows in the well of my mind.

That scream was gutting.

That scream won't quiet in my thoughts.

I look down at his spine again. My eyes watering at the pain he must be in. Why would he do that for me? After everything that was just said? He didn't have to cover my body with his.

The screams in my mind echo, bouncing off like an orchestra of anguish, an amphitheater terrorizing me from the inside out. I swallow down the doubts that keep creeping forward.

Of course I will carry him the rest of the way.

He just used his body has a human shield for me.

It could have meant my death.

I grunt, turning around and slinging his arms over my shoulders.

"Okay…I'm going to get us back to the cages, Niklaus. I promise. Just hang in there."

Out of sheer will, I begin my walk across the damp floor. Because of Niklaus's height, his feet drag across the floor. But I hunch over enough to ensure my back is a stable platform for him to rest against.

"I swear to God, Niklaus, I'm going to get us home. I'll get us home, and you'll never have to see my face again. Just please hang in there!"

The trudge down the hallway is dark, pitiful, and tragic. I pass other prisoners who somehow made it out and curl up in their cages—howling as they attempt to get some sleep.

"I'm so sorry…" I whisper to Niklaus again, though I believe he passed out from the pain. I should hope so. At least it's a bit of relief.

Every muscle vibrates and screams in distress, stretching and swelling from the overexertion of carrying his soaking wet weight. I trip, crashing to my knees, and gritting my teeth as the sharply textured brimstone floors cut into the skin of my knees.

"Almost there," I say to him and myself.

Droplets of sweat run over my brows and into the corners of my eyes as I nearly pop every vein bearing down to stand up again.

I manage to get one foot on the ground.

Good, Sapphire.

Each breath is a match struck and snuffed—hot, quick, shallow. I put all my weight into my left thigh to lift myself, just enough to get the other foot planted again.

One, two, three!

My spine is a rope pulled taut, and it nearly snaps as I fold forward again. It takes everything I have not to yelp, fighting now to let his mass collapse on top of me. The muscles in my core turn molten, burning and pinching my ribs.

I blow the wet hair out of my face and try again.

This time, the task feels impossible. I grate my molars back and forth, building a balloon of pressure behind my eyes as I slump forward again.

"*Fuck!*" I hiss.

I'm another failed attempt from falling to the ground and sobbing until I pass out.

Niklaus might as well be a mountain on my back.

He went through hell shielding me from that shower. And I can't even carry him back to our cage so he can suffer in private.

Krimson could do this without question. My dad? Absolutely. Even my mom could probably carry Niklaus back.

I am a fucking colossal disappointment to everyone! Fuck!

Dad! Oh, please! Wherever you are, please lend me your strength. Help me carry Niklaus a little longer.

No one responds in my head the way Dellilian would. But there's a rush, like a supercharged river power-housing through my chest, stampeding through my nervous system. It's a familiar glow of warmth. The same sensation I get when I hug my mom. When I'm angry and Krimson finds me sitting alone outside. Or when Uncle Warrose places a reassuring hand on my shoulder.

It's all of that, and an implosion of confidence.

I know I can lift him. I know I can make it back.

Clamping down my teeth and every muscle, I force myself up to both feet and continue marching forward. There's blood coming from my heels and knees. I'm drenched in sweat. And my legs are numb to the touch.

But I keep going.

"How is he?!" Sophia asks as I limp into Niklaus's cage.

She helps balance his weight as I slip out from under his chest, quivering as I lower him to the ground. Before his upper body lies flat, I wedge myself under him. His face is cradled in my lap. His arms draping around my hips.

"It's a temporary acid. They call it Jester Mist. He should heal up by tomorrow night," Sophia whispers, patting me on the shoulder. "You did so good, carrying your husband so far and on your back…"

Tears well in my eyes, but I don't let them fall.

I didn't do it alone.

She scampers back to her cage, then returns with a finger to her mouth.

"Hide this in the corner when you wake up. It's contraband, but I've managed to keep it from the sentinels." Sophia hands me a ratty, torn up blanket and a tiny metal jar.

"What's this?"

"Rub it on his back. There's not much in there, but it should help him sleep."

I peek around my bars to Jack huddled in his cage, taking deep breaths.

"What about Jack? He was hit with the acid too."

Sophia shrugs. "We're used to it. I promise, we've been through much worse and for longer too. Take it. Your husband needs it."

That's…that's my grandmother.

I can't even begin to comprehend her kindness. Especially after being locked in the prison for God knows how long.

"Jack?" I call out.

"Take it, Sapphire. *Please*." His boyish voice is a thin, exhausted rasp. He continues shuddering in his cage. "I'll be okay."

"Thank you so much," I barely mutter through my tight throat.

I apply a thin layer of a silver jelly as Niklaus stirs and groans, waking slowly from his pain-induced sleep. My fingers work quickly, applying small amounts to sections of his flesh that bear the brightest scarlet color. Then, I cover us both with the large heavy blanket that smells like rust and an old attic.

Niklaus shivers against my lap, curling his arms around my hips a little tighter.

"Tell me—we made it home, Spitfire."

I sigh, dropping my head against the bars.

Disappointment.

Disappointment.

Disappointment.

I have failed us again.

"No." My voice breaks, accompanied by a trembling chin. "Not yet."

He doesn't seem all that surprised. The agony of the chemical burns strikes again, convulsing his body tightly together as it racks through his core. He growls into my lap, grinding his fingers into my back.

"It'll pass," I whisper, stroking the spots on his sides that were saved. "It's temporary acid. It'll go away soon."

I don't tell him that he'll have to endure this for another twenty-four hours most likely.

"Tell me something," he grunts against my thigh.

I hold my breath as he moans again, louder this time—though it blends in with the orchestra of inmates bellowing at the top of their lungs from the horror they're experiencing too.

I quickly dig through thoughts, memories, or stories I can tell him. Peering over at Sophia holding Jack's hand and humming a song close to his ear, I find that something I can tell him.

"My middle name. The S doesn't just stand for one name. It stands for two." I lean down to his ear, stroking his hair away from the side of his face. "My mom couldn't decide when she named me. It stands for Scarlett…*and* Sophia."

I check to make sure Sophia didn't hear me, then watch Niklaus's eyebrows raise while his eyes remain closed.

"Scarlett was your mother's sister who died," he murmurs.

"Her twin."

"And Sophia…"

"And Sophia," I repeat warmly.

"Hmm. That's—so much more special now."

"It is."

Niklaus grasps at my back as he squirms and grunts against me again. I run a finger along his clammy, chilled skin and pull the wool blanket up higher to trap my heat inside and keep him as comfortable as possible.

I frantically reach for Niklaus's hands. Like pressing a button in routine placements, I find the special pinpoints that help relieve pain.

Niklaus's exhale is loud and deliberate. "That—helps."

"One night during those winter campfires, Krimson and I begged your mom to let some secrets of the prophecy slip. Instead, she told us about a time in prison when Uncle Niles was moaning in his sleep from the burns on his back…" I say, reminiscing about that night under the stars in the Emerald Lake Forest. "She showed us how she hit pressure points on his feet to take away his pain. Showed us how to do it on someone's hands too."

Niklaus hums as I continue massaging him.

"I was so disappointed when she was finished. We told her that was a lousy way of distracting us from our original question. And you know what she said to me?"

An epiphany stitches into my thoughts, as if it was there all along.

"Hmm?"

"She said it wasn't a distraction. She let me in on a secret that I'll need one day."

Niklaus is quiet for several seconds. His breathing growing heavier as he ponders this.

"I think she's known this was going to happen—for a long time, Spitfire."

"That what was going to happen?"

"This. Us. Traveling back in time. I think it was—part of the prophecy. It explains why I wasn't allowed to hear it." His gravelly voice is less strained than before but still hurting.

"Are you angry with her for not warning you?" I ask.

I don't want to fill his head with ideas, but I can't help feeling betrayed by Aunt Marilynn. If she knew this was coming…why wouldn't she warn us? We have experienced tragic event after tragic event. We've been starved, beaten, abused, and tossed through time like rag dolls. We've been sexually violated. We've seen so many things that our parents worked hard to protect us from.

How could she not warn us?

"No," he mutters, swallowing against a dry throat.

"Oh."

"The result must outweigh the journey," he adds.

"You think?"

Niklaus sighs with a light shrug. "My mother was born into the Crimson Kres Colony. They memorize the prophecy as soon as they learn how to read. They're sworn to secrecy and are devoted to their beliefs that the historical figures who play out vital events are precious to the future. All I know is that the future is precious to them because for at least fifty generations after the prophecy's end, there will be benevolent leadership."

I look down at him skeptically.

"I don't know how much of that I believe, but…"

"But what?"

"But we've seen how ugly the past is, Spitfire. I have to hope that my mother's people are right. That everything our parents went through, everything we're going through is going to lead to a future that—that isn't going to hurt people the way the past does now."

My face and neck lose blood as I hear his thoughts play out loud. They carry more weight now that he's been scarred and tortured from the past the prophecy has aimed to be free of.

"I see your point."

"I do think Mom tried to prepare me, though," he muses sleepily. "All the training. Rigorous history lessons. It was for this, I think."

I blow out a breath. "That must have tortured her. Do you think she told your dad?"

"No." The left corner of Niklaus's mouth curls up. "He has such a big mouth."

I chuckle.

"She definitely has been bearing these secrets all alone."

I wonder if my mother knew. Would she be able to keep all of this from me? I take in a quick breath to ask him, but Niklaus burrows into my leg sweetly. My fingers forget themselves, tracing over the spikes of facial hair along his jaw, smoothing the longer hair on his head, and stroking his cheekbone.

Niklaus stiffens at the intimate gesture. His cheek hot against my inner thigh.

I pause my hand nervously.

"Keep going," he whispers huskily. "I love your hands on me."

Something warm and light wakes under my ribs.

"No, you don't." My cheeks burn.

"Oh, yes I do."

My heart takes the bait.

"That's not how our conversation went before the shower," I retort.

His arms clutch me tighter at the memory.

"I know."

I feel nauseated at the sudden images that are shoved to the front of my mind. Niklaus finding me in the packed room of screaming inmates. Niklaus barring his body around me. Niklaus taking the punishment for the both of us.

His screams impale my mind once again, leaving me breathless with my tears blurring vision. The smell of chemicals and burning skin.

I look down at the blisters on my arm as a tear rolls down my cheek.

"Why did you do it?" I ask thickly.

"Hmm?"

"Why did you shield my body with yours?"

I feel his eyes open as those long, dark lashes tickle my leg.

"You know why," he murmurs.

I'm flooded with feelings of confusion and that radiating crush that died in my heart so many years ago. It's foreign, but still recognizable. Still warm to the touch.

"No. You made it clear how you feel about me."

Anger, fear, dismissal, longing, yearning… *Not good enough. Not good enough. Not good enough.*

"You set the stage first, Spitfire."

"No—"

"In the cave. You shut me down after we escaped the asylum…after things *changed* between us," he adds.

"Well, because—"

Niklaus places a single, warm kiss on my thigh. It's all-consuming, carrying a current of tingling feelings up my arms and back.

"I'm not good with rejection, my darling wife."

I blink repeatedly, choking on my own breath.

"You lied?"

He kisses my leg again. "I lied."

He lied. He didn't mean what he said. He was reacting to my dismissal of our time in the asylum. I run through it all over again. That part of my brain that has spent so long despising him tries to reel me back in, then wavers as I take in the damage to his back and arms.

"And you won't change your mind?"

"No."

"Sapphire? How is he holding up?" Sophia asks from Jack's cage.

Niklaus pretends to be asleep.

I smile. "He's hanging in there."

Sophia squints her eyes to examine his back, pressing her forehead to the bars. Her nod is sweet and sincere, and something about it wilts my heart. Knowing her fate and being powerless to stop it crushes me.

"Your vision isn't clear, is it?" I ask.

"My whole life. Everything's always been a little fuzzy."

"You would look very nice in set of round bifocals."

A somber expression crosses her face. "Maybe when the prison gets a physician for the eyes."

One day, I think. *One day, you'll get your glasses.*

"Can I ask you something?"

"Sure," she says warmly.

Niklaus's breathing grows heavy and deep, limbs relaxing as he falls asleep.

"What kind of experiments does Crow Ivast do on you and Jack?"

I'm afraid to ask. I have a feeling…I mean, I know what was done to my parents to some degree.

"Different methods of torture mostly. Long, rigorous hours of finding ways to bring us suffering without killing us."

"Why?"

She closes her eyes. "He has been testing theories that if twins suffer from mental and physical trauma at a young age, their minds break, and they could *potentially* be capable of immense new abilities."

"And has it worked?"

"Nope. My sister, Story, died for a *theory* that will *never* pan out."

"Story? When did she pass?"

"When we were eleven. The doctor lost his temper after she tried to stop him from burning the bottoms of our feet. She took the branding iron and threw it at his back. He—" Sophia's gentle voice cracks. It's still fresh. "He pinned her down and burned her face off and broke her nose with the iron."

I pull my lips and look away.

She was eleven.

"I wish she died on the spot, but she didn't. My sister survived for a short while, a few days, screaming from the melted skin on her face. She couldn't even cry tears because her eyes were burned shut."

An ache rises in my throat. This was my great-aunt. Story was my father's aunt he never got to meet.

"Oh, Sophia…"

She wipes her runny nose with the back of her hand. "Anyway, she ended up passing away from an infection from her injuries. I remember asking if someone could bury her with my parents in the mountains. You see, when the Doctor discovered sets of twins, he abducted them and had their families murdered."

"I—I didn't know that."

There's never really been much conversation about my father's lineage at all actually.

"The Doctor's wife was there when I asked. She desecrated Story's body with holy water. Said that bad little girls didn't get proper burials. That her body would be tossed in the cremation pit with the other dead inmates," Sophia continues, now sobbing into the back of her hand.

"Absinthe," I say between my teeth.

"You've heard of her."

"Yes."

"She was wrong. My sister was strong. She'd take punishments for me. She'd distract me with fairytale stories when the terrible doctor was torturing us. Story was the best, most brave little girl. And with her death, I lost my whole family."

Jack comes in and out of sleep, giving her arm a soft pat.

"Except for Jack, of course." Sophia smiles sadly. "We'll always be family."

"How long have you two known each other again?" I ask, hoping the subject change will dry her pretty brown eyes.

"Since we were children. His village was close to mine in the mountains. We'd play together because we thought we were so special, the four of us being twins and all." She chuckles, wiping her face. "I used to call him Mr. Leather Man because he'd always wear this leather jacket Jeb made him. Even in the summer."

"And Jeb was Jack's twin brother?" I ask.

Sophia lowers her eyes sadly.

"Similar fate as Story?"

"Very similar."

Tears swell in my eyes.

I wonder if my mother knew any of this.

"You'll see them in heaven one day, Sophia. You both will. I know they're up there waiting and watching," I say.

"Jack and I always say Story and Jeb are probably the most stubborn guardian angels."

A lingering silence passes between us as sleep lowers my eyelids. Niklaus is like a warm weighted blanket that makes sleeping in a cold, eerie cage not so bad.

"Sophia?"

"Hmm?"

"I don't know how much time with you I have left, so I want to tell you this now…I can't say I know, but I hope you'll remember it for the rest of your life."

"What is it, Sapphire?"

"Absinthe and the entire Ivast family will get what they deserve one day. There will be someone far more powerful than you can imagine who will make them suffer fates worse than death for a very long time. That is, of course, before they are actually put to death in gruesome ways." I swallow, drifting to sleep. "Story and Jeb will be avenged. I promise."

56. The Blood of The Prison

Sapphire

Krimson stands on one side of my father's bed. I am on the other. It's midnight. The fireplace sends a smoky aroma of burning wood, cloves, and cinnamon wafting through the bedroom. This space used to scare me, encourage rage and bitterness… Now, it's the sweetest place in the whole world. My father sleeping in the center of the room. Krimson watching me with his silhouette outlined by the amber blaze of the fire.

"Tell me where you are," my brother demands.

He is usually so calm and level-headed. But not right now. Under his eyes are swollen and dark. His forehead strung together. I've never seen him so stressed.

"The Vexamen Prison, at least fifty years in the past," I say quickly, unsure how long I have with him before the dream disappears again.

"No way…"

"I've been to asylum when Mom burned it down. I've been to Uncle Niles's house when he was being influenced by Absinthe and Albatross. I've seen Aurick Demechnef when he was living with Mom…I can't control it, Krimson!"

"Okay, slow down—"

"Niklaus is hurt. I need to get us home, but I don't know how this works. It happens when I'm in danger or when I'm emotionally distressed. I cannot do this anymore. I won't survive it. Our parents grew up in a horrific form of hell!"

"I bet I have the gift too. I will come get you. I will find you!"

I run my hands through my hair. "You could get lost too though. Have you told Mom what's going on?"

Krimson's gaze slides to the door and back to me.

"Yes. She's with me now."

"Good. We can't do this alone."

"She got Uncle Warrose, Aunt Ruth, and Aunt Marilynn involved."

Chills rise each hair on the back of my neck.

"Aunt Marilynn?"

"Yes." He gives me a knowing look. "She knew this was going to happen. She's trying to teach me how to access the Nightlung to come get you."

I sigh. "Oh, thank God."

"But Sapphire, is Uncle Niles okay? It looked like he was in the Blackspire Ward of The North…"

My eyes throb from the sudden purge of tears. I stare at my brother, battling that little girl inside me that just wants to fall to pieces and let him fix everything for me.

"I don't know…" I sob, throwing my hands to my side. "Fuck, I don't know! I think he is there, but I'm a prisoner now too—and I can't seem to control where I go or when. If he is a captive there, we have to save him. I'll never forgive myself…"

"We'll get to him, Sapphire. He's smart and has been through much worse. He'll know how to survive until we get there."

As I observe my brother standing there, I can see now that we don't look much alike. I'm far more resemblant of my mother. But he is the spitting image of our father from what I've seen of the past.

"And Mom doesn't know how to travel through time?" I ask.

Krimson shakes his head. "Just the Void. Apparently, it's like a sibling of the Nightlung."

I knew the answer, but disappointment still pours through my body like an ice shower.

"It's ironic, isn't it?" Krimson watches our father sleep. "He's probably the only one that could figure out how to save you, Niklaus, and Uncle Niles before any of us."

I watch out father's chest rise and fall.

"Then maybe it's time I woke him up…" I say.

"Are you sure you're up to eating in the commissary?" I ask as we walk down the hallway with the other wounded inmates.

Dirty looks. Shoulders slamming into us. Cruel remarks in Old Alkadonian.

We are the new enemy to these men and women wearing the same uniforms. Not the sentinels and guardians that pulled the trigger to the Jester Mist. We are the ones who refused to kill each other in that fighting ring.

So, the punishment continues for us.

"Yes," Niklaus rasps, breathing heavily. His back is far from healed, but he isn't in as much pain this morning as he was in last night.

"I can bring you a tray, and we can eat together in your cage," I whisper.

He looks ahead, visibly shaken at the sight of the showers.

"I'm not letting you walk around here alone." Those stern, chilling blue eyes flick down to me.

I scoff. "How could you be worried about me right now? I'm not the one who's hurt."

Niklaus smirks though the joy doesn't reach the quiet room behind his eyes. His large hand slides up the nape of my neck, fingers tangling into my hair. He leans down to my height and kisses the top of my head. The pressure of his lips to my scalp lights me on fire with minuscule tingles that spread like a dustbowl down to my toes.

I give him a surprised, sappy smile, and he laughs.

"Because you're my girl. That's why."

"He does have charm, I'll give him that," Jack says with his red back facing us.

Sophia gives him a playful shove, and they both snicker.

"We have to get them out of here," I whisper to Niklaus. "I've been thinking about the Vexamen history books since we've been in here. Before our parents, there have been documented cases of other escape attempts here, remember?"

Niklaus keeps his head lowered so I can continue speaking to just him.

"Do you remember the log about a couple of teenagers who escaped? The notes were that they had help. They didn't do it alone. What if we were the help? What if we're the ones that freed them?"

His pupils shrink as the shower gets closer.

"It's risky."

"I know. But…" I watch Sophia help Jack along as he winces and limps from his injuries. I watch my grandparents lead the way down this tunnel. "I can't leave them in here."

Niklaus tilts his head to look at me. To *really* look at me. There's a quiet hunger there. He watches me the way someone would watch a candle in a storm. Careful, reverent, and ready to risk it all to keep that small flame in his sight.

"Okay, Spitfire."

"Okay, what?"

That expression is a low, sustained ache. It pulls at a string in my chest.

"I promise. We'll get your grandparents out."

I'm elated and desperate to touch him all at the same time. My hand reaches for his, curving my fingers into his shape, and holding on tight.

"*Viézteix! Demechnef!*"

Niklaus pushes me out of the way before a heavy baton can land on my back. A Guardian strikes him across the shoulder. Once, then again right on the burned, raw flesh of his upper back.

He flashes his white teeth as he growls, twisting his head to the side and taking the quick beating without flinching.

I try to pull Niklaus away from the Guardian, but he won't move. And as I twist to tug him forward again, I see why. We're next to enter the showers.

He's unable to step foot inside.

"*Niéxv! Niéxv!*" the Guardian shouts, winding his gigantic arm up again and slamming the baton back down on Niklaus's back.

And I know the fear of stepping foot back into this shower must be all-consuming and eating him from the inside out—because the pain of the baton striking his wounds aren't enough to make him budge.

He's a statue, hand hardening like concrete around mine.

"That's enough!" I shriek at the Guardian. "Give him a minute!"

But the Guardian attacks again and again. And Niklaus takes it.

"Stop!"

I'm not thinking. I forget where I am and the consequences of certain actions in a place like this. My hand rotates out of Niklaus's stone grip, and I block the next hit with both hands, using the gargantuan man's weight against him—unsheathing his other weapon hooked to his belt and slicing into that veiny forearm. A spray of hot blood finds my chest and face.

And the Guardian fails to contain his disbelief.

"He's not ready yet…" I try to justify my actions, but it's too late.

"Spitfire!"

What have I done?

"You silly, moronic little bitch!" The Guardian throws his long whip of black hair over his shoulder and backhands me. The force is that of a galloping bull. My teeth clack together. My body spins and smacks to the floor.

"*She opened the flesh of a Guardian!*"

Hands are shackled around the base of my neck, under my arms, stapled into my rib cage as I'm hauled from the damp, mildew ground and dragged like a dog. Chains are hooked to my iron collar. My legs and core scape along the brimstone, textured ground.

I scream as my skin is torn and grated raw.

"Krimson!" I cry out.

I believe in you, Krimson! Come save me. Please.

I hold my head up as the great mammoths continue to trail my flopping body behind them like a fish on a hook. The cuts and burns take such a beating against the rough floors, I start to go numb.

What's going to happen to me?!

Aunt Ruth lost her legs.

Oh god. Please. Please, don't take my limbs.

57. Black Widow

Niklaus

It's my fault.

My fault.

My fault.

"Where have they taken her?!" I step into Jack's personal space.

Jack puts his hand on my shoulder, and I shove it off.

"Your wife harmed a member of the Blood Family. A Guardian. It depends on how angry they are with her. The punishments vary…"

I push him to the wall. "Give. Me. Your. Best. Guess."

Jack is just a teenager here. A *child*. But it doesn't make a difference to me right now. He could be a sentinel standing in my way for all I care. I see a tunnel of red. She cried for her brother as they ripped her from me and dragged her body like a corpse…

"Uh, the Black Widow Room?!" Jack blurts out in exasperation. "But it'll be more extreme than that probably. A Marionette Theater *within* the Black Widow Room."

Fury and hatred warp my memory recollection.

"What the fuck does that mean?!"

"Well, it…it means…"

It all comes back to me.

Marionette Theater is the House of Jester Night when a female inmate has to let a line of men please her in front of an audience. The Black Widow Room is where they drug the female inmate to be so aroused she touches herself in front of a small, intimate audience of soldiers.

"No."

"Niklaus, I know this is bad, but—"

I could slam his head against the granite wall.

"*Bad?!*" I growl, balling my hands into fists. "Bad? That's my wife they just hauled away from me. My. Fucking. *Wife*. If you think I'm letting another man touch her, you're either experiencing psychosis, or you are an idiot."

"They are not going to kill her," Sophia says, as if for a moment that makes it all right.

"No? But they are going to sexually assault her."

Jack and Sophia have nothing to say to that.

My world burns around the edges, going up in a hazardous storm of smoke and debris. I can't let this happen to her. Christ, she was only trying to protect me. Why the fuck didn't I just go in? Why was I being such a coward?

This is my fault.

My fault.

My fault.

Sapphire, baby, I am so sorry.

I'll fix this.

I am going to fix this.

"Tell me where they've taken her so I can fucking kill them."

Sapphire

"Wait. Please someone just explain to me what's going on!"

Sentinels chain my arms to a table. A soldier in black leather and cables prepares a crow's mask, connecting it to some sort of tank. It holds that fucking arousal drug…doesn't it?

The room pulses with an oppressive rhythm, like a heart that continues to beat after death. The charcoal walls glisten with moisture and centuries old blood.

My legs are spread, and my ankles are shackled down.

I feel sick.

"Hold on. I won't do it again, okay? I made a mistake!" I try to keep my voice steady, but the panic leaks into my tone, quivering my speech.

A hand swings into my jaw, hard enough to sink my teeth into my tongue.

"*Speak when spoken to, Demechnef Whore!*"

Tears involuntarily flood to my eyes.

My red uniform panties are ripped off, making me scream, and leaving a pink mark around my hips. I drop my head to the table and hyperventilate, staring at the yellow and red bulbs hanging from the ceiling like the garland of a grotesque carnival canopy.

I know what this room is now.

Soldiers are seated and standing, flicking their tongues between two fingers to taunt me. Their dull lip piercings, tattoos, and brown teeth send a pulse of bile splashing along the back of my throat.

The vulgar words and belittling jabs all blend together with the wheezing moans of the glitching music. An organ and trumpet playing off key in obnoxious intervals.

This is the Black Widow Room.

Crude circus masks meant to scare me are pulled over their faces. I focus on the sulfur-halos around the men's boots.

My face wrinkles together like a young girl. And I don't even feel the fiery sting of the glistening wounds from being dragged through the halls anymore.

I know I am about to be assaulted.

I know I will be powerless to stop it.

The table gives a low, metallic groan as my straps and chains are secured.

I inhale sharply, pulling in the unforgettable stench of grease, copper, and burned sugar.

My mind wages through a million possibilities. I could try and travel right now to get myself out of this. But what if I end up leaving Niklaus behind? I'd never forgive myself if I lost him. I'd never be able to look his mother in the eye and tell her I left him in the Vexamen Prison to die.

I watch with pleading eyes as they walk the tank and haunting crow mask to my table. Cheers. Laughter. Applause.

Screams.

My screams.

The shrieks are broken and hoarse, stinging my vocal cords until I make unrecognizable, animalistic noises out of sheer terror.

This isn't like what Apple May did to me in the asylum.

That was with Niklaus.

He is no stranger to me.

These men are brutes. Wild and cruel.

I'm howling words. Sentences strung together out of begging for freedom. And nothing—*nothing* in this world can compare to praying not to be molested.

A blast of air hits the sensitive skin between my legs.

A brass door crashes against the wall.

I lift my head off the table to stare into Niklaus's red, devastated eyes as he sees all of me exposed on the table.

A commander shouts at him, pointing and drawing a weapon to attack the unwanted intrusion.

"Niklaus!" I wail, crying so hard my brain swells and pulses against my skull. "Niklaus, please! Don't let them hurt me!"

His deep-sea blue eyes fill with tears.

"I will take her punishment."

My stomach drops.

Wait…

That'll never work.

They won't want him for this.

The sentinel glances back and forth between us with intrigue. A curly eyebrow is lifted as he points to me with his baton. "*This your wife?*"

"Yes."

The sentinel translates to the small audience of high-ranking officers.

Their reactions are both disappointed and humorous. They shout and laugh, throwing their masks off.

I perk up. Maybe this is a benefit of being mated in this prison? Maybe this just saved me! I watch the leading sentinel like a hawk, waiting for the verdict.

He strokes his beard, thinking, weighing his options. And with a lift of his chin to the sentinels behind me, I'm unstrapped, and the chains are unlocked. My backside squeaks against the table as they pull me off it. My hands shield my lower half, fingers shaking and twitching while I pinch my thighs together.

Men shackle Niklaus's hands together, holding them outward. He's directed to the table I was once exposed on.

"*He will take his wife's punishment!*"

58. Spitfire

Niklaus

The punishment, no matter how severe, is of little consequence to me.

Barging into this Black Widow room to find Sapphire strapped to this table, legs spread, and bawling hysterically?

That is the greatest punishment I could receive.

The anguish and wrath entwine together, hollowing out a space beneath my ribs where my heart use to beat normally.

I walk to the brass table like it's a sacrificial altar. The room is quiet—with an anticipating silence that stretches, trembling like glass about to shatter.

The edge of the table grazes my fingertips.

She looks so relieved. Terrified for my fate, but still—so relieved.

A Guardian enters the room, adjusting that ridiculous headdress that he wears like a silver crown, so tall and pointed, it could be a cranial cage. The broad man saunters over to me, observing my upper body with a strictly analytical expression. His stillness is almost impossible to read and terribly deceptive.

"No—I'll do it. This isn't right…" Sapphire says with a shaky voice. "Niklaus, I don't like this. I can take the punishment, okay?"

"I'll be okay, Spitfire."

The Guardian who carries out these punishments flashes a doll-like grin, then does a signal with two fingers to someone next to me.

My hands are slammed against the table.

They use metal clamps to nail down three of my left fingers, splaying them wide, and tucking away the other two.

The Guardian unsheathes a weapon.

And it doesn't register how bad this is.

It's doesn't fuse into my thoughts.

My heart fumbles outward.

Three.

Two.

One.

My eyes fall to a wide slayer sword slamming down to the table and chopping off my fingers.

The rusted silver is so sharp and precise, it separates the flesh and bone in one swing.

I stare at it.

The hand. The dark pool of blood. Fingernails. Severed nerves.

I stare.

Left hand.

Crimson red puddle.

Fingers separated from hand.

A wrist.

Shackled wrist.

More blood.

Slayer sword glides away, screeching against the table.

Fingers.

They're still lined up.

I blink a few times. Ice spreads into my eyes, down my cheeks, splintering into my throat. The world hums and booms with chaos. But all I can see are the fingers no longer attached to the hand.

I sway a centimeter from the table and pull the hand with my body, leaving a sad streak of blood in its movement.

My hand.

That is my hand.

My fingers.

They've taken my fingers!

My name is screamed.

Again and again. Her voice is a broken shard of glass that splits through the noise. I find that sound through the static, through the fire raining from the heavens.

Niklaus.

My hand. They took my fingers.

"Niklaus! NO!" Spitfire howls.

I look up.

I look at *her*.

I find Spitfire's heterochromatic eyes.

I stare at them long enough to watch her get sucked away in a black hole of shadows and ink.

Without me.

59. Imaginary Friend

Sapphire

"No! No! No!"

I pat the ground under my feet, feeling the cold concrete floor under my fingertips.

All of the light has been sucked out of my vision.

There's a wall behind me.

Two walls connected. I am in a corner.

It's drafty. Cold. Empty

"Niklaus…" I utter his name like it's the last time I will ever hear it said out loud. "Oh, God…Niklaus…"

I shake violently in this dark corner. I can't believe I fucking left him behind! Why didn't he come with me? How could this have happened? I have to get back…

"Who is Niklaus?" A small child's voice enters the darkness, jolting a force of shock to my nervous system. My hands slam against the walls to my left and right.

I search the room blindly.

"Dellilian?" I whisper.

The room pulses with a hesitant thoughtfulness.

"Who is Dellilian?"

I brace myself. Flashbacks of a dark room piece my mind and prepare me for physical violence.

"Are you going to hurt me?" I ask.

The little voice answers almost immediately. "Are you going to hurt *me*?"

"Are you going to keep repeating my questions?" I push again.

The little voice sighs.

"What's you name?"

"Skylenna Winter Ambrose," she says.

My gasp is loud and throaty. I cough. My hand presses to my lips.

"What—are you doing sitting in the dark?" I choke.

Skylenna Winter Ambrose.

As a little girl!

She clears her throat, sniffling. "My father got mad."

I pinch my brows together.

"Why are you in my basement?" she asks.

I look around at the stale nothingness. I'm recalling a piece of my mother's childhood that she only briefly glazed over. It was something about waiting in the cellar for my dad. He would save her when her father would undergo another Mind Phantoms treatment.

"I was chased in the woods by a pack of wolves. I let myself in through the cellar door to hide out until they're gone." My lie might be convincing to a…five-year-old? "How old are you, Skylenna?"

"Six. And those wolves were lucky my puppy DaiSzek wasn't there to eat them!"

"Awww." I can't even imagine DaiSzek as a cute little pup.

"Hey, I have a question," Skylenna says.

"Okay."

"Are you my imaginary friend?" she asks.

My heart melts. She is so adorable.

"That's right. Your best friend."

Little girl Skylenna makes a funny noise in the back of her throat. "No, no, no! Just my imaginary friend. I have a best friend."

"Oh yeah?"

"Yeah." She adjusts on the floor across the basement. "Kane will always be my number one bestest friend."

My body sears with the misery of leaving Niklaus behind and of hearing my mother as a small child talk about my father.

"I'm glad you have him," I say with a lump in my throat.

"You have a best friend too?"

I haven't thought about it. But Niklaus has become my best friend between each era of time we pass through. After every torturous event we endure. He is the one person I am dying to tell I met my mother as a little girl about. He is my best friend.

"Yes."

"Hmm…my best friend is better."

I chuckle. "Oh?"

"Does your best friend have alters in his brain? Mine does!"

"That is very special," I agree.

Little Skylenna hums and then sniffles again, like she's been crying recently. She was being locked in a basement by Jack since she was six years old? God, what the hell were they doing to him?

"Skylenna, does J—your dad lock you down here often?"

Her breathing is labored because she has a runny nose.

"Uh-huh. He gets real mad a lot," she says with a voice like fairy dust and wind chimes.

That breaks my heart. Jack was a good young man in prison. I could sense that deep down he wanted a family just as bad as Sophia did. It's not fair that they made him a villain against his will and to his own daughter.

"Will you do me a favor? As your imaginary friend?" I ask.

"Uh-huh. Yeah. Sure. Okay." She snorts, most likely wiping at her nose again.

I exhale softly. "Always remember that your father isn't himself when he gets angry. The real dad behind that mean, angry mask is your daddy who loves you so much. He's fighting a battle that you cannot see."

"Okay, Imaginary Friend," Skylenna chimes sweetly. "My daddy does love me."

The cellar ceiling makes a snapping sound, then a metal door groans and swings open. "Kane's here! Kane's here!"

I sit up. "What?!"

A downfall of heavenly light is dumped into the room, illuminating a little girl with long, blonde curled pigtails and a white summer dress.

A young boy's tan arms extend into the basement, reaching for the little Skylenna to clasp. She giggles and jumps up and down excitedly. Her small hands clap at an inconsistent rhythm, and she begins to hum and sing out of pure delight.

"It's my best friend!"

I fall against the wall with my hands masking my sobs of joy and long-enduring, all-encompassing love.

My parents. So happy. So innocent. Finding each other so young.

And to my immediate astonishment, the Nightlung opens its vast mouth and swallows me whole. I tumble into a tunnel unexpectedly, whirling down a long, windy canal, and being discarded in a room in the middle of the Demechnef Mountain.

60. Death Would Be Kinder

Niklaus

Pain comes second. The loneliness comes first.

I never realized how loud loss could be. And you'd think I'd manage to be much louder than it, but I am not. Two people rush me through the muggy halls to the stadium. And I don't scream. I clutch my mangled wrist to my chest with a sopping rag, holding the dismembered fingers in my right hand as twisty vines of blood lace in a webbed pattern down my arm, dripping from my elbow.

I have stopped to vomit three times.

I have stared ahead as my heart, mind, and soul go numb.

I have asked God to let me die.

I have passed our cages on the way, and they are so much bigger without her here.

Two familiar voices speak to me and to each other, holding up my weight, and attempting to add pressure to the open wounds. I come in and out of the monstrous zaps of pain bombing into my hand, all the way to my shoulder. It's a blast strong and loud enough to wake me from this daze of survival momentarily. Each time it unfurls the zing of fire and live, angry wires within me, I can't even make a sound. I hunch forward and take it.

"She—left—me."

"We will find her, Niklaus! Just hold on!" Sophia's voice.

I'm slung over the stage where inmates come and go from my vision. The black and red ceiling spins and duplicates as my hand is worked on.

I should die here.

She left me.

I should die.

"…is going to sting!"

A cold splash of water rinses my hand and arm. But it quickly combusts into a chemical fire, eating away at my flesh and bone. It's so unbearable, for three long seconds I worry the agony will either kill me or send me spiraling into permanent madness.

I yell, flailing off the stage.

Inmates hold me down.

"I know, I'm sorry, I'm sorry!"

"She's—*gone*."

I don't have a grasp on reality. It's a fevered nightmare provoked by my bad karma and some kind of deadly illness. My fingers…Sapphire…

What's going to happen now?

My nerves are pinched, and the wounds are compressed. Arguing breaks out over me. Shouting that takes place between my language and Old Alkadonian. I want to tell them all to shut the hell up. The noise or the trauma has me dry heaving with my head rolling to the right side.

"…if we don't at least try, he'll never have these fingers again!"

That possible future thumps viscerally in and out of my thoughts. Do I even care at this point? She's gone. I've been left here all alone. Would I rather just die? Would that be a kinder fate than what I shall endure living the rest of my life here?

But what if she returns?

There really isn't a chance of that.

At least, not from what I've seen.

But even still, if she somehow, some way, figures out how to control where she goes and when…

"Reattach them," I bark, sweat pouring down my face and neck. "All—three—of—them."

There's an uncomfortable breath of silence.

I stretch my eyes wide to scan the faces around me.

"There are only two fingers we can try to save…"

"No." I look down at my blurring left hand. My index, middle, and ring fingers are gone. "Where's the third?"

Sophia exchanges a look of sorrow with Jack. "The Guardian took it. The one Sapphire hurt before she got her punishment. He kept it for himself."

I drop my head back to the stage and close my eyes and unwelcome tears spill down my temples, into my hair.

"Save the two you have then," I mutter. But I have no hope they'll be able to do it. Reattaching limbs is nearly impossible.

"Drink. It's Honey of Sweet Nectar Valley," Jack orders, tipping a leather-wrapped canteen up to my lips. I chug the sweet, syrupy juice until I feel as though I might puke again.

The liquid doesn't take away the anguish I'm writhing in, but it does help a little. A tingling numbness rolls over my body, starting at my scalp and prickling its way down to my feet.

"I know it's hard, but please Niklaus, try to hold still. I have a chemical that increases the chance of the finger successfully reattaching. But it doesn't always work." Sophia leans so close to my hand; her eyelashes practically graze my knuckles. She applies pressure with a tourniquet above the gashes, taking lead on sewing my fingers back to my hand—and from what I can tell, her focus is unshakable. Surgically still hands. A rhythm that is far more confident and well-measured than I would have expected from a young woman who desperately needs her glasses.

With help, they align my finger-bones, stitching the muscle together, examining tendons and nerve endings. A needle and thread carving through my pulsing, stinging, open dismemberment is a horrific trip to hell and back. I black out and come back, only to realize they still aren't finished. The cramps coil so tightly around my bones, I can feel the lingering effects into the base of my spine. I howl, pray, wish that

God would end it mercifully.

She's gone.

"Done. Now we wait," Sophia announces.

I cry and exhale at the same time. Even though my fingers are sewn back on, they don't feel like mine at all. They are someone else's. Foreign objects attached to me.

"Wait for what?" Jack asks.

"If they get darker. Blue or black. We failed. They weren't attached properly, and they will decay. But if they turn pink, there is blood flow."

I grind my teeth back and forth.

What the fuck is the point? She's gone. Sapphire is fucking gone. And I am still here.

"Oh! Look! Pink!" Jack exclaims, throwing back his head to laugh. "That's pink, right?"

"Yes!" Sophia claps her hands. "Oh, thank God!"

I don't bother looking.

"Niklaus. It's done. We saved the two fingers!"

The ceiling swims in warm, devastated water as my eyes grow hot and burn.

"Which one is gone?" I whisper.

Jack drops to a knee so he can answer. "The ring finger."

I feel broken and obliterated.

"At least you weren't wearing your wedding ring."

The tears spill over.

"Right."

This has to be a nightmare.

"We're going to find your wife, friend." Jack pats me on the shoulder.

No, you won't.

Sapphire is gone.

And I am never going home.

61. Time Consequences

Niles

Twenty-One Years in The Past
Timeline: Weeks before the Dralutheran War

"Dessin would be so proud of me, honestly," I tell Renly.

"Uh-huh!"

Dessin would have rather been baptized in bleach than admit that to me out loud. Though it's definitely true. Renly and I have mapped out the exits, the guard schedules, and the societal timing of when villagers are out and about. I forgot they have a curfew, so the streets are empty after dusk.

Our best chance at getting Renly home is on Sunday morning—three days from now. The next public execution. The plan has been combed through thoroughly at all hours of the night when I should be sleeping. And it's Dessin-approved. Maybe. Probably.

Renly gasps. "Mr. Niles!"

I raise my eyebrows, pausing my terrible drawing of the execution block in the gray dirt.

"Your scalp…it's bleeding again."

A stab of dread and anxiety hit me square in the chest. I tap my fingertips to my hairline. Ruby smears down my hand. I should have known. The pounding migraine was only getting worse, and every time it pulses behind my eyes, my pores begin to bleed.

"Ah," I sigh, wiping the blood away on my pants. "My skin is just attempting to detox the disgusting air in this place. *Blehk.*"

Renly doesn't look as convinced as he usually does.

"But—well, Mr. Niles—your hair too."

I don't have to check my reflection in a mirror to know what he's talking about. Since I've arrived, my dark-blonde hair has lightened to silver and gray at an unnatural rate. I look down at my hands. The sunspots. The skin turning thin and nearly translucent.

"You could be a grandpa!" Renly adds in mild disgust, but mostly pitiful empathy.

Ah, children.

I can only imagine how much my face has been affected. Could it be because I don't belong in this time? Could it be because there is another me alive in this time?

"Just ignore that," I tell him sternly, then wink.

Renly giggles into his hand, careful not to wake the others.

"We'll go over the plan again?" he asks with a small lisp.

"Several times until we can rehearse it backward. Now, give me the runaround."

"Saturday night, when I am sent on waste duty, I pack the rations and water we've been collecting in the waste buckets. When we take turns disposing, I'll hide a separate bucket in the drains. On Sunday morning, when no one's looking—we make a run for it! We hide in the drains until dark, then race to the East Vexello Mountains, say we know Helga Bee and need safe passage to Dementia!"

"He's a scholar, ladies and gentlemen!" I whisper to the sleeping room.

"You made a brilliant plan, Mr. Niles," Renly yawns and curls up in the corner to sleep. "Your Dessin would be proud."

I smile sadly at the ceiling.

"Yeah. He would."

62. "You Are My Only Hope."

Sapphire

Drugged women dressed in their fanciest dresses are hard to look at. Heads bobbing with gawdy hats. Drool seeping past their maroon-stained lips. Eyes cloudy and glazed over.

It's a waiting room.

Tables are set with fine porcelain dishes, scones, and steaming kettles.

Women of all ages wait for their turn to be called.

Their limp hands covered in white gloves fumble and spill hot tea from their delicate cups. The IVs in their arms twitch with each flimsy movement.

"Someone tell me what the fuck we're waiting for," I say, biting back the need to slur.

Demechnef officials caught me wandering around in a waiting room, dressed in my Vexamen Prison uniform. I was detained, dressed like a lady, and hooked up to this IV. I can get out of this, even in my sluggish state. Thankfully, I know where I am.

The Demechnef Mountain.

It's where Aurick Demechnef conducted most of his business. It's where my mother learned Demechnef was his last name. And it's the exact place experiments were usually conducted.

I know it like the back of my hand. But I have to believe I traveled here for a reason. If I'm going to tap into the ability to travel again and control it this time so I can go back for Niklaus—I need to understand myself, the past, and what is drawing me to these timelines.

"No one really knows," an older woman to my right says, sipping her hot tea.

"We hear—l-l-lots of screams," a teenage girl replies.

Screams?

"Why are all of you here?" I ask.

"Got caught sleeping with my neighbor's husband. The Emerald Wife accused me of—being Vexamen spy."

"I wasn't *losingweightinthe* women's ward *oftheasylum*," the teenage girl slurs.

"Same."

"S-s-same."

The woman directly across from me sets her cup down. "Homeless. Living in the Bear Traps."

I look around the room and raise my eyebrows. "Do the women who get called ever come back?"

A few women look down at their gloved hands. One shakes her head.

Fantastic.

I don't recognize anyone here, so I'm not entirely certain who drew me to this spot? Aurick Demechnef? Perhaps because I left his son behind? I'm not really sure who else I would be drawn to.

"Snow Abatora," a short old man calls from the cracked doorway.

The fake name I gave when captured.

The women look to me. Pity. Hopelessness. Sorrow.

"Don't worry about me," I say, rising from my seat and nearly falling to the ground from the intense vertigo.

But really, I just don't have a choice. I have two people who mean the world to me that I've abandoned in time. There isn't an option to die here or there. If I die after getting them home? Fine. If I, myself, don't make it home? Okay.

But not getting back to Uncle Niles and Niklaus? Inconceivable.

As I follow the old man to the next room, my sweaty hand instinctively clutches the IV pole I'm attached to. To brace myself for another cage. A dungeon. A dingy basement.

"You are quite the pretty one," the old man comments ironically. "Too bad he does not care about pretty."

He?

The mahogany door he opens does not lead to a basement or damp chamber.

It's a library.

Less of a room and more of a cathedral for rich bureaucrats and wealthy savants. Oil paintings watch from the mile-high ceilings. The trim of the dark walnut wood gleams beneath its polish. A few rolling ladders trace slow arcs across sparkling shelves. Velvet drapes cocoon the windows. Aged-brass fixtures and a fireplace bigger than the last cage I slept in.

And a young man, fourteen or fifteen, sits in the center of the room.

"Meet your newest guest, Snow Abatora," the old man tells the teenage boy.

As if moping, he keeps his head down, arms draped over his knees as he sits on the center of a nice table.

"Aren't you going to introduce yourself, young man?"

The boy shakes his head. Chocolate brown hair shifting side to side.

The old man lowers his head to make eye contact with me above his small, round bifocals that are slipping to the tip of his pink nose.

"Sit down, madame. Now," he orders.

You don't have to tell me twice. I drop myself down to a comfortable leather reading chair directly in front of the young man.

"If you want to move on to the next step in your education, then you must be cooperative." The elderly man grips his own knees with red, flaky hands, inclining forward to invade the boy's personal space. "I am not a fan of this rebellious behavior. I can tell you that right now."

My heartbeat picks up speed as I begin to suspect who I've been drawn to in the past.

The young man remains hunched, ankles crossed, and allowing this old man to speak to him so callously.

“Shall I ask Mr. Demechnef to make another visit?”

The teenager sits quietly a moment longer, then looks up at me. Those striking, yet toasty warm brown eyes split into me like a throwing axe.

Oh god, it’s him.

“Hello,” he greets. Voice a little lighter and less frightening than the last time I heard it. Smooth as cashmere.

“Hi.”

“Good. Enjoy.” The old man bobs his head contentedly and stomps out of the library.

I suck in a nervous breath, taking in the heavy scent of parchment and old perfume. Why have they put us in such a glorious space? I thought he was tortured and experimented on during his time within the Demechnef walls? What is this?

“Can you tell me what’s happening?” I ask him, heart hammering in my chest.

“An experiment,” he answers.

I don’t think I have ever seen so much sadness in one expression.

“And what is my part to play in this experiment?”

My young father looks my way, then to the fireplace where he rests his gaze on a dying flame.

“I will not tell you. Not because I am cruel or sadistic. But because knowing will cause you so much stress, my heart can’t take it. And if you try to run, it will only get worse.”

I take in his white shirt, gray pants, and suspenders. And based on the way he carries himself, it’s not Dessin.

“That’s fair. Though I won’t panic—I respect your decision,” I tell him kindly.

He stares me down now, lifting an eyebrow and studying my posture with curious, suspicious glances.

“Really? You aren’t going to press for it?”

“Nope.”

He looks positively flabbergasted.

"Now…" I steady myself from the bizarre dizziness rotating my world. "Are you going to tell me your name?"

That small smirk lights my soul. "Kane Valdawell."

"It's nice to meet you, Kane. My name is Snow Abatora."

Kane freezes, shoulders tightening under an invisible weight. He loses focus for a few seconds, gazing off to the side. It's strange to watch what I can only guess is occurring right now. He is both present and elsewhere all at once. Then, blinking several times, clearing away a thought, he returns to my face with narrowing eyes.

"He says that's not your name," he finally says.

My breath hitches.

"Who says?"

"You'd think I'm crazy if I told you."

That makes me sad to hear. "No, I wouldn't."

Kane considers this, and sighs. "I have dissociative identity disorder. There's another alter in my head who just told me you're lying about your name."

And I bet I know which alter that is.

But I can't think of a rebuttal fast enough.

"That's okay," Kane says, stretching his legs. "Your secrets are your own."

"Thank you." *I wish I could tell you my last name is Valdawell too.*

My stomach twists and dips as the drugs leave me spinning again. I close my eyes, holding onto the arm of the chair in hopes it will subside by grounding myself.

The table in front of me creaks as Kane moves, hopping off of it.

"Hold still," he instructs, tugging and readjusting my IV bag.

I peek through my lashes as he swaps the medication with something else.

"This should flush the drugs out of your system."

The nausea is soothed slowly, lessening its violent hold on my gut. I observe Kane hiding my former IV bag in a spot among some loose books. Leaning against the shelf, he crosses his arms and watches my reaction thoughtfully.

"You can try and escape…" he offers with a shrug. "But they've gotten good at hunting women down who try to leave."

Somehow, being in his presence does not scare me.

"I'm not going anywhere," I say.

"No?"

"I am exactly where I need to be."

"Hmm." Kane tilts his head and loses focus again, eyelids looking heavy and tired. After a moment of looking confused, he rubs a hand over his face.

"What?" I ask.

"You have a familiar face. But I know we've never seen you before."

I agree with a nod. "No, we've never met."

He looks down in thought again. "You remind me of someone."

"Oh yeah?"

"Yes." With a quick once-over, he scans my face. "Your green eye. Wavy hair. Your cheekbones."

The inside of my chest runs warm, turning gooey and soft.

"And who do I remind you of?"

Kane stares up to the ceiling, drumming his fingers against his arm.

"My sweetheart."

Mom, I wish you could see this.

"How long have you known her?" I ask.

"A very long time."

"And wha—"

Kane lifts a hand to stop me. "I don't like to talk about myself here. Certain details are used against me if overheard."

I wilt in my seat. But this is my chance to get to know him. Hear all about who he was as a young man.

"I'd rather hear about you, anyway," Kane finishes.

I gulp, feeling less heavy and more alert since he swapped out my IV bag. The smaller details of his face, hands, hair are clearing up. I can see my father now.

"What do you want to know?" *There's so much I want to tell you. Where would I even start?*

"Do you have a sweetheart?" he asks.

The echoing loss of leaving Niklaus is an arrow impaling my chest that I can't pull free. And without that pain? I'd have nothing left.

The motivation I have right now to investigate, to understand the purpose behind my time-traveling journey, to discover how to control it? It would dissolve into thin air. I cling to that anguish like a beacon that will eventually guide me back to him.

"Yes." My eyes water, and throat tightens up. "I have a sweetheart."

"Let's talk about him. Get my mind off this setting we're in," he says as though he is much older than I am. As though he is speaking to a child.

"I've known him my whole life," I confess.

"And have you loved him all that time as well?" Kane asks.

My lips press flat. "Hated actually. He spent our childhood years tormenting me. I only just recently began…*loving* him."

"That's odd."

"Why?"

"You hated him. He was cruel to you."

"Yes."

"I guess I'm going to need more context." My father shrugs, like the love he knows is entirely too simple to be able to wrap his head around this one.

"When we were little, Mind Phantoms were used on him to think poorly of my family. Of me. He spoke poorly of my father, and that's mainly why I hated him so much."

"And how did your father handle that?"

My chest caves in. Everything inside my core crumbles.

"He wasn't around to defend himself. He wasn't there to stand up for me." It all becomes so heavy, the unbearable reality that I'm sharing this with my father as a teenager who has no idea who I really am. I've wanted to tell him this for so long. "He died when my mother was pregnant with my brother and me. I used to dream he would protect me. That he'd never let anyone hurt me."

Kane observes me try my hardest to hold it together.

"There were so many times I wanted to tell him all of the shitty things Nik had said to me. But now, that's not at all what I want to tell my dad. I want to tell him that over the past few weeks I've been held captive with Nik. I've been assaulted and starved. I've been taken prisoner, and I've watched Nik take my punishments that have resulted in him losing his fingers and being showered in acid. And through all of that suffering, I've fallen in love with him."

Kane lifts his chin. "I see."

"What do you think he'd say? Am I crazy for loving him?"

"You're not crazy." My father, though young here, has infinite wisdom in his gaze. "People can change. Trauma does strange things, and no one handles it the same way."

"What should I do then?"

Kane's shoulders tense as he puts more thought into it.

"Keep loving him," he says.

My nostrils sting like I've inhaled cold air too fast. I blink against the shimmering vision.

"Why does this make you sad?"

"Because I've left him in a terrible place. And I don't know how to get back to him."

Kane's chocolate brown eyes dart from one side of the library to the other. He lifts his hands to emphasize the location I've currently found myself in.

"Look where you are. It seems to me he's the one who needs to come save you."

I chuckle. "It looks that way, doesn't it?"

He lifts his chin and stares at me with a rising suspicion behind those cautious eyes.

"You are more concerned for his life than yours at the moment?" Disbelief hangs on his expression.

"Yes."

"Either you don't understand the danger you are in, or he's in a place that might as well be the Vexamen Prison." Kane reads the expression on my face like a book. "You are aware of the danger you're in then."

Unsure of how much I should share with him, I nod.

"Is your sweetheart in the Vexamen Prison?" he asks again.

I stare at him.

"Hmm." He pushes off the bookshelf to pace the rug in front of me. "You're intriguing one of the alters in my head. He really likes puzzles."

I smile. He'd have a ball with the truth I can't share.

"If you know the danger you're in, then you know this is the end of the road for you. Saving your sweetheart isn't going to happen. You seem like a wise young woman. Intellectual beyond your years. You must understand that…"

"I am not going to die here," I tell him firmly.

Kane stops pacing.

"I understand I'm being used as some kind of bait in an experiment involving you."

He raises his eyebrows and freezes.

"But you're not going to hurt me."

Turning away, Kane says, "I won't have a choice."

If only you knew who I am to you. Who I'll be to you one day. Why I remind you of your sweetheart, Skylenna, so much.

I look around the library, itching to tell him everything, but settling on another route. A stack of books on the table behind Kane gives me an idea.

"You read all of those?" I point with my chin.

He shrugs. "I've read most of the books here."

"Have you ever read anything on time travel?" I ask.

Kane blinks a few times. "Only works of fiction and folklore."

I take a deep breath. "Good. Now for the really important question."

"I'm listening…"

"You have dissociative identity disorder, and since you're young—is it safe to assume you often suffer from memory gaps and amnesia?"

There's a flash of dissociation and a sounding alarm that has Kane changing his stance. I worry he's close to changing alters before I've had the chance to get to my point.

"Who *are* you? No one knows anything about my disorder."

I grab the arms of the chair and sit up straighter.

"Please, just answer the question. I'm going to tell you more than I can usually tell anyone if you'll just answer honestly."

Looking off to the left, he listens to the voices in his head. It must be a serious debate because he just listens for over a minute.

"Yes. I don't usually remember much while I'm in here."

I nod. I could really fuck everything up if I'm not careful. I could erase my own existence. But as of this moment, I just need to get back to Niklaus. I'd sell my own soul to save him right now.

"I know a lot about your disorder because I have time-traveled here. I left the man I love in the Vexamen Prison over fifty years in the past. I know this place experiments on you to reach more advanced abilities with your brain. I know your sweetheart's name is Skylenna—"

My father's hands are around my throat before I can blink or take another breath.

"Don't you ever say her name in this place again. I swear to God, I will kill you for breathing that name here…"

"And I know you would never hurt her. You've—looked out for her—your entire life! Please! Look into my eyes and see I am not a threat to you or her. I need your help!" I sputter and gag as he lets me go. That grip was far stronger and more deadly than I would have imagined from him this young.

"I know you—are a genius. I need that mind of yours—to help me get back to the man I love. Please, I am begging you!" I pant and clutch my pulsing esophagus.

Kane stares with a building curiosity behind his expression. His eyebrows pull together as he sees something in me. The caution and hesitation loosen their grip on his rigid posture.

My eyes prickle. *Please, you're my only hope, Dad.*

"If you're playing a game, there's an alter in my head who will play it better than you. And he has a temper. Understand?"

The word "*yes*" is mouthed by no sound comes out. And Kane takes a seat in front of me, rubbing his hands together in preparation.

"Tell me everything."

63. The Bastille of Quiet Rot

Niklaus

Grief swells so wide inside me, I swear I hear it hum. If I say her name out loud, the sound might annihilate me.

Four weeks.

Four.

It's as if my fingers haven't healed at all.

Each finger hurts in a way that is unrelenting and inconsolable. All I want to do is sleep to relieve myself of the suffering. Nightmares are hard but nothing is worse than this existence. Four weeks and no sign of her? It feels like I've been here, in hell, for four years. The devastation morphs into anger, then hatred. But a scent might remind me of the top of her head, and I miss her again. I've made myself sick over the emotional whiplash.

I think about that kiss over and over again. I think about my last words to her. About finally confessing how I feel.

And then she fucking *leaves* me here.

My world is smeared in red.

Where could she have gone?

Will she be lost forever?

I shouldn't be worried about her because look at the agonizing shitshow I'm experiencing a front row seat to. But I am. I am so fucking worried about her.

What if she's been killed? Back in the asylum? What if she's made destructive changes to the future?

I've exhausted every option.

I've fallen asleep at night with knots in my stomach and nerves shooting bombs of anxiety into my chest.

Sometimes, I'll hear a woman laugh in another cage on this floor, and for a fraction of a second—I allow myself to get my hopes up. I become that little boy in the abandoned cottage with the Demechnef extremists, waiting for my father to come save me. I am fooled into believing wholeheartedly that it's her laugh. That she came back for me.

She's gone.

She isn't coming back for me.

Accepting that truth has to be easier than waiting around with a maimed hand.

On week two of waiting, I got an infection in my middle finger. The swelling and pus zinged up to my elbow and made it impossible to think about anything else. Sophia tried to get me to eat. Jack risked his life to find antibiotics.

The Mazonist Brothers visited me on day three of her exit. They confirmed my wife was in fact a witch. I just sat there, surrounded by a reeking puddle of my own vomit, dripping in a cold sweat, and trembling from the constant unbearable misery I've been sentenced to.

Every week since? The kitchen staff has starved me in retribution

She isn't coming back for me.

Just fucking accept it, Niklaus!

Dellilian materializes at my side, nudging her head and wet snout into me. She's been doing this since my first night alone here. Initially, that instinct to banish her from my sight almost took over. But Dellilian is all I have left of her. She's proof I haven't gone mad. She's proof I am from the future. So, I let the snuggly creature curl up against me, soaking her body heat into my skin and providing the only bit of comfort I've had in a while.

With my good hand, I pet her head. The strange wolf purrs and grumbles. And she leaves few words in my thoughts to think on.

"*Don't give up, Mr. Niklaus.*"

How could I let myself get that attached? I had let myself *love* her. I still do. Four weeks in abandonment and I can't uncover how to make it stop.

Dellilian disappears as someone moves a cage away from me.

"If your wife really is a witch, she'll find a way to come back for you," Sophia says through the bars. It's almost morning, and I'm sure she can hear my vicious, dismal thoughts racing from my cage.

"Stop," I growl.

"Sapphire loves you. Anyone could see it."

"Do not fucking say her name!" I pound my right fist against the bar. Anger is what will keep the urge to sob into my hands like a child at bay. Anger is the only resource that's helped me.

"I'm sorry," she whispers weakly.

But even through the anger, guilt and remorse can still beat me to the ground.

"It's okay, Sophia."

I close my eyes and relive that moment she vanished into thin air like a poltergeist invading my personal space to haunt me. One minute she was there, the next…

The cage doors open.

Don't give up, Mr. Niklaus.

Maybe I can hold on a little longer.

I pick myself up, stretch with a long yawn, and follow Jack and Sophia from the cages and down the hall.

64. A Promise Made

Niklaus

One Year Later

The inmate who bleeds out at my feet puts a smile on my face. My spear is stuck in his cheek. The uneven, pointy tip of my weapon cracked into a few teeth before it sank into the oversized tongue in his mouth. I felt the meat split on impact, and his eyes widened before they went slack.

A fountain of blood is a ferocious torrent down his chin, forming a small lake at my feet.

That harrowing, beefy body jerks on the stage as I twist the spear, no doubt hitting a vein.

The two faces I do not want to see in the crowd are not there, and I grin wider.

This inmate was sentenced to life in prison for stealing the animals from the Meat Carnivals. I was hoping it was for a noble cause. But I was wrong. The reasons are far more disturbing and inhumane to repeat.

"*Demechnef búizarx!*" his brother roars, jumping onto the stage without permission from the Ringmaster.

The square jaw and boxed head plummet toward me like a crazed bull. He's twice my size, but sluggish and drunk with his rageful attack.

I don't think any of this would have worked without big brother's invasion of the fight night for revenge. I knew I could drag the fight with Nox out long enough… But *this* is what's really going to buy time. This stupid, sweaty, malignant narcissist motherfucker.

I play with him for a little while.

His fury makes him clumsy and uncoordinated. He flings random weapons at me from the rack. Charges me with a sword far too small for a man of his size. I practically float away from each squawk and powerful swing of his arm.

It's too easy.

His naturally pale complexion is cherry-red. And he fights with all his strength to avenge his brother. But not once can he land a hit. No blood is drawn.

I simply move out of his way, using the stage as a designated platform to make him dizzy and spent from running in circles to get me.

I count the seconds carefully.

Enough time has passed. Just in time, too. The Ringmaster fidgets, clearly getting agitated that no one is being harmed.

The brother releases a hysterical battle cry, fumbling over his own feet and raising that skinny sword to attack again.

All it takes is precision. I throw the spear, and it lodges directly into his square head. The skull cracks. Metal pierces the meat of his brain. And that three-hundred-pound man is nailed to the ground without so much as a whimper.

The crowd chucks food and trash. Cheering and chanting.

The small group of men who followed the brothers raid the stage. Swarming the sentinels that attempt to corral them. And I slip into the crowd of inmates, getting lost in the shadows, and among the chaos—I disappear from the spotlight.

A trap door under the stage leads to the sewage lines.

Blueprints in history books prepared me for this.

I sprint through the putrid gray water, crouching under the low pipe ceilings and following the directions I gave to a T.

"I'm here!" I shout-whisper.

Jack and Sophia have made it to the end.

"Hurry—let's go!" Jack signals for us to jump into the waterfall that leads to the coast. A perfect path to get passage to Dementia.

I don't move as Sophia tries to grab my hand.

"I'm not going with you," I tell them calmly.

Jack's mouth falls open. "No, goddamned you. Your plan worked. We're all leaving together!"

"I made a promise to my wife that I would get you two out of here."

Sophia starts to cry.

"We have what we need for all of us to leave though!" Jack tugs at his backpack in frustration.

"Please," Sophia sobs.

Moonlight leaks across the running water at our feet, highlighting their faces that will forever be etched into my memory.

"I can't leave," I admit. Though there is no sadness in my tone. It's acceptance. I'm just happy they get to start their lives, even if their fate is harsh where they're going. For a short while, they'll know happiness. Jack, when he meets Sapphire's grandmother, Violet. From what I remember, they were in love. And Sophia, when she has her two sons, Kane and Arthur.

"Yes, you can!"

I sigh, hearing the footsteps and shouting down the pipes from where I came. They figured it out.

"If there's still a chance my wife could come back, I can't leave here."

Sophia cries, covering her mouth to muffle the sound. Her light brown hair is greasy and askew across her face. They're both covered in grime and shit. But they're free now.

"Hey—don't feel bad for me." I tap her chin with my thumb. "Now, jump! Otherwise, we'll all get punished!"

Jack and Sophia exchange a final hopeless look, then silently thank me with their eyes. I don't know what I would have done this last year without them. Sophia, although she is younger than me here, was the most nurturing woman I have ever met. She tended to my wounds, was patient when I went through every stage of grief, and never once judged me. Jack became my best friend. Most of the time, he's very serious and a little bitter, but he was also hilarious. He helped me adapt with dark humor and companionship.

Her grandparents became my closest friends.

And I will never see them again.

The two clasp hands and jump into the waterfall, plunging down to the river that empties into the coast. That place where they'll eventually find safe passage.

Goodbye, Sophia and Jack.

As the sentinels swarm the humid tunnels, tackling me into rushing water—I know I will sleep well tonight.

Wherever you are, I hope you can see this.

I kept my promise.

65. Incurable Disease

Sapphire

"And the Nightlung…does it feel like a place or a sensation that you feel when you're moving to another time?"

Kane fiddles with the pages of century-old books he found in a dusty part of the library shelves. He doesn't even need to read through them. Just running a finger along the spine happens to jog his memory.

"Both. But mostly a place. A living, breathing entity."

"Hmm."

I'm surprised Demechnef officials are allowing us to lounge in here. How could this be part of an experiment? I pictured torture devices and chains. We are sitting in a library, next to a warm fire, *talking*.

"Do you feel connected to it at all? Or are there no feelings attached?" he asks.

I sort through each memory. From the first time I was sucked into the Nightlung, it felt like a hook pierced my core and was reeling me out to an open sea.

"Yes. Sometimes it feels like the Nightlung is in sync with my heartbeat. Other times it feels like a person who has just always been there, eavesdropping on my conversations."

Kane mumbles to himself, talking to another alter about a specific chapter in the book at the bottom of the stack. "And you said it always happens when your emotions are high?"

I nod. "I can never tell which emotions trigger it though. Sometimes it feels like fear. Other times it's anger."

"No, I don't think it's adrenaline," he mutters to himself. "Oh, yes. Could be. I'll ask."

I wait for his question, smoothing out the ridiculous dress that they put on me.

"That first time you traveled, you were attacked?"

"Yes."

"But it wasn't just you. Your sweetheart and uncle were also there."

"Mmm-hmm."

"Your uncle used his hands to protect you from being slashed by the swords."

Even someone else saying it out loud, analytically, strikes me straight to the bone. I lower my eyes to answer that.

"And the second time, you were attacked again but an animal that can also travel, Dellilian, protected you."

"Right." It sounds crazy. I'm surprised he's still going along with this.

"The third time, it was another attack—but another animal, that you know from the future, protected you and your sweetheart."

DaiSzek. I wish I could tell my father how brave he was.

"The fourth time, you were about to be—*assaulted*." The muscle in Kane's jaw tics. "But your sweetheart saved you."

"Yes."

"The fifth, what was it?"

I drop my face into my hands, rubbing my eyes. "I don't know, I have a hard time remembering things now since the electroconvulsive therapy. I think it was—"

"It was probably when she met me."

I jump at that voice. The one that sounds like a mangled nursery rhyme, strangely quiet, like he's trying to slip between cracks of time and into nightmares.

But Kane doesn't even flinch. He continues flipping through pages of a book, unfazed by the intrusion.

"It's about time you decided to stop being a peeping tom and join us, Vrath," my father says casually. "Waiting behind the back shelves for that long? I was beginning to wonder if you're afraid of me."

I told him every detail about my interaction with Vrath. From that information given, I suspect my father knew this strange man would be joining us soon

Seeing Vrath again, slightly hunched, and moseying out from the shadows—it's like having to sit still while spiders tiptoe across my bare skin. Is it the flaking paint on his face or the insect-like mannerisms that feel violating to look at?

My father stands, hands in his pockets, at first relaxed—but now dissociating.

"I have been privy to your existence too many times, though I do not think I am frightened of you. Perhaps of you as an older man," Vrath speaks slowly, as if the more words he says in front of my father means the more danger he will be in.

I tremble at the fever invading my immune system. My bones are cold. Each muscle aches and throbs. Puking or coming down with a massive migraine are two realistic options right now. His presence is an infection that pulses like a dying heartbeat within these walls. He's making me sick…

I look to Kane and am struck with terror.

No! What if he dies from being near Vrath?

My lungs rattle from sticky phlegm between each labored breath. Whatever sickness he drags behind him like a cloak hits the air around us hard and fast.

"You will behave, or *he* will die a very young man of pneumonia and—some other peculiar disease I do not recognize." Vrath puts in a little too much effort to ignore my father and descend toward me. "I need your blood. I have had enough of chasing you and will not tolerate your inconsolable desire to be away from me."

My father is unresponsive. In the time it takes him to finally turn in our direction, Vrath is already too close. Each white blood cell in my body is under attack. My skin is molten. The instinct to put as much distance between us is feral and sending SOS signals to get me to listen.

"Does it usually work?" It's my father's voice, only different. The same young man. A raspier, sarcastic inflection. "I bet it feels pretty good, huh? Making people sick."

Vrath doesn't answer, he just peers back at my father, who is lounging in the nearest loveseat, legs crossed and left arm propping his chin up.

"And what would happen if you came across, ah I don't know, a devilishly good-looking man with an immunity to that sort of nonsense? Eh?" Kane smirks at Vrath, then winks in my direction.

"You have split a new alter," Vrath comments, though there is a splash of concern there.

I blink, long and slow, trying to see Kane more clearly.

"Don't you wanna know my name, dickhead?" the alter asks.

"That is an irrelevant fact to me."

"It's Church. I'm immune to disease, plagues, illness…etcetera." He flashes a big smile.

Vrath twists back to me mechanically, deciding to ignore Church and continue his pursuit of me, assuming my father's new alter isn't very threatening.

"Have I mentioned that I'm a savant of moving through time? Yeah yeah, every piece of literature and textual evidence in this library and elsewhere, I have read. It's all I've really retained. No, but it gets better." Church sits up excitedly, tucking his feet under his backside. "The low hanging fruit is that I learned a bit about the Short-Haired Windilas. But what's really interesting is that if they draw blood, even once, they'll forever be attracted to it if it's drawn again."

Church springs from his chair and flicks his wrist near the lower half of Vrath's face. The swipe is so quick, I'm shocked when I see a fast trickle of dark blood spill from Vrath's severed bottom lip.

"I'm willing to bet they've nicked you once or twice."

Vrath stumbles back, tapping at his lip with a black-gloved hand and pulling it back to inspect the blood.

"Do you think they'll come running?" Church plays with the bloody razor between his fingers. "*Oooh,* I wonder if they're fast. Are they fast, Vrath?!"

This alter reminds me of a unique blend of Uncle Niles and Dessin. He uses irony and quick wit to deal with these challenges he's split in response to.

For a moment, Vrath pivots to me with a pathetic, creepy look that asks for help.

Help.

I laugh, then cough so hard, my eyes water hot tears.

"If you were afraid of Dellilian, I can't imagine how frightened you'll be of her pack," I say with wheezing breaths.

Vrath breathes heavily behind clenched teeth, scurrying off to the back of the library. He crouches low to the ground, lifting something heavy behind a writing desk and dragging it out to the main light of the crystal chandelier.

With choppy steps, the white tights and modest, black-strapped heels are revealed. Vrath's hands hook around the ankles as he takes three more steps to the open hardwood floor. Her feet hit the floor with a thud. Her cream-colored lace dress with ruffles and a navy sash bow is sopping wet with blood. A deep red streaks behind her, saturating her blonde hair, and gently gushing from an open wound in her chest with each aggressive form of contact Vrath has with her.

I gasp. Church lifts his chin and watches the vile display closely.

"What are you doing?!" I shriek in a feeble voice.

"No shortage of mothers here."

Vrath places one hand on top of the other on her chest and throws his body weight downward. Her breastbone cracks, and he pulls it apart with a panicked grunt. His hands scoop out as much blood as he can carry without too much overflowing, then splashes it to the floor in a substantial puddle.

There's a sound coming from all around us. It's like a cold winter's night when screaming winds whistle against the side panels of a house and the frigid glass windows.

"They will not get me. No, they will not get me." Vrath mutters numbers and strange, ancient words under his breath, using his finger to make symbols and spiral drawings in the thick pool of blood. "Protect my soul, World's Dark Twin Tree."

After twisting off a strand of the mother's hair, Vrath vanishes in a pit of sparkling black dust and violent stormy winds. Pages fly free from bookshelves and the scones and fireplace flickers.

The sickness leaves my body a little too slowly. I slump into my chair, wheezing, and clutching my chest. I should have jumped into that opening with him and tried to find my way back to Niklaus. I should have commanded the tunnel of moving time to take me to the man I've fallen in love with. I cough and tremble in my seat. Useless. Sick. Stupid.

My eyes flash back to Church. I want to warn him about the coma so badly, but he is a new alter. A child. What guarantee would I have that he would remember or be able to pass along the message for an event that will take place in another decade? I need to get closer to that time he is injected by Masten.

"His trigger is fear and superiority over a parental figure—a mother. That's what gets that asshole to travel." Church stares right through me, working out an equation in his head. "I'm not sure he even needs the gore and theatrics to do it."

"What's mine? I have to get back to him, Church!" I choke on another wet cough.

"Don't you see it yet? It's love, Snow. You have to let yourself feel that protective, everlasting love. Think about each time you've traveled! Your uncle sacrificed himself, using his own hands to guard you from being struck by the sword. Your sweetheart did the same! It's *love*! Use it as a key and the compass to navigate where you're going. Command the Nightlung when you enter it. Love is a motivating factor in your journey!"

An epiphany tingles in my chest, trickling down to my fingertips.

That tremor deep in my bones comes alive. A song that flips and spins within my veins, soaring to make contact with the Nightlung. I can feel it open its eyes and look into my soul. I think about Uncle Niles's shredded hands as he blocked the attacks with his body. A powerful comprehension opens inside me, lifting its head and absorbing the love that is produced from that memory.

I think of Dellilian saving us.

I think of Niklaus beating Albatross to a pulp when he had me strapped down to his bed.

I think of my mother burning the asylum to the ground.

It's so close, I can feel its mystical fingers reach out to me…

"Good. It looks like you have brutalized one without my command. Now, you'd have your fun with Miss…." A slender man with dark gray hair, pinched smoker's lips, and pale blue eyes flips through a few pages on a clipboard. "Miss Snow Abatora. Bring Dai to the front and eliminate this mock threat."

I watch Church dissociate again. It's quicker this time as the new alter is disoriented, looking around to catch himself back up.

"To which alter am I speaking with now?" the brooding man asks. I focus harder on his narrow face with aristocratic bone structure. He wears obsidian velvet and a tailored suit that drips of nobility and old money.

"Kane."

I look back at my father with bulging eyes. They want him to *eliminate* me? What's the significance of the alter Dai again?

"Thought so. It is time for Dai to front now, young man. Do this quickly, and we will put the Mind Phantoms away for a week."

Dai…

My stomach collapses on itself. Dai. I remember Krimson and I eavesdropped on my mother talking about that alter with Uncle Warrose. Demechnef wanted an alter who would ruthlessly murder like an animal. They forced him to rip people apart with his teeth. That's when Dai was split!

Holy shit.

I steady my breathing.

Part of his conditioning must be to bond with the women they bring in and then force him to tear them to shreds. It trains obedience no matter the emotional attachment.

Kane's chocolate eyes dart from me, back to the man making commands.

"No, Mr. Demechnef."

My jaw drops as I stare at the evil bastard who is Niklaus's fucking grandfather.

"You remember what happened the first time you refused, don't you? How painful that was for your system?" The tyrant of Demechnef is unblinking with eyes that look like preserved death.

"Yes." He lowers his head.

"Defy me again, and I will make the punishment on your system last twice as long."

My father flicks his hopeless gaze back to me once more.

"I can't…"

"He said no, Vlademur."

To my horror, I nearly cower and submit as Niklaus's grandfather redirects his razor-sharp glare to me. And I am so much less than nothing to him. I am a woman. Property. Snake bait.

In my periphery, I can see that Vlademur's hold on my father has profound roots. With this simple threat, calm and unfeeling—he was able to influence Kane with little to no effort. My father starts dissociating. It's a survival disorder after all. He is protecting their system. All of the alters.

The trauma response is unstoppable at Vlademur Demechnef's mercy.

"You don't have to do this, Kane." I ignore whatever this

sadistic dictator will say next. My father is all that I see now. "You are the smartest man in the world. There's a reason that you're the only one who could help me! Vlademur can't control you anymore. You and Dessin are far more powerful, and they know that if they lose control of you, that's their death certificates."

Sweat drips down the sides of Kane's face as he hyperventilates. Those pupils dilate. The muscles in his upper back clench and contract.

"Please. Don't let them control you anymore. You are the puppet master."

Vlademur waves a few gentlemen in to observe my demise. But I hold out hope that he'll pull through. That Dessin will come to the front and take over. *Please!*

I rise to my feet, ripping the IV from my arm and back away. This isn't a fight I can win. Not with my father. Not with this type of alter born of forced violence to protect any other alter from having to harm an innocent person who is used as bait.

Kane's eyes are glassy, as if someone blew out a candle in his mind. His breathing changes pitch, no longer at a human rhythm. His spine arches, and he crouches to the ground with knuckles grinding into the floor.

"Kane…" I whisper, standing behind my chair, as if that could protect me now.

From his position on all fours, he lifts his head. Nostrils flare. Black eyes see right through me. Head twitches like an animal hearing sound I'm incapable of catching.

Through the fear, I try to remember what Church told me about time traveling. My trigger. That protective love. But it's hard to internalize it when I'm staring my own violent, gory death in the face at my father's hands.

What if I can't do it? Like so many times I've failed myself, this would top them all. I can't make it back to Niklaus if I'm dead.

That sensation to protect him pulses into my fingertips, and I can taste the windy, cold air of the Nightlung.

"Dai! You are stronger than them! Protect your alters by killing the enemy. Not me!" I scream as he shifts on his heels, moving to me like a predator stalking his prey.

The air around us is heavy and spiked with the ghosts of the innocent women who have died this way. I look at what they've done to my father and choke on a sob for him. He was a child before he was a monster. He was a child before he won the war with my mother. He had only loved one woman his entire life. He was a child when he met her. He was a child when they started turning him into this.

I wish he could see me.

I wish I could tell him.

I sob into my hand as the look in his eyes tells me there is no getting through to him. Nothing I could say. Nothing I could do. Tears pressurize through my sinuses, causing me to hiccup at his current state.

He's a non-human alter. Trained to be this way. Abused. No choice but this disorder made for their own survival. I never put this much thought into my father's disorder. But seeing it up close. Knowing what these adults had to do to him to give it life.

And the murderous, animalistic growls turn into a warning snarl before Dai leaps toward me, soaring over a coffee table and tackling me to the ground. Hands pinning my shoulders to the floor, snapping his teeth in my face as I scream.

"Daddy, please!"

Dai freezes over me.

"Attack!" an old man yells.

Though language doesn't register with him. My words do.

Daddy, please!

They sink into his mind and penetrate that feral, inhuman subconscious. His lashes shudder, and his left eyebrow ticks. A breath is sucked in through his nose, slow and shallow.

And that's the feeling. My heart implodes for my father. The feeling is dumped into my nerves, and a pair of phantom hands throws the door wide open to the Nightlung.

I hold this sensation of love for him so close, my nails draw blood into my palms. Tears don't stop coming down my cheeks. I step into the tear in this reality the way one would step into a lake for a swim. But this time, as I enter its abyss, I tell it where I'm going.

I think of Niklaus in the Vexamen Prison.

I'm coming for you, my sweetheart.

66. Mark on History

Sapphire

I expect to see him the moment I open my eyes and recognize these stained ruddy cathedral walls and acrobatic beams across the vast ceiling.

But I am wedged between the stadium seating during a regale hour, watching inmates interact down below during their scheduled recovery time.

My hand fiddles with the hem of my dress nervously looking for any sign of him—*hem of my dress.* I'm wearing a dress in prison. *Shit. Shit. Shit. Shit.*

I crouch lower behind a rusted, sticky seat. I pull the silky rose-petal pink dress over my head, tossing it off the side. Heels off. Tights pulled free from my legs. Hair unwound from its tight bun. All that's left is a lacy black slip as an undergarment.

It's not the usual red, skimpy uniform, but better than a morning sunlight afternoon dress.

I study each inmate who shows me their face. None are Niklaus.

I'm jittery with nerves to see him again, but there's that daunting fear that he didn't make it. That I'm too late. That I didn't travel back far enough.

Three women converse a few rows below me. I pinpoint their lineage by the branded marks on their shoulders. The peak and stag of the East Vexello Mountains. Additionally, they are big-boned, hefty, husky, hewn from hardship.

I've learned about their people from Helga Bee and Gerta at our family dinners.

"Pssst!" I call to them.

They look around, finding me staring at them with one eye between the crack of the chairs. Their expressions contort into a confused laugh as they find humor in my hiding. Not at all threatened by my sudden appearance.

"What're you hiding from, naked little dumpling?" the middle one asks.

I lift my eyes an inch over the seat.

"Get over here!" I whisper-shout.

The three women laugh. "Bossy dumpling!"

"…and I'm not naked. I'm wearing more clothes than you three are."

They approach and begin inspecting my black silk slip, touching the fabric and lace.

"Oooooh, so soft!" one chimes.

"Mmm-hmm. Definitely naked."

"Pretty, but naked."

I roll my eyes. "I need help!"

They snicker. "Bossy must be snorting too much of the stage fumes! She's on a paranoia ride!"

"I'm looking for a prisoner—he has black hair and intense blue eyes. Good fighter. A few inches taller than you three. I don't see him in here!"

"Yum yum! Big blue eyes, don't mind if I do, Mama!"

"Please. I just need to know if he's alive. His name is Niklaus." I'm shaking from head to toe, unable to sit still. What if he didn't make it? What if I lost him for good?

The women stop laughing and go entirely still. Silent

conversations are had between their eyes, once full of amusement, now undoubtedly curious and slightly timid.

"Niklaus," the middle one repeats.

"Yes!" I blow out an anxious breath.

"He's alive," the woman on the left answers cautiously.

I fall back on my butt and laugh-cry into my hands.

"Did you know him on the outside?" they ask.

"Yeah," I mumble into my hand.

"Oooof. How old are you? Eighteen? Nineteen? You must have been a child when you last saw him then!"

It takes me a few seconds.

One, two, three, four, five…

A child…

"I've always wanted to know what that gloomy knight was like before he got here!"

I rock back onto my knees in front of them, plastering my hands to my chest as I beg for my ears to be so wrong, so incorrect about that subtle hint.

"Go back…" I rasp, tears rimming my eyes. "What…what does that mean? I must have been a child…?"

Please, no. Please, God, tell me I'm wrong.

"That prisoner has been locked up for what?" The middle woman looks between the other two and shrugs. "A decade? You're so young. You must have been just a little girl dumpling when you saw him last!"

My stomach drops and each vital organ threatens to stop working. I double over, gasping into my fist, grunting through the shock of it all.

"No! No! No! I don't know if I can move again to a more specific date! I could end up finding him again years later! Oh god, what do I do?!" I'm hyperventilating, shivering, wrapping my arms around my waist and praying this is just a nightmare.

He'll never forgive me!

The women adjust their feet, unsure how to comfort this breakdown. But nothing they say would matter to me right now. All I can hear is my own heartbeat. The sound of Niklaus's screams when he used his body to shield me from the acid shower. The blank look on his face when the slayer sword came down on his fingers. How easily they were separated from his hand. And he didn't react. He stared at the dismemberment as his brain clearly fought to protect itself.

"…that's what I heard, anyway. He could have escaped with those two teens, eight or nine years ago. What were their names? Soap and Jaspy?"

"Sophia and Jack?!" I blurt out.

"Sure. Whatever. He's known to be a master escape artist here. But he always comes back. No one really knows why."

I'm gripping the back of the stadium seat so hard, my nails are bending and breaking off.

"They haven't killed him for trying to escape?" I ask.

"*Pffft!* No! He's the main attraction on fighting nights. They just keep him locked up in solitary down at the hidden dungeons of the underground prison. Even make him wear a metal cage over his mouth and everything so he doesn't try to outsmart the Guardians again."

The right one snaps excitedly, tapping her head as she remembers another detail. "I hear sentinels aren't even allowed down there too! A team of Guardians have to patrol his isolated confinement at all times."

"And other than the fighting, Blue Eyes hasn't had any real human contact, in what?" the curly-haired middle woman asks.

"A couple years, at least!"

"*Oof*, can you imagine?"

"Golly-giblets, no. My bits don't do well in the dry months!"

"I'll say! What do you—"

"*Please*." I am a puddle of two emotions waging war against each other. "How do I get to him?"

One part of me is annihilated with grief over what I've done to this man, for he will never be the same again. The Niklaus I've grown up with is gone. The man I left behind has been alone in the dark, suffering and manipulated. Forced to fight other inmates as the sole purpose for his existence in this prison. A puppet for them to bring out when they get bored.

The other part of me is the annihilator. Imagining everyone who has hurt Niklaus and savoring a particular fantasy of sticking pins in their limbs and dissecting them slowly, watching them struggle to stay sane through the unmedicated surgery.

That includes me.

I have hurt Niklaus more than anyone here.

Because I left.

And it took me ten years to find him again.

"Dellilian!" I whisper into the narrow, stone hall.

"*Hi, Miss Sapphire!*" Dellilian lies down beside me as I wait in a dark corner to enter the underground prison. Her damp snout prods my heel.

"I know you can't interfere too much—but I need you by my side for what I'm about to do. You'll look pretty terrifying behind me."

"*Dellilian scary?*"

"Oh, yes. You are *chilling*, Dellilian."

The onyx wolf chuffs, blowing a small cloud of dust up from the ground.

I've followed the instructions of the East Vexello Mountain women without getting caught. And now, I am at the entrance of the dungeon. The air down here is stale, and it tastes old. Like warm bodies have existed for centuries down here, unable to escape even through death.

"*Very dark,*" Dellilian comments nervously.

I nod, pulling my lips between my teeth.

And Niklaus has been locked down here for so many years.

The women told me that this dungeon is used sparingly. For the prisoners that are too aggressive to keep around the general public of the rest of the prison. Yet too valuable to kill as they are of a scrupulous interest to the Mazonist Brothers.

As the Guardian manning the entrance wanders off, I jog, light on my feet to enter the mouth of the place no one dares to go. The archway is low with claw marks, and I can picture those who have been thrown down here against their will, fingernails cutting into the stone doorway as they try to save themselves.

Slipping into the pitch blackness, the atmosphere becomes unnaturally thick, breathing in the air of someone else's lungs. The walls were made with black bricks by someone who did not understand human proportions of architecture. At moments, it's unsettling as claustrophobia chokes me—the walkway narrows like an unpredictable cave. I turn to the side, duck, and then suddenly have so much room around me, I'm not sure where the walls are.

"*Mr. Niklaus won't be without enemies,*" Dellilian warns.

"I know," I whisper over my shoulder. "I'm counting on that."

As footsteps echo along with dripping water and long, ghostly moans—I break out into a sprint. The predictions of my sources theorize that Niklaus is in the very back. My instincts tell me that's correct, like a magnet summoning me, I can feel it.

Hold on, Niklaus. I'm coming...

I stop in front of five Guardians, members of the Blood family. And I know I've made it. Relaxed in their seats, they stand abruptly, caught unprepared and disheveled to see a woman out of uniform without any chains show up here of all places.

They guard a dome of bars without so much as a small candlelight to show anyone inside. I attempt to look around them to sneak even a glimpse of Niklaus in there.

I recognize Glinorious and Tycraniz Blood right away. The years have been kind to them. They remain god-like, ancient and majestically tall.

"I'm here for my husband." The protective love that unravels into the palms of my hands links me to the Nightlung with ease. I will die to free him, and that truth alone gives me great power. Dominion over these demons.

Tycraniz does a double take. A quick scan of my upper body, and that flicker of identification spreads a grin over his face. "You are the wife?"

"She disappeared," Glinorious Blood scoffs.

"Wasn't she a witch?" another asks.

I measure the room with my eyes to make sure there is no additional threats. There are claw marks on the rocky ceiling. There are words probably carved by fingernails in the wall next to me. *'They don't let you die here.'*

"If you let me leave with him, I will not come back," I say. Even though the tunnel is ice cold, my skin is set ablaze with a fueling desire to eliminate everyone in my path to get to him.

The Bloods laugh, collectively making threatening steps in my direction.

Dellilian steps out from behind my shadow, growling, snarling, and snapping to warn them about getting any closer.

They stop to silently assess the danger of this animal being in close quarters of this prison. A few words are passed around in Old Alkadonian. I only recognize *Meat Carnival.*

"You only have a few seconds to decide," I add calmly.

There's a vehement charge of an otherworldly frequency buzzing into my bones, spearing into my hands. It's a living, breathing beast that waits restlessly for me to release it.

"No," Glinorious announces firmly. "We will cut off your limbs and hang you next to his confinement so he may watch you bleed out."

"Final answer?" I move forward, holding my arms open to show I bear no weapon. "Because I heard you mate with your brothers and sisters to maintain a pure bloodline. Do you have any idea what that kind of incest does to your offspring over the generations?"

Glinorious is the first to attack me.

"It deforms them."

The Nightlung possesses my senses and erupts me at sheer will. Claws are sunk into their minds, their genetics, each individual strand of DNA. And I fuse into the fibers of their souls. Within the radiating darkness of the Nightlung, I speak to the Bloods like a god commanding from worlds away.

"For every harm you have caused him, I will speed up your generational incest."

The clock is spun and pushed forward in their anatomies. Years and decades leave them. But they do not age. No, that is not what I'm adjusting. I am speeding up the birth defects that will one day come to their children and their children's children. I manipulate each era within their foul mating system. Their skin, once bronze by war, turns waxy and of decaying leather, pocketed with boils and warts that weep a yellow ichor. Foreheads bulge unnaturally, like second skulls are emerging. They lose or acquire more fingers and toes. Teeth rot, growing in disturbing shapes. Armor groans and cuts into their skin, too tight from new bone formations.

And those glamorous, noble headdresses—they melt and harden into small cages around their heads.

Drool hangs from their gaping mouths, a milky goo that flutters from each labored breath. Their human likeness has been buried by an incest-derived monstrous instinct. They move like hypnotized mammoths, disoriented and blind.

I strike while the disfiguration continues to warp their brain chemistry.

Stealing a sickle from Tycraniz's belt, I bring two Blood Mammoths to their knees, slicing into their Achilles heels and kicking them to the ground. They crawl away from me in a daze, and the others follow only after attempting to fight back in a drunk, sluggish form—my sickle cuts into their oddly developed muscles and tendons.

A blizzard of iced blood and frigid arteries hit me at every angle internally. But as I see his cage is abandoned, left without a guard…I straighten my back and set down the sickle.

The only sign of life from beyond the bars and within the cocoon of nightfall is leveled breaths.

We are finally alone.

67. Darkened Knight of The Vexamen Prison

Sapphire

There is no key to open the cage door.

"Here!" Dellilian is now inside the cage, holding the keys in her mouth. Her tail wags happily.

"Thanks, sweet girl."

A five-pound, oversize skeleton key is dropped in my hand. And Dellilian ebbs away in a gust of smoke.

I unlock the door with a wobbly hand. It drops from my bloody, frozen fingers twice, but there is no voice on the other side. No one acknowledging my arrival. No one piercing the veil of this silent dungeon to let me know they see me.

I fight the need to curl into a ball against the hypothermic symptoms slowing my movements.

As the door cracks, I lift a torch from the wall to guide me inside the pit beyond the bars. It's bigger than I thought. The shadows eat up the light of my torch as I can hardly see two inches in front of my own face. And it's too quiet. Not the absence of sound, but a muffling of a haunted, residual noise, like gasps of pain inside a velvet coffin.

"Niklaus…" I whisper.

After everything we've been through, I have yet to be this terrified. Will he remember me after God knows what's been done to him? Has he been harboring a sea of hatred for me since I vanished?

My hand quivers in the damp, icy air as I extend my arm to catch even the slightest glimpse of a man. Of Niklaus.

An exhale.

I freeze.

"Niklaus." My throat swells from holding back a mountain of remorse. "It's…*me*."

Though I can't see anything in front of me, I can sense a person a few steps away. I can *feel* a set of eyes on me.

Holding my breath, I take two large steps forward and lengthen my arm all the way out.

The shuddering flame illuminates a man standing upright, chained to a large pole. Arms bound behind his back. A metal cuff over his mouth, attached to the iron collar around his neck. Black hair swept away from his face in a bun on the back of his head.

My legs falter. It's the eyes.

Everything about him has changed.

But not those silky, sapphire blue eyes.

The beard. How time has added creases and lines to his forehead and around his eyes. The protruding, hardened muscles of a stone masonry, roped with veins and flexing tendons. Sculpted from years of punishment and combat. The raised ink decorating his ribs and chest.

"Oh my god," I weep.

He doesn't move. Doesn't blink. Niklaus, ten years older than the man I knew, just stares at me. The scrutiny. The mixed implosion of emotions makes me feel like a mouse that has unwittingly stumbled into the cage of a lion.

"I—I—oh, Niklaus…"

I come to my senses after seconds of breathing through the shock and regret keeling me over. He's chained to a pole. How long as he been here? How long has been tortured and abused? He is covered in welts, bruises, blisters, and the most jagged, gutting scars I have ever seen.

I fumble forward with nerves ebbing and flowing like live wires crossing through each limb. My chest touches his chest. I'm so close, feeling the brush of his breath against mine as I loop my arms around his body to snap the key into the lock and turn it, hearing the click of cogs being unlatched.

Once the clunky lock topples to the ground, I unwind the chains in a hurry. His eyes bore into me without daring to look away.

The last of the chains clatter to the ground at our feet. And he steps off the post without a moment of hesitation. Metal cuff still attached to his mouth, though he doesn't seem to notice. He advances on me. That glare unreadable. Steady and cold.

I hold my hands up in surrender. Tears swell over my bottom lashes as I look up at him helplessly.

"I am sorry. I am *so* sorry." I can't breathe. The loss of never seeing the man I left behind again blasts my senses. He's no longer here.

I left him here all alone.

My sobs rattle me to my core.

After a quiet pause, Niklaus lunges for me, hands clutching my collarbone—a centimeter away from wrapping around my throat. And he pins me to the bars so suddenly I shriek, crying out at the sudden burst of aggression that is more than warranted and so well-deserved.

"Kill me!" I sob violently, still holding my hands up to show I will not fight back. "I—I can never forgive myself. I thought I made it back—but it's been—it's been, oh God, it's been *ten* years!"

He hesitates to grip the life out of me with that crazed, homicidal look in his eyes.

"I deserve to fucking die for this, Niklaus! I'm so sorry!"

He tilts his head. Each muscle ripples like a coiled beast is trying to tear through his skin to kill me itself. It's as if he's been taunted before with the hope that I've come back. Like he's in complete denial that it's actually me standing here in front of him.

"But—you have to know it wasn't on purpose. I swear to God, Niklaus, I would have never left you behind of my own will!"

A flicker of confusion sweeps across his stoic, callous expression.

His hands are fortified steel around me, rough like sandpaper against my chest. They twitch and tighten, and he observes me like an animal trying to decide how much of a threat I am.

Seeing him again heightens every feeling I've tried to bury since the moments I began to fall for him in that asylum. It's an unstoppable force fusing my soul to his. I am no longer capable of feeling hatred for him. No longer adept at denying the way my heart jumps and writhes in my chest, frantic to feel his body press against mine.

I pant against the metal bar plastered over his handsome lips.

If I am going to die here, there isn't a chance in hell I'll depart this world without telling him my heart is his. After all he's been through, the truth will not be held from him. No matter if he rejects it or not.

"I *love* you." I've carried these words like a knife tucked under my ribs. "I am sorry! I love you, and I've fought my way back to you. I will always fight my way back to you. I love you, Niklaus!"

Each purge of tears is hollowing out my chest with an insatiable yearning that is being horrifically bludgeoned by guilt.

The word *love* strikes him like a bolt of lightning to his chest. He balks back, releasing my upper body, stunned and speechless. His lashes flutter, short, tight bursts of blinking.

Tears form over his eyes like molten glass.

"I fell for you in that asylum," I whisper in an injured, fragmented voice.

Niklaus is dreadfully cautious and probing my body language for any signs of deception. He has had ten years of living with the enemy. Ten years of rejecting hope that I would come back for him. Ten years of getting used to constant lies and betrayal.

"I loved you when you held me that night after Meridei put us through that treatment."

The bits of faded memory dilate his pupils. His breathing is loud and leaden, huffing through his nose as if he has been running up a mountain, as if he is working hard not to cry. That gorgeous stare flares wide, like he's witnessing a ghost no one else can see.

With vigilant steps forward, he occupies the air I breathe once more. Staring down at me to gauge my reaction. And unexpectedly, his forehead pushes against mine, and he closes his eyes.

I whimper at the sudden, inviting contact.

"I've come back to you," I whisper sweetly.

Niklaus's grunt is muffled against the metal cuff, and in a stern frenzy, he anchors his hips into mine, caging me against his body. The impulsive need to be as close to me as possible thrums a hot shiver of desire low in my belly.

I melt into the hard lines of him. My hands act on their own impulses by exploring every scar, every burn, ever beating he has endured since I've been gone. And he doesn't seem to mind at all, in fact, my delicate touch spurs him on. He nudges his nose into my hair, inhaling my scent like he has been waiting years to capture that aroma again.

"*Oh*," I purr as he jerks my waist against him even harder. That rough, primal touch triggers a static pulse between my legs. And I squirm in his arms as the ache to have more of him develops thick and sweltering in my veins.

His hands tear into my undergarment black slip until his knuckles turn white.

"You can have me," I pant against his face. "My love, you can have me however you want me."

My words are storm clouds over a dry wilderness. He lifts his gaze, and something in him, if only a small portion—*heals*. Though a mild hesitation still hovers close by.

I act quickly, guiding his fingers between my legs and dipping his fingers beneath my panties, giving him the shove he needs to feel how wet I am for him.

Niklaus growls, the noise reverberating deep in his chest. I buckle forward at the sound, something inside of me purring and at his mercy. His last thought of caution and restraint clearly snaps as he racks me against the bars, curling his fingers inside me. The act is less methodical and more feral, acting purely on carnal instinct.

Sliding his two fingers in and out has me gasping, then grappling at his flexed muscles along his upper back. And he dips his face into my neck, continuing to breathe in my scent like a wild beast.

"Do you need to be inside me?" I rasp against his ear, delirious from the feeling of his hard cock grazing my side through his pants.

Niklaus's groan is gravelly and ferocious. And I immediately help him unbuckle, taking his pulsing shaft in the palm of my hand. His hands seize the bars behind my head, completely at my mercy as I stroke his warm length.

He is a rabid creature, breathing erratically and grimacing down at me.

After another moment of exploring his visceral reactions to me touching him, Niklaus rips off my panties and hoists my legs around his hips. My moan turns into a howl as the head of his cock pushes into my entrance, testing how much of his girth will ease into me.

"I don't want you to be gentle with me," I tell him, arching my back to give him a better angle. To open me up for him. "I want to feel everything you need to get out from these last ten years."

Niklaus hesitates with only his tip being soaked by my arousal.

"Do whatever you want with me," I offer sensually, undulating another half inch on his cock. "I am all yours. Make love to me as hard as you need, baby."

I have unleashed a monster, starved and filled to the brim with uncontrollable aggression. The raw, predatory energy seething off him is only making me more wet, more willing, and surrendering all control to him.

He doesn't ease into me. Niklaus slams me against the bars and sinking into the hilt. In and out, slow but rough, jolting me upright, and causing my breasts to bounce against his collarbone in the process.

My head falls back, and my yelps can be heard from all corners of this underground prison. It will ensure sentinels and guardians break out in search of us. But none of that matters right now. He fucks me with a war on his shoulders and years of torture sinking into his every thought.

"I love you. God, I love you so much, Niklaus!"

I am so sorry. Please forgive me. I will never leave you again.

His ravaging growls and grunts liquify my spine and induce a gnawing, flesh-starved version of myself that grinds against him, matching his violent rhythm, sawing in and out.

It's minutes or hours of Niklaus taking me to the stone floor, hooking his hands around my ankles, and bending my legs back until the tops of my thighs are parallel to the cold ground. I am relaxed putty under his weight. A contortionist with my legs behind my head for him to twist and fuck without complaint.

The rocking of his hips and head resting against mine pulses into my clit. And I translate a look he gives me. One that urges me to understand what he needs. '*Say it again.*'

"I love you," I whisper against the metal plate.

His eyes roll back into his head, and we fall into an incapacitating orgasm together. It burns into my legs and up my spine.

Niklaus bears no concern for coming inside me.

He pulses his pelvis against my throbbing center, filling me up without a second thought.

Slowly, Niklaus releases the backs of my knees, and my legs return to their extended position, numb and trembling.

The tension in the air does not subside after he sits up to look down at me. The backs of his fingers glide along the inside of my thigh. Lost in thought. Unable to break physical contact with me, maybe out of fear that I'll evaporate into the Nightlung again.

"I can get us out of here," I say hoarsely.

Cornflower blue irises flash up to my gaze.

"I met my father as a teenager. One of his alters figured out how I can control the time-traveling. I'm still learning, obviously, but I was able to return. Here."

He is as still as death.

I swallow. "I can bring you home."

Chest moves up and down in long, noticeable drags.

"You got Sophia and Jack out of here." My voice cracks. "You kept your promise."

Niklaus remains rooted to the ground but closes his eyes for three long seconds. Each breath is full of a decade of knowledge he now has that I do not.

"Will you let me keep mine? Can I bring you home?"

The shadows around his gaze are dull with exhaustion. He bows toward me, running the metal plate across his mouth over my thigh as if leaving a trail of kisses. And needing no additional time to recover, Niklaus scoops me into his lap and slides his tip along my sensitive clit, then eases himself into me. This time it's lazier and without the underlying pent-up anger. His face nestles between my breasts. My hips roll back and forth, the second orgasm much easier to achieve.

And as Niklaus clutches me to him, roaring as he slams upward one last time to spill his cum again, I hold him close and let my love harden like armor around us, like a sword that cracks the door of the Nightlung open, and I throw it overtop of us.

Thirty years in the future.

68. The Carousel of Time

Sapphire

His arms have aged. They are locked around me. Firm and unbreakable. His skin is coarser, not just from the scars, but the way his surroundings and violent environment have called for thicker armor.

I wake in a place all too familiar.

There is a stadium. Rows of seating. Inmates scattered across a stage in a social hour. The uniforms we read about when our parents were in this prison.

I grit my teeth, feeling tremendously embarrassed that I just finished telling Niklaus I can control it—yet here we are…

Still in fucking prison.

"I can explain." *No, I can't.*

I look back at him, only to see him simply communicating with only his eyes. They soften and watch me beautifully, like he's waited eons to witness my fuckups again.

"I need to hear your voice," I say wistfully. He has such a special voice, a velvet and cruel baritone that can command a room.

Niklaus glances to the left just as Dellilian approaches with something in her mouth. She rubs up against Niklaus's side like a cat and drops a piece of metal in his lap.

"A key? Good job, Dellilian!" I praise.

I race to jab the key in the lock on the back of his neck. The chunk of metal falls into his hands. My eyes work to adjust to his short-trimmed beard. Three scars along his jaw. His calloused hand rubs at his mouth in gratitude and soreness.

"Say something," I urge impatiently.

Niklaus's eyes go round. "You have not aged a day."

That kills me.

"I know."

"I'm thirty-one now, Spitfire." And his voice, though still similar, reflects that progression of time. It's matured. Lower. Steadier.

"You're an old man now."

"I am." Though he does not smile. This seems to really bother him.

My hand caresses his beard, and he balks. I pause my affection before continuing, waiting for him to process that it's really me.

"You could be in your nineties, and I'd still be in love with you," I murmur.

That sapphire-stained gaze snaps up in surprise.

"You don't mean that."

"Of course I do."

There's a war buried beneath his thoughts, but his posture doesn't waver. He stares down at me, trying to solve a series of riddles in my response.

"It's the guilt," he finally replies.

"It's not." But I feel I should clarify. "There is guilt, yes. But I used to hate you, Niklaus. If I still felt that way, there would be a hell of a lot less guilt."

I place my fingers around his wrist and bring his hand closer to my face. The jagged scar where his ring finger once was…buries me alive.

I brush my lips against it, kissing softly.

"Given my departure that left you behind, I know it would be difficult for you to feel it back…"

"I feel it back."

My lips hover over his knuckles.

"You do?"

He winds that strong hand into my hair. "I have spent a decade in hell loving you, Spitfire."

I rest the side of my head in his hand and sigh.

"The fading memory of your face was the only goddamned thing that ensured my survival. I replayed your laugh in my head like a broken record. I tried not to love you for my own sanity. I did. But you saved my life every time you'd appear in my dreams."

"You love me back?" I stare into his eyes with so much hope, I bet he can see it lighting up my irises with infinitesimal fireworks.

"I love you back, my darling wife."

Niklaus pulls me to him and kisses me with the passion that followed us through time. His facial hair scratches my chin, but those lips are silk against mine, parting to take more of me. It is the most romantic kiss of my life. It's the one you feel through your entire body like an earthquake. The one with so much vigor it makes a valiant attempt to stop time for us.

His other hand sweetly traces the outline of my shoulder, trying to memorize minute details, to savor the smallest touches between us.

As we part reluctantly, Niklaus holds my face close to his, breathing me in, still in agony as it is clear he harbors the fear of losing me again.

"You took my punishment for me," I say sadly. "Watching you lose your fingers triggered me to travel."

"I remember."

"How…how did you survive that, Niklaus?" I plant a small kiss on his mouth.

"Sophia and Jack. Sophia was able to reattach two of my fingers."

I watch him patiently, waiting for him to get out whatever he needs to say.

"Recovery was horrendous. The nightmares were worse. But…"

"Go ahead. You can say it," I urge.

He sighs, brushing his nose against mine. "Nothing compared to the amount of time I held out hope that you were coming right back for me."

He'll never know that bit of information is a sickle straight through my chest.

"I am still not so sure you are real," he adds.

My hands cover and caress his own, tilting them to my mouth for me to kiss several times. "I'm real. I'm here. Your little fuckup came back."

Niklaus chuckles with closed eyes.

"Even if this is another one of their experiments, I don't care. As long as I get to be with you. I don't care."

His words land like a bruise in my gut.

A woman shrieks from the entrance of the stadium. "WHERE IS HE?!"

Niklaus's instincts kick in, and he is no longer relaxed. He's standing, clutching the back of a rusted metal chair.

"Where is Dessin?"

My head swivels to the voice that called out his name. A young, lighter, more distressed version of the voice that raised me. I'm on my feet, gripping the back of Niklaus's arm to steady myself.

What time have we returned to? That tousled, wavy honey hair is wind-blown and strewn about. She's wearing the one-piece red uniform. She's searching for my father. Screaming. Inmates part for her like the Red Sea. Her lively hands clamp over her ears, wincing in pain with puffy, red eyes.

Someone shares information with her.

But whatever it is, she only panics more.

"Fuck!" she shrieks.

The moment Niklaus and I look into each other's eyes, I remember this part of her story. This…*this* is the moment my father was injected with the Crow Ivast's creation that would inevitably leave Krimson and me fatherless. My mother is looking for him because they've been torturing him with Mind Phantoms.

I remember the location they are keeping him.

"Dessin!"

Bearing witness to my mother's distress calls, to the visceral howls as she calls out for anyone to help—it sets my feet into motion.

My entire life, I've lacked the respect she deserves. Reading about some of her experiences on paper is different than watching it play out in person. Or worse, having it happen to me too.

She worked so hard not to let us see her cry.

But she was protecting us from the long, doomed history that broke her heart many times over. My mother was a force of nature. A God-fearing plague on this world in the best way. And she's had decades of pain.

"Dessin! DESSIN!"

Before I can weigh the downside of what I'm about to do, I graze my fingertip over her trembling shoulder. My mother spins around, heaving and snarling like a wild, deadly beast. My wrist is snatched and I stumble back, bumping into Niklaus's chest.

"Do you remember me?" I ask nervously.

She picks apart my appearance through a wall of tears.

"You're the two I broke out of the asylum."

"Yes," I whisper.

"What are you doing here?"

Niklaus answers for me as I draw a blank. "Apparently the side effect of escaping the Chandelier City is to end up here."

My mother considers this with a tidal wave of rising annoyance.

"I don't have time for polite conversation. I'm looking for someone."

Impulsively, I grab her wrist and hold on for dear life.

"Drop it," my mother growls.

I suck in a breath. "I know you don't know me, but you've done so much for me the moment I needed you the most."

The agitation and limited patience are etched into her brow.

"Let me do something for you now," I plead.

I'm here, Mom. I am so sorry I took you for granted. I didn't know how bad this all was... I was a stupid, spoiled girl. I am so sorry.

"He's in the tower on the east wing. It's a dungeon they use to experiment on inmates." My bottom lip trembles as I am tempted to hug her. To tell her how much I've needed her to come save me.

My mother tries to pull away again before I stop her.

I can't let go yet. Not after everything I've seen.

"Don't hold back on them. It takes something extraordinary to unlock a mind like yours. No one will ever forget this day. Especially not me. Not ever."

You are a legend, and you have made history. I am so proud to be your daughter.

She tilts her head, and squints to get a closer look at the color of my eyes.

"Who. Are. You?" she asks.

The Nightlung surges through veins. And I step away from her, taking Niklaus's hand and channeling all of my energy into my father, not far from here.

Niklaus

It's the ash-ridden aftermath of war.

We watched it unfold on the edge of a cliff. Sapphire's father, Uncle Warrose, Aunt Ruth, my mother, and father cornered by a swamp as the Vexamen army thundered over the barren land to kill them. Aunt Skylenna riding on DaiSzek's back, wielding a sword and balancing with her feet gripping his spine.

And DaiSzek fucking breathed—no, he *roared*—fire.

The battle was long and gruesome. Bodies of both sides indistinguishable in a pile of limbs, blood, and dirt. The battlefield a feast for the Dralutheran. The wet glint of exposed sinew. Burned flesh and copper. Smoke rose in black pillars from DaiSzek's ruin.

Sapphire kept her hand clamped over my leg as we watched it all implode. Dellilian hid behind me, too afraid to watch with us.

Knightingale. My father, Aurick, saving my dad, Niles, and bleeding out in front of him. Aunt Skylenna commanding the Blood Mammoth to annihilate the Mazonist Brothers.

We waited patiently for it all to end. The silence after is almost worse than the screams of death before. And this time, Sapphire didn't look guilty. She did control this jump through time. This is exactly where she intended for us to end up.

And after it was all over, Sapphire turned to me with glossy eyes, still reeling from the sight of limbs and innards jutting from the mud.

"I know you don't approve of me warning my father…" she said cautiously.

I look around at the red-streaked sky raining ash over the carnage. She's talking about a fight, I think. Though it was yesterday for her, it was over a decade ago for me. That argument was buried deep in the archives of my mind. Untouched and preserved since the day she left.

"The argument we had," I clarify, rubbing Dellilian's head resting on my lap. "Ten years ago."

Sapphire tries not to show it, but I've wounded her.

"It was only a couple of days ago for me," she replies sadly.

My hand finds the side of her smooth face. The sensation flutters through my brain like a thousand angel wings. I still am unable to comprehend that she is here, sitting directly in front of me. I have fantasized for years about putting my hands on her. Feeling how soft and feminine her skin feels against my scarred and battered hands. The smell of her hair. Those heterochromatic eyes that make me feel drunk and dreaming all at once.

I don't know if the fear of her disappearing again will ever not be ever-present, crushing me from the inside out.

"A lot has changed for me in that decade, Spitfire. Including the stubborn asshole who wanted to stop you from warning your dad."

Her eyes light up.

"*New history path!*" Dellilian adds sleepily. "*Haven't done this the first time.*"

"What does that mean?" Sapphire asks.

"*Miss Sapphire decide not to talk to Dad. Every time in this loop, Miss Sapphire chooses not to tell Dad.*"

"You're saying we've done this before in a fucked-up time paradox, and I usually don't warn my dad? That this is the first?" Sapphire clarifies with hope sparkling on her beautiful face.

Dellilian hums in our minds.

"Warn him, baby. Consequences be damned." I kiss her cheek,

grazing my nose against hers and sighing. “Warn your father, and then we will go and save mine.”

Sapphire’s grin is wide and determined. The delight does something permanent to my heart. I am a starving man who has been deprived of seeing that smile in the dark, hellish hole I was sentenced to. And now that I am out, I know I will pretty much do anything to see that smile every day for the rest of my life.

She has me in chains, on my knees for her.

69. Dessin

Sapphire

My father isolates himself after bathing in a creek not far from the war tents where my mother is sleeping.

The sun is hovering over the horizon of the mountains. And I wait in the shadows of a nearby cave, praying for God to give me the courage to confront him.

He sits on the bank of the creek with clean clothes and wet hair, elbows on knees and a brooding expression as he gets lost in the babbling brook. As his eyes dart off to the side, it reminds me of when I met Kane in the Demechnef mountain. The concentration it took as he'd listen to other alters in his head. I wonder how traumatizing this war was on his system. The chaos that must erupt behind his eyes.

It feels like a century of me standing in this cave going unnoticed. My foot hovers in front of me to finally take action. But I retract it, losing the nerve.

"You can either come out, or I can go in and hunt you down. Your choice." His voice rolls through the cave, low and resonant, like thunder taking human form.

I hold my breath.

Oh shit.

He'll remember seeing my face in the couple interactions I've had with him. Maybe not the time Kane and I spent together, but definitely the others.

My ribs are beaten internally by my thumping heart. The air in my lungs comes and goes in choppy, anxious gusts.

I step out from the shadows, staring into my father's eyes and praying to God he believes what I am about to tell him.

It takes him a sliver of a single second to analyze my face and register where he's seen me before. Those interactions resurface. His expression flashes darkly with a narrowing grimace, the light being swallowed by something cold and bloodthirsty.

I have no chance to run, to scream, to fight back as he lunges into my space, slamming me back into the cave wall and jamming his forearm into my throat. The pressure cuts off my airways, and I scramble to gasp.

"Three seconds. Once I let go, you have three fucking seconds to convince me not to cut your heart out." It's a growl more than a clear statement. A sound that belongs to old gods.

His forearm drops, and I wheeze, coughing and holding my hands to my throat as if that will help me return the oxygen back to my brain.

"Three," he repeats.

"I am not who I said I was," I spit out as quickly as possible.

My father crosses his arms and almost smiles at the stupidity that came from my mouth.

"Terrible job of convincing me."

I hold a finger up because I am not done, and God help me not to fuck this up.

And. It. All. Spills. Out.

"I was born on February Fourteenth. A twin. My mother gave birth to my brother and I without our father present. I love tulips but hate the smell of any other flowers because they've always surrounded my father's bedside. I dance in the rain during thunderstorms. My favorite color is indigo. On most days, I have a problem controlling my temper. I've been told I get that from my dad. When I was seven, no one showed up for my birthday party, and I cried for hours at the lagoon by my house so my mother wouldn't see. I'm stubborn. I love animals. I'm strong. I'm resilient. And I am here because I cannot return home without healing my mother's broken heart. Without healing mine too."

He must be so confused as my eyes are thick and glossed over with tears. They teeter right on the edge of collapsing down my cheeks in a rainstorm of grief.

"Why are you sharing all of this?" he asks, though there is a divine wisdom giving him pause. An intuition that stops him from attacking.

I suck in a fast breath.

"Because…you used to call her Skylittle. Kane did. You fell in love with her in the asylum, but Kane loved her since they were small children. Because you've never met *me*. Not really. Though I have dreamed my entire life of meeting you. Because…don't you see it when you look at me? When you look into my eyes? Don't I remind you of the woman you fell in love with? Don't I remind you of yourself?"

I'm on the precipice of hyperventilating as I sob the next words.

My father takes an unsteady step away, dark mahogany eyes falling to my feet then back to my face. He's stunned and unsure if he's gone completely insane.

"Because I have loved you my entire life without knowing you. Because I live in a cottage built around a red oak tree. Because my mother is Skylenna Winter Ambrose. My brother is Krimson Arthur Valdawell. Because my name is Sapphire S. Valdawell. The S stands for Sophia and Scarlett. And I am living with my family twenty-one years from right now."

His face falls, the muscles in his jaw slacken, and his features hallow with realization.

"No…" Another step back, though he wavers. "You're trying to get in my head…"

"You are my dad. I've come a long way to talk to you," I cry.

My father shakes his head, but he can't unsee it, can he? My face is everything he could have ever imagined his child would look like. Astonishment ripples through his very core.

"Prove it. Tell me something only your…*mother* would know and tell you about us."

Everything he knows is in question, but he can't bring himself to stop staring into my eyes.

I don't have to think very hard for this request. "Until hell freezes over."

The look hits him before he can hide it.

Every look of composure deserts him. What's left is naked shock.

"And even then," I add in a whisper.

My father turns away from me, holding a fist over his mouth, and closing his eyes. When he pivots back in my direction, he removes his fist and asks, “Your name is Sapphire?”

I sniffle and nod my head.

He releases a devastated breath.

“Can I hug you?” I ask, and the question causes me to bawl.

It’s as if I’m dreaming. A lovely, heavenly, wonderful dream.

My father opens his arms and says, “Come here.”

I throw my body into a sprint, barreling into my dad’s hard chest. He folds his arms around me and holds me tight as I wail against him.

“I’ve got you, kid. You’re safe now.”

I am drowning in bliss and years of childhood grief all at once. My sobs jolt and shake my upper body so hard, I don’t know how my father keeps us so still. This is the warmest embrace I’ve ever had in my life.

Krimson, I wish you were here to meet him.

I can’t tell if it’s several minutes or an hour before I finally let go, wiping my eyes and holding his shoulders to steady myself.

“I have to tell you something.”

“Do I pass away in the future, Sapphire?” he asks calmly.

My eyes prickle with more tears.

“It’s okay, kid. You can tell me.”

I shake my head. “You have been in a coma my whole life.”

His brow furrows, and he breathes in that new information.

“Your mother raised you…and your brother alone?”

“She had some help. Grandpa, Aunt Marilynn, Uncle Niles, Aunt Ruth, Uncle Warrose, and DaiSzek.”

It’s a sad, short laugh.

“How does it happen?”

“The injection Masten and Kaspias gave you. Once activated it will put you in a coma.”

He peers down. “How is it activated?”

Huh. I guess I didn’t think through this part of the explanation.

“It, well, once you’re—hmm. When you and my mom are close—you know, cause—”

This is the first time I’ve ever seen my dad cringe.

“Stop. I think I’m caught up,” he says quickly.

“I’m sorry. I know this is the aftermath of what they did to you, experimenting with your brain chemistry. You think my mother was the cause of all your trauma. Is this right?”

Discomfort fractures him from the inside out.

"It's complicated," he replies.

"It won't last. She'll fix it in the void." I fidget with my hands. "I know it's hard to imagine me as your daughter or even be happy about it because you hate my mom right now, but—"

"Happy? Sapphire, I am *devastated.* You are what…twenty-one? I will miss my daughter's first steps. Your first words. I won't be there to threaten the first man who breaks your heart. I won't be there to hold you when you cry or protect you from the evil of this world." He pinches the bridge of his nose and closes his eyes to gather himself. "I am so fucking sorry you had to grow up without me there to keep you safe. I should have been there. I don't need to spend two decades with you to know how much I already love you."

A rift inside my core stitches itself back together. Not healed but no longer ripped to shreds. I smile with swollen eyes and a red nose, feeling like a little girl.

"I love you too. And so does Krimson."

This time, he wraps his arms around me again, kissing the top of my head and resting his cheek there. It's everything I used to wish for as a child. It's everything I needed desperately.

"Tell me there's a way I can survive this," he whispers sadly.

"There is," I exhale against his chest. "Crow Ivast told me if you drink a tea made of Red Oak leaves, before… you and my mom, you know…"

"Yeah, got it." He releases me from the hug.

"It will cancel out the effects."

My father rubs the side of his face in deep thought. "Crow Ivast told you this?"

"Twenty to thirty years in the past, yes."

He stares at me.

"Your genetics and my mom's did this."

"And your brother?"

I shrug. "Not sure."

"You're risking the future you came from warning me."

"It's not a future worth going back to without you in it."

"Dessin!" Uncle Niles calls from a few yards away. "They're boarding the ships!"

My dad looks back at me and doesn't move.

"Go," I urge.

A web of complex emotions flickers behind his dark eyes.

"Go. You need to get back to the Red Oaks and drink that tea!"

"I don't want to leave you."

"There's not another ship you can catch." I smile, stepping away. "If everything goes well, you'll meet my brother and me as babies in a year."

He nods, pained at the thought of me walking away.

"I love you, Dad," I say.

"I love you too, kid. I can't wait to be your dad."

70. The Meat Carnival

Niklaus

Sapphire has been a grumpy, stubborn, mischievous little asshole since the day she was born.

Smiles were a rare sighting.

I can confidently say, she has never radiated so much childlike joy. At least not that I have ever seen from her.

We travel to a broad range of time in Vexamen—attempting to arrive at a moment as close to the time we abandoned my dad as possible. And Sapphire is the definition of optimism. I smile, nodding and observing her babbling on about how once we rescue my dad, we'll return home and get to see her dad wake up.

"*Bad man no let Miss Sapphire go home.*"

We hide behind a boulder as a tropical storm rolls in, blasting the brittle, black trees, and kicking up dust. Dellilian sits behind us, viewing the storm uneasily.

"*Not Mister Niklaus neither,*" she adds.

I look down at the timid creature with a fondness Sapphire might not expect from me. This animal comforted me in my cage on the most agonizing nights of my life. Some days, she was the reason I didn't try and off myself.

"Vrath won't let us go home?" I ask.

I haven't thought about him in ages.

Dellilian bows her head.

"He's not going to stop us. Did you see what Miss Sapphire did to the Bloods?" I smirk, massaging Spitfire's freckled shoulder.

But Dellilian is grim and pouting.

"*Dellilian sent by lady that has prophecy too,*" she explains.

I tilt my head. No, I guess we haven't figured out who sent Dellilian yet, have we?

"What prophecy?" Sapphire asks.

"*From a book. There's a tale of Miss Sapphire, Mister Niklaus, and Bad Man.*"

"A book? I'm guessing the tale doesn't end well if Vrath won't let us go home. Is this why you came to us, Dellilian? Why the lady sent you?" I ask.

Dellilian chuffs. "*Sacred book. The lady calls it Scarlett Leviticus from her world. The tale ends with Bad Man eating Miss Sapphire and Mister Niklaus's souls.*"

Sapphire and I look to each other with raised brows. "Huh."

"Doesn't sound *great*..." I say.

"How do we stop him?" Sapphire drops down to her knees, losing that intense gaze of optimism.

"*Hide. Must hide. Far away.*"

Sapphire frowns. "We can't. We have to save Uncle Niles. That's why we are here!"

"*No. Must hide now.*"

"For how long?!"

"*Forever.*"

I can't help but react out of aggression. "Bullshit! We are saving my dad!"

"Maybe it'll help if you tell us what Vrath has over us? What makes him stronger?"

"*World Dark Twin tree branch. Obliterates souls. Bad Man need Miss Sapphire's blood to change time.*"

I lean against the boulder and scratch my head. I really don't have a clue what the fuck she just said.

"Maybe if—" Sapphire chokes on her words and has a coughing fit.

My lungs dry and shrivel, followed by a fever bleeding into each layer of my skin.

"He's here," I announce.

"*Hide!*" Dellilian shouts again.

"We aren't leaving without Uncle Niles."

I fucking love her.

Sapphire stands, weak but recharged with an idea. The Meat Carnival has the animals locked up, probably for the tropical storm heating up the skies.

"He's afraid of animals," she mumbles, then takes off in the direction of the cages.

I follow in what feels like a drug-induced hangover. Everything trembles and throbs as we unlatch each cage one by one. I was worried we'd have to defend ourselves, but these beasts of many different species are just happy to be set free.

A crowd forms on the other side of the village, not far from the Blackspire Ward of The North. Where my father is held captive. And we leave Dellilian behind to follow the jeers and shouting individuals over epic, furious winds.

"My parents can figure out how to kill Vrath, I'm sure of it!" Sapphire shouts over the incoming store. We sprint, lethargic but motivated to get to my dad. "Once we save Uncle Niles, we get home and find them. Okay?"

"Let's do it."

71. "And I Have No Way of Getting Him Out..."

Skylenna

Present Day

I shut Krimson's bedroom door quietly.

He has been trying all night, making himself sick to reach his sister. After hours of migraines, crying, panicking…we rested our eyes in his room.

But the nightmares were a tornado terrorizing my brain. Images of my daughter locked away in the harshest events of our past.

I tiptoe to the kitchen to make coffee.

The hardwood is cold and slightly tacky beneath my bare feet. I move carefully, avoiding the loose board near the hallway that always groans if I step too hard. The counter smells faintly of yesterday's grounds—bitter and burnt. I reach for my favorite chipped mug, running my thumb over the cracked rim out of habit.

While the kettle warms, I drift to the wooden table and stare at the grooves carved into its surface, following the scratches and dents with my eyes like they might lead somewhere else. I don't sit. I don't move. I just stand there, hollow, watching dust float through the thin morning light.

At some point, I begin pacing. Three steps to the sink. Turn. Four back toward the fridge. Again. Again. The room blurs at the edges, the hum of the pipes ticking, the wind pouring across the windows into a dull static as I sink into the quiet void. The search has been endless. It's rubbing my mind raw, causing small fissures of open flesh.

The clock above the stove clicks, jumping ahead more than it should.

The golden sun beams through the split curtains, trickling across the dusty shelf over the fireplace. I walk over to it. My daughter's stunning eyes in that middle family photograph hit me like a train.

I am a failure, and Dessin would be ashamed of me.

He would have figured this all out. They don't need me. They need him.

"Fuck!" I hiss, slamming my hand against it.

The frame flips off the shelf, clattering to the wooden floor. As I reach down to grab it, hoping the noise doesn't wake Krimson, I realize I don't even remember this picture…

The kids are seven or eight years old. I'm kissing Krimson on the head. And Sapphire is in the arms of…

The frame slips from my hands.

Glass shatters with broken shards sprinkling like tiny blades over my bare feet.

The sound of time ceasing to exist.

Of bones breaking.

My pulse is calcified in my throat.

He… No… He wasn't there…

This has to be a part of so many of the dreams I have about him. I am still sleeping in my son's room.

His face looks back at me in that photograph, littered with broken glass.

And I feel it everywhere.

My ribs, my teeth, the hollow place below my sternum where grief and hopelessness have been quietly rotting for decades.

"Dessin…"

Christ, it hurts to say his name. Not just hearing it sift through my ears, but to call out to him as though he may just answer.

To feel that gnawing pit of hope again.

My eyes lift to the shelf slowly, stinging from not blinking.

And my body goes numb before igniting on fire.

He. Is. In. *Every*. Photo.

The day I gave birth. Kane holding Krimson up to his face.

Our wedding day under the Red Oaks. Kane.

Sapphire's first time climbing a tree. Dessin.

Family day in the lagoon. Aquarus.

Krimson and Sapphire's first day of school. Dessin.

He. Is. Everywhere.

"Oh my *god.*" My knees hit the ground; split and bleeding.

Not real. Not real. Just a dream. Is it? Yes. Not real!

The woman who loved Dessin and all of their alters was murdered the day he fell into that coma. Her soul tied to his, burned at the stake and gone. Gone. Gone.

The ashes of that woman fuse back into a familiar form.

Resurrecting and searching for him…

"Dessin…is this real?" I whisper, hand trembling over my mouth.

I won't let myself lose tears. Not yet. Not now.

Not real. Not real. Not real.

Could be a trick. Mind phantoms. A sweet, aching, longing, tragic dream.

But I focus on the photograph again. Our wedding day. Kane's yearning, so insanely, cataclysmically in love gaze.

And it knocks the air from my lungs.

"Dessin." His name gains another heartbeat of life in my mind.

I stand up, holding the fireplace shelf for support.

"Kane…" It makes its way past a whisper.

Chills explode up my back as I see a man standing by the windowsill, staring out at the endless red trees and shimmering lagoon. Hands in pockets. Black slacks and dress shirt.

I know right away it's not the love of my life.

In fact, the man standing with his back to me isn't even alive.

"Kaspias?"

Kane's brother glances at me from over his shoulder, a peaceful smile plays over his mouth. There are no words exchanged. He merely turns back to the window and continues looking ahead.

I choke on a laugh of whimper as my body ruptures with a reckoning. An irrevocable urgency to scour heaven and hell to find him. A blinding perseverance I haven't been possessed by since the day he went to sleep and did not wake up.

The world around me dissolves to the background like a fading nightmare.

A shockwave pulses through my chest, and I fly forward.

My bare feet pound against the floor, and I do not open the front door—I burst through it.

No room for careful grief. I sprint with confidence. With certainty.

I am an arrow released into the Red Oaks.

"Dessin!" I scream to the open woods.

Please, God. Please, God. I beg of you! I beg of you! Show me mercy! GIVE HIM BACK TO ME!

A divine animal in my chest snarls and digs its claws into the earth, willing to rip every tree from this earth…just to see him. Just once.

For his brown eyes to be open.

To look into mine.

"Dessin!" A shrill, unbecoming scream ripples across the treetops.

My sprint locks into my place, dying into the dry dirt as someone stops me in my path.

Off to the side, a woman and her son hold hands, watching me with the purest, most sincere looks of peace and overwhelming happiness.

It's Sophia and little Arthur.

The doubt in my soul vanishes at the heavenly sight.

They peer at me on this beautiful morning with misty eyes.

"Sophia…" I say with a lump in my throat. "Is he…"

Kane's mother grins.

My feet move again before I can think. My heart a banging war drum. Twigs scratch against my skin, tearing open spots of my dress.

The earth rolls back. The sky peels open.

"DESSIN!" I bellow at the top of my lungs.

I duck under branches and leap over protruding roots.

There is no world where I walk.

I move like fire consumes a field of dead crops.

My mind hiccups. Briefly shuts down. Goes blank.

There.

A few strides away.

His name unable to move past my lips.

Real. Real. Real.

Death looms close by as the whole of my heart threatens to stop beating.

Dessin.

"My god," I whisper.

The love of my life stands among a pile of chopped wood. A gentle morning breeze moves through his brown hair. Sweat glistens over his bare chest.

He is the axis to which I move.

He always was.

He lifts his concentrated gaze slowly, like waking from a dream he never expected to escape.

Dessin.

Dark mahogany eyes slam into me.

I double over. Unearthed and uprooted at the silent killing and resurrection that becomes me from getting to look into those eyes again.

"Skylenna…" My soulmate's face breaks.

That voice, all-knowing and unlike any other.

It's home.

I wail like the grieving widow I've been all these years. In three versions, he sees me in the dirt—the one who fought for him to remember me in that prison, the one who mourned him even though he never died, and the one who kept going, first out of spite. Then, because our babies didn't deserve to have a mother who couldn't let go of his memory.

Who loved a ghost more than them.

Across the open area of woods, he witnesses me crumble.

And his body collides with mine. On his knees in the dirt,

slamming my upper body to his. Dessin folds himself so tightly around my pain, I can't decide if I've died and this is heaven.

"D-D-Dessin! Oh god!" I bawl into his shoulder.

A long-since fossilized bit of my heart takes its first breath as my one true love says my name. Over and over and over again.

"Do you remember?!" I gasp and sob simultaneously. "The c-coma!"

He kisses the side of my head furiously. "I remember."

I cry harder, releasing every lonely moment I spent in my bedroom closet sobbing into a pillow so Sapphire and Krimson wouldn't hear.

I cry for every second I sat at his bedside and prayed for God to give him back.

I cry for the long days of pregnancy when I would feel a kick and have a breakdown that Dessin wasn't awake to feel it too.

I cry my children.

I cry for DaiSzek.

I cry for Dessin and every single one of his alters.

"Sapphire—she time traveled. She changed something! She saved you!" I am in utter disbelief that Dessin is holding me in his arms. That he's taking on my breakdown as his home. That's here. He's with me.

He is awake.

"I know, baby. I've been here. I've been here to see it all…" Dessin says, low and gravelly against my ear.

"What?!"

"You couldn't see me, but I know you felt my presence. I saw the birth of our children. I watched you cry all alone when they'd go to sleep at night. I was holding you while you slept. I never missed a conversation when you'd hold my hand and tell me about your day."

"*Oh!*" I claw at his back, unable to get enough of him.

The love that pours out of me is infinite, rich in power, and absolute.

"Twenty-one years, Dessin…you were gone… It was so hard. I—died inside."

Dessin pulls me a centimeter away to look me in the eyes. The bridge of his nose brushes the tip of mine, and the chemistry is still there—only now, it's a dam losing its foundation, swelling over to wipe out anything in sight. It's twenty-one years of being apart. The unbearable longing to have him touch me every second of every day is destroying my mind, spiraling my thoughts out of control.

"You did so good. You raised our babies, and you did *so* fucking good, Skylenna."

Tears fall but his thumbs catch them as he cradles my face in his warm hands. He doesn't rush me as he waits, his lips hovering over my mouth. Those dark brown eyes fixate on my mouth then back up to meet my stare.

I inhale sharply, melting in his hold.

I close the distance and kiss the man I've loved my whole life.

And it's so much more than a kiss.

We are two halves of a star torn apart and hurled across galaxies. Our love reuniting could rewrite constellations. It's Dessin. It's Kane. It's our souls melding back together.

And there it is.

Time is a tricky, ever-evolving beast. It is governed by itself, obeying a foreign set of rules. A law that exceeds any living being. And that law splits our minds into two lives. Two memories of existence. We have the one that Dessin couldn't be a part of in his coma.

But time grants us the one he was a part of.

Within this kiss, that new life fills the empty spaces of that split mind. It etches into the crevices and weaves every epic memory of us together into our core thoughts.

In a single heartbeat, I live out our lives together.

Those photographs on the fireplace become my most sacred reminiscence.

After I gave Kane his memories back, we spent a couple of days in bed, making love—then went to see Ruth. We threw Marilynn a baby shower, and she threw ours. For Niles's next birthday, Dessin took him hunting. Niles came back pissed that he killed a rabbit and wouldn't speak to him for three days.

I told Kane and Dessin separately that I was pregnant. Kane found out while we played in the rain. I just told him. "You're going to be a daddy!" In the thunderstorm, Kane dropped to the mud and sobbed into his hand. He thanked me for hours. "Thank you, Skylittle. Thank you for giving me a family." And when I told Dessin under the stars after making love, I gave him baby booties I sewed myself. He laughed. Dessin threw his head back and howled at the moon, picking me up off the ground and spinning me around. And with my permission, he woke Chekiss up to shout that he was going to be a dad. He made love to me all night.

During my pregnancy, Kane massaged my feet every night so I could fall asleep. Dessin scoured Main Street to find the pastries I was craving. Greystone took care of my needs when I hit my second trimester and was aroused beyond belief.

I was in labor for thirty-two hours. The contractions were a form of unworldly torture, but Dessin kept me strong. He held me in every position until I delivered both of our babies. Kane was the first to meet them. In postpartum, Ruth and Warrose came to our home every week to help Chekiss watch the twins so Dessin and I could sleep, as the babies didn't allow us to get much sleep.

Breastfeeding was difficult as I didn't produce much milk at first. And with twins, that was a source of immense guilt and panic attacks that I wasn't feeding my babies enough. But Dessin tore apart the library in the Demechnef mountain to read everything they had on lactation and postpartum. He came back with certain types of oatmeal pastries and herbal drink concoctions that would help me produce more milk. It worked. Kane cooked for me relentlessly, enough meals to ensure I kept myself replenished after giving so much to our newborns.

Ruth and Warrose threw us the kids' first birthday party. Afterward, they loaned us a large boat at the shore. We took a small getaway of two nights to float along the coast and get drunk for the first time since before I was pregnant. Dessin worshipped my cunt at sunrise, drunkenly and lazily ravaging me until we passed out from exhaustion.

Sapphire and Krimson's childhood was a pleasure to watch. Dessin babied Sapphire, treating her like his princess. But Krimson was his best friend. They hunted together, chopped wood, fished, and wrestled on the front porch. Kane let Sapphire dress him up and drink tea with her baby dolls. Dessin chewed Marilynn and Niles out for not disciplining Niklaus enough after the first time he made her cry. He threatened Sapphire's teacher for not doing anything after that group of boys defiled her painting in front of the class. And he never, not once, ever let Niklaus get away with targeting his children.

Eventually, Dessin and I underwent several arguments over the strained relationship between those two. I was ashamed that I didn't take the turmoil as seriously as he did. In fact, he didn't speak to me for several days because of it. Eventually, we uncovered the damage the Demechnef extremists did to him when Niklaus was taken. I helped him heal and recover through the void, untangling and straightening out his twisted ideals of my daughter.

After a long journey of restoration from the Mind Phantoms, Niklaus and my daughter began dating and fell in love. Dessin did not accept this union for years. It took bullying from me, Niles, Ruth, Warrose, Marilynn, and Chekiss to get him to finally come around.

I see our entire lives fleshed out in front of me.

I see the arguments about what kind of mushed baby food to give to Sapphire and Krimson. I see flashbacks Dessin would get from the prison and asylum, the carousel switching, the days of dissociation over situations that would trigger him. The summer afternoons of Kane swimming in the lagoon with DaiSzek. The late-night talks with my husband and reminiscing over our days at the Emerald Lake Asylum when we fell in love.

We have lived two lives.

We remember both.

But the new memories chisel into our minds, attempting so very delicately to mend the wounds that his coma did to us.

"Did you see it?" I breathe against his lips.

"Yes, baby. I saw it."

My kiss sparks a flame in the man I love, pulling us both under. He sighs into my mouth at the downpour of love from the me who lived without him to the me who never left his side. His lips open to me, tasting my tongue with an exquisite patience that sends heat spiraling down the center of my chest. It deepens and I arch against him, so fucking hungry to be with him again. To have all of him.

"So help me God, Skylenna," he growls into my mouth. "I swear I'll fucking rip your clothes off and make you mine all over again…"

"No one is stopping you." I bite his bottom lip, and yelp as he takes me to the ground, grinding his erection between my legs.

I clench at his back, his shoulders, his neck—unwilling to break contact in case he isn't real. In case it's all a lie. I'm soaked through my panties, and his fingers dig into my hips, positioning me to add more pressure from my clit to his cock, then rocking along its length.

I gasp into his mouth.

Dessin grunts. The sound like two fingers massaging me between my legs.

"I have dreamed about this for years," I mewl.

Dessin slides my panties off, clutching them in one hand, and brings them to his nose.

"God-fucking-dammit, I love your scent when you're turned on."

I grin up at him; hair puddled around my head among the fallen red leaves and weeds of the earth.

Right as he pushes his cock halfway inside me, Dessin pauses and begins dissociating.

"What's wrong?" I pant. *Please, don't stop.*

He breathes through his teeth. "They all want you, Skylenna. They're all pushing their way to the front."

I moan at what I am about to say next. "Then let them have me. Whoever wants me. I want all of you to make love to me."

Dessin's eyes roll back as he growls.

And as his cock slides into me, they each rapid cycle to the front, fucking me slow and hungry. Slightly disoriented, like having a wet, lucid dream. They growl against the side of my face. They each have a unique way of loving me. At one point, Greystone pulls out to lick me for several minutes, sticking his tongue as far into my drenched pussy as he can get.

Dessin returns, fucking me hard, propping one of my legs over his shoulder and kissing the side of my knee, my calf, and then my toes.

It's been so long of making love, and yet not nearly long enough. I'm pulsating from two strong orgasms, lying limp and writhing on the ground.

"Flip over. I'm not done with you yet."

I reposition myself to arch on all fours for him, but Dessin lowers me to the ground firmly.

"On your stomach, baby," he says huskily in my ear.

Hooking his arms under mine, Dessin cradles my jaw in his

hand, angling my head up so he can bite my neck while he fucks me.

"Harder, please," I beg.

I want it all. Pleasure. Pain. Euphoria.

"I want you to leave marks all over my body."

Dessin bites down harder, roaring through clenched teeth as he crashes into the hilt again and again, crushing me under his weight as he comes inside me.

"Dessin!" I yelp as he spins me onto my back.

"God, I fucking missed you! I love you so much, baby." He kisses my entire face. My chin, cheeks, eyelashes, the tip of my nose. "Every day. I don't care if I'm sick. I don't care if we just argued. I am inside you every day, praising my girl."

My eyes fill with tears as I nod weakly.

"Deal."

Those dark eyes study me, lying on my back, taking a meaningful mental picture.

"It's confusing," he finally comments.

"What is?"

"Having both memories. Remembering the Skylenna that I had to watch go through pregnancy all alone, cry under her covers in a dark room every day. And then there's the mother of my children I got to marry and fall in love with all over again."

"It is for me too." I still feel high and unsettled that he's back. That the love of my life is awake. "I wanted to hear your voice so bad."

"Mom!" our son shouts in the forest. His footsteps loud and thundering. "MOM!"

I scramble to my feet, slipping my panties back on, and straightening my hair.

Dessin watches me squirm and laughs. "At least this is *our* version of traumatizing our children, hmm?"

I snicker. "Yeah. Very different than our trauma."

Dessin turns abruptly, facing our son who is just staring at him in shock.

"I—I remember when you weren't here too," Krimson stutters, looking like his father twenty years ago. He rakes a hand through the top of his brown hair. "I feel crazy."

Dessin doesn't say anything. He closes the gap between them

and hugs his son.

I hold my hands over my chest and sob. Sapphire should be here for this…

"This has to wait—it's Sapphire. I don't know what—I just heard her! She's screaming! She won't stop screaming!"

Dessin grabs his son's shoulders and shakes him. "Tell me what you know about your gift, kid. Don't leave out a single detail. We are not leaving this spot until you take us to your sister."

72. Make No Peace with Evil

Sapphire

Twenty-One Years in The Past

Vexamen

It's that dream again.

I'm hanging off the edge of the cliff, screaming for Krimson, and hearing him call my name over the bangs of thunder and pounding rain launching toward the sopping mud.

"I NEED YOU NOW!" I bellow over the whipping winds of a scourge.

My fingers slip as the mud grows frothy with gray stormwater. The nacreous clouds descend into a cloak of churning charcoal. A tempest with teeth snarls down at my efforts to hold on before I plummet to an unknown black hole of nothingness.

I know this is a nightmare. I *know* it is.

But there's a sickness that has taken root in me. A virus. A bacterial infection. Wheezing lungs and a fever with the vengeful heart of a leviathan in combat.

"KRIMSON! PLEASE! IF YOU ARE GOING TO COME FOR ME, IT NEEDS TO BE NOW!" I wail as lightning splits the heavens open.

My fingernails are the last to slice into the wet clay.

Can't hold on.

The nightmare isn't strong enough to hold back Vrath's illnesses. It lets the ache bleed into my mind and boil over into my dreams.

My last hope slips on the sludge, and I let go.

"Krim—"

Air meets my palms.

Then a pair of hands catch my wrists.

Strong, rough, older hands.

Not my brother's.

I squint, trying to see past the lapidary sheets of rain. The figure hovering over me on the cliff is my father.

"I've got you, kid! I won't let you go."

"Sapphire! Wake up!"

I can hear Niklaus coughing up a lung beside me. I try to reach for him, but my hands are bound around something, elongated behind my back. My eyes peel open, sticky and dry. The storm wasn't just in my dream. We're outside. Voices are scattered a few yards away. Niklaus is hyperventilating. Thrashing.

I turn my head to see him tied to a pike. As am I. Piles of wood at our feet.

Wait…

"Niklaus," I croak. Sand, debris, and phlegm line and web across my throat. "What's—happening?"

"Dellilian was right!" he coughs. We choke on the swamp of rain firing down at us.

Not too far from our posts, a stage stands in front of uniform rows of people. Rags and shreds of wool clothing. A dismal display of captives being forced to watch an appalling event. A gallows without rope.

I try to travel, to call upon the Nightlung, to dip my hands into its vast, fulminate energy.

But I stumble upon the same obstacle I was in when Meridei weakened me with electroconvulsive treatments and starvation. That river of power that usually floods my senses is now parched and dead.

"Dellilian!" I gasp against the diseases killing us. "Help—us."

"Sapphire, to your right." Niklaus cranks his head to point with his eyes past me.

And I refuse to accept what I see through my feverish gaze. Dellilian is caged, bound, muzzled, and unconscious. That is the only details I let myself linger on.

I search the area frantically, trying to pinpoint the source of our capture.

It's not the ropes around my wrists and midsection.

It's not the guards.

It's *him*.

Vrath stands oddly on a bird's nest above the stage, watching the scene below with detached curiosity. A short tower: a watch post with splintered beams for those who try to flee.

Where the fuck are we?!

"It's okay. We can—we can get out of this," I tell Niklaus, fighting a strained, raspy voice.

I assess what's crippling us so outrageously. Vrath stares down at us without moving, inspecting our current state before being burned at the stake like insects being pinned behind glass. A psychotic mathematician of time. His coal pinstripes, bowler hat, and pocket watch set him apart from the many Vexamen officials and keepers down on the ground.

And in his twiggy hand lies the branch of that tree Dellilian told us about. The frequencies soaring off its crooked stem is a quiet malfunction of pure evil.

A plague encased in a wooden rod.

And Vrath sets its eyes on us.

"Sapphire!" Niklaus roars over the enraged symphony and treacherous winds. "My dad!"

I rip my eyes away from Vrath and look to the stage.

There's a wooden block.

A man standing behind it.

An executioner with a black hood and an axe.

I scour the stage for Uncle Niles, but I trail right past him. Because my eyes don't want to believe the state he's in. My eyes can't accept the shape time has carved him into.

My Uncle Niles stands woodenly behind the block. And he is much older than when I last saw him. My Uncle Niles has white hair, wrinkled skin, and is beaten bloody. Swollen cheekbones. Blue smudges over his jaw and right eye.

Leaving Niklaus's dad here, in the same timeline as his past self, has taken a toll on his health, and sped up the aging of his body.

"We can fix this…" I whisper. Numbness pulsing through my bones.

My focus flicks back to the block at his feet.

No…

"Dad!" Niklaus's deep voice booms through the apocalyptic chaos around us. "Dad, we're here!"

Uncle Niles, though staring death in the face, doesn't seem afraid. His aged cheeks pull back into a somber smile as he sees us across the courtyard.

"We can get you out!" I yell.

But my plans of escape are burned to a crisp, just as we are about to be. A few guards below us, prepare torches of fire.

How can I get my uncle out of this if I am executed right along with him?

Krimson! Mom! Dad! Please, help us!!!

I avert my eyes and find Vrath staring down at me again.

"Vrath! You can have me! You can fucking have me! But please, spare my uncle! I swear to God, I will give you all of my blood! Please, don't take him from us!" I scream past my swollen, battered throat, through the fever and clogged lungs.

It's *Uncle Niles*. He wasn't even supposed to be here. He has never had the combat training of Uncle Warrose or Aunt Marilynn. He dove in to protect me even though it was almost certain death. He was cast into this awful decade of Vexamen brutality, held captive, and aged prematurely

"Don't take my father, Vrath. *Please*. We will work with you! Please, God, don't let him die!" Niklaus shouts, bucking and thrashing against his pike.

A guard kicks Uncle Niles to his knees, hovering his upper body over the chopping block. But he doesn't take his eyes off his son.

I cry out, not saying any known words. My cries are weak and guttural all at once.

"You take care of your mother, okay, son?!" Uncle Niles hollers.

"Spitfire!" Niklaus begs.

I nod and concentrate, mentally shoving past that insurmountable barrier of the boundless, godless, mephitic relic in Vrath's hands. As I shove harder at its primordial barricade, my power streams up my spine, ready to ignite—only to collapse in on itself like a dying star.

A sound of frustration and helplessness slashes out of me that doesn't feel quite human.

Niklaus gapes at me in unwilling defeat and denial.

"I can't get us out!" I cry.

I try again and again until my skull cracks apart into a migraine.

"Dellilian!" I try to wake our friend, but that sinister instrument of Vrath's is keeping her down too.

The executioner's footsteps are sonorous tremors beating like a war drum into the stage. Boots splashing through the massive puddles. A mountainous human being positioning himself in front of my uncle and measuring the accuracy of where to place his precise swing to align with the neck on display for him to cut.

Niklaus shouts for Vrath.

I beg Dellilian to wake up.

My thoughts lock onto Krimson's, finding him through the grand stretch of time between us.

As the axe anchors high to prepare for the swing, the official in charge asks, "Any final words, citizen of Demechnef?"

I strain against my ropes until my limbs turn purple.

Niklaus bellows profanities, begging and pleading.

And just as Uncle Niles lifts his gaze to the crowd, to his son yards away…something to our left gives him pause. I follow his focal point to a black rift spilling into this world, gashing through the merciless storm.

A deafening silence.

Then an iron pulse of an almighty.

A gulf of creation opening, where only angels may tread.

The same fissure of time undone by the Nightlung, and out of the cosmic ink seeping from the torn seam—Krimson steps forward, then to the side, unveiling my parents and DaiSzek.

"*Impossible…*" Niklaus mutters.

My chest throbs at the incredible, majestic sight. I exhale a sob and whisper, "Dad."

"Any final words?!" the Vexamen Official repeats.

Uncle Niles locks eyes with my father, grinning with tears spiling over the dimples in his cheeks. That watery gaze shoots to me in astonishment. He lets out a small airy laugh of delighted disbelief, then back to my dad. He parts his lips, as if there are a million words he wants to release so that his old friend may hear all he's had to say over the years.

My uncle smiles, not an ounce of sadness in that golden look he gives my parents. A knowing glint in his eyes, because he told us this would happen. *They'll come for me.*

"Yes," Uncle Niles announces. "Long live my family. And long live DaiSzek, the one true king." And then he shifts his focus to Niklaus, tears emerging as he mouths, "*I love you, my son.*"

The executioner throws his weight into the swing.

No.

The axe comes down on Uncle Niles's neck.

The sound of his neck snapping.

The instant scarlet fireworks of blood.

Screams.

My own.

Niklaus.

A head with golden-white hair hits the stage.

Shoulders and an open neck still in place.

"NOOOOOOO!"

Chaos.

Blood.

So much blood.

Rainwater dilutes it at the boots of the murderer.

I twist my head to my parents as the rift of time closes behind them. My mother's eyes turn crimson lacunal—not just pink, but filled with old blood, wide and with a god-eater fury, pupils expanded planetary black.

The world recoils around her as those lips peel back. And her chest heaves upward, arms casting out, erupting in a scream that wakes the heavens and weakens hell.

That scream is a command to the one true king, DaiSzek.

The sky cracks with a tinnitus of gods, as if even the air above recognizes a superior sovereign has been unleashed to be the ruin of cities, the massacre of civilizations.

DaiSzek's ears and fur stand upright at the death of his old friend.

And he opens his maw, drawing from the abyss of his lungs—a celestial flame that is stronger and unlike what we saw in the battle of the Dralutheran. His draconic shriek destroys the oxygen around him, blasting so ferociously, it turns the courtyard into a womb of annihilation.

A pyroclastic lungful that shoots out of his mouth.

Bodies sublimate to ash mid-scream.

Captives are spared as they scatter, chasing freedom far from here.

The torrent of rain vaporizes in a spectral mist and steam.

Before his fire can reach the stage, my father crosses the distance with a stride fueled of vengeance, moving the way a predator strikes. And the flames do not outpace him, they follow his lead, covering his six and any other blind spots. Dad flies over burned corpses, over barriers meant to hold captives in. Boots rattling the ground, sending gravel flying like shrapnel. And as he reaches the stage, his right hand unsheathes the sword strapped to his back.

The executioner does not see him coming. The inferno tidal wave stuns the man in place.

And as he wields the sword, a shockwave pulses the air, shuddering within the marrow of my bones.

The blade whips straight through the executioner's stomach,

separating his upper body from his hips.

And DaiSzek does not stop.

The tendrils of the hot blaze eliminate all life but leave Uncle Niles's body *untouched*. And the dragon-like roars can be heard from oceans away.

Among the burned carnage, I find Vrath frenziedly drawing his equations out in blood, checking DaiSzek's movements with tantalizing doom.

I do not try to contain my fatal, murderous urges.

Vrath will die today.

Krimson cuts down Niklaus's ropes first. Then releases me from mine and catches me before I can fall.

"I was too late," he cries, holding me up. "I'm sorry, Sapphire! I was too fucking late!"

My brother never cries. I've seen it happen maybe once or twice, so the quivering of his chest against mine has me whimpering against his chest.

"I tried to save him, Krimson! I—I should have gone back further! I got it wrong!"

Niklaus guts me at his position on the ground. One hand on his stomach, the other sinking into the mud as he stares out at the bloodbath. He—he just lost his father.

We all did.

Before we move to the stage, I free Dellilian just as she begins waking up. I kiss her on the head once, leaving her to recuperate on her own.

After the fire dies down a little, we gather on the stage.

Niklaus stares down at his father's body, for only a moment, before looking up to the bird's nest. Vrath is gone.

"Niklaus?" I touch his shoulder.

"I can't look at him," he mutters.

"Okay." I hold in my sob.

"I want him." He directs to where Vrath once stood over the execution. "I want to kill him, Sapphire."

This part of the village is nothing but embers and unbearable silence and the torrent of rain lightens to a dewy mist.

My mother sits next to Uncle Niles's arm, gently moving his

head back to his shoulders and neck. Her whimpers harbor an excruciating laceration in all of our hearts. She doesn't push Niklaus to come near his father. Doesn't pressure him to confront this tragedy.

My mother simply cradles her lifelong friend in her lap, and my father kneels beside them both.

"Krimson?" she calls, voice wounded and bludgeoned like an animal that has just survived a natural disaster.

My brother steps forward, making an effort to lift his head in strength.

"Take us home." She looks into his eyes with a downfall of new tears. "Take us home so that I may bury my brother."

73. "I Will Fear No Evil If You Are with Me."

Sapphire

Over One Thousand Years in the Past

If today I die, I hope my family will understand why I've done this. Why Niklaus and I had to slip away, to make it look like we were going into the Nightlung with them to return home. Why we have been chasing Vrath through time, following his scent like a bloodhound, into the gorge.

And he knew we were coming.

He knew DaiSzek would not follow and that he would be safe.

But all it will take is for Niklaus or me to draw his blood once. One time for the Short-Haired Windilas to appear and hunt him down.

"The golden lamb has been slaughtered!" Vrath sings in a monotonous nursery rhyme tune from within the forest we've been dumped into.

Niklaus keeps his face unreadable as we spring to follow the sound of his voice, though I know these taunts are killing him inside.

"I silenced your yellow songbird!" he chimes again.

My blood bubbles over in hatred.

The night is young under a full moon. It's ice cold out, somewhere close to the North Sapphrine Forest with sharp-needled pine trees and the bland scent of snow. Our breath heaves from our chest in white clouds of fog.

"I killed you father, Niklaus Demechnef. I killed Niles Offborth!" Vrath's howl through the trees is baiting and unnatural. "The last thing he tasted was rain. *Rain!*"

Niklaus and I stop running as the sickness comes back in full force, meaning we're close. So close I can hear Vrath's excited breathing.

"Come out and fight me like a man, coward!" Niklaus growls.

My mind won't block out the image of my uncle's head. The way his shoulders stayed angled over the chopping block. I feel nauseous and dizzy. But it gives me that bit of fire I need. I know I will not return home until I end Vrath's life. Until I watch him bleed enough to drown out this memory that I will never forgive myself for.

"There is no fight to be had. I was less confident of my footing in the face of your RottWeilen." Vrath steps out from behind a pine tree, meandering, that gnarled, black stick in his hand. "Hence, why I beckoned you to follow me here. And now that your beast is gone, I maybe collect the blood that will help me find my way back home. You understand, don't you?"

I'm on my knees now, vomiting blood.

Niklaus remains standing, hunched and clinging to a dying tree.

"You are right, Vrath, you took my father from me," he barks, suffocating on swollen lungs. "You could have stopped it. He was—a good man. With a big heart."

Vrath twirls the stick and avoids eye contact. "You made me do it. Why did he not beg do you think? Why become dead without a single plea?"

As the sickness drains my body, I hold Uncle Niles's face close. I remember the hugs. I remember the nights he would make Mom laugh after she had clearly been crying for our dad. I remember the look of absolute awe he had for Aunt Marilynn.

He was too good for this world.

And his death has given me wings. Ones that materialize behind an invisible veil, side by side with the Nightlung. Ones that contort into cascading plates of volcanic black. They give me strength as if the Void is pumping enough power to withstand the symptoms Vrath curses me with, opening a window to the ability I need the most.

I crawl forward, with a low harmonic rumble cracking the tectonic plates beneath my hands. My world is sheathed in a layer of black and red as I aim for him.

Vrath stumbles back a step, caught off guard by my persistence to eat away at the barrier his World Dark Twin tree branch has ensnared me with.

I am a holy furnace of revenge that refuses to tear my gaze away, though blood and tears drip from every pore. My body losing its life force with each movement.

But I can't let him go.

My broken heart will always be tied to him.

"We *begged* you to spare him," I call out, now inches from his languid, insipid posture.

"Yes, you did," he replies.

The ancestral beast that has formed wings sends forth every drop of power to break the ceiling of his hold on me. An exiled seraph cast out of heaven and willing to risk it all.

I rise to my feet, levitating until my toes hardly touch the dirt.

"You may keep your body," I say, low and bruising. "But I will have your mind. I will move it through time until you are nothing but the mental scape of a little old man. You will forget *everything*."

He isn't fast enough to overcome my daggered talons as they plunge into his neck and puppeteer the strings of time in his brain. I fast-forward seventy years. Giving my uncle's assassin every ungodly mental illness one can obtain in the end years of their life.

Only, externally, he hasn't aged a day.

"Goddamned you, child!" he whines like his tongue has gone numb.

Vrath swipes his hand across my bloody forehead, streaking the red color down the brittle stem in his hands. The gore of my body absorbs into the wood, and my world is sunken in a sea of hell. I'm on my back, unable to move. Niklaus inches closer as blood gushes from his ears.

Whatever he is doing, we are dying.

Dying.

"Niklaus!" I cry. "Get out of here!"

Though in my heart, I know he will never leave.

I should have done more.

It's my fault.

Uncle Niles should live, and I should be dead!

I should have done more!

"Undeserving! Undeserving! Undeserving!" Vrath enforces every pain upon us.

My heart sputters and slows, unable to keep up, unable to survive—

A portal of darkness stretches open from above our heads, and in a blur of white teeth and a mist of onyx fur, Dellilian dives forward, chopping her jaws around the branch. It snaps. It breaks. Its other half is whisked off in a soft breeze.

"NOOO!"

"Dellilian!" I stutter, unable to let a smile spread to show my undying love and gratitude for her. Because she came. Despite her fear of the bad man. She came! She came for us!

But as she lands on her feet, Vrath uses the broken branch to slice into Dellilian's chest.

Her blood is red like ours, but with stardust and an opalescent shimmer.

It is everywhere.

"DELLILIAN!" Niklaus bellows.

This…*this* paired with his father's death…

He is not grieving. He is becoming a mausoleum.

The Morphing Onyx Short Haired Windila falls on her side, air thumping out of her lungs from the tumble. And she lies so still, each small breath invisible.

74. Guardian Angels in The Form of Dellilian

Niklaus

"What happened—what has happened!" Vrath smacks himself in the head, fighting an unseen battle with his own rotting mind from old age. "Where am I! What has happened to my precious tree?!"

I rise despite my body deteriorating from Vrath's plague of a presence. My walk is heavy, willing to lose everything for the vengeance of my father—for striking down my dear friend who stayed by my side in that prison. The gentle friend who tucked herself against my cold skin on long winter nights. The one who found a way to bring me food when I was being starved by the kitchen.

A chord is struck behind my half-crest stare. Every word I hold back trembles in my jaw.

It hurts to move.

To breathe.

To think for too long.

But this atomizing wound that turns leaden in my chest is

stronger than any disease Vrath spreads to me.

One hand scoops the other half of the branch from the ground, and I jog up to Vrath who is spinning in confusion, throwing his bowler hat to the ground.

Pitching my arm in an upward motion, I hook the splintered, frayed end of the abominable wood up Vrath's throat, splitting into his esophagus. Severing tendons and puncturing his windpipe. Heat gushes over my hand.

It's a fountain of spurting blood shooting from Vrath's painted mouth.

"You took *everything* from me!" I say through my teeth, then twist the branch until it crumbles to dust in his bloodstream. "BURN. IN. HELL. YOU SON OF A BITCH!"

That tree's poison floods Vrath's veins, causing him to convulse before it turns the whites of his eyes black, then decays every cell and organ from the inside out. His corroding skin decomposes to mold and mush at our feet.

And the sickness lifts like a wet, moth-eaten veil—but not without lasting damage that we may see for years to come.

Sapphire and I rush to Dellilian still on her side, unmoving and bleeding into the frosty dirt.

"Hi, sweet girl!" Sapphire murmurs.

"Dellilian. You're fine. You're okay. That was amazing!" I kneel in front of her face, sliding my hands around her snout.

"Come on, girl. Tell us you're okay."

Dellilian's eyes are open, and they blink slowly. Still breathing.

"*Dellilian still hurt?*" she asks.

I touch her furry chest, examining my hand as the steaming blood blankets my palm. The crimson glimmers in the moonlight, warm and thick. I am unable to look back into her eyes as I calculate how much she's lost…

We sigh. "Yes."

I did not know animals could shed tears, but they appear in the saddest drizzle, leaking into her soft fur.

"*Move Dellilian away…*" Even that small voice in our heads is a ghost of its usual volume. "*Move Dellilian from Bad Man.*"

My hands shake as I scoop my friend up in my arms, wincing as more blood splashes to the pinecones and dirt. The lesion grows in size as if it's being eaten by an acidic, live virus of the wooden instrument that Vrath used to hurt her.

Sapphire offers to help, but I reject it, fighting for dear life to hold my emotions together.

We walk until we reach a small nook in the North Sapphrine Forest. A hidden alcove where we can see the full moon, and a dazzling show of stars.

After laying her down, I hold the back of my hand up to her nose and silently thank God for the light puffs of air tickling my knuckles.

"Dellilian?"

"*Hmm?*"

"You were…so brave."

"*Yes?*"

"You are a fucking hero… A hero!" I stroke her ear as my eyes begin to water.

Sapphire sits at my side quietly, keeping a warm hand on my upper back.

The small wolf with a big heart whimpers. "*Dellilian hurt bad.*"

"Tell me how to fix it," I beg.

"*Bad tree. Poison.*"

I pinch the back of my neck, pleading with myself to hold it together. For Dellilian. For Sapphire. But I'm coming undone like a loose shoelace.

"*Mr. Niklaus? Can Dellilian say something?*"

"Anything."

Her breaths sputter in and out, choppy and inconsistent, fading, like a song winding down until the final note is gone forever. I press my hands against the wound, buying as much time as I can manage.

"*Dellilian watch many brave human and beast. Save many sad souls. Rescue lost children. Thousands of years. Long, long time. Remembers every name. Every good deed. Hero tales live forever and ever.*"

Each sigh she expels drives a knot of anguish through my gut. Her dark fur loses its star-shining sheen, like a dull sky with no moon.

"*Will Mr. Niklaus make sure Dellilian name—live long? Dellilian been so scared. But Dellilian not so scared—when Bad Man going to hurt—friends.*"

My jaw and chin quiver, but I clamp it shut. My warring emotions battle each other under a pile of rubble within me. Her words… Her words are needles being stabbed and rotated in my heart vessels.

Sapphire's nails dig into my shoulder as droplets of blood appear from our small friend's nostrils. I push my hands harder against her chest.

"I should have protected you." My voice cracks and collapses on itself. "Please, forgive me. I was afraid of you when we first met. You reminded me of bad part of my childhood. But even though I wasn't very kind—you held my sanity together in that prison, my brave girl. Remember that night they barred my mouth closed? I was going to lose my mind. But you spoke with me all night, sharing stories about your adventures, and it made me feel like I still had a voice."

Sapphire trembles against me as she loses it quietly, and it tugs at a loose string holding me emotions together. Slowly, I fight to grasp it again.

"Thank you for protecting us against the bad man. You—you were a *hero*. You showed no fear. Without you, that prophecy would have come true, and Miss Sapphire and I would both be dead."

A muscle in her chest twitches. And the wound opens wider past my hands, like paper being eaten away by a fast-moving flame. But I don't give up. I hold on to her as my triceps burn from being locked in place.

"To answer your question…" I look into those small, sleepy, dusky eyes that block out the rest of the world to capture her last memories of me so beautifully. "Yes, I swear to you, I will make sure your name lives on forever. Do you hear me, Dellilian? Just like the many stories you've told me of great, brave figures—your name will *never* die."

Her tail gives the smallest thump in the dirt. The movement, simple, yet ripping my chest open and plucking my heart clean out of its cavity. And that's it. The breach gapes wide. Everything else follows. I bend forward and disintegrate in place, crying into the back of my clenched fist.

Sapphire guides my shaking hand to her paw.

"Thank you for being my guardian angel… I love you, Dellilian!" I sob so hard, Sapphire has to brace her body against mine, keeping me in place.

That small paw twitches, once, then twice—the muscle memory of galloping through the Nightlung on her many exciting adventures. Time itself seems to hum around her, cradling this brave little Short-Haired, time-traveling, Windila. And those ears tip back, as if to say she loves me back. As if to apologize for not being able to stay with me any longer.

I bring her soft paw to my lips, wet with tears, and kiss her fur.

The poison of that tree does not boom through her. It sings a quiet end. This wolf has seen more centuries than kingdoms, more wars than the trees that have lived through them. Yet she lies here looking so terribly fragile.

Her pulse flickers under my hand. The world keeps moving, though Dellilian does not. And the world quietly shuts the door behind her.

I cry so abruptly, it breaks the respectful silence in the North Sapphrine Forest. The tears welling from my eyes do not touch my skin as they drip endlessly onto her dimming fur.

I'm so sorry, Dellilian. I love you, girl. I love you. Please, take care of my dad. Tell him how sorry I am. Tell him I love him. Tell him I forgive him for the basement. Tell him I am proud of the man he became. Watch over him, Dellilian!

The cold settles into our bones as we sit with our dear friend for what feels like hours. I hold her close, unwilling to let an ounce of warmth leave her body. The moon hangs over our heads like a glimmering vigil candle we never lit. And we don't speak her name. We don't say anything at all.

Sapphire knows there isn't anything she can offer verbally. I cannot wrap my mind around what I have lost. I cannot begin to put thought into how I'll tell my mother that my father is gone. I don't know how I'll ever live without my sweet Dellilian.

"Niklaus…" Sapphire nudges me.

My cheeks and eyelids are frozen as I look up to see something of a miracle. In a burst of silver light, her body weaves into the soil, like roots find their home in the earth. Of stardust and celestial smoke, she returns to the world as if she never meant anything—

"Look! They're trees!"

My eyes fight to adjust to the moonlit spindling trunks emerging from the dirt. The wood curling into unruly helixes, branches stretching wide and crooked, draped with pine needles that glitter like shattered constellations.

Four trees canopy the stars.

Four trees cast a blanket of warmth and everlasting love.

And with it, I know they hold a special meaning for Dellilian, myself, Sapphire, and my dad.

"What should we call them?" Sapphire asks breathlessly.

I smile through the tears.

"Dellilian's Hearts."

75. Coming Home Again

Sapphire

My fingers are hard, frozen marble. I drum them against my trembling arms to try and funnel blood back into them. Niklaus comes and goes as he admires these beautiful, sacred trees. In and out of a daydream, or a waking nightmare as he relives being helpless to watching those he loves dying right in front of him.

"Niklaus?" I whisper, mouth dry and sticking together. "Please, let me take you home."

He shakes his head. "I don't deserve to go home."

"Of course you do! None of this was your fault. It's mine. I am so sorry."

"Doesn't matter. They're gone. Both of them."

Dellilian's blood has dried over his hands and knuckles, splitting with frost. I hold his hands in mine, offering little body heat until I bring those hands to the center of my chest.

"I won't tell you what to do. But…I think you need to be home when your mom gets the news. I can't imagine her pain if she thinks she has lost her son too," I say quietly.

This reaches a place in his core that has remained silent. That hasn't even considered his mother quite yet. And who could blame him? After witnessing these two gruesome, soul-wrenching events…

Niklaus flicks his tired, tormented blue eyes to me, then back down to the soil he clutches in his right hand.

"I don't want to leave her."

"Dellilian's Hearts will be here in this form when you return home." A voice enters our minds the way Dellilian's used to. A female voice that scrapes the air as if being dragged across stone. Slightly jagged like broken obsidian. A voice that gods may kneel to. Commanding. Seismic. Interstellar.

Neither of us move.

A bird caws from the sky above, flapping its massive wings and dipping mid-flight to soar low, inches from our faces.

I flinch back as a folded piece of parchment lands in front of us.

Niklaus unravels that crisp paper between his numb fingers, and we read a small message inside.

Thank you for loving our Dellilian so well.
She has witnessed many great stories but never been a part of one the way she has now.
I come from many worlds away. A place where we catch wind of interesting prophesies.
And I have sent you a Morphing Onyx Short-Haired Windila out of good faith.
My people face a great evil that only your parents and a great beast can stop.
One day, I will ask for your favor to sway them to our side.
For our survival in our war will depend on them.

When Dellilian's species perishes out of magnificent heroism, the magic of their bodies give back to the Earth.
Whether a tree or a burning rose bush, their form will never perish.
It will live on for thousands of years, untouched by fire,

by water, by any element.
In fact, no one will have the power to cut her down. She will only give to those who are worthy.
She will only allow a pure of heart to take her from the ground and repurpose her for what she deems admirable and fueled by love.
You'll hear from me again one day.
Sincerely,
Vindawolf

I guess that answers the question we had about who sent Dellilian to aid us.

Niklaus and I read the message again to ourselves before he drops against my chest in exhaustion and defeat of the icy breeze that picks up against our exposed skin.

I cradle him to me, wrapping his body against my own, and harnessing that love to carry us like a feather in the wind back home.

Skylenna
Present Day

DaiSzek guards Niles's body under the shade of a red oak tree while I walk with my family back to our house.

Moments after we arrive, so do Niklaus and my daughter. Both shivering, covered in a dark blood and their skin a tint of blue. Dessin ran to Sapphire first. My daughter appeared numb and in a dissociative daze until she saw him coming. Her arms flung around his neck, and she bawled into his shoulder, sounding like a little girl again. My husband rubbed her back rigorously, chasing the chill from her bones while he whispered many things that only seemed to make her cry harder. I've dreamed of this very moment so many times. Dreams that seemed to dwindle away in an effort to protect my sanity. But as I watched them with tears running down my soot-covered face, I grabbed onto Nile's boy.

He stared blankly as I rubbed his ice-cold back. I asked him if he wanted to be the one to tell his mother. He shook his head.

As we reach the lagoon, Dessin takes my hand in his and sets a firm kiss against my fingers. I grind my teeth to the point of searing pain blooming up the sides of my face. All to keep from breaking apart in front of my children.

But this is Niles.

My brother.

How am I supposed to hold it all together?

"You're not leading the family alone anymore, baby," Dessin whispers, stroking a thumb over my cheekbone. "I'm here now."

I want nothing more than to fall into his arms and cry until my lungs go up in flames. Every ounce of self-control I have is keeping me on a tight leash. He's my soulmate, and he's back. There is no way to explain how I cannot settle on a feeling or thought when it comes to the sheer joy I feel about getting to climb into bed with my husband tonight and how I will ever mentally say goodbye to Niles.

Thinking about his name makes me want to watch his captor burn all over again.

Thinking about that last smile he gave me breaks a steel wall that's keeping my meltdown held away from the public eye with a neat little bow.

Niles.

Niles.

Niles.

That's my brother.

My brother.

I hear DaiSzek howl in the distance, and Dessin has to clutch my waist to keep my knees from buckling.

I hold on tighter, protecting my unpredictable emotions in a hidden cave of my mind.

Get through today.

Just make it until you're all alone tonight.

Dessin inhales softly against my hair and kisses my temples.

Not alone.

Niles would be so happy for me.

I can do this. My children are behind me, sniffling and holding onto one another. My family is hanging on by a thread. I can do this.

A few steps away from the front porch, my front door swings open, and Chekiss quickly walks out, followed by Warrose and Ruth.

"You two made it home!" Chekiss cheers in a rusty voice. He jogs with wooden, short strides to Sapphire and Niklaus with open arms. They appear dazed and drowning as they accept his hug.

"Thank God!" Ruth sighs.

Warrose points at Krimson. "Never doubted you, buddy."

Their smiles of relief pummel my chest. I feel stunned into place like a small animal being cornered by a lethal predator. I can only observe the short moments of them not knowing and live here a few seconds longer.

"How far did you go back in time?!" Ruth asks Sapphire.

Chekiss breaks their hug to rub their arms. "You two are making me cold. Are you hurt? Is that blood??"

"Is everyone okay?" Warrose asks.

Our family looks to my children for answers. But their eyes are magnetized to the ground. My family looks to Dessin and myself all at once.

Marilynn steps out of the house, staring firmly into my eyes. She has always had that all-knowing stare about her. Her eyes are archives—star-deep with unrecorded history lying dormant. But this gaze is much different.

She knows.

She knows what I haven't said.

What I am about to say.

And grief needs no language as we share these last seconds. It sits between us, enormous, heavy, and breathing death into our souls.

"Wait…" Ruth says.

"Where is Niles?" Chekiss's tone changes drastically.

There it is.

That three-worded question cleaves me in place. A question so razor-sharp, I am desecrated and pulled apart like an old doll.

Dessin's hands steady me, acting as iron crutches. That support, that stability as I stare at Niles's wife sends blood rushing to my face.

Chekiss is suddenly next to me. "Where is Niles?" he asks again.

I hear Ruth gasp.

Warrose looks to Dessin for confirmation.

"No…" Chekiss steps back as my eyes begin dripping.

"Niles?!" Ruth shrieks.

"Oh my god…" Warrose covers his mouth and turns away from us with his other hand on his head.

"No!" Chekiss's scratchy voice rakes over us. "NO! Not my boy!"

Chekiss was the father neither of us had. Niles and I were the children Chekiss never got to raise.

I blink more tears in his direction but cannot bring myself to say anything. I hear my children sob behind us. But it's Chekiss's howl that makes me lose it. It's raspy and dragged out to a long, raucous moan.

His sun-spotted hand spreads over his chest in shock, denial, then another collision of reality sinking in. He cries out as though a sword is lodging in his ribs.

"How did it happen?" Ruth cries.

"He was—executed," I tell them in a faint whisper.

Ruth squeezes her eyes shut as Warrose drops to a knee and hugs her.

Krimson holds his grandpa up, murmuring reassuring words as Chekiss sobs.

I find Marilynn still standing, watching me with streams of tears drizzling over her freckled cheeks. "My son…" she gets out.

I turn my head to Niklaus. Sapphire lets him go as he bolts to his mother, back shaking against her arms as she whispers in his ear, nodding and crying along with him.

Dessin is behind me now, arms a protective wall around my upper body. And my head falls back against his shoulder for just a minute. I look up to the vast sky, at the shifting clouds, and rustling leaves. Niles is here somewhere, watching his family fall to pieces over him. And I know that must hurt far more than his death.

Marilynn finds my eyes again.

"Skylenna?"

"Yes, Marilynn?"

She wipes her face and reaches for my hand.

"Take me to my husband."

76. The Golden Funeral

Skylenna

A closed casket sits among a still surrounding of red oak trees. Silent onlookers mourning with us.

According to Marilynn, Niles wanted to be buried here one day. He assumed he would pass of old age and outlive all of us, then when it was time, he would want to be buried close to where we held family dinners on Sundays. He would want a resting place close to where DaiSzek would rest too. He wanted to be close to family.

Dessin stands on the other side of Niles's grave, an open rectangle six feet under.

I choose to look at my soulmate, and not where Niles sleeps.

"Niles would be very happy right now. In fact, he wouldn't let us live it down." Dessin has his hands in his suit pockets, peering down at Niles's grave. "Why? Because today, imagine being the main character in a funeral full of main characters."

I look at the people who have gathered for his funeral. At Warrose and Ruth, at Marilynn and Niklaus, at my children and

Chekiss, at DaiSzek. I smile at the thought of Niles taunting us with this. All the attention is on him today.

"Marilynn told me last night that Niles would have wanted me to give his eulogy, so I spent all night writing and rewriting how I wanted to do this. How does one put into words…their final goodbye to their lifelong best friend?" He looks at me with a sad smile before continuing. "I want to start by saying that I couldn't stand Niles when I first met him. I did my best to avoid him. But my time ignoring him actually had the opposite effect. Niles worked hard to get my attention and to be my friend."

I remember those days in the prison when their bickering became a source of entertainment for us. A little bit of light in that dark hole.

"The first time he wore me down was when I found out Niles dove through pikes of fire to break DaiSzek out of his cage during a battle with Vexamen. Before that, DaiSzek would growl at him if Niles tried to pet him. And now? Look at the way my boy won't leave Niles's side, even now that he's gone."

We all look to the spot DaiSzek is lying in, right on the edge of the six-foot hole. If he could lie in there with him, he would.

"Niles knew how to bring humor to a dark situation. He could always make my girl laugh. But through that humor, Niles was a magnificent friend. Loyal. Heroic. Strong. I knew all of this about him for years, but I gained a new, profound respect for him when I learned how he saved my daughter's life. My friend never had the same training I had, but he used his own hands to protect my daughter from a sword. That is a debt that I can never pay back. I will never get to the chance to hug him again, to tell him thank you."

I don't know how I'm still standing. How I'm still keeping my emotions strapped down and kept quiet. But I listen to my husband keep going in awe.

"In the Vexamen Prison, on Niles's birthday, he made the annoying request to have a best friend handshake with me. Eleven humiliating moves. And now that he is gone, I didn't realize how much it would hurt that I'll never get to do that with him again." Dessin's dark mahogany eyes land on me, and he pauses, as if knowing what he'll say next will both mend and break my heart. "So, last night, I tattooed the moves on my arm…for Niles."

Everyone leans in as Dessin rolls up his sleeve, revealing an outline in fresh ink of each movement to the handshake. The fist bump. The pinched fingers. The hug. All of it.

I drop my face into my hands and cry.

A symphony of sobs, sniffles, and whimpers echo through the forest. The wind carries each beautiful sound in swirling gusts, kicking up dust and leaves as if Niles is answering this great act of love with a smile and a wave from heaven.

I look up in time to see Dessin turn to his left, opening his arms as Marilynn collides into his chest. Her pale skin turns a deep shade of pink, and her grieving moans makes Dessin look to the sky for answers. He leans down and whispers something that makes her cry harder.

Ruth's chair bumps my leg, and she takes my hand with a smile.

"I brought something for Niles too," she says.

She moves to his lowered casket, pulling out a stunning golden crown from her bag.

"For the many times you stole my crown and said it looked better on you," she announces to his grave.

Our tears are interrupted by surprised laughter.

"I've been saving this for your birthday, Cupid. But I'll leave it here, and you can wear it in heaven."

Warrose places a hand on her shoulder as he towers behind her. Off his weapon's belt is a golden sword, glinting in the sunlight.

"And for all the times you told me you deserved to be a knight of Vexamen because your muscles were bigger than mine…" Warrose lowers the sword to his casket.

"And because you knew how to pick a lock which made you smarter than us," Ruth adds, cheeks wet and rosy yet chuckling along with the rest of us.

Chekiss approaches the daunting space with a cane and a heavy, wide book.

"I know you used to accuse me of favoring Skylenna and calling you a little shithead behind your back—and I did." We laugh, and I know that this is what Niles would have wanted. He would have begged us to mourn, yes, but also to laugh. To tease. To remember the good memories too. "But…I also kept all of your accomplishments here, in this book."

The laughter is gone. As Chekiss's rough voice cracks, and he cries into his fingers, we all lose it once again.

"The article clippings of you rebuilding the blueprints for a women's sanctuary. The first photographs I took of you and little Niklaus. The confetti from the Christmas ball you threw. I kept your best moments because you are my proudest moments as a papa, Niles. This is not the first time I've had to bury a child. So, my only regret, is that this should be you here—burying me."

Niklaus does not say a word as he drops a letter on top of the casket, leaning down to graze its glossy finish with his fingers.

I walk straight to Marilynn leaning on Dessin for support. My offering isn't for Niles.

"In two days, you and Niles would have been married for twenty years. Niles had enlisted my help for three months to help him write these words to surprise you and renew your vows in a ceremony we planned."

Marilynn closes her eyes and lowers her head, nodding somberly at the dreadful fact that they were days away from celebrating their twenty-year anniversary.

"When you're ready, you can read it. But it's between husband and wife."

I hand her the pristinely folded envelope, wrapped in an adorable pink bow. Marilynn holds it to her chest, as if exposing it to the air will make the pages dissolve in a cloud of dust.

"Thank you, Skylenna."

I don't know how much she knew of the prophecy. But I do know Marilynn tried for a long time not to fall in love with the most lovable man in the world. And she failed, despite her greatest efforts.

She must have known enough.

And I cannot imagine a heavier burden than knowing your soulmate was going to die and not being able to stop it.

As Marilynn leaves a delicate kiss on Niles's vows, I remember something I watched him do after he finished tying the bow. My face cracks a big smile. There isn't any doubt in my mind that Niles pushed this memory forward to tell his wife. To make her smile one more time.

"If you're wondering what that smell is, it's Niles's cologne. He sprayed it, and said, I quote, *my wife needs to get a whiff of my sex appeal thus she will never leave me, and our marital bed shall be iron clad.*"

Marilynn and Dessin fall into a fit of laughter. Though her laughs are harmoniously entwined with her distraught whimpers.

I tuck Marilynn into a long hug, feeling Niles's spirit and his love through her embrace.

"You knew your whole life, didn't you?" I whisper.

She nods slowly against my shoulder.

"What a burden that must have been."

"No," she mutters. "At first, I thought so too, yes. But after falling in love with our golden boy, I was so grateful to know how it all ended. I cherished every second with him, Skylenna. I held each millisecond of his time with me like a coveted holy grail."

That's all he wanted too. To be loved and to love someone.

"If you knew, why wouldn't you do something to warn him?"

I hate that I am even asking that question now at his funeral, but I have to know.

She looks down at our black heels and shakes her head grimly.

"I did. Even though it was forbidden for our colony to warn or interfere in that way…I did, Skylenna. A couple of years ago, I broke down and warned him. I told him everything. I begged him not to go, even though I didn't have an exact date to give him. I put your daughter at risk by warning him because he protected her that night! But Niles…Niles was too noble not to go. Not to be there when our kids needed him the most."

That fucking hurts so much more. What was I thinking? No amount of warning would ever keep our sweet Niles from doing the right thing.

"And…he saved someone important while he was out there in the Blackspire Ward of The North," she adds, wiping her pink nose.

"Is this Niles's funeral?" Two men approach from the shadows of the trees.

Everyone stops talking. I scope out their appearance, recognizing the older one with dark skin, and gray hair in long braids down his back.

They are from the Naiadales.

"I helped Niles once after he was burned," the older one says, speaking to me.

I lift my chin. "Rydran?"

He nods, flicking his gaze to the grave site.

"I'm sorry," I tell him, feeling uncomfortable for how to say this. "This is just for family."

Rydran bows his head. "I understand. But I am not here for me, I am here for him."

He places a hand on the young man's back, perhaps in his early thirties. With heavy tears filling his eyes, the man makes his way to Niles's casket in the ground. Not yet covered in dirt.

"Niles was a father to me when I was taken from my papa," he says with a tight throat.

I look at Marilynn with confusion. Though her chin trembles as she already knows who this is.

I hesitate. "When was that?"

"Twenty-one years ago."

I think back and look to Dessin.

"In the Vexamen Prison?" he speaks up for me.

The man shakes his head. "The Blackspire Ward of The North."

Collectively, our family calculates this in our heads. We exchange looks. We shift on our feet. He was with Niles as a captive? He knew our Niles before he died?

As questions swim and float through my mind, I can see that for this man, his memories have been preserved over many years. This event happened for us a day ago.

"You were with him in the end?" Niklaus asks quietly.

The man's black eyes lower to the casket. He thinks long and hard before he responds, taking a knee out of respect.

"I was the youngest captive there. Taken from my family by the Breed when I was only six years old. Niles said I reminded him of his son. He looked out for me. Took the beatings I was supposed to receive. He'd force me to close my eyes during the executions. He'd shield me with his body when the mob threw stones." Those round eyes dart to Marilynn. "I wouldn't have made it out of that terrible place without him."

Marilynn places her hands across her chest. She's read the pages of this chapter. She's read the words without the emotions coloring the page.

"He came up with a plan to get me out, to hide in the drainpipes until nightfall so I could escape to the coast and find safe passage home. I fled during the execution. Niles had to make a big scene, to give me my best chance at making it out. It's why he was on that chopping block in the first place. I was just a little boy, and he saved me."

One by one, we each hug and thank Rydran and Renly for coming. For sharing with us what Niles went through in his final days. What was going through his head when he was up there on that stage. That he saved a little boy's life. I could not be prouder of my brother.

Before the end, Renly speaks with Ruth quietly, asking for passage back to the country that held him captive. He let her know that Niles told him that one day, he might meet the next Mazonist leader, and if he wanted to learn how to govern his own people with wisdom and kindness, to look no further than his best friend, Ruth Mazonist.

She hugged him and agreed to take him back with her, allowing him to pay Niles's kindness and sacrifice forward by doing good in the country he lost his life in.

After covering his casket with dirt, and moving his headstone into place, we stand around it and admire the words engraved there.

Niles Offborth
Friend
Brother
Husband
Father
We'll see you again, our Golden Boy

Before everyone departs back to my house for dinner, I move to the other side of his headstone to speak. "I have something I'd like to close with."

My family waits with dried cheeks and anticipation stilling their movements.

"When I met Niles in the asylum, he insisted on telling me all about his belief in soulmates. He was so passionate of the idea that there is that one person for everyone. That divine other half who was aligned with the stars. Well, he gave me a definition of soulmates that I have agreed with every day since…until today. Soulmates: when you find them, there is no life without them. Now on this day, as I stand in front of Niles's soulmate and beloved wife he has left behind—I can tell you, like many things, he was wrong. There is life still. Because he is not gone! Not really. He lives right here…" I hold one hand over my heart, and the other over Marilynn's. "He is that warm feeling when you hug someone you love. He's the snide comment. He's the inflated egotistical thought you'll get when you look in the mirror. He's in every joke you hear. The laughter of children. He's the wind and the trees. And he's cheering his wife and son on, every second he's gone."

I touch Niklaus's cheek and break apart. "He was your mother's soulmate, but he loved being your dad more than anything in the world."

Niklaus's eyes fall closed. In peace. In guilt. In sorrow. In complete and utter loss of words.

"Now, we're going inside to eat all of Niles's favorite foods. We'll drink and tell his most embarrassing stories. Because our golden boy isn't gone. He's just waiting for that special group hug when we're all ready to join him."

As Rydran, Renly, Krimson, Sapphire, and Niklaus enter the house—my lifelong found family remains at Niles's grave. Kane comes to the front just for this.

With a confusing mix of smiles and tears, we complete the group hug in honor of Niles. And it's sad, every group hug merged so delicately into these passing seconds. It's the hug around Ruth when she lost her legs. It's the hug when Dessin broke me out of captivity with Absinthe and Albatross. It's time on the Fun House stage when we'd catch each other and drop Niles just to embarrass him. It's a ray of sunshine and a dark storm cloud perfectly aligned.

It's a Niles group hug that will not be whole for a long, long time.

77. The Talk

Niklaus

It's midnight, and I have quietly snuck out of the Valdawell house to stand over their lagoon and stare vacantly at the reflection of the moon rippling along the indigo surface of the water.

Sapphire is catching Krimson up on everything that's happened.

My mother has fallen asleep in Aunt Skylenna's arms on the couch.

And I had to get out of there. It's impossible to navigate these conflicting feelings combating in my chest. My love for Sapphire and my guilt for those I've lost. I'm numb and in so much pain all at once. I am ten years older than the woman I love now. Ten years of experience being tortured and beaten in that prison. Of getting to know Sophia and Jack and mourning them because I know the fatal endings they both met.

I'm fucking confused and distraught and screaming alone in the middle of that prison cell, locked away like a rabid animal no one wanted to go near. I'm still there. And I don't know how to get out. I can still smell the strange, toxic algae that clung to the walls. The rotting corpses they'd forget about in the less important underground cages. My misery hanging in the damp air like a sword over my head.

I'm still there.

Even though I'm technically out now, I can't sit with my father and tell him all about it. Let him make ironic jokes to get me to laugh. Then eventually empathize with me. Share his own demons so that we may compare them.

He's gone.

"I know that look very well."

My eyes leave the moon's reflection, finding Sapphire's father watching me from his leaned stance against a tree. Hands in pockets. A calm, considering expression. Reading different features on me.

"What look is that?" I ask.

"The look of man who hasn't escaped his imprisonment yet."

My jaw twitches, and I turn back to the lagoon.

"Among other things, you're back there in your head, aren't you? Trying to process loss behind bars."

My Adam's apple shifts.

He might be the only man on earth who can understand what I'm going through right now.

"You don't know how to talk about it. I understand that. I knew how to escape the asylum, but I couldn't leave my Skylenna. You're the prisoner who made multiple escape attempts but kept coming back, aren't you?"

His words summon that memory of tasting freedom, then rejecting it to go back to my cage.

"It must have been. You grew up with the blueprints of that prison. You excelled in Vexamen and Dementia's history. Of course, you knew how to escape. But why did you always come back?" he asks, though the tone in his voice suggests he already knows the answer to that.

I sigh. "If there was any chance Sapphire would return to me, then I needed to remain a prisoner."

Dessin continues to watch me knowingly.

"I remember reading that it was reported that prisoner was the greatest swordsmen the Mazonist Brothers had ever seen. They used him in fighting rings for ten long years. And no one saw where he was locked up."

Hearing this historical figure dissect my role in history is not something I'd ever picture would happen to me. I have both memories. The one life of him being in a coma. The other of him hating me when I started to court his daughter.

And there was no possibility of him ever looking at me like this in either life.

"Ten years, Niklaus."

The backs of my eyes sting. So, I continue training my stre on the water.

"And I also read that the prisoner took his wife's punishment. That he lost a finger for her."

"I lost three," I admit. And with a quick glance, I say, "Someone very kind saved two of them."

Dessin narrows his stern eyes at me. "You did that for my daughter?"

Before I can answer, he keeps going…

"In that fighting ring, the infamous prisoner was pitted against his wife and refused to hurt her. He even covered her body with his own when all inmates were punished and hosed down with an acid invented by Crow Ivast. Did you do this for my daughter?!" he asks again, pushing off the tree.

I wave him off. "Don't give me an ounce of praise. Please. Christ, I don't fucking deserve that."

"Why do you think that?"

"Because!" I explode. Not many people yell at the man standing in front of me, but I guess I've lost all access to my sanity. "You know how I've treated her half our lives. In both of them. I was…fucked in the head after they took me. I—took it out on her. So yes, I did those things for your daughter. Of course, I did! I fucking love her. I am in love with her. But I don't deserve her. I had to do horrible shit in that prison. I almost committed suicide so many times. I don't fucking deserve that wonderful, brilliant, beautiful girl." I point to the house with glowing windows and twinkling porch sconces.

My eyes are throbbing from not allowing myself to release these pent-up sentiments unwinding at the seams.

"I was so arrogant growing up learning about what you and your wife, my parents, all of them went through. The asylum, the prison, the whole fucking city! I read it all on paper. I didn't get it! I didn't fucking get it. But now that I've lived through it—now that I've seen and felt what my own dad went through…it makes me *hate* myself. How fucking disrespectful was I? How fucking incompetent and deranged to make light of these disgusting moments in history you all had to endure?!" I clasp my hands on the back of my neck. "So no. No, it doesn't matter that I did those things for your daughter. Because I couldn't even save him…I let—him—die!"

Sapphire's father crashes into me with a fatherly embrace that pushes me into a full-blown breakdown. I cry like a fucking child into his shoulder, wrinkling his suit coat into my hands and pretending I'm hugging my dad. One last time.

"I was there too, Niklaus. I couldn't save him either. And in time, we will both forgive ourselves. You hear me? Because you know what your dad is thinking right now? He's thinking, there is nothing to forgive. You are his only son, and he loves you."

We sit outside talking for hours until I calm down. He tells me about the time my dad cut through his own palms to rip off barbed wire from around Dessin's ankle in a prison Fun House Night. He laughed about a few of the terrible jokes my dad shared with the group at his expense. I got it all off my chest too. My days in the prison. Meeting Meridei in the asylum. Absinthe and Albatross.

Eventually, Kane comes to the front to share his own experiences too.

"I wanted to tell you about what happened to my fingers in the prison," I tell him.

Kane examines the two crooked ones and the ring finger that's missing.

"I wanted to tell you about the woman who reattached these two for me."

"Oh?"

"Her name was Sophia," I say gently.

Kane blinks in surprise.

"Your mother was the kindest, most motherly woman I have ever met. I wouldn't have survived many days in that prison without her."

"She was—in prison?"

"She was also experimented on with her twin sister, Story, by Crow Ivast."

Kane parts his lips. "How old was she?"

"She was only fourteen when I met her," I say, rubbing the exhaustion from my face. "But she was sixteen when I freed her and Jack, Skylenna's father, from the prison."

His chest rises and falls rapidly in surprise. "What was she like?"

And I tell him every detail I can remember. Hearing about his mother so young seems to repair a small, broken piece of his heart. About how badly she wanted a family. To be a mother.

After we get up to leave, I stop him.

"I know I'm not ready yet. I know it'll take time to heal after all that's happened. But one day, I'm going to come to you, and I'm going to ask for your daughter's hand in marriage. And by then, I hope I'll be worthy of her."

Kane wraps me in a big bear hug with a smile.

"You already are."

Two years later, that's exactly what I do.

And he says yes.

78. Our Home in The Red Oaks

Skylenna

Three Years Later

My screams go on for miles, scaring the birds from their nests. My feet hit the ground in a panic as I sprint through the woods. My skin is still wet from the lagoon, sticking to my dry clothes.

Almost there.

I can hear the thundering footsteps behind me. As they catch up too fast, my pulse ruptures under my skin.

The trees open up to the purple lavender and swaying trees. Tall blades of grass dance. The spring sun beams over the opening in a cloudless sky.

I scream again as I can hear that voice gaining on me.

"NO!"

A large body plummets into my back and tackles me to the ground. Hands grip my sides and tickle the soft underside of my ribs until I'm bucking and shrieking in a delirious spell of laughter.

"You're so slow!" I holler, turning my bright red face into an arm to bite.

"Slow?!" Kane barks out a laugh.

"And *old*!"

"We are the same age, my love."

He stops tickling me as I feign offense, recoiling back in disgust.

"Same? Same—I'm sorry—I thought you just said *same* age."

Kane lifts an eyebrow but continues to watch his front seat performance.

"You are *two* years older than me," I clarify sweetly. "Some might even say twenty years older with the pace at which you run."

Kane's hearty laugh is perfection. The rough sound burns in my heart.

"But I caught you," he adds.

"Great point, I'm glad you brought that up." I try to wiggle out from under his weight with no success. "One, I was jogging, practically speed walking. Two, you ran with every bit of old man energy you had left in the tank. Every bit of it. Our family is blessed, Kane. Do you hear me? *Blessed* you didn't keel over from cardiac arrest. Or high blood pressure. Maybe even arthritic complications."

"You are beating the joke to death." But he's still barking out more laughter.

And the tickling starts back up again. He kisses my neck, between my breasts, then back up to the tip of my nose.

"Why're you running from me, honey?"

Now I'm laughing. "Because we had sex twice this morning, and now, you're trying to go for a third!"

"Was it twice?"

"Yes!"

"No."

"Yes, it absolutely was."

"No, I don't think so."

"You're not counting it because you were a little too quick at the draw at five a.m."

"That did not happen." He kisses my jaw, then cheekbone.

"I was there."

"That must have been Greystone."

I snicker. “Oh, no. You can’t blame other alters when you had a gentleman’s misfire.”

“*Mmm*—I’m pretty sure it was him.” Kane gives me a silly smirk. “And of course I can blame these misfortunes on Greystone. What other purposes does he serve?”

I squirm as he unbuttons my dress.

“Are you going to let me reclaim my dignity after you regrettably *blinked* this morning and missed my entire performance?”

I cackle. “I am so sore, Kane! I’m not twenty anymore.”

Mid-forties is off the table. We refuse to acknowledge it.

“Honey, I saw you swimming in that lagoon, and I got so hard again. All jokes aside, I really need you to open your legs for me.”

Despite my soreness, I’m already getting wet.

“Give it forty-eight hours,” I say.

“Are you that sore?”

“Yes.”

Kane’s lustful gaze furrows in concern. He props himself up an inch.

“I don’t want you to hurt.” That frown drops to my open legs spread around his thighs. “Will you let me lick you to make you feel good?”

I drop my head back and groan.

I really am sore, but fuck, that sounds so good.

“I’ll be so gentle, I swear, honey,” he murmurs.

And I nod, lifting my dress to expose my glistening cunt. With bent knees, I widen myself for him. Kane massages my thighs as he angles himself to a comfortable position in the grass. One he can rest in while he enjoys my taste. There’s no doubt in me that he might have a small obsession with eating me out. But not quickly. No, he likes to go for quite a long time. We’ve been locked in our room for hours before as he massages me until I’m so relaxed, I could easily float into a lucid dream. Then, he’ll lick me slowly, and it goes on so long that the sensitivity becomes a live wire of sparks and short-circuiting fires inside me.

It’s one of the most out-of-body experiences that he begs of me weekly.

He starts off peeling my lips apart, humming as he gets a single taste of my arousal on his tongue. He's careful with the pressure, kissing me with an open mouth as that one taste drills an unquenchable need in his brain.

I breathe heavily from my mouth, getting a better set on my elbows to watch him.

And he just keeps going, lapping away at my soaking cunt. My thighs vibrate over his shoulders, and I fight against his hold on me to rock against his mouth.

"Don't fucking rush me. You taste so good. I'm in heaven."

I moan, grinding like a needy, desperate virgin who has simply never felt an orgasm before. Because it always feels like the first time. Almost half a century of knowing each other, it will always feel like the first time.

Except now, we are addicted to each other. You'd think that would fade and dim like a dying campfire over time. But it doesn't. Quite the opposite. We have trouble keeping our hands off each other. I find myself fantasizing about the next time we're alone again. Our kids often yell at us in amused disgust.

"Kane, I am so close."

He chuckles against me, then growls as he dips his tongue inside me. Once, twice, and then begins fucking me with it. I grip the back of his head and beg to come. Scream. Howl. The fire of my orgasm spreading too quickly. Its overwhelming pins and needles kick me off the edge, and I buck like I'm possessed against his mouth.

Always like the first time.

"Oh god!" I'm slick and unnaturally sensitive against his tongue that lingers. "I love you. I love you so much."

"Again."

"Give me a minute."

"I want to taste more of it."

After half a minute, he sucks on my clit, pulling each orgasm so much faster than the last. I'm covered in grass and dirt by the time it's over. And we lie under the sun, sleeping for an hour, then gathering a handful of lavender before we return home.

Kane carries me on his back, making additional jokes about how much better in bed he is than Greystone, and how I should definitely tell him that.

We make lunch and set it out of the front porch table to enjoy with Chekiss. Kane plays a record, and as we finish, we get to work on the garden. Chekiss orders us around with an iced tea in one hand, pointing and organizing where each seed should be planted.

At sunset, we give DaiSzek a bath in the lagoon. It's a failed effort as he takes a nosedive in the mud. Afterward, he sleeps on Niles's grave, just as he has done the last three years since the day we buried his old friend.

In the late evening, we get a visit from Sapphire and Niklaus. Her late-night cravings kicked in during her second trimester, and now she begs for my freshly baked cinnamon sugar cookies. Krimson and his girlfriend, Clara, show up not even ten minutes later. He somehow always knows when I'm baking something for his sister.

At midnight, Dessin gets peer pressured to drink with Krimson and Niklaus. And they end up seeing if Niklaus or Krimson can take Dessin, even now that he's a bit older and not as fast.

The conclusion is that Dessin remains undefeated.

His last remarks to them are, "Maybe when I'm dead, boys."

As I feel a kick in Sapphire's belly, she watches me thoughtfully, mouth pulling down at the corners.

"What is it?" I ask.

She taps her belly. "Bringing a baby into this world…it's not as scary."

"What do you mean?"

"I'm having a little girl," she says thick with so much feeling behind it. "If I were to have her a few decades ago…I would have been sick over it. Thank you for changing this world to be a better place for my daughter, Mom. For me. I still get nightmares over how it used to be. I can't imagine my daughter having to grow up in that fucked up society."

I hold her hand and smile.

"One day, you'll make it an even better place before you leave it too."

Sapphire and Niklaus run Demechnef together. They've built a golden lamp post in front of the new women's sanctuary in memory of Niles. They've funded housing for older women who have been trapped in abusive marriages with their husbands.

They've already done so much, and they're only getting started.

As much as it still guts me that my daughter had to travel to the most horrific moments in history, it's made her and her husband better people with fuller hearts.

"Are Aunt Ruth and Uncle Warrose still coming next week?" she asks.

"And Renly."

"Still apprenticing her?"

I smile. "She actually decided to name him her successor."

Her brows lift. "To the Mazonist throne?!"

"Ruth doesn't believe in bloodlines leading a lineage. She wants a well-deserving, pure of heart leader to take her place when she's gone. And she couldn't think of anyone better than the man Niles gave his life to save."

As my children leave and the house grows quiet, Dessin reads to me on the couch. It's two in the morning, and he ends up carrying me to bed. DaiSzek is already lying in his own cot on the other end of the room—never missing his bedtime.

"Want to stay up all night and talk again?" Dessin asks.

I chuckle. "No."

"Final answer?"

The humor quickly turns sour in my stomach. He sits up in bed, caressing my hip. Dessin is usually unreadable, but this is his give away. Something is bothering him, and he'd rather stay awake all night than go to bed and see it in his nightmares.

"Is it the children?" I ask.

He glances down at my worried expression, then shakes his head.

"Has something happened?" *Please, don't make me dig for it.*

"You and I have had a lifetime of loss," he whispers into the dark bedroom, voice a low baritone of rough bark and the tremor of an earthquake.

"We have…"

"I don't know how much more we can take."

"Why would you say that?" He's getting to a point. It's like watching a tsunami build into a tidal wave over your head, a breath before it wipes out all life around you.

His throat elongates as he swallows. "It's Chekiss, baby."

I sit up. My breath catching like a butterfly in a net.

"What? What happened?"

"His lungs."

"Did he tell you something and keep it from me?! Has he been to a doctor? We can get more than one opinion. He's really not *that* old!"

"He doesn't know, I don't think. It's something I've been keeping an eye on. I listen to his breathing, his laugh, his cough. It's gotten worse. I'm not sure he has too much longer before the lining of his lungs thins and gives out."

"Gives out?" My eyes widen.

"He's seventy-eight years old."

I wave a hand dismissively. "People can live past one hundred."

"Not all people were drowned by Meridei for several years. And he was in the asylum for twenty years. Who knows what else he saw in there."

"But…things have been good. They've been good! It took us so long to stop hurting after Niles. We can't—no!" I remember the first treatment I saw. Chekiss was barely hanging on in the hands of Meridei. Why didn't I notice he was getting worse?!

"Neither of us wanted to see it, Skylenna."

I ball my hands into fists, but Dessin pulls me against his bare chest to quell the firestorm of guilt, grief, terror, and hopelessness that is threatening to take me down.

"How do we—what do we tell the kids?" I ask numbly.

"Chekiss can decide that. We'll talk to him about it tomorrow."

I shake my head. My stomach folding over and crouching down with nausea.

"I—can't. Please, just talk to him first."

Chekiss is the only father figure I've ever truly had. I love him unconditionally. Unfortunately, I am not strong enough to have that conversation with him. But I know my husband is.

"Okay, baby. I'll take care of it."

79. Angels Suffer Long

Skylenna

1 year later

No one prepares you for the moment you start memorizing someone's face.

People come and go. Members of his gardening club. His book club. His humane society he started a decade ago. My children have stayed by his side most of the day. DaiSzek refuses to leave the foot of his bed, keeping his legs warm. Now it's Ruth and Warrose, holding his hands and telling ridiculous stories from their home to make him smile.

You'd think watching someone die would be loud.

It isn't.

It whispers.

It weeps quietly in the dead of night.

Because Chekiss can no longer speak. He nods. He coughs. And coughs more. And wheezes. And gags from coughing so hard he can't catch his breath.

The fluid in his lungs rattles, webbing across his lungs and denying fresh oxygen. When hacking fits get too violent at night, he makes me leave the room, so I don't have to see him suffer. But I hear it from behind his door. I slide down the wall and pray. I pray until my mind goes fuzzy and dazed. I pray that God will spare him the pain. That there are a great many people in this world who deserve to die a long, agonizing death—and Chekiss is not one of them.

I haven't slept in four days.

Neither has my husband.

We've waited.

We've paced the length of the house.

We've gone outside for fresh air, and Dessin holds me as I scream.

Because how could God punish such a kind old man? A man who has dedicated half his life to caring for my family and me? A man who visits Niles's grave every single day with fresh flowers from his garden. A man who goes to Marilynn's house every morning to cook her breakfast and make sure she's eating plenty of nutritious foods. A man who went to the library and read dozens of books on herbs that he could grow in his garden for chronic pain relief and made it into a supplement Ruth could take for her inflammation.

Why would God hurt such a wonderful man so badly?

These days have been quite difficult for Sapphire as well. Her postpartum has been brutal on her, and visiting Chekiss while he's in such a deteriorating state has sent her in a depression.

And even though I see Dessin go on walks at night, rapid cycling through his many alters—he avoids telling me about how hard this is on his system. My husband will do anything in his power not to add on to the burden of loss we all have felt. He will bottle it up. He will walk his desolate road alone if he means sparing those he loves.

If God is watching this all unfold, he is too quiet.

"I miss hearing your laugh, Chekiss," Ruth comments, massaging his limp hand.

He nods in agreement, blinking slowly as sleep tugs at his eyelids again. Chekiss breathes as shallowly as he can muster, because he knows the deeper he takes in a breath, the harder he'll cough from the fluid splattering around in his lungs.

"You made a promise to me years ago that you'd outlive us all, Chek," Warrose says, and although his words are dipped in humor—the worry lines on his forehead are abysmal and haunting.

Chekiss smiles and shakes his head, patting the back of Warrose's arm lovingly.

This goes on into the night, and we do our best to keep Chekiss comfortable. I bring him hot tea with Honey of the Valley that Ruth brought from Vexamen. But nothing helps the panic of drowning internally.

Eventually, all that's left is me, Dessin, Marilynn, Warrose, Ruth, and DaiSzek.

Dessin checks his pulse and looks up at us with that wise gaze I've been hoping for and dreading. It's a confusing feeling. I can't stand the thought of living without Chekiss. But as I've watched him grow weaker, endure long nights of no sleep from choking on his on phlegm, it's hard not to wish for a merciful end.

I sigh as Chekiss's eyelids flutter open.

We all stiffen as he needs assistance to sit up and cough wetly, then heave and spew his soup back up into the bucket Warrose holds for him. Ruth weeps to herself as she holds one of Chekiss's feet in her hands.

He gasps repeatedly, the sound bubbles and sloshes, thick and sticky. Each panicked breath trying to push past glue. There's a river of mud trapped inside him. And I want to help, to do anything. But all I can do is pray to a God who won't listen. My hands fumble and claw into my own chest, unable to breathe because he can't.

"Chekiss, please let me take you to the void so you won't have to hurt!" I blurt out in a long sob. I can't take this anymore! None of us can.

But Chekiss shakes his head. I thought that maybe in the end, when it got bad enough, he'd change his mind. But my father by choice is stubborn and didn't want to miss a single moment with all of us together.

"No!" he yells, gurgling against the slow drowning.

He spoke.

Chekiss's eyes water as he stares ahead, blinking past tears, and completely fixated on a focal point beyond the door.

"Oh my god…" he rasps, grabbing on to Dessin's wrist and my forearm.

"Oh, Chekiss, please, please let me—"

But Chekiss begins to cry, loud, beautiful, happy tears.

"I see my wife!" He falls against the bed with a peaceful smile. "I see my daughter."

For the first time since he got sick, the joy in the room flourishes, and I can feel God's presence again.

"Oh! Skylenna!" he coughs, beside himself with delight.

"Yes?" The light of heaven spills over our family, invisible to us, but not to Chekiss.

"My son came!" His dying laugh is a sound I'll never forget. "My son came back for me! Niles, my boy. My boy is here."

I drop my face to Chekiss's shoulder and just cry. Happy he is not alone as death greets him. But already mourning my dear friend. My tears stain his sleeping gown. And Chekiss reaches for me, holding my upper body to his chest in a tight hug.

I hear a single wet rasp enter his chest.

His fingers loosen.

Chekiss dies in my arms.

And the world goes on without him.

80. Neslanox

Skylenna

Three Years Later

DaiSzek scares off three more teenagers.

I'm embarrassed to say it upset me more now than it usually does. They come often, the unwanted visitors. Children, teenagers, and even adults. They have put on theater performances of our lives, Dessin's, mine, and DaiSzek's. And all it's done is turn our home into a museum. Into a circus for freaks.

These three boys came poking around my front porch first, then found me planting flowers in front of Chekiss and Niles's graves.

Kane was out chopping wood.

And I have been an emotional wreck since he returned. No one was hurt. DaiSzek scared the actual piss out of them, but I fell to my knees as they asked whose headstones I was visiting. Not necessarily an evil question. But today is Chekiss's birthday.

And I am so tired of living in a fishbowl.

"Now, please," Dessin commands sternly, opening the front

door to our guests.

Our children, grandchildren, Warrose, Ruth, and Marilynn file inside. The kids who can run off to play, do so eagerly. Krimson holds a four-month-old in his arms, swaying the little boy back and forth as he sleeps.

"During our time in Vexamen, Aunt Marilynn shared a story about DaiSzek and Knightingale, the fae and elven warriors. Before they died, Marilynn, can you share with everyone what their dream was?" Dessin says, standing in front of the seating area by the fireplace.

"Yes, uh—" She adjusts the glasses on the bridge of her nose. "DaiSzek and Knightingale had a dream of ending up on a private island called Neslanox. They wanted to grow old together there, away from everyone after everything they sacrificed."

Warrose and Ruth spin to me first.

"Wait," Ruth spits out. "You're not thinking…"

"Dessin?" Warrose asks.

"A few teenagers harassed my wife while she was planting flowers at Niles and Chekiss's graves this morning. Alkadon has sent a letter requesting to meet Skylenna, me, and DaiSzek. No doubt to ask for our help in another war."

The room goes utterly still.

"Skylenna and I have talked about this for a while, and even though we love our lives here. We love the Red Oak house. We love being so close to everyone… We need to go somewhere to live out the rest of our lives where only you all can follow."

Dessin walks over to me, holding out his hand. I take it with knots in my stomach, anticipating how everyone will take this next part.

"And where is that?" Niklaus asks.

"Somewhere only Krimson and Sapphire have the keys to," I answer.

The relief and joy for our decision outweighs the sadness. Our family rises to approach Dessin and me, surrounding us with hugs. With congratulations. With excitement to see where we end up.

Because we have twins that have the ability to time travel.

And it's time Dessin, DaiSzek, and I find our Neslanox.

Skylenna

Nine Hundred Years in The Past

"Why are you laughing to yourself and staring at nothing?" I ask Dessin.

We've camped here for three weeks. As far from civilization as we can get. Our children were worried about us not having a house to live in, but they soon remember that Dessin and I once slept under the stars when we ran from the asylum. We slept by a fire and kept each other warm.

This is where we are happiest.

I finish off the cooked wild turkey Dessin caught with DaiSzek. It's an early morning with dew sticking to the grass and fog simmering around the trees.

His chuckling tapers off. "We're probably almost a thousand years in the past, Skylenna."

"You think?"

"I made you a promise in the Vexamen Prison. Do you remember it?" he asks.

I shrug. "I've worked very hard to not remember my time in that place."

He challenges me with a look. I sigh, lying on my back and gazing at the way the warm sunrise saturates the fluffy white clouds.

I scan the conversations I remember, and one stands out. We were cuddled up to the bars, and he was telling me about all of his alters…

I instantly understand why he was laughing.

"You promised to build me a castle," I say with a gasp.

"Yes."

I scan the area. The land before us without any architecture. Without any trace of civilization that came from Alkadon settlers when the Chandelier City was built.

"And what would be the perfect name for a castle so special? If not for the heroic time-traveling creature that saved our daughter's life," Dessin says, looking back out at the horizon of endless potential.

I bring my hands to the top of my head, trying to wrap my head around this.

"The Dellilian Castle…:"

"It seems as though we know, without a shadow of a doubt, that I end up building that castle for you after all, baby."

"It all started with us?!"

"They did promise her that they'd ensure her name would live on for a long time," says with a slow smile.

I clap my hands, scratching DaiSzek's head and whooping in excitement.

"You gonna help us build a castle, big boy? You'll get your own room and everything!"

Dessin kneels in front of me, stroking the back of his knuckle along my cheek, memorizing the bliss painted on my face.

"You know what this means?" he asks.

I lean into his touch, my heart soaring at the way he's looking at me.

"What?"

"We made it, Skylenna. We finally made it home. Out of captivity and to our Neslanox. And now, I'm going to build my princess a castle."

81. The Dellilian Castle

Skylenna

Eight Hundred and Ninety-Five Years in The Past

My husband built me A castle.

Though, he did not do it alone.

Our children and grandchildren made frequent trips to help us. Warrose, Marilynn, and Ruth too. Although, Warrose and Dessin would end up doing all the heavy lifting and the ladies would drink wine and critique their mistakes. At the end of the really long days, Warrose and Dessin would have a glass of whiskey on the gigantic balcony they built. The same one I was alone with Dessin on after the ball when he was still a patient.

We met the ancient colonies too, to which they enjoyed venturing out to our work site at sunrise to give us extra sets of hands. They'd bring lumber, beautiful stones, and their finest stonemasons to turn this structure into a masterpiece.

Sapphire and Krimson would bring us baked goods, furniture, paint, and additional tools as well.

Kane carved our bedframe by hand and made the feather bed himself too. He continued drawing blueprints of the ballroom, the designs along the staircase. All of it. And slowly we got there, with only one piece truly missing.

"Where are we going?" I ask Niklaus, leading us on a hike to the North Sapphrine Forest.

"So, I didn't know this before—but Uncle Warrose recently told me how he made Aunt Ruth's chair. Do you remember?" Niklaus helps Sapphire step over a creek, supporting her pregnant belly.

I exchange a glance with Dessin. "No, I don't think so."

We arrive at a small nook in the forest, a spot with four whimsical trees standing crooked and tall in the center of it.

"He cut down one of these four trees. But at the time, he said there were only three trees to choose from," Niklaus explains.

Sapphire sits in front of them, admiring their roots. "He did know that these trees are impenetrable. Over the thousand years they've been standing—they have survived firestorms, earthquakes, extreme frost and war. Now, here's what he didn't know. He didn't know that these trees can only be cut down by those found worthy. That is why he was able to use one for Aunt Ruth's chair. He didn't know that Niklaus and I were here over a thousand years ago when these trees were born."

"What?" Dessin's eyes dart between them suspiciously.

"You still need a front door for the castle, right? Well, Sapphire and I were thinking…if there were only three trees here when Uncle Warrose cut one down, then the fourth must have been uprooted by a person who was worthy. We can't think of a better, more worthy man than one who would build his wife a castle." Niklaus puts one hand on the tree to the far right. "And if that castle is to be named after our sweet Dellilian, then it should have a piece of her built in it too."

I stand up straight. "Is this where…"

Niklaus nods.

"The trees are called Dellilian's Hearts. And this is where Dellilian passed away. These trees grew from her sacrifice." Sapphire smiles sadly, patting the dark soil around her roots.

My eyes fill with tears as I grin at Dessin, holding my arms out to the trees.

"It's perfect. I can't think of anything more special."

We hug our daughter and son-in-law. We admire the trees and take a moment to thank the heroic creature that was there for our children when we couldn't be.

Dessin, Niklaus, and Warrose spend a few days on the front door. It's massive. The spine and heart of our small castle. The wood is the old, burnished brown of the earth after a heavy rain. Warrose carves art into its surface. A RottWeilen with a shadow of wings. Knights and angels in combat. Saints transforming into wolves. And DaiSzek's head as the iron door knocker.

As they install it on brass hinges, the door breathes life into our new home. A pulse that circulates our families' memories into the walls.

One Sunday evening, we invite the colonies to the castle for a peaceful supper. They each bring delicious dishes from their sacred books of recipes. Marilynn helps me prepare a few of our own. During the dinner, we discover that the colonies do not have prophecies they live by. In fact, they hold no stories of the future to come. No prophecies that hold our names and destinies. At what point will they acquire them?

It's then we set our forks down and turn to Marilynn.

She smiles warmly, dipping her head for us to catch on. To gather the last piece of the puzzle that she has always known, but we did not.

The men and women around the table have striking features, as close to fae, elves, nymphs, and other whimsical creatures that were diluted over the centuries. Leaving the descendants we came to know and love in the decade we were born into.

They continue eating, waiting to hear more about our travels from wherever we came from.

"Marilynn?" I ask in astonishment. "Did we…"

"We were the ones to create the prophecy, weren't we?" Dessin finishes for me.

Marilynn downs her drink. She takes three long seconds to respond.

"And now you know everything I do."

Dessin and I lock eyes in disbelief.

"It was us?" I speak.

My husband gazes into my eyes with so much love, it spills over into my body, spreading an everlasting ember of heat to my fingertips and toes.

"It was always us."

Our children, friends, and grandchildren smile and continue their side conversations. And Dessin secures his rough hands around the sides of my face to kiss me fiercely.

"Thank you, Skylenna."

"For what?"

He kisses me again and leans his forehead against mine with closed eyes.

"For giving me this miraculous life. This family. You are my soulmate in life and death. Now let's tell our story."

82. The One True King

Skylenna

Eight Hundred and Eighty Years in the Past

Time is finally catching up to the only beast I ever believed could outrun it.

Even legends grow old, though none of us ever thought *he* would. Once fierce enough to take on a Dralutheran, DaiSzek now struggles to get up from his favorite spot on the dining room floor.

After decades of protecting our children, guarding our home, and comforting Dessin and I through gales of nightmares, flashbacks to the war, and debilitating seas of depression…our boy stayed by our side through it all. Even through one last war from an entirely other world that Sapphire asked us to fight in as one last favor to Dellilian—but that is a story for another time.

A snowy dusting of white fur overtook his chin, brows, and chest. And even in old age, though he limped from the crucial injury from the Dralutheran, DaiSzek still ran. He'd huff and groan as Dessin took him downstream for a bath, attempting to play and knock my husband off his feet. We brushed his shiny black fur every day, snuggled him at night in our bed, and cut up his food when he had a hard time eating.

I've never heard of an animal aging so gracefully. I've never heard of a wolf lasting longer than two decades at most.

DaiSzek has lived for more than sixty years.

After half a century, Kane and I began to believe he would live forever. That eternity flowed in his veins from the ferociousness of his bloodline.

He eventually stopped eating the finely cut meat Kane would prepare for him. The scent of lamb filling the air with its steam, untouched, sent an ache so sharp to my chest, I had to look away. The first time our sweet boy turned his head to the side to reject the meal was when I knew…

What broke my heart more was that Kane refused to accept it. He would prepare different meals. Lamb, rabbit, pheasant. Even the freshly baked blueberry muffins filled with jam that DaiSzek used to sneak off the countertop.

He'd turn his head and rest his chin on the wooden floor.

I let Kane process it without a word. His hands shook. He stared down at DaiSzek, half dissociating, half crumbling to pieces in silence.

On a Sunday morning as the sun rose behind the tree line, Dessin debated with himself in the light misting of rain. He paced down the halls of the Dellilian Castle DaiSzek once galloped through with more distress than the day we were locked up in the Vexamen Prison.

And I didn't have to ask.

I saw the devastating conflict written across his face. The dark shadows under those stunning brown eyes. The lack of sleep weighing down on his posture.

For over an hour, Dessin debated putting DaiSzek out of his misery. And I felt that anguish deep in my soul, piercing my heart with a rusted blade.

It just so happens that DaiSzek understood this too. He limps through the threshold of our favorite wooden door, brushes his head against my thigh, and walks outside for the first time in days. Dessin turns to watch with the saddest, meekest glimmer of hope in his tired gaze. But DaiSzek only looks at him briefly, a silent word that only his best friend could understand.

This morning, we walk behind DaiSzek as he ventures into the tree line to the Red Oaks. Though, this far back into the past, there isn't an ounce of red. The blaze of bright green leaves soars around us. The sky sprinkles its thin rainwater onto the moist soil. Even the trees seem to lean in, sensing an unforgettable event is about to pass us by. And as we come to a stop, Dessin never lets go of my hand.

"I'm scared," I whisper to him.

"Me too, baby."

"Maybe he's feeling better. Maybe he wanted fresh air and a walk," I reason.

I watch DaiSzek stand over Niles's grave. At least, where his grave will be in nine hundred years.

I want to make time stop. To beg for a do-over with our boy. I barely made it out of a depression alive when my brother was killed. When Chekiss passed slowly, struggling to take even the smallest breath in his last weeks of being alive.

But I've known and loved DaiSzek since I was a little girl.

He's covered my body with his own in the middle of a destructive storm. He's come to my rescue more times than I can count. I watched him play in the rain as a pup. I've endured his clumsy stage of feeling small but growing fast and bumping into us when he'd play too rough. DaiSzek was the only family member Kane and I could rely on. The only one alive that would never hurt us.

My grip on Dessin's hand tightens.

DaiSzek lifts his head. Nose quivering at something he cannot see but can feel off in the distance. His ears perk up, listening to a sound that does not exactly belong to this world. The rain quiets. The leaves stop trembling. And the forest exhales as the void pulls a curtain back for me to see.

The tears come as I see her standing there, a few trees away, watching my boy.

Warmth brushes over skin like fingers made of sunlight.

A small but mighty Ginger Wrathbull standing, glowing in the honey streams of light.

Knightingale came back for him.

I throw my hand over my mouth, sobbing at the sight of

DaiSzek's tail thumping, his soft excitement seeing his old friend again.

"What is it?" Dessin asks.

I choke on my words. "It's—Knightingale!"

Dessin releases a slow breath, clenching his jaw and watching stoically.

Knightingale wiggles and gives DaiSzek a happy chuff, calling to him.

"Oh, Dessin. I think she's here to take him home."

Dessin nods, though he cannot speak.

And after a moment, a tall young man steps out from the cluster of trees too. Grinning that golden boy grin we have all fallen hopelessly in love with.

Tears gush down my face as I see my brother, as young as the day I first met him in the asylum. He wears no signs of age, trauma, or ever knowing a life of pain.

"*Niles*. It's Niles!" I cry out, sobbing as I grip Dessin's arm.

I let the void pull him in, sharing my sight as clearly as I can with my husband. Dessin's eyes widen and his chin lifts as he enters the glimpse I share.

My brother flashes his old friend that classic smile and waves to us from his place next to Knightingale.

At this, Dessin lowers his head and pinches the bridge of his nose with a slight trembling of his hand. He's struggling to hold himself together, but I knew that's what does it for him. I've known for a long time that Dessin never really got over losing Niles. I could see it in his somber expression when Ruth and I would laugh at a silly memory with him. An obnoxious thing Niles would say that wasn't funny at the time, but after he left us, we couldn't believe how we didn't notice how humor poured off him relentlessly to brighten our days.

In those moments, Dessin would usually leave the room or go quiet.

And when my husband opens his eyes again to look at the serene view of his old friend waiting to welcome DaiSzek to heaven, his gaze is covered in a thick layer of tears.

The sight is a wound and a miracle holding hands.

DaiSzek lies underneath his favorite tree; the one he will dig dozens of holes around in the future, burying bones, and sleeping in its vast shade on a hot day.

And old age sheds from him like a discarded cloak as DaiSzek's soul steps out of his body. My sweet boy gallops like a young stallion to his friends, Knightingale and Niles, who welcome him home with quiet enthusiasm.

He looks back only once.

Pausing at the edge of the heavenly light, a slow turn of his head.

Suddenly, without a strand of white speckling his fur, our lifelong protector stares into our souls with those big cinnamon eyes. Not out of obligation, but of instinct and undying love. An instinct he's had since he was a pup. The one that urges him to make sure we are safe before he leaves.

This last look nearly brings me to my knees.

He seems to ask us not to mourn, to be safe, and that he'll be waiting to welcome us home one day soon—all at once. I save the image of him firmly into my memory. No longer with a graying muzzle or cloudy eyes. He's young again. And free.

I can feel their love as my long-departed family walks DaiSzek into the light glimmering through the branches. I can feel that Niles and Knightingale will take such good care of our boy until we join him again. And before he takes his last step from this world, I can feel his hesitation. DaiSzek has been with us his entire life. And this will be our first time apart. But even so, his spirit disappears.

As the light vanishes, we rush to kneel at the side of his body. I stroke the fur of his neck as tears dripped from my cheeks to the dirt.

"I love you, DaiSzek!" I cry.

The man kneeling next to me presses his forehead into his fist and sobs quietly with shaking shoulders. His large, tan hand holding DaiSzek's limp paw.

I don't have to see his eyes to know that man is Kane.

"He lived a long, happy life," I assure Kane, rubbing my hand over his back.

Each small tremble of his shoulders fractures my heart. I've only seen Kane cry a couple of times in my entire life. His system has held themselves together so well in front of me. But losing our first baby was bound to leave us in pieces.

"I love you, Big Boy," Kane whispers through soundless sobs.

"You have gotten me through the hardest moments in my life. You've protected me when I was too young to protect myself. You've kept my wife and my children safe…"

He falls short to finish his statement as we both cry at the swift gust of memories from our long life with this beautiful beast. All the years DaiSzek protected Sapphire and Krimson. The silent promise to die for our family if that's what it came to. The time he killed the Demechnef soldiers hunting us down when Dessin saved me from Albatross and Absinthe. The long nights he'd stay awake to guard Kane and I while we slept in the forest. He was always there. Never strayed. Always came when we'd need him most.

"I don't know what we did to deserve you, buddy. You could have left us a long time ago, but you stuck around. Thank you for loving us. Thank you for taking care of us."

"He waited until he was sure we were safe, Kane. Through the years on the run, being hunted down, and until the wars were over. He made sure we would be at peace before saying goodbye…"

We spend hours hugging and crying over his body that is still warm and would remain warm well into the cold night.

I'll never forget kissing those soft ears, and the space between his eyes.

The next morning, we buried DaiSzek next to the space where his friend, Niles, will one day be buried. And we finally understood that the legends of DaiSzek, the fae king's dragon, was wrong.

As DaiSzek's body returned to the earth, that green on the leaves of the trees turned bright red. Like blood seeping into each branch, each twig.

It was not a dragon like the legend stated.

It was DaiSzek. Our RottWeilen.

We waited until Sapphire and Krimson came to visit us again to tell them the news. Watching them cry over his grave ripped our hearts out of our chests all over again.

The Dellilian Castle was never the same after that. The halls lacked the soft pattering of DaiSzek's paws as he'd run and slip through them to greet our children at the front door. The bed no longer had that lasting warmth from when he'd sleep between my husband and me. Yet we spoke about him every single day, keeping his memory alive and thriving.

Even over the next ten years when Dessin and I aged into our seventies…

We felt the absence of our lifelong protector. We mourned our boy that once lay with us under the shade of the red oak trees, ate bowls of blueberries until we scolded him for not sharing, and snuggled into us under the vast night sky of endless stars.

We would never be the same.

Because DaiSzek, the one true king, was gone.

83. Soulmates in Life and Death

Skylenna

Seventy-tree years old

"And remember how I told you Ruth clawed out Apple May's eyes when she threatened me that day?!" I ask Dessin while he's cleaning up the wrapping paper off the ballroom floor.

Our family and friends have finally left after a long week of celebrating Christmas with us. Screaming children filled these halls. Warrose, old and grumpy, wore muffs over his ear to block out the noise. Ruth laughed at his expense. Our granddaughters sat on Dessin's lap while he read the old Christmas tales they beg him to read every year.

I gave a speech about how fulfilling my life has been with so much love and so many children.

And now that everyone's gone home, hundreds of years in the future, I get to tell Dessin the theatrics I get to hear that he isn't privy to.

"I remember."

"Good, good. Your memory has been spotty lately," I explain.

He coughs out a laugh. "My memory is flawless."

"Mmm. I don't think so."

"You think yours is better?" He tosses the leftover wrapping paper in the fireplace.

"Of course," I say innocently.

"Skylenna, my sweetheart, you left the door open last night and tried to convince me we'd been robbed this morning."

I grimace at him. "We don't know I'm the one who left it open."

"I watched you leave it open. When I tried to close it, you said, and I quote—*'leave it open! We need fresh air. You scared of getting robbed or something?'*"

"I think you're making that up."

Dessin throws his head back to laugh, charging forward to lift me off my feet and spin me around to dance.

"Careful! I have arthritis!" I scold.

"No, you do not."

"Yes, I do. I hate when you say that."

"Have you been diagnosed?"

"By who? It's just you and me here, dummy."

He laughs again, kissing my temple. "Me. I could diagnose you."

"I have diagnosed myself, and that's good enough for me."

"I'd believe you if you didn't conveniently complain of that pesky arthritis every time we had to clean the kitchen."

I giggle into his chest, and we continue dancing until I get a little lightheaded, and my husband carries me upstairs to our bedroom in the east wing of the castle.

"You already forgot you were telling me a story," Dessin murmurs in my ear, nuzzling his nose against the side of my head.

"Oh, yeah," I hum sleepily.

He chuckles.

But there's a long pause because I don't remember what the story was about.

"Apple May, sweetheart."

"Oh yeah!" I do a happy wiggle in his arms as he gets past the last step. "When Sapphire and Niklaus traveled to the asylum, Meridei was their conformist for joint treatments, and she let her sick mother watch and torment them too!"

Dessin breathes heavily as he walks slowly into our bedroom. "What?"

"Apple May was a sexual sadist! She was having them—"

"I'm too old and too much of Sapphire's father to hear those details of this story, Skylenna," Dessin grumbles.

"Right, right, anyway, Sapphire ended up manipulating time in Apple May's *scalp* and *hair*! She decayed the top of her head only and made the vain woman bald. Side note, Apple May's hair was her greatest pride and joy."

Dessin sets me down on our bed to laugh.

"And that's why Apple May wore that bath towel around her head," he says.

I flop onto the fluffy pillows and grin at the gold-painted ceiling. I am so tired I could sleep for days. But these memories have me tickled pink.

"Our daughter is brilliant."

Dessin agrees with a hum. And being the gentleman he is, Dessin also undresses me, pulls a nightgown over my head, and massages my feet.

"Remind me of the agenda for tomorrow?" I slur woozily.

My husband kisses each of my toes. "It's supposed to snow in the morning. I was thinking I'd make us some hot chocolate and breakfast, and we could sit on the balcony with some blankets and enjoy the view."

I peel one eye open in the dark. "Is that my sweet Kane?"

"Yes, honey."

My eyes well up as I close them. I haven't seen him in a while, and I've missed him so much. "You promise you'll be here in the morning for that idea?"

"I promise."

"Then continue with the agenda so I may sleep, and we can have a fun day together."

"Well, after that it will be too cold to go outside, so I thought maybe we could get the fireplace going, cuddle on the couch, and read those new books Krimson gave us for Christmas."

I coo happily. "With more hot chocolate?"

"Bottomless hot chocolate for my sweet Skylittle."

Kane kisses me on the head and walks to his side of the bed, getting comfortable under the covers, and scootching my way to spoon me.

"Kane?"

"Yes, honey?"

"I miss DaiSzek."

"So do I. Every day."

"Time travel is so funny. Can you believe we were so drawn to the Red Oaks as kids because that's where our DaiSzek was laid to rest almost a thousand years in the past? Turning the forest red?"

Kane inhales the scent of my hair and hums his agreement.

"Are you asleep?" I ask into the dark room.

"Mmm-hmm."

"Do you know how much I love you?" I kiss my husband's wedding ring with a big smile.

He tries not to laugh, but I can hear it in his breath. I always get a second wind at night when he's here, eager to tell him every detail he's missed since he's been gone.

"How about you tell me just how much in the morning, honey."

I snuggle in tighter. "Tomorrow it is."

"Sweet dreams."

84. Until I'm Old and Gray

Kane

Seventy-three years old

Snow silently falling through a frosty window across a winter sunrise is Skylenna's favorite sight.

I sneak as quietly as I can to the kitchen to prepare breakfast, hot chocolate, and warm her slippers and robe by the fireplace—dancing around the creaks in the floor. Setting cast-iron pots down on the flame as carefully as I can without making a loud clatter. I prepare the breakfast trays with my special handwritten notes I give her when I deliver a breakfast tray to bed. I clean off the table on the balcony, set cushions on the seats, and ensure there is no ice that could cause her to slip and fall.

My wife is usually exhausted after family and friends stay at the castle. She's the sweetest host, ensuring everyone is comfortable and fed, and loves hugging and kissing on all of our grandbabies.

But when they leave, I like to help her relax.

This is my favorite part.

I feel like a kid as I tiptoe up the stairs. Despite my stiff old bones and waning muscles, I am in quite good health for being in my seventies.

And the thought of seeing my beautiful soul mate smile so big at a winter morning just the two us gives me a spark of energy.

I open the door slowly, avoiding the slight squeak of the hinges rotating.

With a cup of hot chocolate in my left hand and her heated robe and slippers under my right arm, I kneel at her bedside, loving the sight of her sleeping so peacefully. Her wavy white hair strewn across the pillow. Those long, curly lashes forming shadows across her cheeks. Skylenna has aged like an angel.

"Good morning, honey." I gently blow the steam and rich scent of chocolate to her face.

But she does not stir.

"Blueberry pancakes, eggs, and a bowl of oatmeal wait by the balcony door."

I consider letting her sleep longer, but don't want the food to get cold.

"And yes, I added cinnamon sticks to your hot chocolate."

I blow the steam in her direction again.

A strand of white hair inches away from her face. And my back goes pin straight. The robe and slippers slide from my grip. I set the cup down on her nightstand.

"Time to wake up, honey." I lean forward to kiss the tip of her ice-cold nose. "Don't make me eat this delicious breakfast all by myself."

Another kiss on her frigid cheek.

"*Kane…*" Dessin shoves his way to the front.

But I ignore him and continue staring down at my wife. Her plush lips are pale. Her chest is so terribly still. I kiss her again.

"Skylenna? I made you breakfast."

A familiar pain and sense of denial bloom inside my throat like a bruise that will never fade. I fold my warm hand around hers and lose my breath at its temperature.

"*Kane? I can take over now,*" Dessin tells me quietly.

I shake my head.

Hope exhales its last as I kiss her knuckles.

"Honey, you're going to sleep the day away."

The other alters gather in a crowd of morbid individuals watching me try to wake my wife. They watch and pray, and their broken hearts suffocate me.

Wetness pools along my lashes before I can control myself.

"Please, wake up. *Please*," I rasp.

My vision tightens at how still she is.

We were supposed to watch the snow fall today. We were going to drink hot chocolate and read our new books.

"*Please, Kane, check her pulse.*" Dessin's deep voice sounds weaker and feebler than I have ever heard it.

I nod once. Sniffling before I press two fingers to her throat. The nothingness that comes from that touch snaps my last string of hope, popping loudly in my ears.

A pressure, hot and volcanic, hits me behind my eyes. I clasp her cold hands in mine and bring them to my lips, kissing each knuckle, each fingernail one last time. Harrowing heartache punches upward, and I begin to shake violently against the bed.

"Skylittle, you were supposed to tell me how much you love me this morning. Remember?" I am a little boy again, buckling under the weight of my cry, though, it is that of an old man now, hearty and full of a lifetime of longing for the woman I love so dear.

My face crumples as I fall against her.

With my head bowed, uncontrollable jerks rack my body.

"Thank you," I sob quietly against my wife. "Thank you for being my sweetheart. For being the only woman I have ever loved."

"*Don't do this alone,*" Dessin says as he cannot contain his cry either. "*I'll take over so you don't have to see this.*"

"NO!" I bellow, eyes squeezing shut so hard, I see stars in the darkness behind my lids. "It's Skylenna! Look at her! I won't leave my Skylittle."

Snot and tears cover the back of my hand as I try to pull myself together enough to say what I need to say.

"Thank you for loving all of us. Thank you for never making me feel ashamed for having dissociative identity disorder. Thank you for making me a hero when I thought we'd only ever be a villain."

My soulmate looks just as beautiful today as she did the first day I met her when we were children. I choose to see that calm expression as sleeping.

"Thank you for loving me so passionately, Skylittle. I thought—I thought I was unlovable for so long. You were my greatest treasure. My most precious love. You gave me beautiful babies. You gave me lifelong best friends. My heart is so full, and I owe it all to you, honey."

I spend a couple of hours right here, kneeling at the bedside of my sweetheart. I tell her I'll take care of her castle until she greets me again in heaven. I promise to tell her children and grandchildren how much she loves them.

I ask her to hug DaiSzek for me.

I dissociate heavily but remain present.

I say my goodbyes.

Eventually, I stand up to walk around from my blood circulation being cut off from my knees. Dessin stays close to the front as I throw away the breakfast I made for her. As I dig her grave next to DaiSzek's.

I don't know when my children will be back again. A part of me hopes it isn't for a while, so that I have time to put myself back together when I tell them their mother went to heaven.

But today, I hold her hand until I lower her into the ground, kissing her wedding ring before I let her go. And even then, I still don't leave.

After seventy years of loving my beautiful Skylenna Winter Ambrose Valdawell, I will stay close until I'm old and gray.

And even then.

85. The Pawn and The Puppet

Dessin
One Hundred Years Old

Letter #3,977

Dear Skylenna,

Today marks thirty years without my girl by my side.

Last night, Krimson asked me, Dad, if you knew the day Mom was going to pass away, what would you change?

What do you think my answer was, baby?

Not a damn thing.

I get to go to sleep every night at peace with the man you helped shaped me into. Why? Because I gave my wife everything she wanted. I was not one of those Emerald Husbands that ignored the mother of their children, neglect, and treat her lesser than. I get to go to sleep every night knowing that I worshipped the woman I fell in love with. I never let a day go by without bringing you flowers, giving you lots of kisses, and telling you how absolutely stunning you looked.

I never took you for granted. Not a single day in our marriage. Not a single moment since the day I locked eyes with you in the thirteenth room of that asylum.

Now, with all that said, I miss you terribly.

I didn't realize how euphoric your laugh was until I'd never hear it again. Kane has not resurfaced since the day he buried you. But he does live a comfortable life in the inner world, dreaming of the day we all get to see you again.

I'm going to try and keep writing these letters, but my hand isn't as strong as it once was, and writing has become a tormenting chore. I'd ask Krimson or Sapphire to write them for me, but I don't think I will. There is something precious and private about letters from a husband mourning his wife, don't you think? Something that should stay whispered between the two of us.

So, I apologize, baby. This may be one of the last letters I'll ever write you.

I've continued adding to the castle in ways I thought you'd like. Different additions I know would have made you smile. I've built in almost every single letter I wrote you into the walls. And then added the ones you wrote me when I was in the coma.

I'm not ashamed to say I've read those letters thousands of times since you've moved on without me. They've kept me going. In the cold winter nights when I needed to feel the warmth of your body next to mine, I'd read your letter about being too warm when you were pregnant. On the mornings I'd visit your grave and didn't know how to leave, I'd read a letter.

Thank you for writing them. I know they were born out of the darkest days in your life, but please know...they've kept me alive during mine.

Marilynn passed on a few nights ago. She asked Krimson to take her back a few decades to when she was pregnant with Niklaus. Krimson warned her that traveling to a time when she was already alive would be fatal. But Marilynn was on her deathbed. She said she wanted to pass on in the arms of her soul mate. And that's exactly what she did. Krimson watched from a distance as an elderly Marilynn woke Niles in the middle of the night and asked that he hold her.

Ruth and Warrose are still kicking. He is far too stubborn to die without her. I wouldn't be surprised if they go at the exact same time, holding hands, warm in their bed.

How badly I wish that's how we met our end. But God had other plans for us.

Thirty years without you. And I'd do it all again to make sure these roles weren't reversed. You have been through too much to be in my shoes right now. You watched me die with that sickle slicing through my back. You raised our babies for twenty-one years without me there to hold your hand and carry you through the hard days.

I've spent these years caring for your castle. Playing with our grandchildren. Giving Sapphire and Krimson advice. Watching your garden grow. Reading books that could fill a hundred libraries.

Thank you for waiting for me somewhere in heaven.

I'll see you soon, baby.
Your sweetheart,
Dessin

I blow out the last candle after I finish sealing this last letter into the wall of our bedroom.

The cane I walk with does little to keep me from falling to the ground now. Warrose made it for me, and it's served its purpose years ago. Now, it's barely keeping me from crawling from one side of the room to the other.

But I didn't want my kids to know how slow I've become as of late. They would have asked to move in with me again. They'd beg me to come live with them.

That's what they tried to do when Skylenna passed away. They sat me down for an intervention after the small funeral we held for her. They begged me to come live with them.

But how could I leave their mother?

How could I leave our home?

Niklaus offered to clear out the Dellilian Castle in the present day and let me live there. But it's not the same. This castle still smells like my girl. It still carries the ghost of her laugh. I can still hear her singing down the hall while she'd take a bath.

I'd never leave the home we built together.

For a long time, I struggled with understanding my purpose after the love of my life no longer breathed. I'd walk through the forest for days, afraid to go home and sleep without her there. I'd spend all day sleeping. All night enduring countless nightmares.

But then I started to write.

All of our lives we have been a pawn on a chess board and a puppet to entertain a live audience. Skylenna and I were children turned monster. We never stood a chance, did we?

We were children.

To fight. To witness gruesome death. To suffer long and cry for our mothers and fathers who would never come.

We were children.

Why us?

I don't know the answer to that.

And even though our story was written into history books, it wasn't written in our hand, in our voice. Skylenna would have wanted that. To leave the world in a better way than we found it.

That is why I wrote this.

And I have left it for Krimson and Sapphire, tucked away in my safe for the day they'll say goodbye to their father and finally stop visiting the past to check up on me.

I close the book and pat it.

"I hope you like it, baby," I say to my wife, somewhere in the clouds, watching over me.

I take one last look at the leather cover before closing the safe.

The Chronicles of The Pawn and The Puppet
Written by:
Dessin
Greystone
Kalidus
Aquarus
Syfer
Cricket
Church
Foxem
And Kane Valadawell

Only a few more steps until I reach the bed. I grunt, passing my weight to one side, and collapsing as the cane slips out from under me—hitting the ground does not hurt like I thought it would. I've fallen before and broken ribs. I've been concussed. I've blacked out for hours.

But this is shedding a heavy, wet blanket. It's unlatching the shackles of the asylum from my ankles and wrists and finally running free again.

This is aging backward and being released of an impossible weight.

"Stand up, my love. Heaven has waited a long time for this."

I lift my head to see that long, wavy, mermaid hair and the golden halo shining down on her. Not a day older than the day I fell in love with her in that asylum.

"Skylenna," I utter breathlessly.

My soulmate grins down at me with misty eyes and rosy cheeks.

"You waited for me," I say in a whisper. Tears are running down my cheeks. And I'm no longer just Dessin, am I?

I am Kane.

I am every alter and none at all.

I am one soul in death.

"I waited for you," she weeps happily. Her kisses come softly, passionately, intimately.

Her words are like ice melting after centuries of winter.

I reach for her with trembling hands, afraid she might vanish if I move too fast, afraid this is another cruel illusion stitched together by exhaustion and old age.

But she's warm. Real. Alive with light. So much light.

My fingers bury into the fabric at her waist, anchoring myself to her body as if gravity itself has finally decided to stop fighting me. I press my forehead to hers, breathing her in—the familiar sweetness of her skin, the echo of home I memorized in another lifetime. My knees nearly give again, not from weakness this time, but from relief so sharp it hurts.

"You're real. You're back."

She cups my face, wiping tears I didn't know were falling, her thumbs steady, reverent.

"I never left. You just couldn't see me," she murmurs softly.

My Skylenna's kiss is devotional. Slow. A reunion written into the bones of the universe long before either of us were born. And God, my heart jolts in my chest, then steadies, beating in rhythm with hers, finally remembering how it was meant to live.

In her arms, the asylum finally dissolves. The restraints fade. The prison is obliterated from our scars. I am home. I am holding my girl again.

My heart explodes from my chest as the others step out from the light around my wife. At first, they are only silhouettes—shapes carved from gold and dawn—but then the glow thins, and faces begin to form. Each one hits me like a wave, stacking grief on top of joy until I can barely breathe beneath it. I stagger back a half-step, clutching

Skylenna's hand as if she is the only thing keeping me upright. My vision blurs again.

Niles first, holding hands with Marilynn. Then Chekiss surrounded by the wife and daughter he lost long ago. Gauranthian's towering form emerging like a mountain next to Asena, their white wolves, and Runa. Knightingale's stoic stance. Dellilian's dark shimmering, eyes reflecting starlight. Each presence presses into my chest with memory—battles fought, blood spilled, laughter stolen between our darkest moments.

I laugh, though tears cool my burning cheeks.

Before I can say anything at all, they part for a woman running to me with open arms.

"My son!"

I break apart completely.

Years of silent rage. Of suffering alone. Of living in an endless cycle of watching this woman lose her dignity and life all in one blink of an eye.

My mother is untouched by time. And she is radiant in ways I only remember in childhood fragments. Tears rim her eyes, glinting against the round glasses sitting on the bridge of her nose. "My boy. I've waited so long to see my boy."

I fall into her embrace, clinging to her small frame like a child again. Shaking and undone. "I'm sorry, Mom. I'm so sorry."

I have waited a lifetime to tell her that.

Though here, in heaven, I know it is not my fault. The sickle. What the evil men made me do. I know. But I unleash my apology just the same.

"Hush now," she soothes, squeezing me tight. "I love you, my son."

Over my mother's shoulder, a small boy stumbles through a meadow in my direction.

His feet barely touch the ground as he charges toward me, hair wild, eyes shining, face frozen in that reckless, fearless grin I memorized before everything was taken from us.

"Kane!" Arthur screams.

I drop just in time to catch him as he slams into me, his arms locking around my neck with the same force he used to tackle me as a child. I bury my face into his shoulder, shaking, sobbing, coming undone.

"I wanted to save you!" I choke out. "I'm sorry, Arthur!"

Arthur clutches me tighter. "I watched over you. I tried my best to be a fierce guardian angel, Kane. You would have been proud of me."

I cry loudly, nodding in approval.

I used to pray I'd see Arthur one day in heaven, happy and untouched by the sinister acts that took his life.

Every hardship I endured was worth it to be here for this moment.

More faces from my past fill the area. Kaspias, Jack, Scarlett, and Violet.

I hug them all. Sins of the past forgotten. How can I harbor any negative feelings now? I am no longer an old man, reading books alone in a large castle. Wishing I could hug my sweetheart one more time.

I'm here.

"Someone's been asking for you," Skylenna announces.

The ground trembles beneath us as something massive barrels forward from the heart of the radiance.

A thunderous sound splits the air.

Lifting my head to see him is a dream. His massive figure is cloaked in darkness and light. God must have welcomed this great beast to heaven with a standing ovation from all of His angels.

I fall to my knees.

"DaiSzek…"

My soul recognizes him before my eyes fully do. No limp. No scars. No white fur dusting his muzzle. Just power. Youth. Strength reborn in every stride.

He roars—not in rage, but in reunion—a sound so deep and joyous it rattles my bones.

He barrels into me, head slamming against my chest. Jumping like a puppy again. Licking my face and wagging his tail in bliss. Those massive paws pin my shoulders as he whines and barks and trembles all at once, overwhelmed by the fact that I'm real.

"I'm here, buddy!" I laugh, kissing the space between his eyes. "I made it. I promised I'd see you again."

Across many battles. Across an ocean. Across enemy lines. Across heaven. My boy found me again. I sob into his mane, and Skylenna joins in, holding us close and crying with me.

"We're just missing Ruth and Warrose," I mention to Skylenna.

Skylenna looks thoughtfully to the happy RottWeilen rolling in the grass.

"They will join us soon. Once they learn of your passing, they will ask Sapphire to move them through time, back to the Dellilian Castle. Renly will take over in her place. And our friends will live out the rest of their days in peace."

I smile. "How will they pass?"

"Together. Warm in their bed."

I sigh in relief.

"Hundreds of years later, Alkadon settlers will find two sets of bones in the castle. They'll never discover who they belong to," she finishes.

"Wow." But another thought emerges in my mind. "What about—"

"Sapphire and Krimson will find The Chronicles of The Pawn and The Puppet. And they will make sure the world hears our story, my love."

I have no words. I sit with my hands stroking DaiSzek's soft fur, stunned at how this has all turned out.

"When I ran out of books to read, I decided to write my own," I tell her.

Skylenna's eyes go round and glossy. "Thirty years is a very long time to survive alone. It broke my heart to watch you. Visiting my grave. Putting a pillow on my side of the bed. Writing me letters. You never wavered in your love for me. You loved me through death. Through thirty years of solitude."

There's validation that she was there. That someone was there to witness every moment that ticked by.

"You're my soulmate. I would have waited three hundred more."

"I know." Her kiss wraps me in warmth.

"I hope I am not dreaming," I say.

"No, baby. We all waited for you."

I gaze at my family, shaking my head in disbelief at the faces I've longed to see in the loneliness I only just survived.

"You've finally made it home," Skylenna adds, entwining her fingers with mine, warm again at last.

DaiSzek leads the way into heaven, opening with an indescribable sun, an endless dawn. And as our family gathers behind us, I feel the youth return to my bones. Whole for the first time since I was six years old.

And now that we've made it out of hell and into heaven…

My soulmate and I can finally go see the stars.

The End.

Thank you for loving this story as much as I do.
If you're in a puddle of tears, like me…
Just know—this found family is waiting to give you a group hug whenever you need it most.

And now, a sneak peek into my next book:

Scarlett Leviticus

A Dark Fantasy Romance Sex Trafficking Trilogy
Trigger Warning: Rape and Emotional Trauma

My face burns as I scream, shoving him off my body with the strength of ten men. Tears spill over my cheeks. My hands fumble to pull out a pair of scissors I hid in my bra. And I'm on top of him now, straddling his naked legs as I hold the scissors to his erection.

Realization smears across his face. His eyes fall on the blade pressed against his most sensitive part. I laugh through my tears as he chokes on a gasp.

"Do you have—children?" I ask between angry sobs.

He doesn't answer. That stare, watching the blade with every ounce of his focus. I add more pressure.

"Yes!" he answers, squirming under my weight, mouth gaping at me.

I nod. "I'm someone's child. And you're *raping* me. *You're* raping someone's child!" I bellow, my tears falling onto his chest. "I'm being fucking trafficked, and no one seems to care! I'm sick of this shit!" I've spun into full-on hysteria, panting down at him.

"I'm sorry—" he rasps, breathless while lying under my death grip. If I was still clueless to how this world really works, if I still believed men were good, and kind—then I might believe his apology was sincere.

"Why won't anyone fucking help me?! I'm only twenty-one for God's sake!" I'm shrieking now, spitting in his face. My sobs are pulsing with every heartache I've seen. The time Freya cried for her dad one night in my arms, the moment we sang happy birthday to Jo and she broke out in a sob, and those aching two seconds that Kimmy looked back at me before jumping from the van.

He takes a breath to speak again, but it's no use, my gates have burst open, and there's no stopping it now. *Somebody fucking help me! I can't do this anymore.*

"You're all going to turn me into a monster! I dream of cutting your dicks off and peeling off the skin little by little." I laugh, tasting the salty tears that slip into my open mouth. "I can't keep living like this! This isn't living! It's *surviving*! It's slavery, and I'd rather die on my feet than live on my fucking knees!"

I've had enough. *Someone. Anyone. Please, help me.*

And I've made the decision now. I'm ready to seal my fate. With all of my strength, I pull my hand back with every intention to stab the scissors into his now limp cock.

But my face cracks against the hardwood floor, and the scissors fly from my grasp.

There's a blur of Pierre's face before a fist smashes in my temple.

Coming soon…

Acknowledgments

The day I came up with the idea for this series was in math class. I daydreamed about a dangerous patient who would kidnap his therapist and lock her in the asylum basement for hours. And then I wrote it into a short story with no intention to build it into an entire six-book series.

This is to that fifteen-year-old girl that was unable to pay attention in school because she couldn't stop daydreaming about soulmates who find each other in a dark asylum.

Thank you for not giving a crap about the Pythagorean theorem.

Thank you for spending over fifteen years loving Skylenna and Dessin and taking such good care of them when so many believed you'd never make a living from writing books.

Well, I am making a living. I am building a legacy for my daughter. I am an international bestseller. A Spiegel Bestselling Author in Germany. I've signed with multiple publishers to translate in many countries.

Thank you fifteen-year-old, Brandi. You made it!

To my family, Mom, Lacey, and Lindsey. I was in the trenches of pregnancy and postpartum with this last book, and you all were instrumental in helping me in any way I needed.

To Lucy's dad, you've celebrated every word count mile marker, every chapter finished, and every new opportunity that these books that brought me. Your enthusiasm for these books helped me through major writing blocks.

To my daughter, Lucinda Bella, I hope one day you see these books and know I was wiping your butt as breast pumps sucked the life out of me while missing these deadlines. *But* it was all worth it, my little squishy. Would I do it again? Mmm, no. Definitely not. I'd grow a brain and get these books done BEFORE you were born.

Oh, and one last thing to my number one girl. If you're embarrassed of these books one day when you're older, that's too damn bad because when I die these royalty checks go to you. Hahahah! I love you, my princess!

To my loyal, passionate, dedicated readers. If it wasn't for you throwing rocks at the windows of my DMs, begging for the last book—it might have been another two years before this book was finished. THANK YOU. THANK YOU. THANK YOU.

To my cover designer, Stefanie Saw—the covers for this series will remain iconic. To my format designer, Amy Kessler—you have been a pleasure to work with! And to my editors, Ellie, Debbie, and Christine—you are ALWAYS so accommodating and flexible around my last-minute requests and crazy schedule. I'd be in deep doo doo without you!

To my beta and sensitivity readers: Danielle Caballero, Kayla Watson, Laura Pena, Ciera Sanchez, Alisha Minhas, Claudia De Chiara, Makudes Jasaroska, Nourah AlMurtairi, Tayor Robison—thank you for such thorough notes and letting me follow along on your reading journey! It was so bittersweet.

About the Author

Brandi Elise Szeker has had a million stories in her head since she was a little girl convincing her baby sister there were killer clowns in the trees that came out after dark. She has four rescue dogs, Louis, Cali, Stella, and Nova. You can find them sprinkled throughout the series so that her love for them will live on forever. And some days, she lies awake at night wondering if she writes the most beautiful love stories, maybe one will find her too. Texas is where she currently resides, but one day, she'll be deep in the mountains, under the stars, writing a thousand more books that will both break your heart and give you life.

To learn more about Brandi, visit her at:
Author website & newsletter:
www.brandibookthought.com
TikTok & Instagram:
@brandibookthought
Author Facebook Page:
https://www.facebook.com/brandieliseszeker/
Spoilers Facebook Group for TP&TP:
www.facebook.com/groups/thepawnandthepuppetspoilers/

www.ingramcontent.com/pod-product-compliance
Lightning Source LLC
Chambersburg PA
CBHW020244030826
48979CB00030B/2546/J

* 9 7 9 8 9 8 9 4 4 3 6 8 0 *